Just another dream. . .

Twist reached one arm around Dad's head and yanked it back, exposing his throat. The other hand held a knife to Dad's jugular.

It was a dream. Just a dream.

"Ethan?" Dad squinted at me and struggled. "Where are we? What's going on?"

"Nice try," I said. "You made me watch him die before, and it wasn't real."

Twist smiled.

"Wait, is that Twist?" Dad tried to look, but the arm had a grip like a vise. "Are we dreaming?"

He had it down. It sounded liked Dad. Moved like him.

He looked right at me. "Get out of here, son. If none of this is real then he can't hurt me. Go!"

But if it wasn't real, why should I run?

"Just go," Dad shouted. "And tell. . . make sure Mike gets the ring. Please. I want him to know I had a ring."

My throat tightened. How could Twist know about the ring? He couldn't.

"Dad?"

The blade flashed in the moonlight. A river of the darkest red I'd ever seen poured out of my dad's throat.

"No!" I rushed forward.

Dad fell into my embrace, blood cascading down his chest and out of his mouth in bubbles.

"No, no, no, no, no." I tried to wrap my shirt around his neck as best I could, but blood soaked thorough the thick material in seconds.

This Special Edition includes
I n t e r s t i t i a l
Step 3.5 in the Tango Triptych

Also by John Robert Mack, available or forthcoming on Amazon.

NO TENGO TANGO

JOHN ROBERT MACK

Special Edition

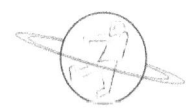

Zen Monster Press

For Lauran. Sorry about all the cuss words.

Part I

Sometimes a story begins in more than one place

Chapter One

Warren lay in a prison infirmary staring at the ceiling, at the beam that ran above his bed. It would support his weight if he could get his hands on a sturdy rope.

"And how are we today?" Nurse Whedon held a Dixie cup full of pills up to him.

Well, he'd been gang-raped by a half-dozen cons he'd put behind bars and was probably HIV-positive. They'd broken his arm and pounded his face into one massive bruise.

"Fine." He took the pills. Handed the cup down to her.

She reached up and wiped the drool from his face. She was the shortest person Warren had ever met. Maybe four-foot tall. Maybe. Wherever the little witch trolled, she carried a tray of Dixie cups.

"You know, a little TV for company will cheer you right up," she said.

"No."

"With the infirmary so empty…" She completely ignored him. "It must get lonely."

"No."

She pointed the remote at the TV on the wall and clicked the damn thing on.

"I said no."

And there it was. That fucking music video from that shitty Austin band with those damn kids dancing and smirking and having a life that didn't consist of rectal bleeding. The local stations played nothing else since Palatino's death.

"Turn it off," Warren demanded.

They cut to a photo of Palatino and called him Twist.

"But it's such a catchy tune," Whedon insisted.

And then the inevitable shot of Warren, smiling in his deputy's uniform from a time before his only outfit glowed orange.

"My goodness, is that you?"

"Turn. the fucking thing off. you deaf. sadistic. bitch!"

She turned the fucking thing off.

Without a word, she left.

Thank God.

Warren would never get his hands on a rope. Maybe a sheet would work. His broken arm would make it harder to string himself up, though.

The lights died.

The infirmary fell into silence except for the soft noises of the monitors.

What had happened? When would Nurse Tiny-dumb-bitch come tell him?

One of the overhead fluorescents crackled and sputtered to life if only barely. It buzzed and tried to stay on but only managed to flicker.

No nurse.

No nothing.

The light buzzed and sputtered.

Oh shit. Had someone paid her to let them finish the job? Warren ripped the hoses and wires from his body and slipped painfully out of bed. He crouched beside it, scanning the room for movement. Those cons were huge. He'd be able to spot them a mile away.

The overhead light sputtered and crackled.

If the damn thing would just stay on!

"Hey," he called out. "Nurse Whedon? What happened to the electricity?"

No response, but a sudden cold breeze brought out gooseflesh on his exposed skin. The thin hospital gown didn't cover much, but who'd turned up the AC?

Warren dropped onto his stomach and slid under the bed, crawling forward to the foot. He glanced both ways. Nothing to see. Nothing to hear. Shit.

Several long minutes passed while he lay on the cold, cold floor and waited for something to happen. Oh crap, what if that nurse was punking him for being rude?

He slid out from under the bed, struggled to his feet and glanced around in the flickering light. The bulb buzzed and sputtered.

His breath huffed out in a soft cloud.

"God damn it, Whedon—"

Something heavy dropped around his neck. It tightened with one sharp yank and pulled him from the floor to hang and spin three feet in the air. He grabbed at the rope with his good hand and kicked his feet, which only set him to spinning faster.

The room whirled and the light flickered.

Wait. Who was that?

—Whedon—

He spun.

—holding the end of the rope in one hand—

He couldn't breathe.

—her face a mask of sheer delight.

What? She couldn't weigh eighty pounds soaking wet. How could she hold him up? With one hand no less!

He spun.

Spots of light appeared.

Ah damn, he mooned her every time he spun. The back of his gown was open to the air.

The edges of his vision darkened.

No! He *didn't* want to die. He wanted to live!

He kicked harder. If he thrashed enough, it would pull on the rope. She'd lose her grip. She was tiny for God's sake! It didn't matter if he had to cope with anal leakage his entire life. And HIV meds worked wonders. He wanted to live!

The darkness at the edges of his vision expanded.

The spinning stopped abruptly.

"Hello, Warren." Nurse Tiny-dumb-bitch's voice sounded too deep, too familiar. "Have a nice time in Hell. Sorry I won't see you there."

Warren couldn't kick anymore. His arms fell limply at his sides.

The entire world shrank down to Nurse Tiny-dumb-bitch's face.

She flickered in the dying light.

A silvery flash of a different face. A man.

He'd swear—No. It wasn't possible.

Palatino had died. Hadn't he?

And then Warren died, too.

Coffee. Oh my God, coffee.

The smell of fresh roasted goodness yanked me out of a sound sleep, the first since my world had exploded at Kamp Lindy-Ho-Ho just over two weeks ago. Kenny had moved back into his own place yesterday, so this was the first night I'd had a room to myself. He figured he should sleep in his house a few nights before moving into Corey's with Dad and me.

About that. Long story short? Corey found out his dad had been cheating on his mom which violated the pre-nup he'd signed years ago. Corey inherited everything and kicked his father out. Kenny, Dad and I all planned to move into the farm which was way too much house for one guy who found himself pretty much alone in the world. That's an entirely different story, though.

Back to coffee.

Since Dad had spent the night at Mike's, that heavenly aroma had to be Auntie Mac's creation. I slipped into sweats and a t-shirt then trundled my way downstairs with a big stretch and a yawn. Winter break had been extended while the town reeled from Twist's rampage, and I had nowhere to be, nothing to do and nothing, really, to worry about. The bad guy had died.

Deep breath. The good kind.

"Hey, Ethan."

Yipes! I stumbled down the last couple of steps and nearly bowled Corey over.

He skipped out of my way, careful not to spill the coffee he held in my usual mug, the one that said, "I was a world championship ballroom dancer and all I have to show for it is this lousy mug."

"Dude, why are you skulking in the hallway?" I took the mug. "You scared the crap out of me."

"Sorry." He shoved his hands in his pockets in his bad puppy impersonation. "I heard you walking around and figured you were on your way down."

"Why didn't you just wake me up?" You know, the way he usually did.

"With everything going on, I didn't want to scare you."

And that had worked out so well. I couldn't say it, though. He'd been through so much and was trying to be polite, I guess.

I padded into the kitchen. "Thanks for the coffee. Were you hitting the bag?"

"No. I just wanted to talk." He sat across from me at the table. "Figured I could wait."

"Dude, you didn't need to wait." Mmmm, coffee. Gotta love a man who knows exactly how you take your java. "It's you. You can wake me up whenever you want."

"Thanks." He sipped his coffee.

Something was wrong. "So. . . what's up?"

He waved his mug at mine. "Drink your coffee."

The front door opened and closed. "Everything okay?" Kenny called from the hallway.

"In the kitchen," Corey replied.

Huh? "Why's Kenny here?" I asked.

"He was watching the front door." Corey said it as if it was the most normal thing in the world.

"Watching it?" I asked. "What did he expect it to do?"

Kenny's hair hung wet down his back and he wore yesterday's t-shirt. What the hell had happened?

"Warren's dead," Kenny told me.

"Officer Friendly?" Wait. Why did that freak them out? "How?"

My best friends exchanged a look I'd only seen the last few days, like they were conspirators on something. They had a secret I secretly knew about, but I didn't confront them on it because I already knew it was bullshit.

Okay, that even confused me. Mm… coffee.

"Apparently," Kenny said, "he was in the infirmary and the night nurse wrapped a rope around his neck and strung him up like a piñata."

Holy crap.

"Yeah, that's the *police report*," Corey said with utter disdain for all things police-y and all things report-y.

"But?" I asked, dreading the response.

"But she couldn't have lifted a goat, let alone a full-grown dude, and. . ." Corey started.

"And *her* prints and *only* her prints are all over the rope," Kenny added. "One hand." He lifted his and wiggled the fingers.

They shared that conspiracy look again.

"And?" I prompted.

"And she says she was forced," Kenny said.

"Like she was just along for the ride," Corey added. "Sound familiar?"

Okay, it was kind of funny when one of them finished my sentences, but they should not do it for each other. Just sayin'.

"Twist is dead, guys," I reminded them.

"You know what that junior dick said," Corey insisted.

"I don't care what the dick said." I pushed to my feet and went for more coffee, glad that the shortcut for detective was dick. "Look, Twist used drugs to make us all think shit happened that did not happen. And now he's dead. That spooky dude from Austin works for Gunner, for Christ's sake. Of course he tried to convince us his client didn't kill his parents."

"He also told us someone would be dead in a week." Kenny's voice sounded the way it did when someone corrected his knowledge of music, and he knew he was right.

"Yeah," I said at last, knowing I was diving into the deep end. "I have to wonder about that little coincidence. I think we should tell the cops about that guy."

An alarm sounded. Spook looked up at the monitor. Blast.

Gunner floated in the air over the parking lot in glorious black-and-white, the camera almost washed out from the ambient supernatural light. Drat. The little douchebag had tried to make a run for it.

Spook headed for the front door, bumping into his buddy Nicci on the way. "I got it," Spook said, hitting the front door latch with one hand. "Shouldn't be too, too hard."

Nicci flashed a hang loose sign. "I will observe from the doorway just in case, little spooky brother dude."

Spook returned the sign. What containment spells did he know off hand?

Gunner spun in the air like a carnival ride, puking and screaming, which would probably ruin his clothes. Well, the clothes he'd stolen.

Spook closed his eyes and centered.

The ghost appeared to his third eye as a silvery figure full of rage and red, shiny hatred.

"*Vix solet graeco dolorum,*" Spook shouted.

Gunner stopped spinning and dropped to the pavement.

Twist's head did a 180 to glare. "Bitch." He rushed Spook, but stopped a few feet away, his body shifting to match the direction of his face. The specter sniffed.

"Yeah, get a load of me." Spook raised his arms and exposed his pits. Wait for it. . .

"What are you?" The ghost drifted away.

"I get that a lot." Spook lowered one hand. "*Summo conceptam.*"

White hot light flared from the upraised hand and hit Twist full in his noncorporeal chest. The ghost screamed and spun into a whirlwind. Once he sorted out his shape, he glared at Spook again. "I'll do you, you freak."

Spook laughed. "Shouldn't that be, 'I'll get you, my pretty, and your little dog, too'?"

Twist scoffed so hard, he'd have choked if he'd still had a throat. "Fag."

The glowing, silvery, smoky figure blew out into nothing.

"Really?" Spook muttered. "You understood the reference, and I'm the one who's gay?" He sighed.

Gunner knelt on all fours, still heaving.

Spook sighed again. "Please realize that ghost keeps learning. He found you. He knows you have protection. Next time he'll wait until you get far enough away that our wards won't tell us to come rescue your pathetic posterior." But what the heck? "Why'd you do a runner anyway? We're not nice enough?"

Gunner rose from his hands but stayed on his knees. "Corey's mom died." He wiped his arm across his mouth. "I missed the funeral. I should. . ." He shook his head. "You wouldn't. . ." He looked up at Spook. "Fuck you."

Spook sighed. Sociopaths. He exchanged a look with Nicci who stood in the doorway. Nicci shrugged.

"We'll send flowers," Spook said.

"Flowers?" Gunner rose to his feet and wiped his hands on his jeans. "Corey's mom was a *saint*. And you want I should send him flowers? He's family."

His eyes burned into Spook's.

Spook stared him down.

Eventually, Gunner looked away and shoved his hands into his pockets. "Cory's in danger, isn't he? My parents dead. Warren." He shook his head. "I don't want him to get hurt because I killed that bastard."

Ah, that made more sense. Nicci nodded and ducked into the building.

Spook grabbed the door before it closed. "Come inside, Gunner. I promise I will do everything I can to keep your friend safe."

Gunner looked up so quickly it was amazing he didn't get whiplash. "Why?"

Really? Well, they all asked that sooner or later.

Spook shrugged. "It's what I do."

Chapter Two

I stirred my coffee longer than usual.

"I found Morrison James," Kenny said.

Stellar. I'd thrown his card in the trash before we'd even left the cemetery the day we met him, which many of my friends applauded and the rest had decried.

"What did you find?" I asked.

He and Corey exchanged that look again. I didn't believe in magic and the two of them did. That's the secret they had. They thought I didn't know about their covert searches into the supernatural, but Corey never closed his Google screen.

Kenny worked his tablet and pushed it across the table to me. A high school yearbook senior photo. Hispanic.

"He seriously needs to get over the Buddy Holly fetish," I said, "but that's him." I tapped the screen. Wow. All the guys had a Buddy Holly thing going on. The girls all worshipped Sandra Dee. What the hell?

Kenny tapped the home icon and the image changed to the yearbook cover: The Kaukauna Galloping Ghosts. Seriously?

"No way." I poured the last of the coffee into my mug. "A kid named Spook is from. . . how do you even pronounce that?"

"Like a crow," Kenny said. "Caw-caw-na, emphasis on the second caw."

"Emphasis on *crap*. He planted it." I pushed the tablet away. "The

Ghosts? Orange and Black? Some made-up town that sounds like a crow puking? The whole thing is a Halloween punk."

"Dude, it's real." Kenny pulled up the city's website. "You can't make up stuff like this."

Well, we did live in a town called Dumass whose mascot was a Rampaging Mule. Go ahead and google. Kaukauna is a real place. Go Ghosts. The photo of the dude in a white sheet riding a horse onto the football field disturbed me.

"Not a lot of Black folks in Kaukauna, Wisconsin?" I asked.

Kenny shook his head. "Look at the year, Ethan."

I tapped over to the cover again. 1961. Fuck me.

"It's a put on," I insisted. "Or it's his dad."

Kenny scrolled through the book. He stopped on a page near the end.

"In memorium," I read, "Morrison James and Ross blah, blah, blah. Missing and presumed dead, blah, blah. Any information blah, blah, blah de blah."

The photo looked exactly like Spook hanging out with a ginger geek, a bunch of Bunsen burners and glassware in a lab of some kind. Total dork central, prophylactic thick-rimmed spectacles and all.

"It's a Morrison James who looks exactly like the guy we met," Kenny said, "and this is the only thing on the net about him. There's nothing about him or the Ross guy and their disappearance. No news articles. No police reports."

"No birth record. No death certificates," Cory added. "Nothing in the town paper about them."

"It was a small town," I offered.

"Exactly. A town that small?" Kenny said. "Half of the paper is obituaries. They'd *run* with a story about two missing kids."

Yeah. Pick up a local paper from anywhere in a hundred miles or turn on any local newscast in Texas and you'd have been inundated with *our* story.

"Finding this was a fluke," Kenny insisted. "They only digitized the yearbook a week ago."

"I bet if we go and look next week," Corey added, "it'll be gone."

"I know this guy's a spook in more ways than one," I said. "But you want me to believe he vanished in 1961, he's somehow still a teenager and has the technological knowhow to erase himself from every database on the planet? Do you not know how insane you sound?"

Kenny turned to face me. "You seemed happy to have my support when you thought Twist was doing a Freddy Krueger on your ass."

"Did you *really* believe me?" I asked.

He did a complete double take. "The *fuck* you say?"

Shit. Oh shit oh shit oh shit. "I'm sorry." I held up both hands. Wow. I'd never seen him actually pissed before. "You did. I suck." I brought my mug to the counter. No amount of coffee would be enough for this conversation. "But that's just it. We all believed it until we found the drugs in my system. Science won. Hands down."

Kenny held out a newly refilled coffee pot, and I offered my mug. He chewed on his lower lip in a way that told me he was holding out.

"Spill."

He raised an eyebrow then sort of relaxed. "Okay, can you keep quiet about something that will benefit you in the long run but makes me look like an asshat?"

Wow. He'd practiced that a thousand times.

"Spill."

"I hacked Dr. Mike's computer." He cringed as if waiting for me to blast him.

"Oh wow." Corey rose to stand beside him.

I laughed. "Dude, that in no way upsets me."

"Sweet." His whole body relaxed. "Twist didn't poison you. It wasn't a hallucinogen."

"What was it?" I asked.

He glanced from me to Corey and back again. "It took the labs a long time to figure out because it wasn't anything poisonous. Vertivert, galingal, patchouli, black pepper and capsicum."

"Wait. . ." Corey said with disgust, "he used some guy's—"

"Capsicum is a flower," Kenny interrupted. "Nightshade."

Nightshade? Oh. hell. That's where he was going. It sounded like the ingredients for some kind of magic spell. Except. . .

"My aunt owns a restaurant," I said. "Nightshade is also potatoes and peppers."

Kenny scoffed. "Nothing in there could have given you those

nightmares. Dr. Mike was certain." Wow. He'd really done his research. "You told me exactly what Twist 2.0 looked like *before* you ever saw him outside your dreams. Darker. Muscles. Long hair. Just like the real thing. At the camp he repeated phrases word for word that he'd said to you in your head."

Wow. Kenny really listened, didn't he?

"Dr. Cherkasky couldn't explain how Twist got so big in just a few months without steroids," he continued, "which weren't in his system when he was shot. So time had to be messed up, hai? Accelerated?"

I raised an eyebrow.

"Okay, I hacked the doctor's computer, too and read the autopsy." Wow. "It's a small town." His face was so intense, his eyes desperate for me to believe him. It was a look that had likely covered my own face when he'd pulled me out of the pool and breathed life back into me.

"Okay, you're a better friend than me," I admitted.

He scowled.

"But I'm trying," I said. "I just don't want to fall for any bullshit again."

He nodded, but his eyes remained desperate.

"Okay, when all that happened to me," I said. "I had every good reason to want to believe it. Why is this so important to you?"

Even Corey seemed curious about that.

"Hai." Kenny took his mug across the room. "Do not make fun of me in any way."

I held up a hand.

Corey glanced at the gesture then did the same.

"My Papa Karela," he said quietly. "My mom's father. He was Romani and had all these great legends about monsters and magic and golems and stuff. He said they were stories from the old world, from Europe, handed down from a time when my people wandered Europe in wagons."

He stared at the floor. "I loved all that, but my mom hated it. Said it was all lies. He died when I was little, so I've forgotten more than I remember and Mom won't say a word, pretends she doesn't know."

It all made sense. If Twist had really used magic on us, then Kenny could believe his granddad's stories.

"Um. . ." Corey fidgeted with his coffee cup. "What does being Roman have to do with it? I mean, are you descended from some kind of Roman god or something? 'Cause that would be awesome."

I cringed, but Kenny smiled. "Other people call the Romani something else. They say gypsies." Kenny shrugged. "Most people hate being called that, but I don't know. I kind of like the word. Papa wore it like a badge of honor." The memory of his grandfather shone out like a light. "All those years I felt like some kind of loser freak, Papa's stories made me feel special. When Mom took all that away, when I started to forget the stories? I lost the last thread I had to hang on." He met my eyes. "I know it's totally uncool, or whatever, but I've actually believed in the supernatural my whole life."

But I never had, and it had taken so much for me to believe in the first place. When I found more logical answers? Much easier to accept. I wanted to ask if he'd seen anything supernatural with his own eyes. Had he *seen* it or was it just stories? But I couldn't ask that. That would've just made it worse.

Spook's favorite place in the whole world was a bar called Bitter Sweets in one of Austin, Texas' shadier East Side neighborhoods. It was the kind of place you entered through the back alley.

Spook sat in his favorite red velvet booth, a recessed two-thirds circle with black curtains that could be closed for privacy. He watched the early morning crowd while Billy, the manager who still waited on Spook because he tipped ridiculously well, made his way across the dance floor.

Half the crowd bobbed and waved and bounced perfectly in sync. Hm. Must be some kind of flash mob. Wait.

Spook opened his third eye. Waves of energy lapped across the floor, wrapping the dancers and moving their limbs. The spell centered on four small globes, one on each side of the floor. Dance balls. Part and parcel for online virtual communities. Click on the globe and your avatar danced to a preprogrammed series of moves while you chatted and tried to find someone for one-on-one action.

"We're trying them out," Billy said. He wore a black tuxedo with blood red vest and bow tie. His blonde hair and blue eyes were a trifle Ken doll for a place like Bitter Sweets, but he managed to pull it off.

"How do you keep the tourists from knowing there's actual magic involved?" Spook asked.

"Oil." He pointed at the nearest globe. "We tell them they're covered in a drug that opens them up to the collective unconscious." Billy opened wide his eyeliner-darkened eyes and sold it.

Spook chuckled. Stupid tourists.

"The usual?" Billy asked.

"Nah. I'm expecting a guest," Spook said, "so let's go with a bottle of something mellow made by nuns or priests."

An amazingly pretty Asian girl danced on a raised platform. Her dance complemented the dance globe choreography but took it a step higher. When the lyrics came in, the girl lip-synced along—wait. She wore a headset. Was she singing live? Incredible.

"Who's the singer?" Spook asked.

"Jem. Korean dragon."

That explained the vocal range. "She need dancers?"

"You know some?" Billy leaned against the divider.

"You looking?" Spook glanced up.

Billy smiled, leaned over and kissed Spook's head. "You have dancers need work, I'll make a spot."

"That's just because I tip well." Spook swatted his friend's butt.

Billy raised an eyebrow. "Married."

"Metro." Spook handed over several bills.

"She's a big deal in Korea, you know." Billy shoved the bills into a pocket without looking at them.

"I'll google," Spook said. "My meeting here? She's a nun."

"Like, a *nun* nun?" Billy smiled and looked toward the door. "Known or Unknown?"

Spook shrugged dramatically. "Not sure. She's *Santería*, so even if she's not Unknown she's likely seen her fair share of our world." Normal humans were Known. Everyone else, and that included a plethora of species, was Unknown. Bitter Sweets was one of very few places where the two mingled.

Billy's eyes glassed over. "She's here," he said. "Wow. She is a *nun* nun."

Spook turned to the doorway as a tall, handsome woman in an old-fashioned habit entered. She even wore a wimple. Spook hadn't seen one of *those* since the seventies.

Oddly, walking through a room full of demons, werewhatsits and, ugh, Goth vampire-wannabes, her ancient costume fit into the cosplay atmosphere. She spoke to a young man with blue puzzle pieces tattooed from the horns on his shaved head to the oversized belly-button ring on his bare torso. Was his look genetic or affectation?

The young man turned and scanned the crowd. His eyes glowed yellow for the shortest moment then he met Spook's gaze, smiled and pointed. Not an affectation then.

The nun thanked him and headed Spook's way.

"How badly do you want to impress her?" Billy asked.

"I have no idea." Would she even know the difference if he blew the money?

"Blue Nun it is." Billy gestured her into the booth opposite Spook.

She smiled and nodded. "Mr. James, I presume?"

"In the flesh," Spook said. "Sister Liberata? You're younger than I thought you'd be."

She huffed into the seat and had to move the table a few inches to fit her rather expansive waist. Billy helped her then melted into the crowd.

"I didn't know they still made y'all wear the full get up," Spook remarked.

"Oh, they don't make me." She adjusted the wimple. "It's just a habit."

So, one of those. She wore a rather simple smile while she took in the dance floor where fangs, horns and wings were as common as kohl around the eyes.

"Singer has a wonderful voice." She bopped along for a moment in a way that reminded Spook of himself back in high school before he'd been de-geeked, deflowered and transformed into the Unknown.

The singer undulated in a decidedly reptilian fashion. Did she even have a spine?

"You don't seem very out of place here," Spook said to the nun. "I was a bit concerned how you'd take it." He'd chosen their location as a test.

"I assure you I'm just at home here as you are." She didn't take her eyes off the dance floor.

He opened his third eye. Whatsa Jesus! What *was* she? Her energy radiated red and charcoal grey. Not evil, but. . . she rode the line.

"Ah, is that the reason for the habit?" he asked.

"It's amazing what a girl can hide under one of these things." She laughed and adjusted her dress. "I could have a bazooka in here and no one would know it."

"Do you?"

She winked.

Nope. He wouldn't think about it. Not one little bit.

Billy arrived with an open bottle and two glasses. He poured. He left.

Spook took his glass and waved a hand over it. "*Etiam partem temel.*" The wine sparkled and not in a bubbly way.

The nun raised an eyebrow. "That's awfully open."

"In here?" He sipped. "It's nothing."

"And with me?" Her tone dripped feigned innocence.

"I doubt I could surprise you." He sipped again.

"What did you do to it?" She took her own glass and drank it down in one draught.

Whoa.

"Alcohol has no effect on me without a little jump start," Spook told her.

"Oh?" She refilled her glass. "So you're hiding as much as I am?"

"Mine's just easier to conceal, I suspect." He finished his glass, not wanting a nun to outdo him. "I'd never need a whole habit to hide what I have going on."

She snorted.

Thank goodness he didn't have blood coursing through his veins to redden his cheeks.

"Why are we here?" she asked, thankfully letting his dork move slide.

"I understand you met with this man a few months ago." He pulled out a photo of David Palatino, aka Twist, and placed it on the table between them.

She hissed—actually *hissed*—then pushed the photo away and spat on it. Good aim.

"If you're an associate of that monster. . ." Her voice had dropped half an octave and filled with venom. And *that* coming from *her?*

Chapter Three

"I think we need to get the crew together," I said. "Talk through what everyone saw." I met Kenny's angry eyes. "If this is a ghost we're talking about, he's taken out Gunner's parents and Warren. That pretty much leaves us as the next logical targets."

Kenny's eyes softened a little.

Corey rubbed his back.

Fine. We hadn't danced since the camp. I hadn't talked to Katy since then either. Not really. Crap. That brought up another set of emotions that sucked. I missed her. Really truly missed her, but could I trust her after all that? I was certain I'd seen the love die in her eyes that last day, but she kept asking to talk.

I guess I wouldn't know how I really felt unless I saw her.

"Get the crew together?" I asked. "Sound like a plan?"

Both guys nodded.

"I wish we could contact Spook," Kenny said. "What I found doesn't really help locate him."

Corey nodded.

Time to admit my own secrets. "I did some digging, too." I moved back to the table and accessed my cloud from Kenny's tablet. "He hangs out at this place called Bitter Sweets. It's kind of a Goth hangout from what Jimmy Russo tells me."

"Wait. You've been digging, too?" Kenny took his traditional spot over my shoulder. "And you didn't tell us?"

Because they'd been so open with me. Ugh.

"On a hunch, I asked Jimmy to try and find the weirdest, spookiest place in Austin. He found this place, says it's wa-a-ay underground." I pulled up the photos.

"Whoa." Kenny clicked through the shots. "They take cosplay to an entirely new level."

Indeed. The photos showed a dark, spooky dance club with folks made up like angels, demons and pretty much everything in between. There was one funny pic of some shirtless dude made up like a sparkly vampire getting a swirly.

"How'd Jimmy hear about it?" Corey asked.

"He hangs out at a hardcore underground fight club." I'd been pretty surprised to find out about *that,* too. "Guy he knows named Muscle knew Spook, knew the club." I pointed at the big Asian dude in one photo.

"Whoa. Big dude. Kinda spooky looking, hai?"

"You have no idea," I said. "Weird thing is I met him once."

"Hai?"

"A coupla years ago." I freaking *hated* coincidences. "He saved me and Monika from muggers. Took a bullet to the shoulder like it was nothing."

"Are those horns on his head?" Corey zoomed in.

I scoffed. "It's Austin. I had horns."

They both pulled back with raised eyebrows.

"It was a costume," I said. "An angel/devil thing Monika and I did."

Corey laughed. "Red tights and a pitchfork?"

"*Anyway,*" I redirected before they asked for photos. "I thought I might head there this weekend and check the place out. I didn't say anything because. . ."

"Because what?" Shit, even Corey seemed annoyed with me.

"Because I feel stupid entertaining the possibility that this is all supernatural." I jabbed a thumb at the tablet. "Look at how seriously they take it. I mean, it's like a comic con."

Kenny crossed his arms, back to petulant and likely to get angrier.

"You want honest?" I demanded. "I was going to check it out myself to find out he's full of shit, and then come back and prove this whole thing is behind us."

"Except it's not," Kenny said, his voice cold. "People are dying."

"Except it's not," I admitted. "I don't know what it is though."

The anger in Kenny's eyes made my heart hurt.

Corey dropped a meaty hand on my shoulder. "You just want it to be over."

At least *he* understood. "I just want it to be over," I admitted.

My phone vibrated. A text from Saundra: *Happy Birthday, Mr. Fox the younger. Any chance you can drive up to the big city for a visit? I have a present for you.*

What had I just thought about coincidences?

Wait a minute. Happy Birthday?

"Holy crap, is it the fifth already?" I checked the date on the screen.

"Yeah, why?" Corey released my shoulder and patted it.

"It's my birthday," I said. "I'm an adult."

"Wow." Kenny stopped looking angry. "Happy birthday."

Corey hugged me. "No more sex with minors."

I accepted the hug and forced myself to laugh at the joke, but I'd told everyone I didn't want to celebrate this year. I wasn't in the mood for a party.

However. . .

"Okay y'all," I said, pulling out of Corey's hug. "Let's get on the line and gather the troops."

Corey saluted. "Aye, aye captain."

"He's dead," Spook blurted.

"Good." The nun rose from her seat. Things clicked and popped, and Spook couldn't help the curiosity over what hid beneath the habit.

"But I suspect he's not gone," he told her. "And I want to stop him. I am *not* his friend."

She stood by the table, breathing fast with fire flickering in her dark eyes.

Spook sat quietly, meeting her gaze and letting her make the next move.

She lowered herself into the booth.

Thank the gods.

"Ah, see?" Spook drank his wine and offered to refill her glass. "I had a feeling we had something to discuss. Why do you hate him so much?"

She waved the bottle of cheap wine away and raised a hand.

Billy appeared.

"Your best Scotch," she said. "Neat."

Billy swallowed. "Our *best?*"

She held Spook's stare and raised one rather shaggy eyebrow.

"Your very best," Spook said without hesitation. He suddenly had a feeling this "nun" was so much more than she seemed.

Billy raised a bottle and held a glass under it, but the nun grabbed the bottle itself and sucked down half of it in one long draught.

Billy winced and made an apologetic face to Spook.

Spook waved him away with a reassuring smile.

Billy startled, bowed deeply and vanished. Yipes. The tip alone on that bottle would likely match a year's salary for the bar manager. No big. Spook's compensation for living life outside polite society was vast financial resources.

After chugging half the bottle, the nun set it down.

Should he offer to spell it for her? Chances were her nature was as much a liability in the booze department as was his.

"The little prick killed my best friend." Everything about her had changed. She'd lost every ounce of nun persona. This was a hard-nosed professional. "He visited me a few months ago. He came off as a complete boob, looking for a witch to help him 'get someone out of the way.'" She shook her head and sucked down another slug. "My friend Delilah lived out in the desert. I sent him to her. It was a mistake. I underestimated him."

"Why send him to her?"

"She's one of the most. . ." Her face pinched tight for a moment, and Spook could tell she missed her friend." She *was* one of the most powerful witches in the country."

Huh? Spook thought he knew everyone. "I've not heard of her."

"No huge surprise, she's been in isolation for a whole lot of years."

"Isolation?"

She pounded the bottle on the table.

Spook jumped.

"When you say he's back," she asked. "What do you mean?"

"I think he's killing," Spook told her. "I think his spirit is possessing people, and he's using them to exact revenge."

She sighed a deep, contented sigh. "Oh, well, as long as that's all it is."

"That's *all?*" Spook asked sardonically. "Three are dead so far."

Billy appeared.

"Keep it coming, bright eyes," the nun told him, dropping a handful of gold doubloons on the table. "This rounds on me. Don't skimp."

Holy. dratting. feces. How old was she?

Billy's eyes grew wide. He bowed and produced a rather dusty bottle and two glasses.

She laughed a dry laugh, almost a cackle. "Things could be far worse. If he'd gotten her spell book. . ." She let it hang.

Spook hated dangling clauses. "She wasn't out there of her own free will, was she?" He took a swig of the Scotch. Big daddy smooth. Just. the. best.

Spook glanced at Billy, who smiled like a serpent. Spook smiled back and winked to tell his friend to remember that bottle, no matter how expensive. Billy nodded and evaporated.

"No." The nun swirled her drink. "She was cast out. . . by the Cloaks." She glanced up at the velvet curtains at the edge of the booth, and they dropped closed.

"Wait. The actual Cloaks? What did she do?"

The nun set her drink on the table, but the Scotch kept swirling. It glowed and then poured out of the glass into the air above the table, creating a liquid screen between them. Images appeared. A middle-aged Black woman and the bloody corpse of a man.

"Her husband died." Sister Liberata narrated as the images played out the story. "She was too smart to reanimate the body, but she was also too smart to think there didn't have to be another way."

The *telenovela* showed the Black woman pouring through ancient texts.

"She brought him back," Spook foreshadowed.

"Yes. . . Sort of." The nun waved at the image. "He went hinky."

They always did. The spell showed a different man, rather grey and decomposed, attacking and killing an entire family, ripping bodies apart as if they were wet tissue. Apparently, she'd found a way to incorporate the husband's soul into a new body. That rarely worked.

"He ate a couple of villages." She waved at the image and it showed a montage of grizzly cannibalistic murders. "It was messy and *public*."

Which explained why the Cloaks got involved. They kept all knowledge of supernatural activity away from the general public using any means necessary. Spook had suspected for years they were the truth behind the "accident" at Chernobyl.

"They destroyed all evidence," Sister Liberata said. "Called it a plague. That sort of thing wasn't so uncommon then."

Just how long ago had this happened?

"Why didn't they erase her?" Spook asked. "Why cast her out to the desert?"

"She was the most powerful witch in the country," Liberata said as if he was simple. "They had uses for her."

And then Spook's real question. "Why did you send Palatino out to her?"

She waved a hand over her glass and the liquid dropped back into it, erasing the images. She took another drink. "One of the things she did was scare off potential trouble. Tourists come to me seeking dark arts because they assume all witches are evil. If they seemed focused enough to cause trouble but not bright enough to be of any use. . ." She shrugged. "I sent them to her and she scared them off the path when she could."

Ah. "And when she couldn't?"

"They were sent off the path one way or another." Her eyes sparkled. "She worked for the Cloaks, not the Welcome Wagon."

And there it was. People who wanted to do evil—but weren't smart enough to be of use—disappeared.

"What happened with Palatino?" Spook asked.

"I honestly don't know. I sent him out to her. A few days later, I heard her scream in my mind." She shuddered. "She died violently. Her shack was nothing but ashes. From the hole in her skull, she'd been shot. If she underestimated him as much as I had, he could've gotten a shot off before she could stop him." She stared into her glass. "I sent him out to her, and he killed her. That makes it my responsibility."

She spat on the photo again.

Spook understood. Every life he'd failed to save weighed on his soul.

"How'd she bring her husband back?" he asked.

"Doesn't matter." She smiled a fake, ecclesiastical smile. "The hut was burned to the ground. Her methods were lost."

Yeah. If only, if only. . . Spook pulled a stuffed grackle out from under the table and plopped it on the table.

She gasped. "Where did you get that?"

Where indeed. "There's a farmhouse in Middle-of-nowhere, Texas. It burned to the ground shortly before Palatino went on his killing spree at the Boy Scout camp. I found this there. It survived the fire. The entire place reeked of dark magic." He leaned closer. "*Dark* magic. And not just his."

Her eyes narrowed. "He wasn't alone?"

Spook shook his head and gods help them all if he was right about the accomplice.

She touched the feathers. "This was Delilah's. If he had this, it's hard to say what else he took."

"And if he had her books. . ." It was Spook's worst-case hypothesis.

She sighed and met his eyes evenly. "If that sick little twist has Delilah's books, you're all in mortal danger." She met his gaze. "More from the Cloaks than from him. He doesn't seem to have the good sense to keep things quiet."

Not just danger. *Mortal* danger.

"I sort of figured." Spook shook his head. He sometimes hated when he was right. Had Fox found the yearbook photos he'd planted or would Spook need to make contact on his own again?

The singer finished her song on a high note no human could hit without FX.

The spell released the dancers and they applauded madly.
Hmmm.

Lucky Fox walked up the steps to the front door as his son and entourage left the house. "Hey, straight son."

"Hey, gay dad." Ethan hugged his dad, but the affection seemed perfunctory.

"Anything wrong?"

The smile that instantly lit Ethan's face had to be fake. "No, just going for a dance crew reunion."

Well, Lucky could tell it wasn't a lie, exactly, but it also wasn't the complete truth. He hugged his son tight. "Good luck." He'd fess up when he was ready.

"Thanks."

Lucky bumped fists with the other guys as they passed.

"Hai, Mr. Fox."

"Yo, F-bomb. Ready for the big move?"

"You know it."

Corey's smile showed Lucky the kid was stoked he'd agreed to chaperone three teenagers for the rest of the school year. It hadn't been a hard decision. Lucky had too many lousy memories in Mac's house to really consider it home. Plus, looking after Corey and Kenny would help him feel he was earning his keep. They wouldn't need much in the way of supervision, although if Ethan was any indication, they'd all need to learn to pick up after themselves.

The three of them piled into Corey's Challenger.

Lucky's biggest job would be fending off Corey's greedy relatives and that bastard of a father. Lucky had known Harry in high school, back when he and Lisa had first started dating. He'd done a bit of running around behind her back then, too.

Bastard.

Lucky sighed deeply and waved as the car pulled away. The fact that

Ethan noticed and waved back made his day. How many teenage sons would take the time for a second glance?

Kenny waved, too. There was a boy with some issues. His conviction that Twist had returned from the grave scared Lucky a little. He was so sincere.

Anyway, time for chores. Lucky walked through the house and into the backyard.

Some pretty bizarre things had happened. . . but ghosts? Lucky's explanation was much simpler: Gunner killed his parents, and those cons threatened the nurse into confessing. Lucky had to admit he was grateful to that little sociopath for blowing Twist away but not so much that he'd let himself be swayed away from the obvious.

He grabbed the net and moved around the edge of the pool, dragging it along the bottom. Back and forth. Back and forth. The bad thing about having a pool was all the work even when the weather was too cold for swimming. Ah well, all things considered he had far less work on this old place than he'd had on the Austin house. He missed that house though. All the memories.

Fortunately, Corey had people to do that sort of thing on the ranch, so Lucky could help Mac with her place without doubling the workload.

"People to do that sort of thing," Lucky muttered. Man. Weird. No matter how much money he'd made in Austin, he'd always cleaned the house himself. The gym, too. Heh. Ephraim had made jokes about that.

Back and forth. Back and forth.

Poor Ephraim. *That* kid would be in therapy for years. For his sake, Lucky wished magic *had* been involved. How the hell had Twist convinced that poor kid he'd been the one to shoot Lisa?

Back and forth.

Ethan's birthday and no one was celebrating. So much was about to change for him. Well, Ethan might have expressly forbidden presents, but Lucky had found what he hoped was a pretty damn good one. He couldn't let his son become a man, well, legally anyway, without commemorating *somehow*.

The best part was that, as far as he could tell, Corey hadn't spilled the beans. Ethan's friend was pretty much a genius with anything that had an engine and had made the entire project possible.

As Ethan would've said, stellar.

The gate creaked open, distracting Lucky. Mike hurried across the grass.

Wonderful. Lucky hadn't expected to see his boyfriend until later that day. "Hey, Mike. Just can't keep your hands off me?" Wow. Boyfriend. What a concept.

A strong shoulder crashed into Lucky's side, knocking him off balance.

"Mike, honey, it's awfully cold—"

Too late. Splash! They tumbled into the pool together. Fuck it was cold!

Mike's entire body wrapped around Lucky's. Okay, Lucky enjoyed good-spirited hijinks as much as the next guy, but the water was damn cold.

An arm tightened around his neck. A fist pounded into his kidney.

What the hell?

He yanked on the arm around his neck. The move had absolutely no effect whatsoever.

Wait. It *was* Mike, right? He wasn't nearly that strong.

The bottom of the pool bumped Lucky's hip.

Christ, what was Mike thinking? They could both drown.

He grabbed the fist slamming into his kidney, but his attacker just threw it off and slammed the side of Lucky's head.

Stars flashed. The only thing stopping him from sucking in the pool water was the arm choking him out. He struggled harder, but it was like a Navy SEAL had latched on and wanted him dead.

It couldn't be Mike. No way.

The flashing lights flared more brightly.

The world faded to black.

Chapter Four

The bell tinkled in its merry way as I led Kenny and Corey through the studio door. Everyone looked up in a silence I could tell had lasted awhile.

Tango, who still answered to Tango, Trudy (formally known as Juicy) and Cosita (who refused to give me any other name) sat together on the dance floor.

Ephraim, Lizard and Woody (who'd made a brief appearance as Sam before returning to Woody) sat at the bar. Lizard's presence surprised me a bit, although he'd been at camp and bonus for Ephraim that he'd come to visit.

Retro stood with the guys, yet on the other side of the bar.

Hm. Factions. Damn.

Tango's eyes searched mine.

My throat tightened, but I stuck to my guns and refused to show anything at all.

Whatever she'd been looking for, she didn't see it. She looked away.

Double damn. I couldn't deny it. Still had the feelings. I loved her.

"You've all heard about Warren?" I led my entourage to the edge of the floor, halfway between the two groups.

"He was a jerk and kind of a waste of skin." Trudy shook her head. "He didn't deserve that."

"What even really happened?" Tango asked. "Some tiny nurse pulled him off the ground and lynched him? That's bullshit."

"What do y'all think happened?" I asked.

"Do you know why he was in the infirmary?" Trudy countered.

Huh. I didn't. Apparently, no one else did either.

"I talked to his mom." Trudy was his ex-girlfriend, remember? "He was a cop in gen pop with tons of *pendejos* he put behind bars. Five huge guys jumped him and made him their *perra* all night long."

Aw. Shit. Even he didn't deserve that.

"He was recovering in the infirmary when it happened." She shook her head and kissed the back of Cosita's hand.

"Did he narc them out?" I asked. "Was it retaliation?"

"That makes the most sense to me," Tango said, and I could tell she really wanted me to land on the same side.

"A tiny little nurse was holding the rope," Woody said. "She weighed nothing, *chica*. Do the math. There is no fucking way *pequeña mujercita* could've done it."

Tango rose and walked right up to him. "So the giant bruisers who assaulted Warren ganked him for selling them out and told her she was next if she didn't take the rap." She glanced my way and rolled her eyes before giving Woody her full-on glare. "Who are *you* saying did it?"

"I'm saying it was Twist." Woody leaned back against the bar as casual as could be.

Ephraim and Lizard exchanged a glance that said they agreed one hundred percent. Well, they had reason. Truth.

Tango, Retro and Cosita scoffed.

Trudy remained decisively neutral. Huh.

"All y'all heard what that Spook guy said," Woody insisted. "Gunner might've killed Twist, but that doesn't mean he's gone for good."

"Oh dear God," Tango exclaimed, "are you serious, *Santería?*"

"What, this is an episode of *Supernatural?*" Which told me where Retro stood.

The volume increased as they yelled it back and forth.

Yeah, that'd be productive.

"Shut up!" I shouted.

They shut up. Huh.

"Look. We haven't talked about this," I said. "We have radically different theories, and we should hear them all, and we should be God damned *nice* to each other because the rest of the world is going to do *jack all* for us, okay? Please." I tried to meet every pair of eyes. "We're friends here. No matter what anyone believes. . . or doesn't believe."

Tango breathed heavily, keeping her mouth shut.

Woody hooked an arm around Ephraim's neck. "Sorry, Tango. I know you don't buy any of this, but. . ." He squeezed Ephraim. "Just try to keep an open mind?"

She melted and nodded. "Sorry, Effy."

Effy nodded.

"Lock in?" Kenny suggested.

"No." Ephraim shook his head and pulled away from Woody to go back to Lizard. "I can't. I'm all keyed up the wrong way. I want to talk."

I'd guess I'm the only one who noticed the very brief flash of disappointment on Woody's face. By the way, his last name was Madera, so Woody was actually a riff on his name and had nothing to do with dick. Ironic, huh?

The ladies took chairs. Me and the guys, too, but I kept my seat in a neutral position. Kenny and Corey flanked me.

"Stereo Hearts" played on someone's cell.

Cosita grabbed hers. "*Lo Siento. Es Stereo.*" She read the text. "She heard we were here. She wants in."

"Stereo?" I asked.

"Mono's twin sister," Corey said as if that should mean something.

"Mono had a twin sister?" I asked.

Okay, *everyone* muttered at that.

"Jesus, Ethan," Trudy said. "Really? She was at every funeral."

"What?" I said defensively. "We all know I'm a douchebag, right?"

Oh. *That's* where Mono's nickname must've come from, and I'd always assumed it was Spanish for monkey. She must've been the older of the two.

"I say we let her in," Kenny insisted.

"She wasn't there," Tango objected.

"She has a right." Kenny rarely stood up like that.

Tango scoffed. "That's just because she already had one foot in your psychotic new age gypsy world before this whole nightmare, and you know she'll side with you."

"Jesus, Tango," I said without even thinking, "that's kinda harsh, hai?"

She glared at me.

Oh, wait. Tango's less than politically correct description helped me remember the girl from Mono's funeral: a pretty punk rock/hippy chick with combat boots, blue and white hair and lots of leather who seemed to belong more at an Austin drum circle than a Dumass funeral.

That was Mono's sister? Wow. They were twins? Double wow. Oh. I got the name, too. She was sort of the Dolby 5.1 surround version of her sister.

"Tell her she's welcome to join us," I said.

Cosita nodded and texted.

"We're not waiting," Tango said. "Ephraim. You said you want to talk. Floor's yours."

Lizard gave him a squeeze.

"You all know I'm the most cynical mean-spirited son of a bitch in town," Ephraim said.

Well, yeah.

"I can't explain what happened to me." He looked at Corey.

"It's okay, bro." Corey gave him a rather stoic thumbs up. "We've talked. I get it. I don't blame you at all."

Effy nodded and turned to Lizard, who faced the crowd.

"We were kissing," Lizard said, "in my room, and he jumped. I thought I'd tickled him or something." He looked at the floor. "Then he pushed me off and just started walking. I thought, maybe he was shy, maybe I'd done something, since he wouldn't talk to me, wouldn't say a word."

Ephraim shook his head. "I remember it. I was there, but I couldn't do anything about it." He faced Tango directly. "It wasn't like being drugged. I didn't hallucinate or anything. It's like I was on a roller coaster, where they strap you in so you can't really control where you go. It just drives you around the track. I didn't want to shove him away." He pulled Lizard closer.

Yeah, walking away from a guaranteed make-out session didn't strike me as an Ephraim thing to do.

"I didn't want to stop kissing him. I mean, I hoped. . ." Effy blushed. *Effy*. "I hoped it would go further."

"That's what *she* said."

Everyone slowly turned to Trudy. Really? Not quite the time to tease him.

She rolled her eyes and scoffed. "No. I mean, the *nurse*. That's what she said happened last night. It's exactly the same thing she's saying. She was there. She remembers doing it, but she couldn't stop herself." She shrugged. "The cops assume she's going for an insanity plea, but it's exactly the same thing Effy just said."

"It gets weirder," Lizard muttered. Under everyone's stare, he sort of shrank down.

Effy hugged him tight. "I know you don't know them that well. They're good people though. Even the skeptical pretty boy." He glanced at me.

"I didn't know what was going on," Lizard said. "I just thought he was blowing me off. You know, that he'd changed his mind. Maybe I sucked at kissing? What do I know?"

"You do *not* suck at kissing," Ephraim said.

Lizard sort of almost smiled. "Anyway, I felt horrible, so I wanted to talk to my big brother, to Ben, er, Whiskey." He glanced up at Tango. Hm. "I heard he was at the command center, so I ran there. What I saw—" He shook his head and stared down. "Whiskey was beating the *snot* out of Mono and Teddy and they just *let* him. Just stood there and took it." Tears ran down his cheeks. "I thought it must be another big set-up, so I didn't say anything, you know? Then I saw he was crying, but he didn't stop pounding on them. It's like he was begging himself to stop, but he just kept hitting them and they just took it." He sniffled. "Then they sat in the chairs we'd used for the fake gunshots. There was dried fake blood, and it looked totally different from what was on Mono and Teddy." He wiped an arm across his face. "He tied them up. I was so shocked, I just watched. I mean, it had to be some kind of put-on, right?"

He looked right into my eyes. For some reason, he seemed to want to make sure I believed him.

"Then Whiskey walked into a corner, like he was a naughty boy or something. He just stood there, staring into the corner." Lizard looked down again. "None of them said a word or moved. It freaked me out. I mean, what the heck? I finally went up to Ben and asked him what was going on, but he wouldn't talk to me. So I punched him in the arm. These tears were running down his face. . ." He hiccoughed and wiped his face again. "And I told him what Effy did, and I yelled at him and told him to stop messing around, it wasn't funny, and then I hit him. I mean, really punched him. He just cried more."

The tears poured down his face. How did he keep talking?

"I said *fine*," he choked out, "*fuck you then*, and I left. It was the last time I saw him alive." He could barely speak. "Fuck you was the last thing I said to my brother."

And then he lost it. I think Effy only held it together so he could comfort Lizard.

Was Twist some kind of mind control genius? Was it hypnotism? I mean, what Lizard saw, that was. . . Shit, I couldn't explain *that* away.

I moved close and stroked Lizard's hair. "He understood."

He looked at me with red, red eyes.

"I saw the two of you together," I said. "He loved you. You loved him. You both knew it, and you *showed* it. Those last minutes weren't your fault no matter how messed up they were. That's what you need to hang onto. That last time didn't count. Neither of you could control what happened."

Lizard nodded then buried his face in Effy's shoulder.

Effy took over the stroking of his hair. "See Lizzy? It's what I told you. It's the same thing I said." He smiled at me through his own tears and mouthed, "Thank you."

I still didn't know what I believed, although I knew what Lizard needed to believe in that moment, and I would do whatever I could to help.

"It never made sense to me," I said, and that was the truth, "the way he ran headlong into the building. It was reckless, and he may have been a lot of things but Whiskey planned everything carefully. I don't think he was reckless."

"Are you saying you think someone, *Twist*, mind controlled him to kill himself, Mono and Teddy?" Tango's voice was so quiet. I couldn't read her expression at all. No tears. Angry? Why angry?

I shrugged. "What else do we have?"

She moved away with a noise that went way beyond scoffing. "You have to be kidding me."

Everyone jumped in and the volume rose.

Effy pulled away from Lizard. "It wasn't a hallucination," he shouted over the rest of it, "what I did. I didn't imagine it. I did it. I shot her." He turned to Corey. "I am so sorry."

Corey hurried to him and wrapped him in those big arms. "It wasn't you, Effy. It wasn't you."

"*Jesus Christo, chicos,*" Tango whispered, "do you hear yourselves? What you're saying?"

"There's a lot of shit we can't explain," Woody said.

"I can't explain Justin Bieber's popularity, but that doesn't mean I think voodoo is involved." She shook her head and crossed her arms. She looked at Trudy, who didn't seem to be on her side on this one. She glanced at me.

I shrugged. I didn't know what to believe.

"This is bullshit." She walked toward the door.

"Katy," I called. "Tango!"

"No!" When she spun to look at me, tears finally fell from her eyes. "I thought we were coming here to *dance*, not indulge in insane mass hysteria. I will *not* be involved in this." She turned to the door. "Lock up when you're done." She left.

Silence ruled the studio. All eyes turned to me.

Stellar.

I dashed after her.

"Tango!" I ran flat out to catch her before she reached her car. How the *hell* did she move so fast? "I don't know what I believe, okay? Right now, they *really* need to believe this."

"What about me?" She crossed her arms and the tears poured down her cheeks. "What about the rest of us? People died. That sucks, it *sucks*, but trying to make Gunner's parents and Warren about Twist? That means we keep relieving what happened out there day after day. Aren't you a little tired of reliving all that? Wouldn't you rather move on?" She stepped closer. "I just want to pretend it never happened."

Her eyes told me she was talking about so much more than the people who died. She was talking about what had died out there between us. She wanted to pretend *that* had never happened either. To move on as if she'd never kissed Whiskey, as if she'd never fallen for him.

Could I do that? Could I forgive her? Yeah. Probably.

Move on? Maybe.

Could I pretend it'd never happened? No. I wasn't built that way.

What I really wanted was to hold her in my arms and kiss her until all the pain and angst disappeared. Before I could do that though, she grabbed the door handle, slid into her car and started it up.

She looked in the mirror at me, as if hoping I'd stop her.

"Let her go, douchebag," an unfamiliar voice said. "That girl is dealing with a host of demons."

I turned. The blue and white hair told me she was Stereo, in a black trench coat. The sun sparkled off the pentacle. . . pentagram? With the star-shaped thingy between her boobs.

While I tried to gather my thoughts, Tango drove off.

"I know," I said.

"No." She smirked. "You don't."

I didn't like the sound of that. "I know about the kiss."

She laughed. "Kiss? You think all *that* is about a *kiss*?"

Oh. . . Shit.

"Do I get to say it, douchebag?" She sauntered closer as if enjoying herself. "Do I get to say the words? I will if you want me to."

Katy had sex with him. When we'd talked about the kiss, she'd already had sex with him. She lied to my face as if it didn't matter. In my mind, I heard Twist accuse her of it. I saw her shake her head in denial. I'd believed her. What a fucking *chode* I was.

"There we are." Stereo held her hands behind her back and smiled in a way that reminded me of Monika. "Good. Does it hurt?" She raised one heavily made-up eyebrow. "Does it? Good."

I took a step back. "What the hell?"

"You killed my sister, you asshole." She advanced aggressively. "She was there because of you, and Twist killed her because of you." She shoved me so hard I almost fell. "No one will tell me different, so finding out your little girlfriend screwed the rock star behind your back? Yeah. That's just the start."

Blank. Total blank.

"We were going to the same school next year," Stereo shouted. "When our parents split up, Mom kept Jane here in Dumbass and Dad took me to Houston. . . but we were going to Austin together. Six months and we'd have been together!"

She raised her hands to shove me again.

I'd have let her.

She pulled back. "You know what?" She stalked around me toward the studio. "I don't want to infect myself touching you. People who touch you die."

Chapter Five

Lucky fell limp in Mike's arms. Christ on toast! Why couldn't he stop? Why was he choking the life out of the biggest miracle in his life? Mike felt the cold. He felt his lungs burning. He saw the lights flashing in his eyes, yet he couldn't do a thing about any of it.

He couldn't even close his own eyes to shut out the sight of—

Hands grabbed his head, squeezing at his temples.

A voice in his mind: *Vis facer legim uset.* We want to do. . . what?

A brilliant flash of orange light.

Something sucked Mike out of the pool. . . like a vertical drop waterslide in reverse!

His arms released Lucky. Thank God. . . but had it happened in time?

A violent wave tossed him into the air. He tumbled to the grass and rolled several times before landing on his hands and knees.

The world's largest football shoved its way out of his stomach and forced its way up his esophagus. That's what it felt like. Huge and painful, worse than the biggest booze-filled frat party in college.

Projectile vomit.

Green and glowing. . . no, not vomit. Something green and liquid glowing bright light screamed from his mouth and poured into the air.

It swirled overhead in a glowing tornado before tearing off faster than a rocket. It shrieked so loud, Mike covered his ears to block it out.

Glass shattered.

Lucky. Where was Lucky?

Some kid in a soaking wet trench coat knelt over Lucky's unmoving body.

"Get away from him!" Mike tried to shout, only managing a hoarse rasp. He couldn't stand. He crawled. "Don't you dare hurt him!"

The kid met Mike's eyes.

Christ in a tabloid.

His eyes. Golden. Glowing, fucking *glowing* like the stuff that had puked out of Mike's own body. The same glow surrounded the hand the kid pressed onto Lucky's unmoving chest.

"*Nostro prompta molestiae.*" The kid's voice sounded far too old for his face.

Our. . . what? What messed up language was that?

"You in any danger of dying?" the kid asked.

Okay. That was English, anyway.

"*Estás en peligro de morir?*" he added.

"No. I'm fine." Mike scooted over to Lucky's side, grabbed his hand.

Lucky's entire body spasmed into life. His back arched. His eyes opened wide as he sucked in the biggest breath ever. Oh, thank God.

Mike pulled Lucky's hand closer, and the big guy focused. His eyes opened wide in terror and he scooted away.

And Mike died a little. He released Lucky's hand.

"What the fuck just happened?" Lucky pointed at the kid whose eyes had stopped glowing. "Who are you?"

Mike couldn't move. He'd tried to kill the most important person in his life ever. If Lucky thought. . . hell, what else could he think? Mike saw it in his eyes. Fear. Confusion. Had he lost him? Did Lucky believe Mike would hurt him?

"Mr. Fox, *really*. . ." The kid rose to his feet calmly and brushed off his hands. "Apart from being psychologically incapable of harming you, do you actually think this man could physically overpower you?" He gestured from Mike to Lucky. "I don't think so." The little jerk smiled at Mike. "No offense."

But what he'd said made sense.

"It's what Ephraim Miller described," Mike said quickly. He had seconds to salvage Lucky's trust. "What that nurse last night said. I couldn't stop. I swear it, Lucky. I'd never. . ." He had to wait a second.

Was he going to throw up again? He swallowed. "Jesus Christ on toast, Lucky, I couldn't stop." His eyes burned. "I would never. . . I couldn't. . ."

Ah, Christ on a pogo stick. He couldn't even say it. He could never hurt Lucky. Never.

Lucky's eyes changed. He closed them, shook his head. He shook out his entire body. When his eyes opened, they were calm.

What did that mean?

Lucky scooted closer and grabbed Mike with both hands. He yanked Mike in and wrapped his arms around him.

Oh, thank God. Thank God.

Mike choked back a sob and latched on. "I'm sorry, Lucky. I'm so damn sorry."

Lucky kissed him, shushed him. Pressed his forehead to Mike's.

Okay. Anything like skepticism would be delusional. Magic was real. Something had played Mike like a puppet.

"Who the hell are you, kid, and what are doing here?" Lucky kissed Mike again, and they helped each other to their feet.

"My name's Morrison James." He produced a business card that was, miraculously, dry. Well, Mike had seen him resuscitate Lucky with glowing gold hands. "I assume Ethan has at least mentioned me."

Lucky took the card, holding Mike tight with his other arm. "The Winchester sidekick from the cemetery?"

"Ha." The kid's lips pressed flat. "Yeah. Ha. He is both clever and original that boy of yours." His face lost all trace of emotion. "When I heard what happened to the officer last night, I came to town as quickly as I could."

"Not a moment too soon," Lucky said.

Mike held tight with both arms. He couldn't touch his boyfriend enough to feel satisfied. They'd almost died. How could Lucky be so matter-of-fact?

"So what do you know about all this?" Lucky asked.

"Are the two of you as skeptical as Ethan?" the kid asked.

Lucky turned to meet Mike's gaze. He'd been the more doubtful of the two. Lucky had never really embraced the possibilities of magical. . . stuff, yet Mike had discounted it from the beginning, working his professional detachment for all it was worth to avoid insulting Ethan when he'd stated rather abruptly that he thought Palatino stalked him in his dreams.

"After today?" Mike kissed Lucky again. "Not so much with the skepticism."

The kid shifted uncomfortably in his trench coat. Perhaps the PDA was awkward for him? Then he shook water from his arms. "Look, I'll explain what I know, but is there any chance I can borrow some dry clothes, and can we all go someplace a little warmer?" He shivered from head to toe like a dog. "I don't regulate heat very well."

"Yeah. Yeah, of course." Lucky's perpetual host instinct rose to the occasion.

Mike stopped him with both hands on his face. "Okay, I didn't go through everything you did at that camp." He forced Lucky to match his gaze. "I just tried to kill you." He had to swallow. "That doesn't make you hate me?"

Lucky's face melted. "Mike. No." He held Mike so tight he could barely breathe. "I'm sorry. I get that it wasn't you. I'm sorry I didn't say. Jesus. . . no."

Mike shook his head. He held Lucky at arm's length. "We're fine. I just. . ."

The kid's hand dropped on Mike's shoulder. "Look. You're going to need time to adjust. I get that. Can you just blow him later and make it all better? We have shit to deal with."

Against all odds, Mike chuckled.

Lucky, too.

"Fine." Lucky led them into the side door of the garage. "I did laundry. There'll be dry clothes."

They made their way around an unfamiliar car to the washer and dryer. While the kid shook out his coat, Lucky yanked clothes out of the dryer and threw them into a basket. He tossed James some of Ethan's things.

Mike grabbed towels and handed them around. "What happened to me?"

"What do *you* think happened?" James lay the towel on the car and unbuttoned his shirt.

Mike exchanged a glance with Lucky who knew how skeptical Mike had been. "I think it was some kind of mind control. My professional side wants to say some kind of drug or hypnosis, but that's not possible. The kind of complete control?" He grabbed Lucky's shirt, which turned into helping him out of it. "I've never heard of anything like it, and I've been researching everything I could find since they all came back from that camp." He met the kid's eyes. "I can't explain what happened here, not with anything like real world, scientific stuff." His wet clothes suddenly seemed doubly cold. "The theory going around is that it's David Palatino's ghost."

"Something like that." James dried off and pulled on Ethan's clothes: designer jeans, a t-shirt and a hoodie. Dressed like that, he looked like any teenager. Mike could almost forget that he'd seen the kid's eyes glow gold.

Man, the kid's eyes had *glowed*.

Mike pulled on oversized sweats and tied the string tight.

"We should find Ethan and his friends," Lucky said. "They're all in danger."

Mike pulled out his cell. Soaked and dead. "I'll take the land line and—"

"Not necessary." James shoved his hands in his pockets. "They're at the studio."

Mike wanted to ask him how he knew that, although they'd kind of bypassed that sort of question after the kid had jumpstarted Lucky with glowing hands.

Twist punched his way into the bitch who lived next door to Fox, upstairs in her bedroom. She gasped and fought for half a second. Seriously? Fuck that. He yanked control of the body by force then walked in front of a mirror so he could see what he looked like.

Blond. MILF material. He caressed her torso. Possessing women was weird. On the one hand, it felt just plain wrong. He was a dude. On the other hand, it did provide a few toys to play with. She had nice breasts. Still firm.

Okay, playtime was over. What. the hell. had happened?

He spun to face the direction of Fox's house. Something had forced him out of the gay shrink before he'd been able to kill them both. And it'd hurt. It'd fucking *hurt*. What'd been the freaking point of getting himself killed when stuff could still hurt?

And getting literally puked out? Gross!

Twist moved to a window and looked down over Fox's front lawn. After a few moments, big Fox, the gay shrink and some scrawny Mexican kid hurried out the front door and to the car in the driveway. The shiny BMW screamed rich fag.

Twist refocused his meat suit's eyes into a supernatural spectrum, and the kid climbing into the car popped. Almost literally. He glowed a bright, bright orange, as if *made* of magic. What the hell?

Twist shook his head to clear his vision, and there the kid was, climbing into the gaymobile like any other scrawny teenager in town. Not a local though. Twist knew everyone, and that kid? Not from around here.

Wait! He was *the guy*… Twist had tried to kill Gunner, and that guy had saved him. In Austin. Wow, in normal clothes he looked like nothing.

Fine. Mary had warned him about do-gooders. She'd even mentioned an enemy gathering forces. For all he knew this was that guy, too.

His boobs distracted him, standing out in his peripheral vision. He touched them. Hm. Not much feeling. Boob job?

And she needed to pee. Yikes! He pushed out of her and hovered in the middle of the room while she staggered a few steps and sat heavily on the bed. She brushed her hair out of her face and looked around.

Twist flitted through her, wiping her mind. Too many locals with a memory of his control, and the new guy might take notice. Well, *more* notice.

The MILF looked surprised then fell over sideways onto the mattress, eyes staring vacantly.

Oops. Too much. Twist hadn't quite adjusted to his powers. When he'd had a meat suit of his own, that touch would have just erased a few minutes.

Apparently, he'd wiped a bit more.

Yeah. She wasn't coming out of that any time soon.

Oh well.

He slipped through the wall and searched for a dude to possess.

Playing with titties entertained him, but he always missed having junk.

"It's not true, you know." Corey walked across the lot to my side. "None of this is your fault. Stereo's hurting and I get that, but it's a total bitch move to lay it at your feet."

"Is it?" I demanded.

He touched the middle of my chest with one finger. He shrugged. "Still breathing."

Good ol' Corey.

I closed my eyes and had to swallow again. "Did you know?"

His finger fell away from my chest, and I opened my eyes.

"I thought maybe." He shook his head. "I didn't want to believe it."

Him and me both. "Well, you told me so," I said.

"That's not why I'm here. To say I told you so."

I met his eyes. No. He'd never do that.

His mom was dead. How selfish was I to think. . . "I love her, Corey." A hand clamped down like a vise on my chest. "I still love her."

His eyes grew moist, and he nodded.

"With everything else that's happened," I asked, "how does this even matter?"

"It matters because she hurt you." He squeezed my arm. "And she hurt me, and. . . and so just cry and get it over with."

But I didn't. "No." Over his shoulder, vague shadows moved in the studio. "Not right now."

"Later?" he asked.

"Most likely." Did I have any tears left to cry? "Stereo. She knows about ghosts and stuff?"

He shrugged. "Seems to. There's a lot more of *everything* in Houston. Kenny asked her to help us figure stuff out."

"Come on." I pointed with my head. "Let's go learn something."

He fell in step beside me.

You know, there's a certain advantage to dealing with one more thing than you can handle. After that, you just go numb and keep moving forward, getting shit done.

The door tinkled as we entered.

Kenny's eyes found mine first.

I nodded.

He half-smiled.

"So what do you think?" Ephraim asked Stereo.

"Well, it's more than a poltergeist," she said very matter-of-factly. She sat in the middle of the dance floor on a chair turned around, her arms resting on the back of it. "Sounds like a *chindi*. They're way nastier than regular ghosts."

"*Chindi?*" Ephraim asked.

"It's a Navajo word for a ghost created by a witch to mess with the living." She certainly seemed sure of herself.

Retro and Shilling sat together in a corner exchanging skeptical glances.

Ephraim and Lizard hung on her every word.

"My guess is he's had his fun and is done with y'all." She leaned back and held the chair with both hands. "Except for douchebag. I sincerely hope he's still going to mess with you." She winked at me.

"Oh my God," Corey said. "Get off his back."

"I didn't ask you here so you could make Ethan feel bad, hai." Kenny flanked me. "Do you actually think he's going to mess with Ethan. . ." The doorbell tinkled. ". . .or are you just messing with him."

She shrugged. "A girl can always hope," she said. "But my guess is you've seen the last of your friendly neighborhood *Chindi.*"

"*Chindi* infect the target with illness." Morrison James walked in flanked by Dad and Mike. "They don't hang someone, and they sure as hell don't whack you with an axe like what happened to Gunner's mom."

What the what? My jeans. My hoodie and t-shirt? "Why are you wearing my clothes, you little creep."

In my clothes, he didn't seem mature or spooky or anything. Just like any other skinny teenager. He smiled. "Because in a world that sucks as much as yours, that's the thing to take away? The fact I had to borrow your clothes because mine were soaking wet from saving your dad and his husband from certain death." He looked at Stereo. "Who's the tourist?"

"Um. Boyfriend," Dad corrected sort of sheepishly. "We're not. . . we're not married."

Mike turned to him. "We could be."

"What?" Dad's eyes went huge. "Is that your way of proposing?"

Holy crap! What was this all of a sudden happening?

"It's my way of saying, we could get married." Dr. Mike seemed to realize that a bunch of eyes stared at them. "You know, if you wanted."

It's like Dad had asked if he wanted to have dinner and he'd said, "I could eat."

"Okay, *Modern Family*," Stereo interrupted. "This is touching and all, but did the little metro just call me a tourist?" She rose from her chair and clomped over to Spook, where she towered over him because of her platform combat boots. Standing there, chin to nose, she did look far more the part.

"Who the hell are you?" she demanded.

Spook crooked half a smile, shook his head vaguely and turned his attention to me. "You're being haunted by Twist's evil spirit. . . although. . . something's off. A ghost should be tied to a place or an object or a person, not free range."

"Like a chicken?" Woody asked.

Stereo scoffed.

"Pretty much." Spook smiled all the way. "Nothing connects the places or the people, except Twist himself. That's pretty much unheard of."

"Says the metro in penny loafers?" She looked around smugly, as if hoping we'd support her on it.

Yeah, she had the look down pat, yet something about Spook, now that she was trying so hard, seemed to change. Something in the dude's eyes. Like he'd seen things. Dark things. He didn't seem like such a kid all of a sudden.

Wait a minute. Rewind.

"You saved Dad and Mike from what?" I demanded.

"Nothing gets past you, does it?" He turned away from Stereo. "Twist possessed Mike and made him pull your dad into the pool. They almost drowned."

Folks muttered and made noise.

All I saw was my dad, standing there with an arm around Mike.

He'd almost died?

Dad. Dead. What then? What would I have done?

Nothing. I had nothing. That. could not. happen. Ever.

And Stereo. . . she'd kind of almost predicted it. She'd wished it on me.

She met my eyes and a slow, subtle smile curled her lips, as if she were saying, "See? Just like I said. And I wish it'd happened."

She did. She really wished my dad had died so I would feel her pain.

The world slammed into me like a burst floodgate or something.

I shoved past Woody and Shilling toward her, a deep-throated snarl growing in my chest.

What would I do to her when I reached her?

No way to know. Dad jerked me away.

I tried to pull out of his grip, but, well. . . Dad. He held my arms and made me look into his eyes. "I'm fine," he said.

Air wheezed through my lungs. I still wanted to pound on her, to punish her for wishing my father dead.

He shook me again. "Breathe." He held my face. "Breathe."

I breathed. I breathed some more.

Twist had almost killed me in the pool, too. We'd both almost died in the same pool.

He must have seen the change, because he pulled me close and wrapped his arms around me. "We're fine, Ethan. We're both fine."

He smelled like a dryer sheet.

I forced myself to calm down. "I'm not apologizing," I whispered.

"To that bitch? No need."

I pulled myself together and away from Dad. Too many eyes.

All staring at me.

Except Stereo, who stood a few feet away pointedly adjusting her makeup in the mirror. No. She stared at me, too, in the mirror. Not such a big secret after all then, the mirror trick.

"Mike?" I asked.

He moved closer.

"You're the biggest skeptic in town," I said. "You believe it was the ghost of Twist?"

"After James yanked us out of the pool, this giant green. . . *thing*, a glowing nuclear mucus came pouring out of me, shrieked enough to break a couple of glasses on Mac's patio, then. . . then flew off into the sky." He shrugged and looked around at the wide eyes of my friends. "So, yeah, I'm pretty much sold." He looked at Spook. "Plus. . ."

Out of the corner of my eye, I saw Spook shake his head ever so slightly.

"Plus nothing," Corey said. "I don't need anything past the giant ball of snot flying off into the sky."

"Ectoplasm," Stereo called from her corner of self-indulgent land. "It's called ectoplasm."

Spook rolled his eyes. "I'm going to drive out to the camp to see what I can figure out. Twist has a high degree of control. Jumping into Mike to attack Lucky, that's. . . that's some serious magic." He glanced at Ephraim. "And it seems like he could do it when he was alive. That kind of energy leaves a vapor trail sort of thing. I can learn a lot about him from what I find there."

He swept the entire group with his eyes. "Can you guys go to Austin? All y'all? I have equipment there and might be able to enlist a bit of help. My team has a place. . . it's big enough for everyone for a couple of days. You'll be safe there."

More noise and questions.

"You think we're in danger?" Retro asked.

"What part of 'a ghost is trying to kill people connected to Twist's death' has not gotten through to you?" Spook strode over to Retro and would have been tons more intimidating if his shoes hadn't squeaked. "People are dying. I want to protect you. I can't do it here."

Retro slunk over to the bar. "I was just asking."

"I want to go with you to the camp," Stereo said.

"No." Spook didn't even look at her. "Everyone. Go to Austin tomorrow. I'll text you a meeting place when you get there." He turned to leave.

"James." Mike held Dad close. "Thank you."

Spook gave a salute and left. Jingle, jingle.

Chapter Six

Who the hell did that numbnut in penny loafers think he was calling her a tourist? She read tarot. She'd studied with more than one Wiccan high priestess. She knew. . . stuff. Stuff that would. . .

Well, she'd *seen* stuff, too. Real stuff. And her Tarot readings? *She'd* seen Twist's return in the cards. She had.

Kenny believed in her, anyway. He had to, right?

Stereo walked up to his front door and punched the doorbell. Nice house. Not as big as the farmer's, but nice enough. It had a porch.

A baby started crying. No, a baby screamed as if someone was boiling it into soup. Yikes.

Footsteps approached the door. The curtain on the narrow window twitched aside.

"*Ajapa!*" The curtain fell closed. The voice had sounded like Kenny's. "Just a second."

Glass shattered.

Well, it was always nice to have that kind of effect on a guy, no matter how dire the situation.

The door opened. Kenny wore a crocheted afghan like a toga, but she could still tell his boxers had some cartoon character on them. "It's okay, Mom. I'll pick it—" His shout turned into a smile for Stereo. "Hey there, Stereo. How can I help you?"

Suave. Lol.

"Nice dress." Damn. Why did she always have to go for the sarcasm?

"You like it?" he asked with all seriousness. "I was going for a neo-Brady Bunch retro chic. I work it?" He extended a bare calf and pointed his toes.

She couldn't stop the chuckle. "Nice save. Sorry about the lamp."

He glanced over a shoulder. "It was an ugly lamp and deserved to die." He met her gaze. "Did you just come to trade jibes or. . .?"

"I want you to try a Ouija board with me." She held up the box. "I brought Parker Brothers." She hoped that with someone like Kenny, who believed so damn much, maybe she could get the stupid board to work.

He stared at her with wide eyes and an open mouth. Why?

"I thought we could go over to Twist's grave and see what we can find out." If she could discover something—anything—before that *Supernatural* reject did, she'd prove she wasn't a tourist.

Kenny didn't move or speak. Oh crap, had she read him completely wrong? Was he too much a fan of that Fox bastard to even talk to her?

"Unless that's a bad idea?" She held the box across her chest like a shield.

"Sorry." Kenny shook his whole body out. "It's a great idea." He stepped forward then glanced at his toga. "I probably need pants."

Stereo shrugged. "Don't bother on my account."

His cheeks bloomed red. Aha, so *that's* why he'd frozen.

I awoke with a gasp. Giant flying monkeys had been trying to drown Dad in a river of monkey poo. Thank God it hadn't been anything freaky.

Deep breath.

My clock read 11:00 p.m.

My stomach read hungry.

Since I had no school tomorrow, a midnight snack wouldn't wreck me. We hadn't set an early rise for the trip to Austin.

Oooh, we had ice cream.

In the kitchen, chilly linoleum shocked my bare feet. I grabbed chocolate-mint and a giant spoon then jumped onto a stool at the island. Smooth, creamy goodness. Mmmmmm. For five whole minutes my brain thought nothing apart from, "Dig, lift, open mouth. Mmm. Repeat."

"Is there enough for two?" Dad leaned in the doorway, arms and ankles crossed.

"How long you been watching me?" I asked around a mouthful of ice cream, and he most likely only understood me because he was my dad.

"Just a couple of minutes." He sat beside me. "Dad privilege." He took the spoon and shoveled ice cream. "Mm."

Indeed. Wait a minute. . . "Are those Boss?" I asked.

He glanced down at his boxer briefs and shrugged. "Some fancy, gay designer like that, yeah. Clearance sale." He got in a second spoonful of my sugary salvation because he'd shocked me. A) Boxer briefs and not tighty-whiteys on *my* dad? B) *Designer* boxer briefs?

I grabbed the spoon after he'd already scooped out his third shot.

"Hey." He faked a snatch at the spoon.

"You can scoop more than me." Yum. "Is Mike turning you into an actual, real homosexual?" Wow. Homosexual was hard to say around a mouthful of ice cream.

He threw an arm across my shoulders and kissed my head.

"So are you actually engaged?" I asked, working my balance to prevent his affection from knocking me off the stool.

He released me and took the spoon. "I kinda think I am." The goofy grin on his face was nice to see. Not a lot of those going around these days.

I stared down at the silver ring on my right hand. It'd been my. . . my biological father's wedding ring. Dad had found it right after Corey's mom had died, when he'd nostalgically gone through a box of old stuff he'd been saving for when I turned eighteen.

"Is that all right by you?" Dad handed me a spoonful of sugar, and the grin had been slaughtered by concern.

"Yeah!" I said quickly because I could tell he'd read my silence as hesitation for all the wrong reasons. "I think it's great." I held up the hand with the ring.

"Ethan. . ."

Would he let me do this for him?

I ate the ice cream, handed him the spoon and slid the ring off my finger. "If you want it, then you gotta put a ring on it." I shoved the ring into his hand.

"I can't take that. I just gave it to you." But the look on his face made me resolve that he would take it. As much as his conscience had insisted I should have it, his eyes told me he really, really wanted it for Mike.

I pushed his hand away and took the spoon. "He was your best friend, Dad. You should have it." I dug with the spoon, but that middle part had frozen solid.

He took the ice cream out of my hands and attacked it with his massive strength. "There's more to this decision. Spill."

Damn. We'd been on this merry-go-round before.

"Don't hate me, Dad. Seriously, but *you're* my dad. Karl was just. . ."

"The man who gave you life?" He handed me the spoon.

I heard calliope music in my head. "He was your best friend. He was this huge part of your life stolen away just when you were getting to really know him." So, yeah, there'd been some long talks with a lot of new information after Mrs. VanZeeland's funeral. "I never knew him. He isn't even real to me. But he was to you, and from what you've told me recently? You're the one he'd want to have this."

Ice cream oozed down my fingers, so I licked. "You gave up all this relationship shit your whole life because you always put me first." I handed him the last of the ice cream on the spoon. "Let me give you this one thing so you'll never, ever doubt that I support you and Mike."

He sucked up the ice cream.

"And don't you cry, you damn baby," I said, hoping it was funny.

He laughed so hard he spit minty chocolate chips across the linoleum. Ha!

"You still don't think this is too fast?" He didn't even get up to clean his mess. Wow. Strange times.

"You're not married," I said. "You're engaged. That means you hope he's the right one, and you want to test drive the idea a bit to see if you like it."

He smirked. "Test drive, huh?" Dig, dig, dig.

"It's late, okay?" I rolled my eyes. "No jokes about driving."

He glanced at the clock. "It's still technically your birthday." He handed me the spoon. "Happy Birthday."

"Thanks. I really don't want to think about it this year."

"I know, I know." He waved a hand. "Did Saundra get a hold of you?"

"I got the text." I passed the empty spoon back. Hey, if he was going to keep scooping. . . "What's that about anyway?"

"Just general legal stuff now that you're eighteen." Dig, dig, dig. "You know her, she wants to make sure every I is dotted and every T crossed. It's nothing bad. Maybe we could drop by since we'll be in Austin anyway."

Yeah. We were going to Austin for protection from the violent, evil ghost that'd almost killed my dad. Might as well make a stop at the lawyer's crib.

I shivered and not from the ice cream. Just thinking about Dad's close call freaked me out.

"You know. . ." I refused the spoon so he'd get some ice cream. "I kinda get where you're coming from every time you go all *Lifetime Channel for Women and Gay Men* on me when I get hurt." Since his mouth was full I could keep talking. "Knowing that you almost died today, that you were almost, just, *gone*." I shivered. "And that stupid girl. . . *wishing* it on you."

"World o'crazy, that one."

Understatement of the season.

"I can wrap my head around just about anything," I said, "but I can't even *imagine* what life would be like if you died." I leaned on his shoulder. "Can I still tell you I love you, even though I'm all grown up now?"

Huh. No instantaneous massive hug. That was odd.

"I got you a present." His tone gave me the willies. He knew I'd be upset.

"No," I said, sitting up straight. "Dad, we don't have the money."

"Shut up," he grabbed me around the neck and pulled me in. "I want to give my son a birthday present for his eighteenth birthday, I can God damned well do so." He ruffled my hair and released me, wearing his adamant face.

"Fine," I relented.

He pointed at a small box on the table next to the garage door. At least it wasn't anything big. Don't get me wrong. Presents = Stellar! But we were really freaking broke.

The box was really, really light. The lid lifted off easily.

It held a key. A *car* key.

My heart pounded in my chest. "Dad? What did you *do*?"

"Don't get too excited." He leaned against the island and ate ice cream as if this was the most boring day ever. "It's a piece of shit, but I figure—"

"You bought me a *car*?"

Dad shrugged and ate ice cream.

Holy shit! I ran into the garage.

There she was. My new baby. Yellow. A. . . Toyota. Cool. They lasted forever, right? It kinda reminded me of Kenny's ancient Civic. Oh! A Matrix. Cool name for someone whose life was pretty much one freaking run down the rabbit hole after another.

She had a few dings and stuff, but she seemed clean and solid, but. . .

"Dad. We can't. . ."

"Shut up, Ethan." As usual, he leaned in the doorway. "Corey knew a guy who wanted training and couldn't afford the cash, but he had this laying around." Laying around? "It didn't even run, until Corey had his way with her."

I stopped my examination of the car. "Dad, no sexual innuendos with my new baby."

He laughed.

"Corey fixed her up?" I opened the door and jumped in. Wow clean. How had he made it *smell* like a new car?

"That's *his* birthday present to you, since you told us we weren't allowed." He seemed happy with my enthusiasm. I could tell he'd been worried she wouldn't be good enough.

Wait. "When did all this happen?" Mrs. Van Zeeland's funeral had been, like, a week ago.

"Last couple of days."

Holy shit.

"Wait 'til you see the before pictures," he said.

Not a lot of bells and whistles. Handles instead of buttons for windows, but. . . score! MP3 player hookup.

"How does it have an MP3 dock?" I asked. She seemed too old for that.

He rolled his eyes. "A normal straight son would be checking out the engine block."

"And a normal gay dad would've painted her sparkly powder blue."

He cuffed me. "Mac sprang for a new radio. Her present. We know how important your tunes are."

Holy crap. Wait. Where was Auntie Mac?

"She knew the nurse involved in Warren's death." Dad always read my mind. Spooky. "She's with her family tonight."

He leaned through the window while I checked out the glove box and made sure the sun visor had a mirror and a light.

"This is really mine?" I asked sort of rhetorically. "All mine?"

"All yours." He leaned in and looked around. "I know it's not a Roadster—"

"Your turn to shut up." I left my baby's bosom and wrapped Dad in my arms. "This is the most *amazing* present ever. I freaking love you." I squeezed him as tightly as I could and tried to pick him up, but he had, like, three hundred pounds of solid muscle or something.

"Yeah," he said. "Maybe when the other one drops."

I boxed him a little but of course he blocked every punch and grabbed me in a headlock. I mean, no matter how much you tell everyone not to give you birthday presents, there's that tiny part of you that is still a five-year-old and hopes they will anyway.

"You need to look at the engine," Dad said, dragging me, still in a headlock, to the front of the car.

"Because looking at it will mean something to me." But I didn't waste any energy trying to prevent his lead.

He chuckled and released me. "Corey worked damn hard on that engine, son. The least you can do is look at it, in case he asks." He wandered over to the driver's side and reached through the window.

"Can't we just *say* I looked at it, since any question he asks will mean. . ."

The hood popped.

". . .jack-all to me?"

He padded to my side and did a thing with the hood release and lifted.

Fuck. me. On the inside of the hood, Corey had hung a poster. It *had* to be Corey.

Happy Birthday ROOMIE!!!!!!

He'd drawn a house in crayon, like a little kid house, a square with a triangle on top and a square for a window. He'd drawn four stick figure dudes. One had tall black and red hair: Kenny. One had short blond spiky hair: me. One was twice as big as the rest: Dad. And the fourth was halfway between the little dudes and Dad, and that one had a third leg drawn even longer than the two usual legs.

Ha! That had to be Corey joking that we'd have to get used to the fact that he never wore pants in the house.

My eyes burned. My chest hurt so bad I couldn't breathe.

"Yeah," Dad said. "I figured you'd want to see that."

I couldn't move, so he slowly and carefully removed the poster and set it on the washing machine, because, you know, I'd totally forget it was under the hood and spark her up and start a fire. And you know what? The fact that I had a dad who *thought* about that? Who knew me that well. . .?

Once again, I grabbed him and held on as tight as I could. "It's like my life sucks worse than anyone else's possibly could," I said into his chest, "and at the same time, I'm the luckiest bastard on the planet."

His shoulders joggled with his chuckle. "If you quote Dickens to me, I'm taking the car away."

I kissed him then pulled away with a scoff. "Dickens was a talentless hack who got paid by the word."

"That's my boy." He closed the hood with a bang.

We had to take her for a ride.

"Come on, come on, come on." I jumped behind the wheel again.

He slid into the passenger side.

She had a garage door opener. I pushed the button and started the car.

She ran smo-o-oth. Corey'd gotten her purring like a kitten.

Wait. "Corey helped you with this and didn't let the secret slip?"

Dad nodded and shrugged.

"That is *so* awesome."

A-a-and reverse. I pulled out of the garage.

"Er, Ethan?" He glanced around. "Don't you think we're a little underdressed to go for a joy ride?"

I backed her into the street and gave him my best sarcasm face. "Yeah, because *you've* only gone running around this town bare ass *naked* a thousand times."

He chuckled and nodded. "True."

You have no idea how cool it is to have *that* dad.

Unless you do.

Booyah!

Kenny stood in the living room wrapped in an old afghan.

Holy light and lively crap!

Stereo, the hottest girl he'd ever met in his entire sexually deprived life, had shown up on his doorstep and invited him to sneak into a cemetery in the middle of the night.

Okay, her visit was likely sloppy seconds since Spook had made fun of her after she'd tried to run off to the camp with him.

Kenny was cool with that. He bounded up the steps three at a time and threw the afghan onto his bed. What should he wear? He glanced at the mirror. Was there time to jack up his hair? No, it took time to dry.

Oh Christ, Naruto underwear? He stripped them off and ran to the dresser. He had to own something without a cartoon character on it. There. Basic black. Nice.

"Who's the hottie?" Ed stood in the doorway.

"Her name's Stereo and she's. . ." At a loss, Kenny just pulled on jeans and a plain t-shirt.

"And she's a hottie." Ed grinned and didn't move out of the way.

The baby screamed in the background.

Kenny ran to the door. Maybe Ed would get the hint.

He pointed at Kenny's t-shirt. "Why are you wearing a plain t-shirt?"

Kenny pulled the fabric out. "It's just a t-shirt."

Ed shook his head. "You haven't been around much lately, but even I know that's not you at all. Is that Ethan's?"

Busted. The t-shirt had found its way into Kenny's laundry one day. As welcome as he felt at the Fox house, he still brought his laundry home to wash.

Ed pushed past and hobbled over to Kenny's dresser. He pulled out Kenny's *Black Butler* t-shirt. "If that chick isn't interested in the real you, don't even waste your time." He held out the shirt.

Kenny stared at the shirt, then yanked the designer t-shirt off.

"How's the leg?" Ed asked.

Kenny froze. No one in his family had asked that before. "It hurts sometimes," he admitted.

Ed nodded. "Mine, too."

What the hell could Kenny say to that? He pulled on his shirt.

He stared at his brother and couldn't think of another thing to say.

Ed scooted out of the way. "Go get her, killer. Don't need that leg to satisfy a woman. Don't let anyone tell you different."

Wow. But what the hell to say? Kenny brushed past and hurried to the stairs. . . then he stopped.

His brother waved at the stairs. "Go." He smiled. "One warrior to another? Tell me what happens later."

Kenny laughed. "I'm no warrior."

Ed pointed at Kenny's hobbled leg. "That says otherwise, little brother." He shrugged. "Maybe we have something to talk about now?" Oh Jesus. Ed hadn't wanted to talk to Kenny since he'd come home from the war. Ed waved. "Go get her, tiger."

"Hai," Kenny said, nodding, then ran down the stairs.

As much as all his friends had to deal with horrific tragedy, Kenny's life continued to improve. How messed up was that?

Chapter Seven

Twenty minutes later, Kenny sat across from Stereo at Twist's grave.

How stupid was that? Well, damn stupid, but Kenny kept reminding himself. . . he sat across from Twist's grave with *Stereo*!

She pulled the board from the box. "I never get over the fact that the same business that makes Monopoly and Life sells the means to communicate with the spirit world."

A plastic triangle with little feet and a clear window rested on a board with letters, numbers and the obvious *yes* and *no* options. Kenny rested his fingers on the planchette.

Stereo didn't.

He looked up.

"You've used a Ouija board before?" she asked.

"Grandpa had one," he told her. "We played with it when I was a kid." Papa Karela's had been a solid oak board with a crystal planchette, but whatever.

A smile crept across her face that made Kenny hard. Hopefully, she wouldn't notice.

She touched the planchette. "So you know. . ."

The planchette moved, started turning figure eights, the basic neutral position for a Ouija board.

Stereo gasped. "It works." She looked up at Kenny. "Are you doing that?"

He shook his head. "Isn't that what it's supposed to do?"

She stared into his eyes. Her eyes were blue even in the darkness of the cemetery. "It's exactly what it's supposed to do." She glanced down at the board then met his eyes again. "Why can't I lie to you?"

Kenny shrugged.

"I've never made a board work before," she admitted.

Kenny's face grew warm. "So why. . .?"

She looked down. "I sort of hoped it'd work with you."

Oh. Wow.

"So what do we ask?" she asked.

"You really want to contact Twist?" he asked. "That doesn't seem dangerous?"

She shrugged. "What do you think?"

Kenny closed his eyes. He would do pretty much anything Stereo asked of him. She was about as Wiccan as they came, and she'd come to him. Because she thought he had some kind of special connection.

Nope. He didn't care why she thought that. It worked for him.

The planchette spun out its figure eights while Kenny thought back to things his Papa had said to the board.

"Is anyone there?" Kenny asked.

The planchette slid quickly and easily to the yes.

Stereo gasped.

Kenny sat up straighter with pride.

The planchette spun figure eights.

"Who are we talking to?" Stereo asked.

The planchette spun a couple of eights, then spelled out: *S-a-t-a-n*.

Kenny and Stereo both yanked their hands away. Holy crap!

The board flew into the air and burst into flame, and Kenny skittered back.

Stereo leapt to the side with a shout.

Smoke poured out of the ground and the temperature dropped.

A silvery image rose from the smoke.

Twist! Holy shit!

Kenny leapt across the smoking ground to Stereo. He grabbed her and blocked Twist with an arm, as if that would help.

"You really want to ring my bell?" Twist said.

Wait a minute! Kenny had a charm he'd bought from a nun in Austin. It was designed to protect against evil spirits. Would it really work?

He pulled it from a pocket and held it out.

The spirit screamed, its arms blocking its face.

Holy shit! Was it working?

But nothing happened. The spirit lowered its arms and glared down at Kenny. "What the seventh hell of Asmodeus is that?"

Then the entire ghostly image evaporated in a puff of silvery haze, and the tread of heavy boots announced someone's arrival a split second before a familiar form appeared, tromping through the last of the spirit.

"What the hell do you think you're doing?" Spook bent over Kenny and pulled the charm from his grasp by the leather thong. "You buy this at some New Age bookstore. . ." He scoffed in disgust and waved it at the smoldering Ouija board. "Get a God damned Parker Brothers witch board, and you're what? Buffy the vampire slayer?"

Kenny and Stereo scrambled to their feet. Had Spook just saved them so he could berate them like naughty children?

"The board was working," Stereo insisted.

"No, it wasn't," Spook said. "I did all that for show, to see just how far you'd take things." He shook his head and then confronted Kenny, shoving the charm into his chest. "You should know better."

Kenny took the stone and shrank. It'd all made sense when he'd had an erection.

Spook waved at Stereo. "I get that the tourist doesn't know any better, but you know what could have happened here. You were at that camp." His eyes spat disgust at Kenny. "If Twist *had* appeared for you, he'd have possessed you and killed her, most likely after raping her with your body while you got to listen to her scream."

Jesus Christ, what'd Kenny been thinking? "But Stereo knows what she's doing." Even as he said the words, he heard his own lie. She'd never made a board work before. She'd said so.

"I can take care of myself," Stereo shouted.

Spook panted a few times. He sucked in a deep breath and his entire body relaxed. "No, you can't." His quiet voice was even scarier than his shouting. "Mike Lopez choked out Lucius Fox at the bottom of a swimming pool. Had I not shown up, they'd both be dead. A four-foot nurse hauled Palatino into the air one-handed." He met Stereo's gaze. "The reason tourists are dangerous is they read a few books, attend a few

Samhain rituals and suddenly they think they understand the Unknown. They lose their fear of the things that go bump in the night because they think they can 'blessed be' it all away."

Stereo clenched her jaw, but her eyes watered, and a single tear slipped out.

"Okay, Spook," Kenny said. "We get it. We suck and you hate us, hai? Can you just. . . can it just be enough? Please?"

Lights swept the tombstones, and Spook grabbed the others and pulled them down behind a large monument. "We don't need cops finding us here, either."

Kenny leaned back against the cold marble with Spook against one shoulder and Stereo against the other. She looked about as miserable as Kenny felt. Impulsively, he grabbed her hand and squeezed.

She looked at him with moist eyes.

Since Spook had his back to them, peeking over the monument as a car crunched gravel, Kenny nodded in the hardass's direction and rolled his eyes.

Stereo smirked and nodded. She squeezed Kenny's hand then released it, frowning at Spook's back. Yeah, no reason to give the jerk more fodder for berating them.

The sound of the car stopped. Doors opened and closed.

"It's Fox and son," Spook muttered. "Going to a grave over there."

"What?" Kenny started to rise.

"Stay down," Spook insisted.

Kenny sat back down. "It's Ethan's birthday," he said. "They're probably visiting his parents."

"You mean his mom." Stereo's eyebrows pinched together.

"His biological parents died when he was a baby," Kenny said. "Mr. Fox raised Ethan on his own. He's technically Ethan's Uncle."

Stereo leaned back against the stone, apparently running that through her head a few times. Well, if knowing Ethan was an orphan helped her get over her anger with him then the trip out to the cemetery wasn't a total fiasco.

Kenny held up the stone charm. Would it work against a real spirit? He sure as hell hoped so, in spite of Spook's doubts.

Car doors opened and closed. The engine started up, and Ethan and his dad drove off.

"Okay," Spook said when the sound of the car had fallen distant. He rose.

Kenny also rose and offered a hand to Stereo, who hesitated at first but accepted his help.

Spook stared at them in silence.

Kenny waited for the next tirade.

"I'm sorry I yelled," Spook said. "I don't hate you. But you have to understand the gravity here. People are dying and there's only one of me. I suspect Twist has help. I do not."

"What kind of help does he have?" Stereo asked.

"I'm not sure." Spook wandered in the direction of Stereo's car. "I hesitate to say until I check out the camp."

"Why aren't you there already?" Kenny asked, but that could sound rude. "Not that I'm complaining. I mean. . . thanks for stopping us." Although he hadn't needed to be such a dick about it.

"I had a feeling someone would do something stupid like this," Spook said. "I can only hope that you guys are the only idiots out tonight." He stopped at the car. "Go home. Sleep. Meet me in Austin tomorrow." He walked away.

Stereo watched his back until he vanished in the darkness. "Do you think I'm a tourist?"

Why would his opinion possibly matter? "Compared to him," Kenny said, "we're all tourists."

She frowned but didn't seem insulted. She pointed at his hand. "That's the one you had made for him, isn't it? For Ethan."

Kenny held up the circle of rock. "Yep."

She opened her car door, shaking her head. "I still say you should keep it for yourself."

Kenny walked around to the passenger side. At least she hadn't called him That Fox Bastard.

Stereo put the key in the ignition but stopped short of turning the engine over. She sat back and looked at Kenny. "When we thought it was Twist," she said, "and he was about to attack us. . . you threw yourself in front of me."

What else would he do? Would that bother an independent woman of the twenty-first century?

She shook her head and reached for the key. "I don't quite get you Kenny Valentino."

But at least she was smiling.

I climbed out of the car and met Dad near the garage door. "I love her," I said with another hug. Duh. "Thanks."

"So I'm pardoned for breaking the no present rule?" He grabbed a basket of laundry and followed me into the house.

"Yeah," I said as casually as possible, "especially since you let me give you the ring."

He passed through the door I held and made his way into the kitchen.

He was engaged. To be married. Wow.

"Dad?" I grabbed a sponge from the sink to wipe up the mess from his forgotten mint ice cream.

He turned.

"Congratulations," I said. "I don't think I actually said that before."

He smiled down at me as I wiped the floor.

"I'm ecstatic for you," I told him. "And I really like Mike, too, not just because you do. He's a stand up guy."

"Thanks for cleaning up." He turned with a smile and headed up the stairs.

"You still don't get to cry, you big baby!" I called out.

I cleaned up the rest of the ice cream mess, really wanting to text thanks to Corey, but he was likely banging Theresa and I didn't want to interrupt. Yeah. That's Corey. In the middle of the planet's best sex, he'd stop to respond to a text about my birthday present.

Gotta love him.

I texted Kenny: *U up?*

U hav no idea.

Uh-oh. That was fast. *U okay?*

Stellar. Whats up?

I snapped a photo of the car and sent it. *B-day present from dad*

Holy shit! Can I come see it?

Cool! *Absolutely. See you in five. I'll even put on pants*

Lol don't bother on my account

Um.

Pls delete that comment from ur phone, he sent.

Lol

I ran upstairs and into Dad's room. "Kenny's coming over. That okay?"

He held the phone to his chest. "No problem. Still your birthday. Try to get at least a couple hours of sleep. Tell him hi."

"Hai." I lunged out of the room, then grabbed the doorway and hauled myself back. "Hi to Mike. He can come over, too, if he wants."

I dashed away without waiting for a reply, grabbed sweats and a t-shirt and trundled down the steps. Hm. You know what? It was my fucking birthday, after all, so I grabbed a bottle from the bar and two glasses, texted Kenny: *In the garage*

k

I shoved the bottle in the back seat and hit the garage door opener just as Kenny drove up.

He parked and walked over with a whistle.

"Yeah, I know," I said. "She's a piece of shit but she's mine all mine."

"Bro, you've been in my car." He walked over to the passenger's side and joined me. "At least this baby was manufactured in the current *millennium.*" He rubbed the dashboard. "So things are going better for your dad?"

"He traded coaching." Wait. "Did you know about this?"

"Nope." He checked to see if the passenger visor had a mirror and a light. Ha! Not just me.

"Okay, because Corey helped him fix her up," I said.

Kenny's eyes opened wide. "Wow, and he didn't spill?"

"I know, right?" See? Also not just me! I touched stuff to look like I was, you know, doing something guys do in a new car.

Kenny did the same thing, but with him it seemed like he was working up to say something.

"Speaking of spilling," I said, "What's up tonight?"

"What? Nothing, I just. . ."

"Ed?"

He took a deep breath and leaned back in his seat. "No. Ed's cool." He rubbed his face. "The baby on the other hand. He's just fussy, but he's been crying, like, twenty-four hours a day, and I have gotten no sleep." He closed his eyes. "We actually got him quiet for a few minutes tonight, then. . ." He smiled. . . then he lost the smile. He opened his eyes and looked over at me.

"Then?" I asked in my usual leading fashion.

"So I think there's this girl who likes me," he said, only kind of smiling again which seemed odd since a girl liking him so soon after Kiki had dumped him should be major grin-worthy. "And she stopped by and woke up the baby."

"Stopping by is a good indication of liking," I said, waiting for the shoe to drop. "Are there other indications?"

"She liked the Black Butler t-shirt. . ." The grin grew large and forced. "And she totally gets the whole magic thing."

Seriously? What the hell? I dropped my head onto the headrest. "And I'm going to guess she wished my dad would die." It had to be Stereo.

"Sorta, yeah, but—"

I held up a hand. "But that pretty much sucked." The bitch had wished my dad *dead*.

"Yeah, that was shitty of her." He stared at the dashboard.

Understatement of the millennium.

I fought to get my breath to slow down and waited for the excuses.

But he made none. No apology for her. No excuses. He let me process it.

Because she was also perfect for him in a lot of ways. As much as he'd hurt when Kiki dumped him, it'd been for the best. Kenny needed someone loud and exciting who'd drag him kicking and screaming out of his shell before he headed off to Austin for school.

Stereo certainly had the loud part and exciting seemed to go with the fashion choices.

But she'd wished my dad dead.

Deep breath.

Even I'd let him down with my lack of faith in the supernatural until Dad and Mike had seen green goo fly into the sky. Stereo had believed from the beginning. In some ways, she was a better friend to him than I was.

Okay, even if I didn't agree with all of his choices, I had to do my best to support the not-eternally-dangerous-and-damning ones. Maybe he saw something there I couldn't.

"If she says anything like that again," I said, "I will bitch slap her."

"Obviously."

"And that won't be a problem between us?" I opened my eyes.

He shook his head. "She's way hotter than you, but I've known her one week."

Deep breath. Supportive friend then. I could do that. "So she stopped by?" I asked full of friendly curiosity.

He nodded. "When I showed her what I got you for your birthday, she actually called you Ethan instead of That Fox Bastard. So that was nice."

Indeed. Wait. "You got me a birthday present?"

"I bought you a birthday present."

"Dude. I told you not to."

"Yeah, whatever." He dug into the back of his pants and held out a small paper bag. "I'm not so much into the wrapping thing."

Wow. Everyone who mattered had given me something.

"Thank you." I swallowed. He had no idea how much that meant.

"You don't even know what it is yet."

So? Couldn't respond. I opened the bag and some sort of round stone on a leather thong dropped out. A necklace?

"I know this nun in Austin who does *Santería*." He spoke fast, like he knew I had no clue what the gift was or what it meant.

"Santa whatsit?" The stone felt cool and smooth. Hadn't Tango mentioned that word?

"*Santería*," he said. "It's this cool blend of Catholic church and traditional Mexican religion. She. . . blessed that, and if you wear it, evil spirits aren't supposed to be able to hurt you."

Because that was normal now.

Some sort of symbol had been cut into it. I had no idea what it meant.

"You think it's stupid." He shrank.

"No. No." I slipped it over my head. "I think it's stellar." God, people were so used to me mouthing off all the time that taking a moment to think made them assume I was all critical. "This is still hard for me to process but this is *really* thoughtful." I held it in one hand, waiting for it to glow or sparkle or something. "You think it works?"

Big silence.

"I wouldn't give it to you if I didn't," he said very quietly.

And there I was being a douchebag again. I reached across the stick shift and grabbed hold of him as best I could. I got one hand around his neck and pulled him close. "You are the best fucking brother a dude ever had. You know I don't understand any of this and you make sure I'm protected anyway." I squeezed him hard and released him, holding his gaze. "I believe, Kenny. It just takes me longer to process, and I don't. . ."

I didn't what?

He smiled. "And you don't know what's real now and what's still in the column with Santa and the Easter Bunny."

What would be the absolute best thing I could say?

"What did Stereo say about it?" I tried.

But he kind of grimaced. "She said I should keep it for myself." He shrugged. "Sorry."

I smirked. "At least that means she knows it'll work." Okay fine, he liked the girl who wanted me dead. Was that sort of thing even unusual anymore? "It's cool you found someone who knows all about this magic stuff." Ah crap. "I'm not trying to be dismissive."

"We're good." He tapped my shoulder with a fist. "And. . . yeah. . . she doesn't know as much as she wants us all to think." He shrugged. "Spook's kinda right about her being a tourist. But it'd be cool if you didn't pass that along."

I laughed and rubbed my hands over my face. "You realize that chasing this girl means you have balls the size of Godzilla, especially all things considered."

He turned red. "You've seen 'em, dude. You know that's not true."

Ha. Good. Maybe the time he'd been spending with Corey was a good thing after all. He'd lost a lot of his shyness already. Okay, more supportive friend time, but on a different front.

"She's in Austin, you said? This nun?" I turned the stone one way and the other but it just looked like a rock from any angle.

"Yep."

"Maybe we should visit *her* this weekend, too." Since we had so little going on, you know. But I wanted to leave no stone unturned in the effort to protect my friends. . . my family.

"How are you really coping with all this?" He leaned back. "I see you trying and shit, but. . . truth?"

Deep breath.

"I'm just riding the wind, bro." I dropped the necklace onto my chest. "I need more info to have an opinion. It's crazy as shit, though."

"Hai."

"You wanna stay over?" I asked, because duh.

"If it's okay." He still needed to seem sheepish.

"And I'm taking this bad girl to Austin tomorrow." I patted the steering wheel. "You in?"

"Like Flynn!"

"You sure? 'Cause there's these comic book stores I know," I said, "and a steampunk store and this restaurant called Zen that plays anime all day."

His eyes grew wide. "Hai?"

"Yeah, I figured I could start, you know, showing you what you have to look forward to. I mean, I know a ghost wants to kill us, but what the shit, we might as well take a moment to explore the city, hai?"

He smiled. He seemed to really get that I believed now.

"Unless you had plans with Stereo," I threw in.

He snorted. "I just found out she likes me, bro, it's not like we're dating or anything."

"Yet?"

He smiled, blushed and shrugged.

I reached into the back seat and hauled out the bottle and glasses.

"Bro!" A big grin lit his face.

"It's still my birthday." I glanced at the watch I wasn't wearing. "Close enough, anyway. You have a hot freaky chick interested in you, and I have a kick ass ride and the best fucking brother on the planet." I handed him a glass. "Here's to moving on."

"Here, here."

Clink. Drink.

"Ethan? What about this Spook guy?" Kenny asked.

I opened my mouth to tell him exactly what I thought about the clothes-stealing jerk then remembered that he'd saved Dad and Mike. And that Kenny likely worshipped the guy.

"What do *you* think about him?" I asked. "You know more about magic than I do. Is he the real deal?" Notice how I'd avoided the word *stuff?*

He made this complicated combination of shrugging, nodding, smiling and sort of grimacing, the upshot of which seemed to mean Kenny thought Spook was the real deal but he knew I was still skeptical.

"I say we meet Spook in Austin," Kenny said, "and see what he has to say after the camp. I say we talk to the nun and see what she thinks of it all. We can use them to check against each other. I know Spook saved your Dad and Mike. . ." He smiled and sat forward. "Okay, I have to say that whole sort of, kind of proposal was about the sweetest thing I have seen in my life."

"Yeah?"

"It gives me hope, you know?" His eyes grew all soft and sentimental.

"What do you mean?"

He glanced at me, at his booze.

I clinked his glass with mine. "Go ahead Dean, be mushy. Ya ain't driving,"

Huge grin. "All right, Sam." And the smile evaporated. "My folks? They don't like each other much anymore, and that's my experience of marriage." Sip. "So seeing these two middle-aged guys all goofy and dorky and in love like that? It gives a man hope, you know? Shit, we're only eighteen. There's plenty of time for us to find love." He took another sip. "See? Stupid."

"Not at all, dude. Not at all." It was about the smartest thing I'd heard that day.

We clinked glasses.

I gripped the necklace. "Thank you for this. Seriously."

"Thanks for letting me come over," he said.

"Let's get some sleep," I suggested. "Something tells me tomorrow is going to be a big day."

We left my new baby, and Kenny ran a hand along the hood as he made his way to my side. "Dude, if Corey helped with the car, you need to invite him to ride with us."

He was right. I texted. *Bro. For Austin, you, me, Kenny and the new car, you dog. What did you name her?*

Kenny and I made our way through the kitchen and to the stairs.

Corey sent a huge smiley face. *Foold you bro? Your dad told you that was my bday prezzie right? The work I did?*

Yep. And the poster. What could I possibly say? *Stellar. You rock.* Okay, lame. I was tired. *What did you name her?*

Dude. Your car. You name her

I know you. You had a name for her while you did the work. Spill

Kenny and I reached my room.

Bessie junior, Corey admitted.

Awesome.

Kenny pointed at the uninflated air mattress, but I just waved him to the bed. Too. tired. to deal.

Ha. Perfect bro, I typed. *Meet here tmrw?*

Fuk yeah what time?

Kenney and I stripped to our skivvies.

Please let me sleep til 8am

You got it

Hi to Theresa

;-) hi to Kenny

Huh. I glanced at the shoulders beside me.

How did you know? I asked.

Back atcha

I nudged Kenny's back and held the phone over his shoulder so he could see it.

"Shit. Have we become Ethenny?" he asked.

"Or Kenthan?"

"Fuck it," we said in perfect chorus then, "Night."

I turned out the light and settled in. Kenny's weight on the mattress beside me calmed me. With everything going on, I didn't care what people thought. Having someone watching my back meant something.

I touched the charm at my neck. Hopefully, it would work.

Chapter Eight

The camp was a cliché. It was a set out of every tacky slasher film made from 1986 to 2000. Spook loved it. The sun rose over a lake, a pontoon raft and a bathhouse with boarded windows. The boathouse sagged half-submerged in the water.

What seemed like the main building lurked in shadows on a hill above the lake, a U-shaped thing with waist-high weeds crowding the central courtyard. Spook had made a point of not learning where this bizarre creature named Twist had been shot. He wanted to let his senses figure things out on their own.

It was, what, about 6 a.m.? He stepped to the middle of a narrow bridge that linked the main building with the rest of the camp. He took a deep breath, closed his eyes and opened his other senses.

Ow! Double damn!

Residual energy lit the camp bright as day. Brighter. Shining vapor trails crisscrossed the sky like the aftermath of an air show. Whatever this guy had done, he'd been all over the place, throwing his power around as if he had no limit.

Drat it. He probably didn't. Dratting natural born magic user with little to no limit and someone had taught him how to tap into the source of his magic. Bad luck there. Spook didn't have as many limits as most folks either, but for the magic thrown around the camp to glow that brightly two weeks later? Gluttonous.

Spook wandered in the direction of the big cinderblock building where the energy centered. The side door was locked but clicked open with a wave of Spook's hand. He navigated the corridors by heading toward the hot spot. Energy radiated through the halls away from some kind of vortex at the center, most likely the place where Twist had died.

Yowsa, lots and *lots* of sex had happened in this building.

Cheap chairs, tables and dressers littered the hallways. Stains dotted the ugly carpet.

Someone most likely had distressed it so it appeared even shabbier than it had—

WHAT THE GOBSTOPPING HELL?

The thrice-damned lobby nearly blinded him. A massive event had occurred there. He damped down his senses and separated the signatures. This had to be where Twist had died, but why expend so much energy? And it hadn't worked anyway. Gunner had just blown him away.

Maybe he'd been setting up a major trap and had been interrupted, so the energy. . .

What the whatsit?

Spook opened his eyes. No, they weren't visible in the normal spectrum. He closed his eyes again. The silvery spirits of rabbits and birds and even a blasted Bambi dear stared at Spook, as if wondering why he'd invaded their home.

Why in the seven eternal hells of pain and suffering had an ethereal petting zoo set up shop in the lobby of a Boy Scout camp?

Was that a beaver?

Spook adjusted his senses.

Okay. The kids from Dumbass were the cast from *Glee*, but they'd stumbled onto the set of *Buffy the Vampire Slayer*. Oops. Ancient reference. *Teen Wolf? Supernatural? Hemlock Grove?*

Anyway, dere was some messed up shit in dat room. The animal spirits centered on a circle drawn in blood near the opposite doorway. Spook wasn't their loci so they simply watched him as he approached. He knelt and held his palm over the dark line.

Blast and what the hell?

He yanked his hand back and sucked on a finger. That ridiculous ignoramus had no damn idea what kind of power he was messing with. He'd made a simple containment circle for hell's sake, why dump so much power into it?

Spook took a deep breath. *"Pro an alter umper cipit liber aviss."* He held his palm out again. The energy poured through his hand, but it no longer seared him.

He analyzed the energy.

Well, *that* explained the ghostly petting zoo. An over-amped containment spell that "contained" the spirits on the plane, not just in the circle. Which explained all the ambient energy around camp. Twist must've made his zoo and used them as spies. From what the kids had told him, the animals also likely acted as conduits for Twist's mind control.

So Twist was a natural born witch who could perform freakishly amazing magic and had no clue what he was doing.

Gorgeous.

But why the hypercircle here in the lobby? What the hells had he been trying to contain?

Spook prayed to all the gods he'd ever met he was wrong in his speculations. There'd been magic at the farmhouse where he'd found the stuffed grackle. Familiar magic, and if Spook was right about the source of that magic, the intended victim of the containment circle would never have been trapped there. Maybe that's what had gone wrong?

Spook closed his eyes and explored deeper. The advantage to the fact that Twist was a natural born witch was that he was less likely to cover his tracks. Spook sank his teeth into the circle itself.

Huh. Deeper containment.

He searched the true matrix of the spell.

Blood magic. *Tying the witch to this plane. . . even unto death. . . and beyond.*

Drat!

Holy drat!

No. It wasn't possible.

Triple Drat!

No! Why, the flying *monkeyballs,* would anyone do that to himself? On *purpose?* Why force your own death in the hopes you'd manage to come back as a shadow of your living self? What the blazes was he hiding from? Or whom?

Spook sniffed the air.

No trace of her here, but if he were trying to escape her. . . but would it be worth it? Seriously? What kind of existence would he have?

Something tickled his knee. A rabbit. A silvery ghost rabbit nudged his calf and glanced over one shoulder.

Ghost bunny? Huh. And Spook had been pretty sure he'd seen everything.

The rabbit took a few steps away and looked back at Spook over one shoulder.

Okay. He'd followed stranger leads. "Okay, Mr. Bunny," he said, not even sure why the name seemed right. "What do you want to show me?"

The rabbit headed out of the building and down a clear path, pausing to glance over his shoulder.

"I can keep up with a ghost rabbit," Spook said. "Just go."

The rabbit vanished in a silvery flash.

Huh. That was odd. Had it understood him?

Well, he could follow the vapor trail.

The woods were pretty, other than the vapor trails and mists of blood magic covering everything Spook could see with his sixth sense. What had happened between Twist and the dancers had not been the first time magic messed with folks here at Camp Kill-Me-Slowly. Something long ago had gone down here, too, something. . .

Spook stopped.

The rabbit stood in a clearing on its hind legs.

The energy swarmed with the residue of a powerful, deadly witch.

One of the most powerful Spook had ever met.

The witch who'd made him back in 1961. His ex-girlfriend.

Mary.

"Shit." From the signs here, they'd fought. And if Twist had been afraid of Mary's wrath, then yeah, there were so many, many options on the table far, far worse than death.

"Oh my God." Kenny held out his cell phone and poured coffee. "Have you seen the new promo for *Consequence of Folly*? If this steampunk store you know doesn't have t-shirts I will *die*."

I grabbed the cell and watched the promo. Movie looked stellar.

"You sure you don't want me to give Bessie Junior one more check before we go?" Corey took the coffee I offered. He grabbed two of Auntie Mac's kolaches.

"Dude," I said. "The ride she is cherry. Relax."

He grinned.

You'd never know we were heading to Austin for protection against the evil undead. I guess that's just the kind of thing that takes a while to sink in. As far as our brains were concerned it was a road trip.

"Oh my God, we have to go to Pluckers for hot wings." Corey nearly jumped up and down. "They are the best."

Kenny nudged him. "You are such a jock."

"Bro, everyone loves hot wings."

The doorbell rang. Who the heck?

"But," Kenny asked, "do we need to eat hot wings with every freakin' TV on high alert for football season?"

"Bro, we're totally going to Anime central Japanese restaurant." He gave Kenny a playful punch to the ribs. "You can't indulge my passion for bashin'?"

Kenny punched him back.

I opened the front door.

Woody. And he looked like shit.

"Dude. Hey." His smile was fake.

He'd never been to my house before. Did he need a ride? Cool.

No. His car sat parked on the curb.

"Is Dr. Lopez here?" he asked. Wow. So formal. And the casual way he said it was as fakey as his smile.

"Uh, no. He and Dad are running errands for the trip to Austin." I also suspected Dad meant to do the proposal the right way.

"Oh, well. . ." He turned away and crossed his arms tight over his chest. "Okay, um. . . do you have a cell number?" He turned back to me way too quickly. "I know you shouldn't give it out."

What the hell? I closed the door and stepped onto porch. Woody would likely bolt if he saw the other guys. Something about him said an audience was not what he wanted. I waited a while, but he said nothing.

"Dude, what's going on?" I prompted.

He stared at his car. Wait. He'd worn the same clothes at the studio the night before. What the hell? He was as metro as me. Same clothes two days in a row was a mortal sin.

"Nothing," he said at last. He shifted so much I knew he was lying.

Someone inside broke a glass.

Woody glanced over. "*Ese*, your boyfriends are over. I'm sorry. Y'all must be getting ready for the big trip."

Something was wrong. Seriously wrong.

"Woody, damn it. Stop." Was someone pregnant? No. That didn't explain the night in his clothes. "What's wrong?"

He sputtered with fake nonchalance. "Nothing." He kind of turned to go. "You know what? *Pardone me*. Never mind."

He only took two steps.

"*Ese. Non,*" I said.

He laughed, probably at my horrible accent, but he didn't leave.

"Woody?"

I ran through what I knew. Ephraim had a guest, so Woody had no one to talk to. I couldn't let him leave.

He stared at me. He looked at the ground. "My parents found out about the website."

The site where he whacked off online for cash. Shit. But. . . I glanced at his clothes again. Oh Christ. No way.

"Where'd you sleep last night?" I asked, although I already knew.

"What?" He scoffed. "Where does anyone sleep?" Wow, lamest attempt ever.

"I've never seen you wear the same shirt two days in a row." I glanced around him at the car.

He followed my gaze and sighed. He looked at me for a long time.

Nope. I was not going to say a thing.

"In my car," he muttered. "They kicked me out." I could tell it was the hardest thing he'd ever admitted. "I need to talk to Dr. Lopez. He'll. . ." He made a broad sweeping gesture that said he didn't know what else to do.

Poor Dr. Mike. We all assumed he could solve the world's problems.

Effy's wouldn't be an option. Too complicated.

Well, this I could fix.

"You'll stay here," I said.

Woody jumped a foot. "Dude, you don't know me."

"Sam." One particular conversation in the woods at the side of the creek came to mind. "We're going to Austin today so Spook can protect us at his hideout, or whatever. After that? I will *not* let you get shoved into some stupid foster home when there is no reason whatsoever you can't stay here." I made sure my tone brooked no argument.

He crossed his arms over his chest, and I watched the non-existent traffic while he got his emotions under control.

"Just a day or two," he said, "until I get something figured out."

"As long as you need. Whatever. You have anything?"

He shrugged and looked back at his empty car.

"Okay," I said. "Look, the three of us are going to Austin together, and you're coming with. Should we get Effy?"

"He's hanging with the Lizard." Which was why Woody had slept in the car in the first place.

"Please tell me I can make jokes about that," I asked, hoping humor would work.

He choked out a laugh. "See, *ese*, that's what I asked you for in the first place."

Jesus, he'd asked me about helping with jokes back at the camp, in an entirely different lifetime.

Deep breath.

"Look, we're getting out of town because the spooky guy says we need to," I told him, "but we're going to make sure we have a little fun there, too. I'm guessing you could use that."

The smile slid off his face. "I got nothing, *ese*." He meant no clothes and no money.

I dropped a hand on his shoulder. "You got one thing that means a hell of a lot around here."

He smiled. "A big dick?"

Oh my God, really? I removed my hand. "Friends. What the hell do I care about your big dick?"

He burned bright red. How funny that he could still do that.

Corey and Kenny sat in the kitchen sipping their coffee as I led Woody inside.

"Hey, guys," I said. "Woody's coming along with us."

"Woot!" Corey shouted and gave him a high five.

"Is Effy coming?" Kenny asked.

"Nah, he's riding the Lizard all the way to Austin today," I said.

Woody chucked my shoulder. "See? *That's* the kind of thing I need help with."

Corey poured a cup of coffee.

Woody took it. "Nice place."

"It serves its purpose."

So. How to make this lack the awkward.

"Throw your stuff in my car, guys," I said to Corey and Kenny, all nonchalant in the newfound ownership of my own vehicle. "I'll be right down."

I gestured for Woody to follow me upstairs with his coffee. "I'm guessing you want a shower." I passed through my room to the bathroom and yanked a towel out of the cupboard. "If my hair care products aren't good enough for you, you can fuck yourself." Grinning, I threw him the towel and opened my closet and a few dresser drawers. "When you're done, go through and borrow anything you want. If it's not on the floor it's clean." I glanced around. "Coffee. Shower. Clothes. You need anything else?"

He stared at me blankly.

Shit. Didn't know what it meant.

"Look. Ethan." He stared at his hands. "I was shitty to you when you moved here. . ."

Oh. That. "I was a douchebag when I moved here." No point in hitting the nostalgia button. "This is my way of saying I'm sorry." Whatever it took to get him on board with the assistance.

He grinned. "You *were* kind of a douchebag." He lost the grin. "*Gracias.*"

"No worries." He wasn't Kenny. He didn't want the whole hand-holding and love thing. "Get moving. You know Corey. He was milking cows, like three hours ago. He wants to get on the road."

I left him in my room.

The guys stood in the kitchen again, their eyes full of questions.

"His parents kicked him out last night," I said.

"We figured." Corey sipped his coffee. "Look, Ethan, we're all planning on moving into my house anyway—"

I waved him off. "I wasn't about to offer him your place, bro. Even I'm not that rude." I glanced up at the sound of the shower upstairs. "He doesn't need to think about any of that right now. I mean, absolutely invite him, right? But let's just go to Austin and see what happens there. We'll worry about the sleeping arrangements when we get back."

We all drank our coffee.

"He has a ton of money from the site though, right?" Kenny asked. "I helped him reconfigure the server, so I know what he was raking in."

Corey shook his head. "You know his parents. As soon as they figured it out, I bet they realized where the money came from he was throwing around. Unless he hid it somewhere, I bet they went to the bank and snatched the money before they even said a word to him."

Holy shit. His parents were like that?

"Hey. . . Ethan?" Woody called down.

I exchanged a look with the guys then ran upstairs.

Woody stood there in the worst clothes I'd ever owned. Avoiding laughter took much strength.

"Um, I hate to ask. . ." He shifted nervously. "But can I grab a change for tomorrow?"

Ah, damn. All thought of humor vanished.

"Yeah." I tried to play it off all casual. "And feel free to pick something *not* in the Goodwill rejects box." I tugged the collar of the tragic shirt he wore. "Seriously, we're going to Austin, dude. Sweet honeys. Oh wait." I grabbed a pack of unopened briefs from the drawer. "Emergency stash left over from when I was rich and threw stuff away every couple of months." I tossed them to him.

He just kind of stood there.

Okay.

I looked him up and down.

He wore the absolute worst of my horde.

"Holy shit, dude," I said quickly. "We're almost exactly the same size." I went to the closet and grabbed two snazzy button-down shirts, trying to get him moving. "This or this?"

"Uh."

"It's going to get cold," I said. "Indian summer's over. You like them both?"

He nodded a lot. "Sure. Whichever."

Damn. Not working.

I handed them over. "You can decide later. Jeans. Designer or casual?"

He made a face.

"Yeah, casual it is."

He seemed embarrassed at his opinion.

I handed over two pair and rummaged through a drawer for t-shirts. I grabbed a couple. "Here." I gave him a belt. "Your waist is smaller than mine, you piece of crap."

Woody hesitated. He wasn't used to charity.

Yeah. Me neither until Dad had lost his job.

I grabbed more clothes and pulled a duffle bag out of the closet. "Okay, I know we're not all that tight yet, but this is an emergency and trust me, the socks are clean."

He stared at the pile of clothes. "I can't let you give me all this." His voice sounded almost dead. It was hitting him, what it really meant to be homeless.

I remembered exactly that feeling.

What would Dad do?

"What give?" I said with a scoff. "Look, do you think my dad and Dr. Mike aren't going to at least get your *clothes* for you? I can't wear three hundred pairs of jeans at once. It's a loan." I picked up the plastic wrapped briefs. "Except for the underwear. Those are a gift. I don't want those back."

Woody tried to smile but it didn't quite work. He shoved stuff into the duffle.

I watched him, remembering the shock of finding out Dad had lost the gym, the money. But even then, we'd known we had a place to go. A roof over our heads. Yet it'd pissed me off to no end that we'd had to move out to Dumass.

Damn, what a douche. Not wanting to go where you can is one thing. Not having a place to go? Utterly different story.

Woody would know he was wanted.

I would fucking make certain of that. "*Ese?*"

He needed a few moments to look up at me. The humiliation he felt at having to accept my help bent his back into a question mark.

"I live in my Aunt's house," I told him. "Until we had to move here, Dad had always let me know she was a homophobe who'd made it clear he would never be fit to raise me. They hate each other." I pointed at the bag. "That's not charity. It's pay it forward."

He stared into my eyes a long time. A million thoughts ran rampant across his face.

"I don't know which was worse to them, the porn or not telling Effy to go fuck himself when he came out." He zipped up the duffle. "And now I don't even have a way to make money." He stood there, breathing heavy and scared. "Do you know how lucky you are with your dad?"

"Jesus, Woody, every day proves it to me more and more."

Chapter Nine

Trudy sat cross-legged on Tango's bed. That girl redefined the word *terco*. She refused to go to Austin, even though she was in more danger than anyone else involved.

Cosita had already given up and left to wait in the car.

Shilling hovered in the doorway, as if trying to stay out of the argument.

"This was Dr. Lopez, Tango," Trudy insisted for the umpteenth time. "You didn't see him. He was to-tal-ly fa-reaked out."

"You're right." Tango sat at her dressing table, brushing her hair. "I wasn't there. So I didn't see it. So it's bullshit."

"*Cabezona.*" Trudy made one of her famous noises of disgust. She pushed up from the bed. "I need a *Jaritos*."

"Get me a Coke." Tango finally met Trudy's eyes in the mirror. Sure, when she wanted something.

"*Lo que.*" Trudy stopped in the doorway at Shilling's shoulder. "You want something?"

"Coke?" For such a big girl, Shilling knew how to make herself almost invisible.

"*Sí.*" Trudy touched her shoulder as she made her way into the hall. "Maybe she'll listen to you, *chica.*"

"You know she won't," Tango called as Trudy navigated the maze of hallways to the kitchen at the front of the house.

Mamá Montez cleaned the mirrors in the dining room adjoining the kitchen. "You know she won't believe any of it until she sees it with her own eyes."

Trudy walked around the enormous island in the kitchen and opened the fridge.

Mamá wiped and wiped in little circles.

"You still clean those every week?" Trudy asked.

Mamá smiled. "No excuses for a dirty house."

Trudy examined the room. The kitchen wall had been taken down to hip height and the entire dining room lined with mirrors. Dance parties had been a regular thing back in the day, but they hardly happened anymore.

The hardwood floors shone, too. Oh. *Mamá* was stress cleaning.

"You want a Coke?" Trudy asked.

Mamá smiled. "That would be nice. With ice?"

Trudy transferred the sodas to the island and grabbed glasses. "Do you believe in magic, *Mamá*?"

She came to the island and folded her arms on it.

Someone screamed. Deep in the house. A full-throated shriek of terror.

Trudy froze. "No. Not here."

Three of Tango's brothers ran in from the porch.

Shilling's heavy tread rattled the wooden floors as she ran toward the kitchen, shouting in Russian at the top of her lungs. She reached the open space and met Trudy's eyes for one second, her face the picture of terror.

Then her head twisted 180 degrees with a loud crack.

Her legs slammed together and wrapped around each other with a quick series of snaps and pops. Her arms reached overhead and braided.

Mamá screamed.

Shilling fell to the floor in a puddle of blood.

"Katarina!" *Mamá* hurried around the island to the hallway.

"*Non*," Trudy muttered. She tried to call out but couldn't get the breath.

Mamá reached the hall and stopped. "Katarina?" Not a shout. A simple question.

High heels trod the hardwood floors, but Trudy didn't recognize the sound. She knew every possible sound Tango's feet could make. That was not Tango.

Mamá's eyes opened wide and she opened her mouth to scream.

Her arms reached up to cover her face.

And she exploded.

Warm blood spattered Trudy. She sucked in an involuntary breath and tasted salt and copper.

Blood covered the walls. Katy's brothers froze in shock, covered in their mother's blood. Carlos, Ron and Cisco.

"Katy?" Cisco asked. He was the oldest.

"*No es Tango*," Trudy whispered, backing into the fridge and sliding to the floor.

At the first scream, Trudy closed her eyes.

The brother's screams overlapped with the sound of bones breaking and something that sounded like rubber stretching and snapping. They screamed and screamed and screamed.

Trudy covered her ears with her hands and scooted around to put her back to the island. *Por favor, no dejes que me vea aquí!* She opened her eyes when the screaming stopped.

The top half of the mirror in the dining room peeked over the hip divider. It showed the upper walls and ceiling beyond the island that hid Trudy from the rest of the kitchen.

The walls glistened red.

Katy strode into the kitchen with entirely the wrong walk. She stumbled on her heels. She cursed in a deeper voice than normal. The shoes clattered across the floor.

"Fucking heels."

Blood dripped down the white, white fridge door.

Por favor, keep Cosita in the damn car.

"Wow. That was cool," Katy's wrong voice said. "I am definitely stronger now."

Twist. It had to be Twist. He'd taken her, controlled her.

Bare feet made quiet sucking sounds as Twist walked Katy around the blood-covered kitchen.

Trudy held her breath, eyes locked on the mirror in case Katy might come back into view.

"I could use a Coke," Katy's wrong voice said.

Mierda. Trudy opened her mouth to make her breath quieter, and she waited to die.

Bam! The front door blew open.

A hot blonde strode into the front hall, her dress red, velvet and slinky. An unnatural wind followed her and blew her hair every which way.

It also covered the sound of Trudy's vibrating cell.

Cosita: *¿Qué coño?*

Stay there! Trudy sent back. *Call cops*

She turned off the phone.

Twist and the woman faced off on the opposite side of the island.

If they so much as glanced in the mirror, they'd see Trudy. As long as she didn't move, she'd be fine. Unless they were dancers, most people thought of mirrors as walls unless movement attracted their attention.

"Is that you in there, David?" The woman squinted closer.

"Hello, Mary." Twist grabbed her and kissed her soundly.

Dios mio, caliente. With the horror all around her, how could Trudy be turned on by that?

"Hm. Minty." The woman touched her lips with the tip of one finger. "But I'm going to guess that was a lot sexier for you than it was for me."

Twist chuckled in Katy's body.

Mary wandered around the room and out of sight.

"I thought I told you to keep a low profile," she said. "Shredding a family is not low profile."

"What do I care?" Twist asked, turning away from the mirror. "I'm *dead.* No one can hurt me." Then Katy's hands jumped to her throat, and she coughed. She lifted from the floor and burst into flame! She screamed, but in Twist's voice.

Trudy clamped her hands to her mouth to keep from calling out.

The flames flashed and flickered, but Katy didn't burn. A flash. Twist! Silvery and pale. *He* was burning, not Katy. His spirit flickered. He screamed again.

Then the fire went out and Twist and Katy fell to the floor.

Trudy started shaking and couldn't stop. The room had fallen so, so cold.

"Do-gooders, Twist. They will hurt you far worse than that." Mary moved into sight and looked down at him.

Twist rose to his feet, then faded into Katy again. She leaned against the island, panting, her eyes filled with a hatred completely foreign to Katy's face no matter how pissed she'd ever been.

"I hear there's already one snooping around here." The woman moved away. "He seems to imagine himself one of the Hardy boys."

"Who?"

The woman appeared at Katy's side again, one hand raised to bitch slap Twist. Then she stopped. "Wait a minute." She sniffed Katy. She made her way from her shoulders down to her abdomen.

"Sorta creepy," Twist said.

Mary laughed. "That gives me an idea."

What?

She walked around Twist, and, thankfully, Katy's body held her complete attention because she'd have seen Trudy easily if she'd looked down.

Trudy held her breath.

"What?" Twist demanded. "What?"

"The girl you're wearing is pregnant."

Trudy almost gasped. *No era possible.*

"What?" Katy's hands went to her stomach.

"Just barely." Mary leaned against the island, her back to the mirror now. "I'd bet even she doesn't know yet. "

"Wow." Twist walked Katy away from the island and stared at her reflection in the mirror. "Must be the rock star's."

Soy invisible. Soy invisible. If he so much as turned her head.

"I don't care who the daddy is," Mary said. "That baby is mine. It's so new, I'm sure we can use it. It'll be perfect."

"Perfect for what?" Twist turned this way and that, gaping at the reflection.

"Get away from the mirror, you idiot," Mary snapped. "You can't *see* anything after two weeks."

Twist glared at her but moved away. "I was just admiring her tits."

Trudy breathed again.

Sirens sounded in the distance, closing fast.

"Well, David." Mary glanced in the mirror and touched Katy's lips. "The Bible tells us we must be born again. You up for it?"

And with that they left.

Trudy sat frozen in her spot.

If she moved, she'd see things. . . things that would prove to her everything that'd happened was real. Then thick smoke poured into the kitchen and flickering shadows covered the sitting room across the hall.

Trudy jumped to her feet and hurried around the island. Her socks slipped on something pale and rubbery, but she caught herself on the counter.

Blood and guts covered the floor worse than any horror movie she'd ever seen. When the smell of burning meat hit, her stomach heaved violently and spewed her breakfast onto the floor.

Carlos' eyes stared up at her a foot away from her own vomit. His face seemed very surprised. Where was his body?

She threw up again.

The heat grew. She heard voices shouting outside and the gentle roar of the biggest bonfire ever. And there, covered in blood, Mrs. M's wedding rings and the necklace from Katy's great, great grandmother. She needed to get them to Katy!

Trudy finally moved. She grabbed the jewelry and ran down the hall.

The smoke choked her, but the central hallway was free of fire. The flames must have started on the outside wall at the front.

Since the fire was eating its way in, she could get to the back.

She stopped in Mrs. M's room and grabbed the jewelry box. Katy would want it, and they'd need the money to start over. She grabbed Katy's laptop from her room, with all her music and dance videos. If she lost those, she'd be *so* upset.

Trudy looked up. The fire ate its way toward her, like a ravenous mouth devouring the hallway. The smell of burning meat hit her again, but she was past vomiting.

A distant scream reached her.

The loudest crack in the world broke through the roaring of the fire and the floor itself shuddered. A wall must have collapsed in the front of the house.

The floor shook again.

"*Mierda.*" Trudy looked around. Why was she just standing there?

She threw the locked jewelry box out the window as hard as she could, then backed up for a running start and leapt through, cradling the laptop in her arms.

A wall of heat sucked the air out of her lungs, but she dove to the ground with more oxygen than she'd had in the house. She rolled and came up on one knee. "Cheerleading sucks so much, does it?" She grabbed the jewelry box. "Learning how to roll out of a fall just saved my life."

She stumbled away from the burning building. *Mierda*, how had she made it out of that alive?

Voices shouted at the front of the house. What would she tell them? All the evidence was ash and smoke.

She looked at the stuff in her arms. "And here I stand looking like a thief." She backed away from the inferno.

Then it hit her.

Katy's mom was dead.

So were Carlos, Ron and Cisco.

Dios mio. So was Shilling.

Dead. Never coming back.

Tears had been pouring down Trudy's face for a while now, but her stomach twisted, and her heart pounded in her chest.

She had to get away. She couldn't be there anymore.

She fled.

Twist stepped through a glowing portal of light into a cemetery, his cemetery, and there, a few feet away, stood his gravestone and six feet under it lay his corpse.

"Thanks, Mary," he muttered, "You know how to make a guy feel special."

As she stepped out of the light, it sucked into the abyss with a quiet thwip. Seriously? What happened to not drawing attention?

"Completely different," Mary said. So. . . not even pretending she didn't invade his mind. Brilliant. "No one saw it there." She waved an arm. "No one to see it here. Whereas that. . ." She waved at the spot where the portal had led from Katy's house. "Was something every God damned person in the town saw."

Twist faced her. "Saw what? A burning building? No one's going to be able to tell a thing from those charred corpses. Cops won't—"

Mary grabbed him under the chin, lifted him from the ground and slammed him into a tree. Ouch.

"I don't give fetid rhino's crack about the cops." She pressed him into the tree.

If he'd been in a dude's body, he'd have sported major wood.

"There are so many things worse than cops," Mary snapped.

"Yeah, yeah," Twist wheezed. "Do-gooders."

She pushed her nose into Twist's face. He felt warm between his legs. Huh. So that was the chick equivalent?

Her eyes studied his face for half a second before she scoffed in disgust and released him. "Even in a woman's body you're a pig."

Twist chuckled.

"Worse than do-gooders." She pointed at the portal no longer there. "That kind of display is going to attract the Cloaks."

Somehow, Twist had heard the capital C.

"As much magic as you now know exists in the world," she said, "have you never wondered why the world doesn't know about it?"

Actually, he'd never wondered anything of the sort.

She rolled her eyes. "There is a group of the most powerful Unknown beings in the world who make sure no one finds out. They clean up the messes idiots like you leave behind." She stared him in the eye. "And by clean up I mean incinerate everyone involved and erase the memories of anyone remotely associated."

"Sounds like the Men in Black," Twist said.

She raised an eyebrow, nodded and turned away. "That's aliens. We actually sometimes call ours the Men in Black Cloaks." She looked at him. "They often do wear black cloaks."

Twist stood over his gravestone. Could his mom have been any cheaper? He undid his fly to piss on it. . . wait. How did chicks pee in the woods?

Mary let out a deep sigh behind him. "We squat."

Twist looked down. He tried to imagine it without pissing all over himself. Nope. No clue. He missed his junk.

"Are you listening to me?" She grabbed him and spun him to face her.

If he'd had a pecker, he could've pissed right on her.

"Yeah, yeah, big scary freak police hate us having fun." He buttoned up his pants. He'd have to come back in a dude. How many people had a chance to piss on their own grave? "Tell me more about reincarnation."

"Not reincarnation." She smiled. "Rebirth."

"Wait, so I come out a drooling, shitting brat, or I come out as me?"

"Is there a difference?" Her hands settled on her hips.

Ha ha.

"While in the womb, you'll sleep," she said. "I'll weave a spell around you at birth that will keep you asleep and will age you a few years in a short time."

"Why not just age me all the way?"

"We're not fast forwarding a VCR," she said. Wow old reference. "If I get it wrong, you end up with a fetal dick and balls the size of lima beans."

Okay. That would be bad. "Why take the chance at all? I'm kinda getting into the whole being dead thing."

"All spirits eventually go insane."

Oh crap, now she sounded paranoid.

"*Eos et id que num quam suav itate.*" She raised her arms and mist rose from the ground across the cemetery. With it, pale silvery ghosts shimmered into view everywhere. Hundreds of them. Wailing and moaning, some of them flickering and fading in and out.

"Where is my daughter?"

"Why can't I see?"

"Why, why, WHY!!"

They soared through the air and around the trees, screaming, bleeding. Some of them reeled from being shot over and over again. Some of them hung from ropes, kicking and screaming.

"Huh. Cool. Can you teach me how to make them all visible like that?" It would be fun at parties.

"What?" She waved both arms and all the mist and ghostly images sucked back into the ground.

"Okay, okay, point taken," Twist lied. Point so not taken. He wasn't anything like those rubes. He'd done all this on purpose, but he needed to humor her for the time being until he figured out just how powerful he really was now.

"Fine. We make me a baby," he said, "but not before I destroy Fox."

"Of all the infernal wastes of time. . ."

"*Dicat possi mut quo.*" He waved a hand.

A purple swirl of oily mist shot from the ground and engulfed her.

When it cleared a moment later, a grackle fluttered its surprise.

Twist jumped up and down. "Hot damn! It worked!"

She squawked and beat her wings.

"Don't worry, sweetheart." Twist waved and walked away. "I'm sure you'll reverse it in a couple of minutes. Just let me have my fun, then I'll crawl into my womb and be a good little baby."

Twist pulled out Tango's cell phone. He had unfinished business. He tapped the icon for Daddy Fox.

"Katy!" gay Fox shouted. "Are you okay? Where are you?"

"Sorry Fox, you big gay bastard." Twist gathered energy in a vortex around himself. "Katy doesn't live here anymore."

While he waited for Fox to do the math, he teleported to Juicy's house to steal a change of clothes. Something a bit more substantial for the weather.

"Twist," Fox said at last.

"What? I was hoping for 'If you hurt one hair on her head, I'll kill you?'" He barked a laugh. "Whoops. Already dead."

"What do you want?"

Nice. To the point. "Meet me at the studio—"

Mary flapped in through the window, landed on the floor and swirled into her normal form in a whirl of purple smoke.

"In an hour." Twist hung up the phone. "We can do this together my way," he told Mary, "or we can fight and waste time and neither of us gets what we want."

The hands clenched into white fists at her side showed Twist just how much willpower she needed to avoid a massive battle right then and there. The fact that she *hadn't* just attacked told him more about his newfound ability than any amount of experimentation would've revealed.

"Fine. The do-gooder who saved the father. I know him." Mary crossed to the closet and pulled out clothes. "I know how he thinks, and I know what he will try." She dropped the clothes on the bed. "At the risk of offending your alpha male sensibilities, may I offer a plan that I know will work to our mutual satisfaction?" She held up a sweater. "And a decent ensemble."

"Sounds good." Twist pulled off his blouse. "You know how much I like it when we both leave the room satisfied."

Mary rolled her eyes.

Twist fumbled with the bra strap. Huh. They were harder to manage from this angle.

Chapter Ten

As we hit Loop 410 to drive around San Antonio, Woody leaned into the front seat and tapped my shoulder. "Dude, dude, dude. There is this little place called Beto's that makes the world's *best* fish tacos. It's right off the highway, and—" He stopped abruptly and leaned back.

Huh?

"Sorry," he muttered. "Never mind."

That's right. He had no money. We'd buy him some tacos, though. . .

Corey sighed a deep, thoughtful sigh then undid his seat belt and turned all the way around. "Okay, look, bro." He pulled out his wallet. "I know I try not to flash my money around even though you all know I'm loaded." He held out a couple of bills. "And I don't know the whole story here, but if your asshole parents hadn't swiped your hard-earned money from you, you'd be fine. So here."

I wanted to make a joke about the porn money being hard-earned, but I shut up.

"I can't. . ." Woody held up both hands. "I can't take your money."

"Say it's a loan, okay? We're going to see Ethan's scary lawyer, bro. She will *totally* get your money back for you." He grinned. "Your parents meet her once? They'll shit their pants and hand you the keys to the house." Which, oddly enough, had pretty much happened with Corey's dad.

Corey shoved his hand into Woody's chest and dropped the bills.

I balanced avoiding accidents with watching in the rearview mirror.

Woody gathered the bills. "I'll pay you back every penny."

Corey turned to face front again and glanced at me. He faked a smile. "Dude, I just want to try those fish tacos. Y'all know there's no way they're better than my mom's." The smile bled off his face. We drove in silence a while.

Corey met Woody's eyes in the rear-view mirror. "Look, this isn't public knowledge right now, okay? I found out my dad's been cheating on my mom for a year."

"*Cojeme, ese.*" Woody's eyes went wide,

"Yeah, on top of everything else that sucks, I kicked my dad out of the house 'cause he's an asshole. My mom left everything to me, so Ethan's scary lawyer lady helped make that happen. Long God damn story." He turned to look at Woody directly. "My life kinda sucks right now, bro. And y'all have been there for me the last couple of weeks. That money? I found it in a drawer in the kitchen. It's like change for the day, you know? So keep it and forget about it because it makes me feel good to help someone else, and there's not a helluva lot that makes me feel good right now."

Time to swing the mood around. "So what's our fish taco exit, *ese?* I'm freaking jonesing now."

Woody smiled and nodded. "Broadway south."

Kenny elbowed him. "Always told you guys I'd make it to Broadway."

Corey and Woody laughed, and the guy talk resumed.

Kenny avoided meeting my eyes in the mirror. I was the only one who knew his shot to the leg may have removed the Broadway option. It'd looked like it hit the same way mine had, but what did I know about anatomy? He might always have a limp.

He finally met my eyes, smirked and raised an eyebrow as if to say, "My real passion has always been the tech, hai?"

Hai.

My cell rang as we pulled into the parking lot. I put Bessie Junior in park and grabbed it: Ephraim. I tapped it on speaker.

"Hey, Effy—"

"Do you have any idea where Woody is?" He sounded frantic.

Woody closed his eyes and sat back in his seat.

"He won't pick up his phone," Effy said. "I called him at home and—"

"And his parents kicked him out." I left the car.

The other guys followed suit. Why did Woody look so stressed?

"Uh, yeah," Effy said. This long, weird pause happened. "How do you know that?"

We all congregated at the hood of my car. Does it totally ruin the flow of this conversation if I reiterate how awesome it was to have my own car again? Deal.

"He's kind of standing right here with me," I said.

Woody crossed his arms in a very uncomfortable manner.

"Oh, your place. Perfect." And now Ephraim sounded all lightness and fun. "I'm on my way."

"We're not at my place," I said. "We're in San Antonio."

Woody cringed so hard I almost missed the fact that Ephraim didn't speak for a couple of seconds.

"What the fuck?" Effy asked. "Why don't I know any of this?" His voice sounded hateful, and that's not a word I throw around a lot.

What the fuck?

"Why don't I give you to Woody?" I suggested.

I held the phone out.

Woody smiled a huge smile fakier than any I had ever seen and tapped the phone off speaker. "Hey, Effy! How're—" He glanced at me, slightly embarrassed. "Yes. Dude. . . I knew you were with Lizard, I didn't want to—" He closed his eyes. "Well, I thought I was—" He took a deep breath and I saw the frustration building. "*Mijo*—" He took a few steps away. "*Mijo!*" He glanced over apologetically.

Then he turned his back to us and stopped trying to keep his voice down. "Would you shut up for one God damn minute?!" He took a quick breath. "I got kicked out of my fucking *house* last night, slept in my car and Ethan God damn *Fox* was considerate enough to let me shower and borrow some clean clothes." His whole body started to shake. "I don't know where the *fuck* I'm going to live, so I'm sorry if I made a mistake in thinking you might want some alone time with your *boyfriend*." He held the phone to his mouth in that way that said he was about to hang up after a tirade. "Oh. That's *right!* You have a God damn *boyfriend* now, so pardon me for thinking I might get one fucking day to myself for a change."

Effy's voice came over the cell, but I couldn't hear what he said.

Woody looked at the phone, then held it to his face again. "*Ese.* He has a call." He held the phone away and I could hear shouting. "*Ese. . .* It's not my *phone!*"

"Don't you dare hang up on me," came over the line oh-so-easily heard.

"It's not my phone," Woody muttered. He clicked through, took a deep breath and created a voice far calmer than I'd have managed. "Foxtrot's phone. Woody." His whole face lit up. "Trudy!" His face blanched and his eyes opened into giant plates. "*Santa* fuck!"

I'd never seen someone's face switch to horror that fast in my life.

He found me and handed the phone over, but Trudy launched deep into speed Spanish. I had no idea what she was saying, so I clicked the phone over to speaker.

She kept ranting.

Corey and Woody turned so pale it scared me.

Woody grabbed the phone out of my hands and tapped it off speaker.

"What the fuck," I asked.

"I'm not sure," Corey said.

Woody put the phone to his chest. "The spook was right," he said. "Twist just *possessed* Tango, killed like, half her family, I think. *Seriously.* The entire house burned down. Trudy was there. She saw it. She. . ." He shook his head. "Mrs. Montez *exploded.*"

Really long pause.

He shook his head again. "*Ir a Señor Fox,*" he said to the phone. "He'll protect you."

Jesus, why did everyone think my Dad was Conan the Dadbarian?

Well, fuck, he kind of was. But damn it, he was my *dad*.

Woody closed the call and held the phone out to me.

Shock wouldn't come close.

For any of us.

Corey nudged Woody. "Did I hear right? *Que está embarazada?*"

Woody did this bizarre shrug, nod, hands up in the air thing.

"What?" I asked. "That's way beyond my Spanglish."

"Katy's pregnant, *ese*." Woody grabbed my arm. "Congrats."

Kenny and Corey froze.

"Can't be mine," I said. "We never had sex."

Lucky Fox paced the dance studio floor, wishing Twist would hurry up and show. So much depended on the next few minutes.

Katy's home had burned to ash. Her mom was missing but presumed dead, along with three brothers and the poor Russian girl. Cosita would need therapy for years, and no one seemed to know what'd happened to Trudy or Katy.

Lucky wanted to call his boy but didn't have the time. Besides, Ethan had driven off to Austin which kept him well and truly out of harm's way. Exactly where Lucky wanted him. A single phone call would bring him running back to Dumass and that was the last thing Lucky wanted.

He stopped pacing and took a deep breath.

It was a thing he'd learned from Ethan.

"Take a deep breath," his son always said. "It'll relax you."

Lucky sucked in again.

Didn't work.

He looked around. Man, the place hadn't changed in twenty years. No wonder Ethan had thought it was lame when they'd first moved back. It looked like something Liberace would have designed back in the seventies.

Lucky had taken dance classes in high school. He'd been dating Cheryl Plumber. She and her girlfriends had insisted Lucky, Mike and Karl take lessons before the homecoming dance junior year.

Huh. Even then, he'd wished he'd been dancing with Mike rather than Cheryl. How crazy that he and Mike had finally had that dance together in the old alma mater twenty years later.

And Mike had almost died because of Twist.

Damn.

Lucky paced some more. Don't think about it. Focus on what he could do. If he followed that Morrison kid's instructions, he just might rid them all of their Twist problem.

Lucky had no idea how the kid had made the trip from the camp to the studio in a matter of minutes. He'd never, ever ask. But the bizarre circle he'd drawn on the ceiling seemed to be the real deal.

When the young man had arrived nearly an hour earlier, he'd started drawing on the ceiling and spouting instructions to Lucky. Had he not already experienced Mike's possession, Lucky never would've bought the young man's sincere directions.

Would Morrison's plan work?

He glanced over at the storage room—

Boom! The front door exploded in a fury of glass.

Lucky turned away from the blast and covered his face. When he could look again, Katy stalked through the wreckage and stopped just inside. Bright light streamed around her, forcing her shape into silhouette. Smoke blew in and swirled around her feet, glowing a sickly purplish green.

The bell jingled and jingled.

She glared at it, grabbed it and threw it to the floor. "I have always hated that thing."

Not Katy. Wrong stance. Wrong voice.

Just wrong.

Twist.

The special effects subsided. They had to be meant to scare Lucky.

They did, but he wasn't about to show it.

"You know. . ." Katy—no Twist. It was Twist. He moved into the seating area. "The last time I stood in exactly this spot, Ethan was out cold because Warren had clubbed him." He crouched down. "I can still see the blood stain." He looked up at Lucky and smiled an evil grin. "If I'd've just killed him right then and there, none of this would've happened." He rose. "How many innocent lives would've been saved? How many people died because I didn't have the foresight to just kill him right then and there?" He shrugged. "Of course, I was more worried about Katy." He held out his arms and looked them over. "More worried about me." He laughed.

Lucky didn't worry about a thing Twist said. He'd fought enough men to know trash talk when he heard it. "I see you finally grew that vagina we all assumed you had."

Twist glanced up, and his eyes flashed with a red fire.

Fuck. Fire eyes meant all kinds of bad.

Twist moved closer, to the edge of the dance floor. Grey smoke swirled around him. An image, like a shadow, grew out of Katy's body, a grey shadow that hulked behind her for a moment then sucked back in.

She shook out her hair and the eyes lost their fire. "A sexist fag? That's messed up."

Lucky had hit a nerve. Interesting. He stepped closer. Everything in his soul wanted to move away, to run into the storage room and hide, but if he played his part correctly, Twist might be ended for good and Ethan would be safe.

That's all that mattered to Lucky. His son would be safe. Nothing else. Nothing.

"For all the shit you said about how much you wanted Katy," Lucky said, "how much you loved her." He waved a hand at Twist inside Katy. "I guess the whole time you just wanted to *be* her."

Twist's eyes flashed red for one second then he smiled. "Yeah, sure, try to piss me off." He stepped onto the dance floor. "We both know you aren't leaving this building alive."

There it was.

He'd said it.

No more dicking around.

No. Move forward. For Ethan. The rest didn't matter.

"You told me you had a proposition," Lucky said.

"I lied." Twist waved an arm casually.

Something hit Lucky and tossed him as if the heaviest fighter had punched every square inch of his body at the same time. He flew across the dance floor and smashed into the mirror.

Glass shattered.

Lucky fell to the floor on his hands and knees as glass rained down around him.

Get to your feet!

Shit! Had he heard that? Or was it a memory from his fighting days?

Didn't matter. He was a fighter. He pushed to his feet and didn't worry about the warm wetness across his back. Just blood.

Twist stepped closer.

Lucky set himself, ready in case another blast hit him.

"Holy shit," Twist said. "That was the best. bitch slap. ever."

Lucky grinned. "I had teenage girls in my classes that would've made you look like Honey Boo Boo."

The eyes flared again, and the shadow burst out from Katy like a billowing cape. It cried out in anger loud enough to rattle the chandeliers.

Twist moved forward to the middle of the floor.

There!

Lucky dove to the side and rolled up to one knee.

"*Has dico null ainvid untut!*" Morrison rushed from the storage room.

A circle of green fire ignited the floor around Twist. Foom! A chorus of something dark and scary sang a loud high note while flames leapt to the ceiling.

Mary mother of Christ! Lucky fell onto his ass, scooted back as fast as he could then jumped to his feet.

Twist jumped back and swore a list of profanity that would need googling.

So. . . a girl who looked like Katy Montez but was inhabited by the spirit of the psychopath that Gunner had killed stood in a circle of magical fire in the middle of a dance studio that looked like something Liberace had puked up in 1973.

Damn.

Morrison strode to the edge of the fire circle that cast no heat.

And thank God threatening Lucky had kept Twist from looking up.

"You!" Twist pointed at Morrison. "You tiny-dicked spic! You really think this can hold me?"

Morrison shrugged. "Good work, Mr. Fox. You okay?"

Lucky waved. "Fine. Call me Lucky."

Morrison laughed. "Indeed you are." He walked up to the edge of the circle that trapped Twist. "I do think it can hold you," he said to the spirit.

Panting, Twist strode to the fire and glared at Morrison.

The kid smiled. "You're my little bitch."

The shadow flared again, and Twist raised both hands in clenched fists.

If the plan was going to work, they needed Twist to run through the circle.

Or. . . something? Lucky didn't exactly understand what would happen.

Twist examined the fire with quick, sharp movements. He reached out and touched the flames with one finger. His brow furrowed when nothing happened. He extended his arm through the wall.

He smiled. "I fink you fucked up wiff your wittle wall." He wiggled his fingers in Morrison's face.

Morrison stepped to Lucky's side.

Twist withdrew his arm. "Just tell me what it does."

Morrison's smile sent a shiver up Lucky's back. Thank goodness they worked for the same side.

"It's a soul cage." Morrison crossed his arms. "Only one soul may ride this ride. Please keep all stowaways inside the protective circle."

Twist raised one eyebrow.

"So here's how it's going to go down," Morrison said. "You're going to leave her body and see if you can figure out a way to escape the circle in ghost form. There's no way you're getting out while you're hitching a ride. Any secondary souls in her body get sucked out and trapped in a handy crystal."

Twist sniffed a quiet laugh. "Wow." He retreated to the center of the circle. "She really knows you, doesn't she?"

Something about Twist's sudden calm sucked.

Morrison seemed less than thrilled as well.

"She knew exactly what you would do." Twist clapped his hands slowly and dramatically.

"She?" Lucky muttered.

"Drat." Morrison held his hands out to his sides, and they glowed. "I'd kind of thought you'd already had a falling out."

"Oh, we did." Twist rubbed his hands together. "We kissed and made up."

Balls of fire engulfed Morrison's hands. "Really? That's kinda rare for her."

Lucky moved away. Fireballs! In his hands!

"Can you guess why she wanted you to trap me in a soul cage?" Twist asked.

"Easier way to break up than texting?" Morrison dropped into a fighting stance.

Lucky moved a little farther away. He'd never backed down from a fight, but the kind of battle that included handfuls of fire and a vengeful ghost went a bit beyond his training.

"The slut's pregnant," Twist said.

Time slowed down.

Morrison chanted Latin.

Katy's arms flung straight out to her sides and her head snapped back as a grey, oily shadow leapt straight up from her body.

She screamed.

It was the most painful sound Lucky had ever heard, as if it had built in her all day. It broke his heart.

She spotted him and ran full tilt in his direction, screaming.

"No!" Morrison rushed to intercept her, back to his Latin.

Her fingertips passed through the fire and tiny spots of light scattered.

The oily smoke took Twist's shape and raced circles inside the fire wall.

Katy's arm broke through. More sparks.

Her face cleared the flames, tears pouring down her cheeks.

Morrison shook the fireballs from his hands and reached for her.

Her shoulders crossed the barrier. . . and the moment her stomach touched it, a galaxy of sparks exploded from her, swirling around her and expanding to fill the room.

"NO!" Morrison grabbed her hands.

Too late. The galaxy swirled into plumes and vortices, a spider web of energy that bounced off the mirrors and rebounded at Katy the moment she fell into Morrison's arms.

A tornado of golden light spun down into her, sucking away the entire barrier of fire.

The scream of a terrified infant shattered every light bulb with a shower of sparks.

The mirrors shook.

The floor trembled.

A glowing golden crystal fell to the floor and tinkled.

Morrison did little better than slow Katy's fall.

The world held its breath.

Then time did its best to play catch up.

Lucky ran to Katy and Morrison.

Twist's ghost darted around the room at breakneck speed, leaping into one mirror and zipping from the glass across the room, back and forth, in and out, all the while filling the room with its dark echoing laughter.

Lucky lifted Katy from the floor and held her like a child.

She clung to him, sobbing. "What just happened? What just happened?"

Morrison leapt to his feet, flipping around, trying to keep up with Twist's movement. "God damn mirrors. I *hate* dance studios." He muttered something in Latin and the broken bulbs flickered to life filling the room with a steady light.

The ghostly laughter faded away.

"Predictable." A woman's voice from the shattered doorway. Blonde. Pretty in a 1950s kind of way. She stalked across the broken glass and tumbled furniture with a casual grace that worried Lucky. The scene seemed far too normal to her. "That's what made you so lousy in the sex department, Morri."

"Mary." The fireballs leapt back into Morrison's hands. He threw them at her. Two. Four. Six. Eight in rapid succession.

They fizzled to nothing before they reached her.

His hands met above his head in a clap that reverberated like thunder as lightning exploded from them.

It arced across the room, shattering the chandeliers and grounding on the woman, Mary, wrapping her in a manic cocoon of electricity that changed to dark purple and dripped away from her like water, puddling on the ugly carpet and sinking into nothing.

Morrison clapped his hands in front. "*Salutatus!*" A pulse radiated from him in a circular wave that threw the tables and chairs into the air and shook the floor.

She waved a hand and deflected it.

Morrison stopped, crouched battle ready, air heaving in and out of his lungs.

Mary's words finally registered in Lucky's mind. "She's your *ex*?"

The woman smiled. "Breakups are a bitch." Her eyes met Lucky's and flashed orange. "So am I."

The ghost hovered beside her. "Wait. You fucked that little twerp?"

"Boys." She rolled her eyes. "Always worried about who fucked whom."

The ghost circled her. "You did?" It focused on Morrison. "You little shit."

Mary made a noise of disgust. She waved a hand at Twist. "You." She pointed at Lucky. "Into the girl."

She wasn't pointing at Lucky then—

The thing shot into Katy, who jumped to life in Lucky's arms. An elbow caught him on the chin. A fist hit him in the eye and a foot slammed his gut before he could even react.

"Get your hands off me, you damn dirty ape." The deeper voice again, Twist's voice.

Lucky's arms instinctively opened, and Twist scrabbled away.

Morrison just stood there. Well, everything he'd thrown at Mary hadn't even mussed her hair. What could he do?

Katy, no, Twist ran to Mary's side.

Morrison moved forward.

"Uh, uh, uh." Mary waggled a finger at him. "I'd think you'd have learned that you can't stop me. Even your absolute best is nothing more than foreplay."

"Hey." Twist glared at her.

She closed her fingers at him, and his mouth snapped shut.

"We stopped you," Morrison said through clenched teeth.

"And yet here I am none the worse for wear." She gestured at her body with one hand.

A horrible ripping sound. A jagged line of light appeared behind her and opened a dark tear, like a gash in the air itself. The tear opened farther.

Lucky had to do *something*.

Morrison stopped him with an arm across his chest.

Without another word, Mary led Twist through that black, open wound then the gap closed with a sound like an enormous zipper.

The floor shook yet again, and the spot where Mary had stood cracked open.

Fire poured from the hole like lava.

"Oh shit." Lucky grabbed Morrison, lifted him from the floor and raced away.

The fire spread like oil across the parquet and up the walls.

Lucky crashed through the swinging door into the storage room.

A castle of toilet paper broke their fall.

Morrison rolled to his back and held both hands directly in front, wrists together, right hand on top. The swinging door stopped abruptly as the oily fire hit it and Morrison grunted.

Smoke curled under the edges of the doors.

"Good save," the kid said. "Thanks."

"Except that now we're trapped."

"Not so much." He held a hand out to Lucky. "Take it."

He took it.

"Stay close." He muttered again. *Was* that Latin?

A whirlwind blew into life around them.

Morrison led Lucky out of the room and into a roaring inferno. Their personal whirlwind caught the fire and spun it into a terrifying maelstrom, but the heat didn't touch them.

They walked across the blackened parquet and stopped in the exact middle of the blaze. Flames roared and spit, but the whirlwind sucked all the fire and smoke into one intense column.

Morrison tugged his hand. "I need that now."

Lucky released it, a little embarrassed at how tightly he'd been holding on.

Morrison flung his arms out wide. "Fuck off!"

The fire blew into nothing, leaving the studio a smoking, blackened ruin.

"'Fuck off' is a magic spell?" Lucky asked.

Morrison walked to the empty doorway. "Sometimes the words themselves aren't so important."

"You realize that if you had led with something like what I just saw here," Lucky said, "everyone would've been a lot less resistant."

"If I always led with something like that, I'd be an unwilling resident in a government lab somewhere with a probe permanently lodged up my rectum."

He had a point.

"Let's get out of here," Morrison said,

Outside the ruined building, movement across the street caught Lucky's eye. A crowd had already gathered. Damn it.

"You said you stopped her once," Lucky whispered.

Morrison scoffed. "We scattered her atoms across the solar system."

Lucky grabbed his arm. "With what? A nuclear missile?"

"Sure, we'll go with nuclear missile." He pulled his arm away.

"You hit her with that," Lucky demanded, "and she walked away from it?"

"Nah." He patted Lucky's shoulder. "We pretty much vaporized her." He looked over the wreckage. "Not really sure how she came back from that one. Didn't think she would."

"And. . . your ex?"

The kid's grimace made him seem his age. "With all you just saw, that's still the piece you're taking away from it?" He shook his head. "A lot of guys say their ex is a witch. With me, it's not hyperbole."

Wisps of smoke rose from the ruins of the studio as the sun set behind it. A chill breeze blew over those of us who stared at the gutted home of our memories.

Mr. Montez sat weeping on the tailgate of a pickup. He'd lost so much. His wife, three sons, their home and the studio.

How the hell could I tell a man his daughter was alive but possessed by a ghost?

Somehow, we had to get Tango back.

I ran Dad's report of events through my head one more time in the vain hope it might somehow seem real to me. This was Dad, who'd never been prone to flights of fancy.

And *Trudy.* Hardcore, no bullshit Trudy. The things they'd seen.

Nope. Couldn't get it to seem real.

A group of us stared at the wreckage. Dad, Kenny, Corey, Woody, Ephraim, Lizard, Retro. Huh. Just the guys. Shilling had died. Tango had been taken. Trudy and Cosita had gone to ground because Trudy was in no shape to lie to the police, and Spook remained adamant none of us tell them the truth.

Who would believe us anyway?

"By all that's unholy, now what?" Spook pointed at a nun talking to the cops. Serious nun.

"I didn't realize they still made them wear the whole enchilada," I said.

"They don't," Spook said. "With her it's just a habit."

"You know her?" I pointedly ignored the lame joke.

"I've spoken to her." He surreptitiously waggled his fingers and the smoke moved away from us.

"Me, too," Kenny said. "Remember I said I knew a nun?"

Spook nearly did a double take. "You know her? That can't be coincidence."

Sheriff Olmos scratched his head a lot while they talked.

"It's not," Kenny said. "I. . . found her name on Twist's hard drive."

"Wait a minute." He'd mentioned that hard drive back at camp, too. "We destroyed that thing with a baseball bat."

"Don't get mad." Kenny cringed. "I knew how important that drive would be, so I swapped it out with one I had on me when Tango wasn't looking." Because of course he happened to have one on him. It was Kenny. "But I made sure I deleted all the nasty stuff. I just—"

"Dude." I turned my attention back to the nun. "It so doesn't matter anymore."

"So Twist had some info on Sister Liberata over there," Kenny said. "He called her a dead end because she wasn't willing to teach him black magic. I looked her up after everything at the camp. She's the one who made the present I gave you."

My fingers moved to the charm around my neck.

The nun placed her hand on the sheriff's shoulder, and his eyes sort of lost focus. He stopped scratching his head and listened to her for a full minute.

"Oh, drat." Spook seemed to have noticed the exchange as well. "That does not bode well."

"What am I seeing?" I asked.

Olmos blinked a lot and shook his head. The nun patted his arm and left him there.

"These are not the droids you're looking for," Spook muttered as if intoning some kind of spell. He pointedly turned his back to her. "Everybody, stare at the smoking studio." He turned me forcibly. "Do not speak to her."

And yes, she made her way to us.

Spook growled quietly.

"Mr. James. Mr. Valentino." She planted herself directly between us and the building. "What a surprise to see both of you here. Together?" Her voice sounded all brightness and joy, but something about the habit made me check her hands for a wooden ruler.

The hand I was watching reached for me. "And you must be Ethan Fox." She touched the charm around my neck.

I expected it to burst into flames.

It didn't.

She met my eyes. "If I'd known Mr. Valentino had wanted this for you, I'd have made a rather different charm."

Wait. She knew me?

"I know a great many things, Mr. Fox."

Wait. I said that out loud?

"No. You didn't need to." A tiny spark of green light flashed deep in her eyes. She turned to Spook. "Bringing so many children into this, Mr. James. Shame on you."

We all turned to him, waiting for a response. Wow. He folded his arms like a nervous schoolboy. Bad memories of grade school teachers?

"How deep is the shit we're in?" he asked.

She tutted. "Such language in front of a sister of the cloth."

"You don't need to wipe the city," he said. "We can still contain this. Mary has Known connections to Twist. Vengeful girlfriend is almost a cliché. Austin PD has a criminal file on her."

Sister Liberata smiled and finally released the charm. "And a very creative file she has, thanks to you and your interesting friends in our illustrious capital." She glanced from face to face.

"You can't," Spook said, and I had no idea what that meant. "They need to know they're in danger."

"I can," she said. "But I agree they need to keep their memories for now."

For now? She swept her gaze across us all again. "I've handled the sheriff. Mary is a Known criminal, and he has her description."

Why did I keep hearing capital letters?

"I'm taking them all to my place in Austin," Spook said.

She appraised him with that schoolteacher look. "Keep them there and keep it low profile. If you can't contain these two, you know. we. will." She turned her attention back to me. "Funny. You're taller than I'd expected."

She folded her arms into the sleeves of her habit and walked away. Something about her movement was too smooth, like she glided. . . or slithered rather than walking.

"Seems like—" Woody said, but Spook cut him off with one hand.

When she was gone, Spook let out a deep breath and turned to face us. He looked pale.

"Seems like that old nun costume is a little obvious for someone who wants to keep things low profile," Woody said.

"I suspect her profile would be much higher if she wore something less concealing." Spook stared at me. "How do you know her?"

I shook my head and shrugged.

Spook turned to Dad. "You know her?"

Dad shook his head. "Her I would remember."

"Drat." Spook stared after her.

"Spook," I said as gently as I could. "This is all a million years beyond any of us. What just happened?"

He faced me, but his attention was all about the charm the scary nun had made.

"She's part of a clean-up crew," he said. "We call them Cloaks. Men in Black for the supernatural world. I met her in Austin and had no idea who she was." He met my eyes. "May I?"

I nodded, and he touched the charm.

"Cripes." He pulled his hand back as if it had sparked him. He stared into my eyes. "Kenny met her. I met her, both through Twist. She knows you somehow, or she's heard of you at least." He stared after her again. "I need to get all y'all to Austin."

"When you say cleanup crew," Ephraim asked, "what exactly do you mean?"

"Ever heard of a place called Chernobyl?"

We waited for more.

"There's a singer in Austin," he said, apropos of nothing. "She needs dancers for a gig next week."

Whoa reality.

"You expect us to dance with all this going on?" Retro complained. I had to agree.

"The hardest part of dealing with the supernatural is living your normal life between the explosions and death." Spook glanced at the smoldering ruins. "I make a living at it. It's what I do, but everyone else has to go back to grades and girlfriends and boyfriends and making lunch, all the while knowing deep in the background all this Unknown shit is still happening." He stared at Retro. "So yeah. . . you should do this show. At some point, you'll have to go to college and find a career, and this kind of publicity can't be bought."

"Who's the singer?" I asked.

"Her name's Jem, and no not the sad one from the 90s." He glanced at Kenny. "She was half of Jem-N-I until a few months ago."

"Boing!" Kenny actually said that. "Seriously? They were huge in Korea and Japan." He turned to me. "I'd heard she'd set off on her own and was trying to cross over here."

"And you think it's safe for them to do a show like that?" Dad asked. "What happened to hiding out?"

"Throwing a tantrum in Dumass, Texas is one thing," Spook said. "Crashing a party with hundreds of people watching? It won't happen. Not with Mary at his side. She's the most dangerous witch I've ever met, but even she knows better than to take chances with the Cloaks."

"No." Retro? "No. This is garbage." He was drawing a line? "You're all insane. I'm not going."

"We're not messing around—" I tried.

"No!" Wow. He'd never gone off before. "For the first time in my life normal people like me. . . notice me. Girls! Girls notice me, and not just because I'm the funny one." He shook his head and backed away. "I will not let y'all mess up my life with whatever insane drama this. . ." He waved at all of us and the smoking building. ". . .is. I quit."

"You're in danger on your own," I said. "He'll try to kill you."

"Do you even hear yourself? He? He who?" He stepped closer. "Twist is dead, Ethan. Dead! What have you, personally, seen? You had some bad dreams. You got slipped some bad drugs." He waved at the others. "But with all the crap they keep spouting. What. have. you. seen? *You.*"

I had nothing.

"That's what I thought." He walked away.

Corey moved to follow but Spook stopped him. "We can't force him. It'll just make it worse." He seemed to notice the question marks in everyone's eyes. "Yes. I've done it. Did not go well." He turned to the rest of us. "Anyone else?"

We all looked around. No one moved.

"Okay, folks, let's get going," Spook said. "We have a substantial ride ahead of us."

Part II

There are those who find the magic.
There are those whom the magic finds.
More rarely, there are those who are born to it.

Chapter Ten

Retro drank his smoothie. The newsfeed had blown up with reports on the dance studio fire. If only they could get famous for their dancing instead of all the evil crap that happened to them. While he caught his breath between sets, he dried off with a towel and made sure his friends were all right, that no one new had died.

Wow. What a messed-up thought. So many people dead, and his friends thought it was some stupid ghost. The newscasters reported a girlfriend of Twist on a rampage. She had his mind-rape drugs, too. *That* made sense.

He swiped back to his dance exercises but left the reporters to talk in the background. He played the video and moved into the middle of the patio. His parents had whined a little when he'd asked to move all the furniture onto the grass, but as soon as he'd started using the patio for exercise, they shut up about it. Now that people noticed him, he'd managed to work himself into a pretty regular routine.

Plus, Stacey Williams had picked him for her lab partner, and maybe she liked him. All the motivation he needed to keep working out. Stacey was normal and funny. And pretty. And when he talked to her, he didn't think about death and ghosts and psycho girlfriends.

He set the smoothie on the patio rail and prepped to spin. He had doubles now. He wanted the triple. Stupid triple. It seemed so easy for everyone else.

He fell out of the spin halfway through the third.

Someone clapped behind him. Who?

Tango? She closed the sliding patio door and moved closer. It was her!

"Tango!" He rushed forward, but sweat soaked his shirt. He picked it away from his chest with two fingers. No sweaty hugs. "You're okay!"

"I got away," she said, hands dropping behind her back. For someone who'd just lost her home and half her family, she seemed awfully calm. Could she be in shock?

"And you're okay?" he asked.

"As well as can be expected," she wandered over to the chiminea. "So-o-o-o, I tried to let Gertrude know I'm well, but everyone seems to have fallen off the. . . grid."

Gertrude?

"Any idea where they are?" Tango looked at him over a shoulder. When he didn't respond right away, she lifted her eyebrows.

"They went off with that Spook guy," he answered quickly. "Some hideout in Austin."

She pressed her lips together and nodded. "If they were there, I'd know it." She settled against the railing and smiled. "Spook gave me his card. They aren't there."

Something about her voice was wrong. In fact, everything seemed wrong. Maybe she really was in shock.

"Any other ideas?" she asked.

Retro ran through his conversations with Ethan. "Oh wait, Ethan said something about a place, a club." What was it called? "Bitter Taste? Sour Grapes?"

Her mouth relaxed into a smile. "Bitter Sweets?"

"Yeah. That's it." He closed his tablet. Tango would help their friends see reason. "Give me a minute to change—"

"Not necessary." She held up a hand and moved away from the railing. "I just need to deliver a package."

"I'll go with." Except his feet wouldn't move. What the heck? His arms wouldn't move either. His whole body stuck in place.

"No. You won't." Tango stepped closer. Her eyes narrowed. "You're the doubting Thomas, aren't you? The boy who doesn't believe in magic."

Why wouldn't his body move? Nothing. Frozen.

And now that stupid song would be stuck—

She shook out her hair and ran her hands through it. It shimmered to bright blonde. And her skin paled. She shrugged as her boobs grew and strained against her blouse.

Her face changed. It wasn't Tango at all anymore. Her eyes swirled to blue.

She stepped so close he smelled lavender.

He clamped his eyes shut. It wasn't real. Couldn't be.

"Do you believe now, Thomas?" she whispered in his ear. "They always do, you know, right there at the end."

Trudy said Mrs. M had exploded. And no one had found a body.

Oh, God. His entire body trembled, but he couldn't move a muscle. Was it real?

"They used to say there are no atheists in foxholes." Her voice purred, the air tickling the hairs on his cheek. "I say there are no skeptics when my fist closes around a beating heart."

Warmth poured down Retro's leg. He squeezed his eyes tighter. *Querido Dios, no quería morir.*

Glass shattered. Retro's entire body twitched.

"Tommy?" His mother's voice.

Retro opened his eyes.

Mama stood in the open patio door, a shattered glass and a puddle of purple smoothie at her feet.

No Tango. No terrifying blonde woman.

The vise holding his body released him, and he fell to his hands and knees, gasping. Mama's hands on his back felt real and solid. The pee down his leg grew cold.

Mama talked fast and worried, but he couldn't hear her. Everything his friends had said was true. All that horrifying crap was real.

And Retro had told that witch exactly where to find them.

Bitter Sweets was already hopping at ten o'clock at night. For that crowd, in Austin, ten o'clock was early. I sat with my friends in a booth that would have thrilled the Addams family. We all fit: Corey, Kenny, Dad, Mike, Trudy, Cosita, Woody, Ephraim, Lizard, Stereo and Spook. We'd met there in three or four cars and planned to caravan to Spook's place. He wouldn't give directions or an address. Jimmy Russo had wanted to meet us, but Spook forbade it. Since Jimmy had no reason to be on Twist's radar and no real connection to him, Spook wouldn't risk putting yet another potential victim on Twist's "to do" list.

The weird thing? All the booths seemed to fit exactly the number of people in them, like they'd been made special.

Okay, not the only weird thing. Where to even start?

"Here we go," Spook said, pointing at the dance floor.

Knee high platforms ringed a square, open space where dancers jumped up and down in costumes and makeup even more realistic than in the Facebook photos I'd seen. With everything Dad and my friends had seen in the last few days, was it all makeup?

Two staircases led to a joint balcony at one end of the dance floor before leading up to a catwalk that ringed the entire space. Other rooms opened off the catwalk, but we hadn't been up there yet. A spotlight picked out a tall Asian girl descending to the balcony. A couple of bald, red-skinned women noticed the spotlight and made room for the girl, who had to be Jem, the singer who wanted us to perform with her.

The music changed, sliding into something bouncy and strong.

"The new single," Kenny said. "Has to be the one she wants us for."

As she started singing, several of the dancers ran to the edges of the floor and touched these white glowing orb things. Kinda creepy, but then they all ran into position and started dancing perfectly in sync. Oh. Flash mob.

"What's the deal with the creepy ritual?" Trudy asked. She was holding up remarkably well considering what she'd seen. Mike said she was in shock. I hated to think what would happen when reality set in.

But Stereo squealed. Seriously, squealed. "Dance balls!" She pushed past Spook and ran to the floor, brushing an orb with her fingers as she passed. She faced us and jumped right into the choreo mid-step. What the hell?

"She said she'd never been here," Trudy said. "Is the choreo online somewhere?"

A hardcore bridge prevented Spook from answering. The dancers fell into the tightest hip hop sequence I'd ever seen, locked together as if programmed.

And Jem? Her voice ran through some vocal gymnastics that made autotune weep in embarrassment. She moved like a snake and only barely brought her movements down from the flash mob. Wow breath control.

Wow large mouth, too. I mean, when she opened wide to belt it out, every guy in that booth had to adjust himself. Well, except for Effie and Lizard. Or Dad and Mike.

Anyway, Spook leaned over the table and turned his face away from the rest of the bar. "It's a magic spell," he said. "They have some bullshit story for the tourists, but it's magic."

Seriously? Didn't look like magic. No glowy, sparkly lights or anything. Just tight as hell dancing.

Kenny nudged me. His eyes opened wide, and he nodded at the floor with a hopeful expression. Hard to say what stoked him more, the chance to dance with a K-pop special artist or the idea that he might have a chance to prove to me once and for all that magic existed.

Corey poked me in the back. Didn't need to see his face to know his thoughts. If I didn't jump at the chance to make it up to Kenny, I was the biggest douchebag on the planet.

"Next stop the flash mob express," I called out, and we all piled out of the booth, except for Dad, Mike and Spook.

Even Trudy seemed up for it. "I want to see how this shit works."

"Don't fight it, Ethan," Spook said. "Let it move you."

Really? Did he think my skepticism could completely ruin it?

Corey pushed me past the little junior dick, and I followed Kenny onto the floor, wiping my hand on the glowy dance ball thingy as I passed it.

Nothing. I felt nothing.

The music hovered between songs and everyone just kind of did their own thing.

Shit. See? That's why—

Jem hit the highest note I'd ever heard.

The drums rolled into a techno explosion.

Everyone clapped three times then threw their arms out to the sides, hands in fists, heads down.

Me, too.

Jump, jump, slide. March, march, slide back.

Twist, twist, twist.

It wasn't the best choreo in the world, but. . . well, fuck, I wasn't doing a thing. My body just moved, perfectly in time with everyone else. We ran, ran, slid, twisted one leg, tap, tap, tap the heel.

The music sped up.

So did I, though I tried to fight it, to stop from rolling my shoulders. The music pounded faster, and my shoulder wrenched. Ow, that hurt!

"Ride the ride!" Kenny shouted beside me, performing the best locking and popping I'd ever seen on him. "Don't fight it."

What the hell? Panic welled up inside me. It was like one of those nightmares I'd had. My body was somebody's bitch, and I had no control. I fought to stop my arms from waving.

My bicep wrenched. Ow!

Spook appeared directly in front of me.

His eyes flashed yellow. Bright as day.

His hands touched my face, and the roller coaster crashed to a halt. He caught me before I stumbled from the momentum, yanked me from the dance floor and forced me to face the dancers.

"You want proof?" he shouted in my ear. "Here you go."

His hand caught the back of my neck.

The floor lit up with Disney cartoon fairy dust, sparkling gold and silver. It swirled around the flash mob dancers, guiding their limbs and twirling them through space.

Plus. . .

"What the free-flying fuck?"

Three men on one side sported enormous, flapping bat wings.

A golden halo spun over the head of a red-headed woman in a white suit and fedora. Pure white wings opened behind her, like a dove's but freaking enormous and dripping with gold dust. She caught my eye and smiled.

The most amazing sense of peace and joy filled me for three seconds.

"Magic is real, Ethan Fox," Spook said. "And not all of it is horrible."

He forced me to meet Kenny's gaze. A scattering of black tinged the fairy dust swirling around him. The smile bled from his face as he watched me. Who knows what he saw in my face, but it hurt him. It hurt him a lot.

Deep breath.

If magic was real, it had killed good people.

It'd stolen Tango from us. . . from me. Had devastated her family.

But Corey was out there, dancing ten times better than he could dance, the joy on his face something I'd never made happen. Trudy had her eyes closed as swirls of mist pushed her limbs through the moves and for that one moment she seemed truly at peace.

With all the horrible shit we'd suffered, all of them smiled. Even Stereo. Even Effy.

Only Kenny had seen me pull out of the choreo, had seen me leave the floor. He ripped his eyes away from me and threw himself into a ticking bridge, and I saw him try to memorize the moves.

Spook's hand moved away from my head, and all the special effects vanished.

I spun to him. Why'd he take it away? I wanted to see more.

He raised an eyebrow.

Oh.

He gestured at the dance ball with one hand.

Deep breath.

I touched the oil and jumped into place between Corey and Kenny.

I relaxed and let the magic move me, and the very act of admitting magic moved me required a Herculean effort. I battled my impulse to fight the movements.

Like a puppet, I spun and jumped and clapped.

The choreo was pretty pedestrian, but whoever had made it had needed to compromise for dancers who might not be flexible or athletic enough—

"Stop analyzing it!" Kenny shouted. "Lock in, brother. Just lock in."

He was right. And for him, more than for anyone there, I had to let it be real. He'd brought me back to life. He'd taken a bullet for me. I owed him this much.

Let the music move me. I'd learned that lesson from Trudy.

Fine, why not let the magic do it?

And then, all of a sudden, it was easy, like following, letting a leader move my body, letting them direct my movements. I couldn't see it, but the glowing fairy dust had to be there, leading the dance.

And that's when it turned fun. I mean, crap, wasn't that every dancer's dream? All the moves, all the perfect sync, but none of the work. Heaven!

We ticked, we popped, we spun. And we laughed, God help us all, we laughed and smiled.

Dad and Mike stood off the floor, arms around each other in love and happy.

Okay, fine. Magic was real. And maybe it wasn't all bad—

Then someone screamed.

The doors of the club blew open, flooding the space with light from outside. The dance balls released us, and everyone on the floor stumbled from the momentum.

I fell to my knees, blocking the bright light with an arm.

But the doors hadn't blown open. They were simply gone, replaced by a sharp vertical tear, like a rip in the air itself, exactly like Dad had described in the studio. Bright light poured into the club through the window to somewhere else. I saw dry grass and, in the distance, a wooden fence.

People and other things ran from it, screaming and shouting, racing for the fire exits.

Spook pushed through the crowd directly toward the light, purple fire bleeding from his eyes.

I jumped to my feet and followed him. No idea how I could help, but maybe the charm the nun made would protect me.

A dark silhouette appeared in the light as I reached Spook's side. He glanced at me then grabbed my shirt in a fist. "Smart boys run away from the screams, numb nut." He moved to stand between me and whatever emerged through the magic window.

I figured if I kept saying the words "magic window," they'd connect.

The tear closed with a sound like a zipper, throwing the club into dimness as good as complete darkness for the ten seconds it took my eyes to adjust. Who or what had come through?

"Katy!" Trudy's scream drowned out the sounds of the fleeing club patrons as she flew past me, but Spook seized her and swung her around.

"It's Katy, *pendejo*," Trudy shouted. "Let me go."

Spook threw her at me, and I caught her.

"How do you know it's her?" Spook asked Trudy.

"You think I don't know my own best friend?" Unbelievably, she didn't pull out of my grasp.

Spook waved a hand. "*Tacimat espertin acia.*"

Blue light shone around the figure in the doorway. She fell to her knees, then all the way to the floor. It sure as hell looked like Tango. The glow solidified into a translucent bubble around her.

"She just staggered through a dimensional portal of some kind with glowing, shiny special effects. . ." Spook faced us with his arms held out, stabbing us all with blue, glowy eyes. "And it never occurs to you that somewhere there might be someone with the ability to assume her appearance or mind-control her at the very least, you know, like the flash mob y'all just. . . mobbed."

Spook turned his back to us and pulled something out of his pocket. He muttered more mumbo jumbo and walked through the blue bubble. It stretched with him then snapped back into shape with a pop.

"Oh my God, she's bleeding." Trudy fell to her knees, dragging me down. "Please let me help her."

Woody pushed forward.

"Stay the hell back," Spook shouted. He knelt beside Katy, his body blocking whatever he did. "For all we know there's a bomb inside her about to go off."

"*Dios mio*, just how paranoid are you?" But Woody held back.

"It's how a friend of Mary's killed my brother," Spook said. "With a bomb inside his head."

"*Mierda, ese.*" Woody dropped back to my side. "Sorry."

I helped Trudy to her feet and looked around. The whole gang huddled behind me. Christ, every last one of us had raced into the mayhem instead of running away. Every last one of us. Kinda made me proud.

Dad pushed to my side and grabbed me with one arm, kissing the top of my head.

"It's her," Spook called out, scooping her into his arms more easily than I'd have guessed for a small guy. "Everyone get inside the barrier."

The light faded to green and we dashed forward.

"Don't touch her," he warned as Trudy closed in. He glanced around.

"We're all here," I offered.

He nodded then examined the club beyond the bubble. "I am going to owe Billy a small fortune for this." His eyes flashed. "I recommend everyone close their eyes."

"Why the hell—fuck!" A bright, white light flashed, blinding me.

Several people shouted or shrieked. I will never confess which I did, but I blinked several times and shivered. The temperature had dropped. The wind made it worse. Wind? What the hell?

A parking lot. All of a sudden, we stood outside the shabbiest, most beat to shit nursing home I'd ever seen. Several spotlights lit the place as bright as day. Faded plywood covered the windows. Faded graffiti covered the walls. Weeds filled the space between the lot and the building.

Spook started forward.

"We teleported," Kenny said. "Actually teleported."

We must have. One second, we'd been inside a dance club, an eyeblink later we were who knew how many miles away. It was like so many of my dreams, but real. What else in my nightmares could be real?

"That's his secret hideout?" Woody asked, his voice incredulous.

"What a piece of shit," Stereo added.

I started after Spook, and the others followed.

"Because the God blessed Mystery Mansion wouldn't call attention," Spook muttered. "Stupid tourist."

"Stop calling me that," she snapped.

"Stop acting like a tourist." He paused at the double glass door entrance. "*Clitahabemus sea.*" Tiny lights flickered, and a lock clicked. "Door please."

I pulled the door open and stood aside as everyone piled through.

What the what? Had we stepped through another magic portal?

We piled up together while we took it all in. The lobby was pristine. Dark tile floor, sage green walls and everything trimmed in brushed steel. Bossa nova music. Ikea-style furniture.

A guy behind a reception counter jumped to his feet. "Little spooky brother dude," he said with so much surfer in his voice I'm surprised he didn't have a board under one arm. "You're early—oh wow, dude." He hurried around the counter to meet Spook at a set of double swinging doors. He wore cargo shorts and one of those t-shirts printed with a tuxedo. His long, dirty blond hair had been pulled back in a ponytail.

"She came through a dimensional portal this way," Spook said, handing Tango over. "Temporal displacement up the yin-yang. Get her to the med lab and start an exam."

Without a word, the surfer dude backed through the double doors and vanished.

Arms outstretched, Spook pointedly blocked the doorway.

"No way in hell you're keeping me—" Trudy proclaimed.

His eyes glowed blood red and dripped fire.

"Interesting choice of words, Trudy." He gave us all the once over, probably to make sure we all saw his eyes. "So now that we're well and truly on the same page here, you all know that you are so far out of your depth a sub couldn't reach you. I will try to save her life while you guys stay in this room and do not go snooping around because there are spells in place that will kill you before bothering to notify me. You may have noticed that even I had to come through the front door and had to unlock it."

Bare footsteps slapped toward us from a side hall. Jesus, now what? Well, not Jesus.

Gunner slid to a halt, hair wet and holding a towel closed around his waist. "What's with the alarms, Nicci?" He stopped and looked from face to face. "Oh. Awkward. Hey, Corey."

"S'up Gunner."

Gunner scoffed and shrugged. "Fucking ghost trying to waste me."

"Tcha." Corey nodded. "Me, too."

Gunner nodded. "Sucks."

"As touching as this is," Spook said, "I am not going to deal with it right now. Gunner will go anywhere he's allowed except this lobby. The rest of you will stay put here." He backed through the swinging doors and vanished.

"You want to push metal later?" Gunner asked, his attention still on Corey.

"Yeah, bro. Awesome."

"Kick ass gym," he said as he turned and very casually walked away. "Later."

Yeah. The casual had to be an effort.

Chapter Eleven

We waited. It sucked.

Dad and Mike pulled me off to one side, probably to ask about the dance balls, but before they could say anything, Ephraim's raised voice distracted us. Woody held up a hand, shook his head and walked away from him over to me and Dad and Mike. He crossed his arms with his back to the rest of the room.

"I'm sorry to bug y'all," he said very quietly.

"Not at all." Dad squeezed his shoulder.

"Look," Woody said, "I know this makes me a teeny, tiny kid, but please don't put me in a room with Ephraim. I know you can't let him and Lizard bunk up, but. . . I just can't."

"One. . ." Dad held Woody's gaze evenly. "The middle-aged men I dragged around the country to compete in fights whined about rooming assignments, so don't sweat that."

Woody smiled and bobbed up and down.

"Two. . ." He held out a worn and much-folded piece of paper.

Woody looked it over and did a double take. "Seriously?" He handed the paper to me.

Trudy and Cosita. Ephraim and Lizard. Mike and Lucky. Corey and Kenny. Ethan and Woody. Stereo was penciled in as well as Jem with question marks next to both of their names.

"If those boys want to have sex," Dad said, "I want them doing it in a locked room, not in a corner somewhere or, God forbid, sneaking outside. They're both over the age of consent and keeping them alive is a hell of a lot more important than protecting any remaining virtue."

"You two are the most amazing adults I have ever met in my life." He turned to look at me. "You cool with it?"

"Of course." I held out a fist for him to bump.

Why hadn't Dad roomed me with one of my best friends? Think about it for two seconds. Which one? To be honest, I looked forward to getting to know Woody better in case, you know, we ended up housemates at Corey's farm.

He bumped the fist with a grin then offered a hand for Dad to shake.

Dad shook his hand then folded his other hand over it. "At some point, you need to let Ephraim apologize," Dad said. "Trust me. I completely understand the deal." He glanced at Mike, and I thought about a locker room sucker punch twenty years old. "But there is too much going down for bad blood in the ranks. You and Ephraim need to clear the air."

Woody tried to pull away, but, well, Dad.

"I don't know what he did," Dad said. "But if he dies in an hour, *dies*, do you want this to be how you remember him? With this argument? Think about Lizard and Whiskey. That's the world we live in now."

Woody closed his eyes. He nodded.

"It doesn't need to be now." He released Woody. "But soon."

The double doors banged open and everyone jumped.

Spook was back. "She's fine."

"But all that blood?" Trudy raced to his side. "I need to see her."

"What about what she needs?" He crossed his arms and stood in the middle of the doorway. "You have no idea what she's just been through. I do. She doesn't need a bunch of well-meaning but stupid friends throwing their hysteria at her. She. is. fine. Calm down. Sit. All of you."

No one moved.

After a moment, he pointed at the chairs and raised an eyebrow.

Trudy made a noise, of course, but we all sat. Once we had, Spook hopped up onto the reception counter.

"You just saw her fall out of a dimensional portal," he said, "so I don't want to hear one of you doubting what I am about to say." He looked carefully from face to face. "Mary had her in a dimension where time moves differently. Faster."

Just wow.

"How much faster?" I asked.

"She gave birth to a son. That's why the blood, but she's fine physically." He banged his heels on the counter like a kid. "She's been gone almost nine months." He sat up straighter. "I assume you all knew she was pregnant?"

General noise ensued.

His eyes picked me out. I nodded. So did he.

"What did they do to her?" Trudy asked.

"From what I can tell, they treated her well." He shrugged. "Mary put Twist's soul into the fetus and Tango carried him to term. Of course, Mary was good to her. She wanted the baby healthy."

I didn't even know how to process any of that.

Retro rang the doorbell and waited. He fidgeted and craved chocolate but that was sort of the norm now, anyway, so the fact that the girl who'd likely open the door might laugh in his face was only barely relevant. He had to get word to the crew, and he couldn't find that dance club anywhere. He'd driven all over Austin and asked about it, but no one knew anything.

But the band might.

Jimmy Russo wasn't home, and Retro didn't really know anyone else. Jimmy had stayed in the guys' cottage and had been a standup friend. He'd even hooked Retro up with a girl who'd been totally into some over-the-clothes petting. It was as much action as he'd seen in his young life, which made him a total dork, but maybe, just maybe, the girl might be able to help him find his friends.

The door opened. It was her. God, she was beautiful.

"Oh, wow, Retro." She clutched the bathrobe with one hand at her neck. "This is kind of a surprise." And from her expression, not a pleasant one. Well, that was one answer anyway.

"I'm not stalking you or anything," he said quickly. "I know my friends are dancing at this place called Bitter Sweets and they went to check it out and I can't find it and they're in a buttload of danger." He took a breath. "I think Lizard's with them, so I hoped you'd know the place?"

She smiled and Retro's pulse raced.

"Aren't you the diligent little friend?" she asked.

Little? That's not what she'd said when her hand was—

"Why do you think they're in trouble?" she asked.

He took a deep breath. Was there any way she'd believe his story?

"I really hope you have an open mind, Ginger."

Trudy hurried into the med lab then stopped.

Katy sat on an exam table in jeans and a t-shirt. Her hair had been cut short. Her cheeks showed that she'd gained some weight. Her skin was pale. But she was alive.

"Hey," Trudy said, trying to figure out what came next.

Katy'd had a son. An actual child.

"Hey." Katy sat with her hands in her lap. "I hear I've only been gone a day."

People always said new mothers had a glow, and Katy glowed. Wow.

"I hear you took the scenic route." She moved to Katy's side and touched her hair. "I like it."

Katy's hand rose. She smiled. "I shaved it one day." She lost the smile. "Kind of a bad day a few months ago."

What the hell could Trudy say?

Katy took her hand.

Trudy held it with both of hers.

"I had a baby, Trudy," she said quietly. She snuffed and sucked in air. She gulped. Then Trudy watched her force the emotion away. "I felt him move and I felt him kick and I took care of him for nine months. . ." She shook her head and squeezed Trudy's hand. She swallowed hard. "The whole time I thought for sure she would kill me after he was born. . ."

Tears sprang out of her eyes. "But I ate for him. I exercised for him. I did everything she told me I needed to do to keep him healthy."

Trudy pulled Katy into her arms. What could she say?

"And I loved him, Trudy. I loved my little growing baby." Her shoulders shook. "I named him Adam."

That's when they both lost it. Trudy pulled her off the exam table and they leaned against it on the floor and held each other and cried for the loss of a baby named Adam, and Trudy wept for Katy's mother and brothers, who'd died nine months ago as far as Katy was concerned.

"What the hell did you do?" Trudy asked eventually. "Where were you?"

"We lived on a farm in the middle of nowhere." Katy snuffed. "Mostly, I did chores. I milked cows and brought in eggs from chickens." She snorted. "Mary was born three hundred years ago. I think she's still more comfortable away from the real world. Computers piss her off." She sighed. "I love my baby, Trudy. I would do anything I could to have him with me. Give up the dancing. Run the studio. Anything to make a life for us."

Trudy decided it wasn't the time to tell her the studio had burned.

"He's the only thing left of Whiskey in the world," she whispered.

"Wait. Did you love the rock star?"

Katy shook her head. "No. He was. . ." Her face pinched. "He was a mistake, but he should get to live on in his son. His eyes." She met Trudy's gaze. "Adam's eyes looked just like Whiskey's." She wiped her face. "I messed up bad, Trudy. I messed up so badly."

"We'll get him back," Trudy promised. "We'll find that bitch, and we'll—"

"We can't," Katy insisted. "It's not Adam in there anymore. It's Twist, and when he grows up, he'll be the exact same person Twist was. Adam is dead." Tears welled up in her eyes again. "My boy is dead."

"Not quite dead," some guy said. Spook. He stood near the door, holding a crystal that looked like amber.

"What's that?" Katy asked.

"When I accidently yanked your son's soul from his body, I put it in this shard." Spook held the crystal so the girls could see it, but Katy grabbed it from him.

"He's safe," Spook said. "If—and it's a big if—if we can find Twist and put Adam's soul back into his body, he just might be able to fight Twist out of there."

Katy closed her hand around the crystal and squeezed Trudy. "Is that possible?" She forced herself to her feet.

"It's happened before," Spook said with a shrug. "Maybe it'll work. Maybe it won't." He cleared his throat. "But I will need that back if I'm going to put it into his body."

Katy stared at the shard of amber in her hand. She nodded, then kissed her son's soul and handed it back to Spook.

Woody watched Effy and Lizard for a long time. The new kid looked to be good for the little *pendejo*. Solid. But why didn't having a boyfriend make all the bullshit go away?

Mr. Fox had been right, though. As pissed off as Woody was, the idea that Effy might die with Woody still pissed at him? That damn near ate his gut away.

He sucked in a deep breath and walked over.

Lizard nudged Effy in the ribs and nodded his chin.

"Woody—" Effy said.

"Shut up and listen." If he let Effy take control it'd end up in a stupid argument. "I have shit to say, and I want you to keep shut."

"Sam—"

But Lizard grabbed his arm and shook his head.

Effy shut up. Huh.

"You're the best damn friend I've ever had," Woody said. "I'd say I love you like a brother, but you know what *pendejos* my brothers are. So I love you more than a brother. But this crush you have, or whatever it is. . ."

Effy blushed and opened his mouth to talk, but Lizard yanked on his arm and shook his head. Effy shut his mouth.

"See, that's why Lizard is good for you, Effy. He's smarter than you."

Please God let him be right about Lizard. "He's smarter than me. And he's the one you should obsess about. He's the one you should get twitchy over when you haven't seen him for a few days. Not me."

He crouched down to look Effy in the eye. "Don't ever think I don't love you, but I want to find some girl to freak out when I don't call her, when I vanish for a couple of days." Was any of it making sense? "I know how fucked up everything is right now, but that phone call, that shit on Ethan's phone? That was messed up, too. I can't handle that. I'm not that guy."

Woody met Lizard's eyes. "I hope you're that guy, *ese*. I really do, because you seem totally stand up. But Effy needs a lot, and if you ever hurt him, I will kill you."

What the hell was he even trying to say? A lump filled his throat, and he couldn't talk.

Effy opened his mouth, but Lizard covered it with a hand.

"You are the best straight guy ever made," Lizard said. "And Effy has been so fortunate to have you for a friend, he will never know." He blinked tears away. "You're a lot like my brother. And I'll make sure Effy knows how lucky he is. But it may take a day or two for me to get it through his thick skull. Until then. . ."

Woody nodded. Until then he'd keep breathing.

Spook's hideout was as amazing inside as it had been shitty on the outside. Someone in his little Scooby gang had big bucks, like Batman big. He and Nicci, the surfer dude who seemed to operate like the team's Alfred without the British accent, led the way. We started at the gym, which was bigger than Dumass High's gymnasium.

Blade weapons and things to hack lined one wall. Mirrors covered a second. All kinds of ropes and stuff hung from the ceiling. Oh, and they had weights off to one side. Sure enough, Gunner lay on a bench pushing metal.

"Y'all can practice here," Spook said. "I'll find out from Jem when she wants to do the show."

"Wait," I said. "What about the dance balls? Can't we just program a spell or something to dance us? I mean, they're used to seeing some tight dancing. How can we compete with that?"

"You're thinking." Spook smiled. "I like that. Problem is no one's figured out how to spell more than one dance step in the same space at once. Unless you all do the exact same thing, like the flash mob, I'm not sure how to make it work." He smiled again. "But I'm impressed you went from doubting to working the system in under an hour."

Someone tapped my kidneys. Kenny. "He's always been a quick study."

The locker rooms off the gym were unbelievable. Hot tubs, steam rooms, kitchenettes with fully stocked fridges. TV screens.

"I could live right here," Woody announced. "Fuck my parents, I'm never leaving this locker room if that TV has a game system. Fighting ghosts and goblins makes you this kind of money, count me in."

"I was totally stoked when the Scooby gang moved in," Nicci enthused. "This place is so-o-o much better than it was before."

Silence descended.

"He sort of came with the property," Spook said quickly, silencing Nicci with a look. "He was the custodian before us."

"He swept the floors?" Woody asked.

"Custodian means the person in charge of the property," Corey said, "not the janitor." He blushed when everyone sort of stared at him. "I'm learning a lot of lawyer speak from Saundra."

Saundra! Whom I still needed to contact. Meh.

"Um. . ." Kenny pointed at a corner. A camera. "We kind of have surveillance issues."

"I know," Spook said. "All cameras in locker rooms, bathrooms and sleeping quarters have been turned off while you're here."

"You have cameras in the shitters?" Corey's face told us all what he thought of that.

"Mary is not even close to the worst thing my team faces on a weekly basis," Spook said. "I am ninety-five percent certain that she can't get in here. If she could, she wouldn't have dropped Katy at Bitter Sweets. But

I'd rather have Nicci here watch me take a dump than run the five percent risk that I'm wrong about our defenses. Turning the cameras off is a risk and a favor."

No one criticized his logic.

No one asked him to turn the cameras back on, either.

As pointed out, we had issues.

"What's the most badass thing you've fought?" Stereo asked. "The absolute worst?"

"Hmm. . ." Spook and Nicci shared a look.

"Loki," Nicci suggested.

Spook nodded. "Definitely Loki."

"As in the Norse god?" I asked.

Spook nodded. "It all worked out though. My buddy Muscle saved her daughter, so we called a truce."

"Her?" Kenny asked. "Loki's a guy, I thought."

"Shape shifter," Spook pointed out. "She was a woman when we fought, although she is the daughter's father." He patted Nicci's shoulder. "That was the fight that convinced us we needed a clubhouse."

"Dude." Nicci threw him a hang loose.

"Wait." Trudy grabbed Spook's arm. "You've fought worse than this Mary bitch. So you can protect us, right?"

Spook looked across all the expectant faces. He sighed.

"I hope so," he said. "I learned a long time ago not to make promises."

A long time ago? How old was he?

"Anyway. . ." Spook led us through the locker room to the pool.

"This place is like a tardis, hai!" Kenny ran up to the edge of the Olympic size pool with diving well at one end. His voice echoed in the space. "It's bigger on the inside."

"I assure you it's not bigger on the inside," Spook said. "The pool was here when we moved in. The gym was originally two stories of apartments that we hollowed out."

"Whoa." That was Dad. "You could do that without ruining the structural integrity? I've built a couple of gyms, it's hard to secure a space that large without any support posts."

Spook smiled. He held up a hand and a sizable ball of fire whooshed into existence.

Wow. I took a step closer to check it out, only then noticing that everyone else had taken several steps away. Even Stereo.

"Magic helps." Spook closed his hand into a fist and the fireball vanished.

Okay, magic was dangerous and shit, but fireball hands? Stellar, right?

Our rooms lined one hallway that was the first area since the lobby that looked like a nursing home. Spook gestured at a door. "Who's first?"

"Cosita and Trudy," Dad said.

"One at a time, palm to the locking pad." Spook pointed at the black square of glass beside the door.

Kenny and Stereo peered close. "Palm reader?" they asked in unison.

Kenny blushed and backed away.

"It won't tell your fortune," Spook said, "if that's what you mean, but yes, it's a palm reader locking system." He pulled out his phone, tapped the screen a few times. "Ladies?"

They each pressed a palm to the reader.

"Welcome Trudy," a breathy female voice said. "Welcome Cosita."

He tapped the phone. "No one else can access the room now except for me, and that's because if you both get injured in there—"

"I am not asking questions, *mijo*," Trudy said. "You make fire in your hands; I like the idea of having you at my back."

"*Sí*," Cosita added. She glanced into the room. "So. . . the cameras *are* off?"

"You have my word." He held up a hand with three fingers pointing skyward. You know, he probably *had* been a boy scout. I utterly saw him tying knots for merit badges.

The rest of us programmed our locks and headed in to unpack.

Kenny opened the door to the room he would share with Corey, who grabbed me in quick hug. "We're right next door," Corey whispered. "And you can crash with us any time you want."

I was so glad to hear him say that and not even sure why. But I'm glad my new roomie hadn't heard it. He deserved better.

Our room was cozy. Single beds on opposite walls. Dressers, a sink and vanity. A desk with all the electronic adapters a man could desire.

Small closet with a few hangers. TV with a remote and two video game controllers.

Woody turned to me with a sardonic grin. "Fuck you and your offer. I'm never leaving this place." Then he grabbed me around the neck and punched my shoulder before snatching a controller and turning on the TV.

Ephraim dropped his suitcase on the floor and commenced to pretty much freak out. The room—you know, the room he got to share with his *boyfriend* because that wasn't the kind of thing that should immediately cause the end of the known universe—was so damn nice. Muted colors, soft but understated carpeting.

Oh yeah, and a king-sized bed. It was like someone knew two gay boys would stay there.

Yeah, king-sized bed. It rather dominated the room.

Lizard whooped and leapt onto it, bouncing and landing on his back with his hands under his head and his ankles crossed because he was really, truly that suave. At sixteen.

Ephraim would sell his soul for the boy. Seriously.

But they'd never. . .

"You're freaking out," Lizard said.

"No, I am not freaking out."

"You are absolutely freaking out."

"I am completely and utterly freaking out." Ephraim tried to move closer to his boyfriend, but his feet wouldn't work.

"We do not need to have sex here, you know," Lizard said, "the fact that the gay Ward and June Cleaver have given us their blessing does not mean we need to do the big wonka wonka."

Ephraim managed a breath. "You won't dump me if I don't put out tonight?"

Lizard jumped up and took Ephraim in his arms. "You really assume I'm such a sure thing?" He kissed Ephraim's cheek. "My brother was the slut, not me."

Well, that kind of changed the mood. Offhand comments about dead siblings seemed inappropriate to conversations about sex. Or the lack thereof.

"Effy." Lizard's eyes were always so dark and mysterious.

Ephraim kissed him. "I wish I could be as free as you."

Lizard held him close, more like a best friend than a lover, really. "You are perfect just as you are, Effy. Don't try to be like me. Just be yourself."

Uptight, sarcastic and brutal? That didn't seem appropriate for the room they would share while a vengeful ghost tried to kill them.

"So this is me then." Ephraim moved out of Lizard's arms and stood over the bed. "The whole idea of sex scares me. I came out to the world less than a month ago and here I am with a wonderful boyfriend and this giant bed that screams, 'Do someone on me.'"

Lizard chuckled. "It really does, doesn't it?" He took Ephraim's hand. "Effy. We do what we choose to do. I don't know anything more than you. I'm just as scared."

"Yeah?" What a bizarre thought.

"What if I suck at it? What if I don't know what I'm doing, since, well, I don't?" Lizard sat on the huge bed. "It's just a place to sleep." He tugged Ephraim to sit with him.

The lights dimmed.

Oh, well, that was just too well timed. Really?

They both laughed and fell back onto the mattress. Lizard reached across Ephraim and hit the switch on the bedside lamp, plunging the room into darkness.

They kicked off their shoes and spooned. Ephraim pulled Lizard's arms tightly around his chest. "We can just fall asleep like this? Just holding each other?"

Lizard kissed Ephraim's neck. "I may have no choice but to jack you off in the morning, but we can certainly fall asleep like this tonight."

Oh. . . well. . . Ephraim could live with that.

Chapter Twelve

I woke up in a forest, the ground covered in pine needles. The moon threw a soft white light in distinct lines across the bare forest floor from shadows cast by the tall, straight pine trees.

Pushing to my feet, I looked down. I wore Dad's old sweats. The sweatshirt with his gym's logo hung on me like a sack.

I spun in place. A grackle cawed above me. Another answered it from a tree farther off. A flock of the birds moved and shook their wings and cawed in the branches above.

Wait. Grackles didn't caw, they made that freaky grackly noise.

"Oops." A small boy stepped out from behind a pine tree. "I forgot how much of a hard-on you get for those birds."

The sounds changed.

"It's been a few years since I saw one." The boy stood with his hands in his pockets. "Hey there, Fox."

Twist? It had to be. The boy had his voice, but black hair and dark skin.

"Good thing I'm not racist." He held his arms out and looked at them, turning the hands over and back. "They set the Easy Bake on high for this kid."

Tango's boy. Adam. I recognized her eyes, Whiskey's nose.

"You sick son of a bitch." Anger welled up inside me.

"You say that like it's a surprise." He crossed his arms.

I had to be dreaming and dreams didn't need to follow the laws of physics, but what should I do? Then I remembered Spook, what he'd done to get our attention.

I held up one hand and poured all my anger into the tight fist.

Fire ignited around it.

Yes. Fireball. I pulled the arm back and focused on the boy.

He couldn't be more than a few years old. Tiny. Skinny.

He had Tango's eyes.

The fire sputtered and drizzled from my hand like water.

Even in a dream I couldn't hurt him.

He smiled, and the expression was all Twist.

"I like this game," he said. "My turn."

He held up a hand, and I crouched, ready to dive behind a tree, but instead of igniting a fireball, he waved his fingers in the air before him. Tiny spots of white light spun and danced in a vortex. When they cleared, Dad knelt there, his arms bound behind his back.

Twist reached one small arm around Dad's head and yanked it back, exposing his throat. The other hand held a knife to Dad's jugular.

It was a dream. Just a dream.

He'd only been able to hurt me by knocking me into the pool or trying to push me down stairs. He couldn't actually hurt my dad, who was sound asleep somewhere else—

"Ethan?" Dad squinted at me and struggled against Twist's hold. "Where are we? What's going on?"

"Nice try," I said. "You made me watch him die before, and it wasn't real."

Twist smiled.

"Wait, is that Twist?" Dad tried to look, but the tiny arm had a grip like a vise. "Are we dreaming?"

Twist had it down. It sounded liked Dad. Moved like him.

He looked right at me. "Get out of here, son. If none of this is real then he can't hurt me. Go!"

But if it wasn't real, why should I run?

"Just go," Dad shouted. "And tell. . . make sure Mike gets the ring. Please. I want him to know I had a ring."

My throat tightened. How could Twist know about the ring?

"Dad?"

The blade flashed in the moonlight.

Dad's eyes opened wide and a river of the darkest red I'd ever seen poured out of his throat.

"*No!*" *I rushed forward and grabbed the tiny wrist but couldn't stop him from a second slice.*

I wrenched the arm and Twist jumped away.

Dad fell into my embrace, blood pouring down his chest and out of his mouth in bubbles. I ripped the shirt from my own body and held it against Dad's neck.

"*No, no, no, no, no.*" *I tried to wrap the shirt around his neck as best I could, but blood soaked thorough the thick material in seconds.*

His eyes held mine and he tried to talk, but all that came out was more bubbles.

"*No, no, no, no.*" *What could I do?*

Wait. Dream physics.

What could I do? I pressed my hands to Dad's neck. "*Don't bleed,*" *I said.*

How the fuck did real magic work? I'd made a fireball with anger.

"*Don't bleed.*" *All my love for him, all the fear of what would happen without him, I poured them all into my hands.*

His breathing slowed down. Good or bad?

"*Don't bleed,*" *I said again then kept repeating it.*

He held my eyes and managed a sort of half-smile. Then his mouth fell slack.

"*No.*" *I squeezed to stop the flow of blood.* "*Don't die.*"

The light went out of his eyes and his head fell against my arm.

"*No, no, no.*" *I held his face.* "*Dad?*" *I shook him gently.* "*Dad!*"

Not him. Anyone but him. Please God take anyone but him.

"*Dad!*"

He died. Right there in my arms. I felt his heart stop.

I woke up screaming.

A light. Hands on me. Woody.

I shoved him away and sprang to my feet. Had it been real?

I raced out of the room and across the hall.

"Dad!" I banged on the door. "Dad!"

Jesus Christ, what would I do if he'd really died?

"Dad!" It was a scream.

The door opened.

Dad. In his chaperoning minors PJs. Alive.

I grabbed him and held him as tight as I could. "You were dead." Relief pounded my chest like a horse kick. "I saw you die. And I didn't know. . . I couldn't get you to stop bleeding."

My entire body shook, and I couldn't stop it either.

"Ethan." His hands took my face and moved me away a foot or so, enough that I could see his eyes. "I'm fine. It was dream. You're awake now. He didn't hurt me."

I forced myself to release his shirt, balling my hands into fists as I tried to stop the shaking. The air burned in my lungs and tears stung my eyes.

He was alive. He was fine.

But what if it'd been real? Twist had tried to kill him once.

He wasn't immortal.

I shook my head. "I can't. I can't do this. I can't lose you."

"*Santa* fuck, Spook," Woody said somewhere behind me. "I thought we were safe in here."

"We are." Spook's voice was quiet.

"Then explain how Twist just mind-raped Ethan." Trudy huffed. "Again."

"Ethan's fine," Spook said, an edge in his voice. "Twist has a direct line because he's been there before."

"He's been in my head, too," Ephraim said. "Does that mean he can control me again?"

"No, he can't do that." Spook's voice brooked no disagreement.

"But he got through all your fancy magic to mess with Ethan." Trudy's voice grew louder. "Look at him. Shit."

Dad pressed close to me. "You need to pull it together. Ohio Star finals when Monika changed the choreo on you. You held it for that."

Re-choreographing? That somehow even related?

"No one got hurt," Spook insisted. "Ethan just got scared."

I looked around. We had quite the audience. They stared at me in couples and triples, every one of them but Katy, all touching someone for reassurance. Their expressions ranged from terror to fear to anger. Underwear, pajamas, sweats. No one seemed to care what anyone saw.

I'd freaked them out.

"If he can get into Ethan's dreams, what's stopping him from getting into my head?" Ephraim demanded. "Is he going to hijack me and start killing people?"

"How the hell did you let this happen?" Trudy moved away from Cosita to get up in Spook's face.

"Because Mary is ten times more powerful than I am, and I don't have my team," Spook stepped closer. "Only God knows what Twist can do now that Mary's helping him. I don't know when my team is getting back, so I'm doing the best I can on my own. If any of you think you can do better without me, you know where the door is. I'll call you a God damn cab."

He left. A rather profound silence filled the hallway.

Everyone turned to me.

Stellar.

Deep breath. Dad was right. No one there had my experience with handling shit.

So. The choreography had just changed, and three couples headed into my line of dance. Time to improvise.

"It's not his fault," I said. "I took off the charm the nun made."

Kenny moved closer. "Why'd you do that?"

"I didn't think." I shrugged. "I always take off jewelry before bed."

"That would've done it? Protected you?" Ephraim asked. "Can we all get one?"

Everyone turned to look at Nicci, curled up in a nearby chair. He startled and sat up straighter. "I'll see what we have." He looked so sad.

Crap. I'd freaked out and messed with *everyone.*

How to get it back?

"Okay, look," I said to the hallway at large. "Sorry about that. Now you know what I went through last month. No more surprises." I moved closer to Nicci. "Are you and Spook basically killing time hoping the rest of the team shows up?"

Nicci looked around and hugged himself. He nodded.

Okay. So Spook felt alone and out of his depth.

Well, I could certainly sympathize with that. I headed down the hall.

Spook stared at the photo of him and Ross with Santa. He and his brother had taken the grandbrats to see Santa and had surprised him by climbing up onto his lap themselves. That had been Ross's last Christmas.

"Whenever I mess up, I come and talk to you, little brother." He rubbed a smudge off the glass. "I am so out of my depth on this one. These kids learn about magic and think somehow I can fix everything for them. But this is Mary. . . and Twist?" He shook his head. "He's as strong as her, Daddy-o. If I don't take him out before he learns control, I don't think the whole gang could stop him."

He'd worked cases on his own before. After Ross retired and before the new team, he'd spent some time on his own. That hadn't gone well. He wasn't really the lone wolf sort.

Someone knocked on the door.

"Who is it?" he asked the room.

"Nicci has our guests with him," the room replied with Ross' voice.

Drat. Did he have any way to save face after his tantrum?

No. Not really.

He returned the photo to the shelf and crossed to the door.

Ethan stood in the hall, Kenny at one shoulder and Corey at the other, which seemed to be their accustomed positions. The rest of the crew fanned out behind them.

"We know what it's like to have to perform without the rest of your team," Ethan said. "It sucks and we get that. We're sorry we jumped to the conclusion that you're Superman, and we know we're all tourists, but is there any chance you can give us some training? We're going to go crazy and twitchy if we aren't at least trying to do something."

Huh. Spook started to suspect why the nun found Ethan so interesting. And the father, standing in the background and letting his kid take point. Spook nudged his surface thoughts.

Yep. Lucky knew he lived with a giant bull's-eye on his back. He couldn't leave the building under any circumstances. The kids needed to do this on their own.

"Okay." Spook leaned in the doorway, which made Ethan smile for some reason. "We start training in the morning. Nicci will handle weapons. Mr. Fox can help with hand to hand."

The big man crossed his arms and nodded. He seemed more comfortable with a job to do.

"I'll start with basic protection spells," Spook said, "and do some tests to see if anyone is natural born."

"Wait. What does that mean?" Stereo asked. "Can anyone use magic, or do you have to be born to it?"

So the tourist was trainable. Good.

"It's like music," he said. "Anyone can learn to play the piano, but Mozart was a natural born musician."

That seemed to make sense. A couple of faces lit up.

"Don't get too excited. The chances of a natural born on the team are slim to none, and in so short a short time you're not going to learn anything very exciting. I'll do what I can, though."

"We just want to be as ready as we can if they attack before your team gets back," Ethan said. And he seemed smart enough to know that they needed a goal, something to take control of their own destinies. Even if it was kind of a sham.

"Can we find out where they are?" Corey asked. "Can we take the fight to them?"

Hell no.

"I talked to Tango about where she was," Spook said. "I don't think I can figure it out," he lied. "In a universe with infinite dimensions, Twist could be anywhere. Ask your geeks what that means later."

The truth was that Mary and Twist had settled on a farm out in the middle of Texas. The temporal ripples there were obvious to someone looking for them. Mary wanted him to know. She wanted him to attack. Which meant he wouldn't do so under any circumstances. She'd laid a trap.

If only his team would hurry the hell up and get home.

"Could we lure them out?" Ethan asked. "Go ahead with the show at Bitter Sweets and advertise it so Twist can't possibly stay away. It was the publicity from the shoot at the campground that lured him out of hiding."

The rest of the team nodded and made general noises of agreement.

They had guts anyway. Okay, he could channel that.

"Tell you what," he said. "Start practicing for the show. I'll contact Jem. And Lizard, can you get in touch with the band? I heard rumors of a memorial show."

Lizard blushed. "There's been talk."

"Who would sing lead?" Ephraim asked.

"Me." Lizard glowed with embarrassment.

"I have an idea," Ethan said. "What about a mashup? Jem can use the publicity from the band, and the band can use the built-in marketing from her crossover."

The crew muttered and tossed ideas around. Excellent. Let them stay busy with the mashup and they'd never realize there wasn't a snowball's chance in Hades Spook would let them go up against those two. . . especially someplace so public.

"Excellent idea," Spook said. "Get some sleep. We'll start working tomorrow."

"Operation 'ding dong the witch is dead' is a go," Kenny said.

The group moved off in a clump, teasing Kenny about being such a geek.

Only Lucky hesitated. He caught Spook's eye and winked.

Yeah. Dads knew how to spot someone working their kids.

Hugs and stuff went around before we all wandered back into our rooms. As if any of us would sleep that night.

"You know you're welcome to bunk with us," Corey reminded me.

I squeezed him back. "Thanks bro, but I'm good."

"Don't forget to put the charm on," Kenny reminded me during his hug.

"First thing I do when I get in there," I promised.

Dad waited until the hall emptied. "You think it works?"

"I don't think Spook would have lied about that," I said. "False sense of security doesn't seem to be his thing."

"True." He nodded with bemusement on his face. "So you can tell he's bullshitting us about some of this?"

"Yep. He'll never let us do this show."

"Which is a good thing to my way of thinking." He crossed his arms.

I shrugged. "I'm tired of waiting around for Twist to attack, expecting someone else to save me. I know I'm totally out of my depth on this, but the longer we wait, the more powerful he gets. After Mrs. Van Zeeland shot him, I sat on my ass, hoping he was dead, fully expecting the cops to take care of him if he showed up. Look how well that worked."

Dad scowled. "You had no way of knowing he'd turn out to be some kind of latter-day Carrie."

"I didn't then," I said, "but I do now. I don't have any more excuses."

He wore his vacillating-between-scared-and-proud face. "You understand why I had to make you pull it together?"

I did. On the competition floor, if Monika had ever worried I was distracted, she couldn't follow. She second-guessed every move I made, and I ended up fighting her every step of the way. So I'd learned, no matter how messed up I might be or how pissed at her, when we stepped onto the floor, I was the guy in charge and nothing could phase me. That way, if I had to suddenly ditch the choreo and wing it, she'd trust me and simply follow.

Who knew all those years of ballroom dance would ready me to face a vengeful ghost and his super powerful witch of a girlfriend?

In our room, Woody sat on his bunk. He watched me beeline to the dresser and slip the charm over my head. He wasn't nearly as Lifetime Channel as Kenny and Corey, so hopefully I'd get a pass on all the sympathy and crackers. My emotions were all packed away nicely for the moment, thank you. I wanted to leave them there.

"So. . ." Woody broke the silence. "When you told me you understood about the night terrors back at the camp, I kinda thought you were blowing smoke up my ass."

"Not so much, no."

"What did he look like?" he asked.

"What?"

Woody held up his hands. "You don't want to talk about it, I get it, but from the shit you said, I take it you saw Twist in your dream. And if you can handle it, I'd like to know what we're looking for in case he comes after the rest of us." He dropped his hands into his lap. "I didn't want to ask in front of everyone, but I'd really like to know. If he goes after you in your dreams, he might try for your sidekicks."

I worried the charm with the fingers of one hand. No, I didn't want to talk about it, but Woody's question was different. He wanted to make plans, not get all weepy.

"He was a little boy," I said. "Katy's little boy. About three or four or something." What did I know from how old little kids looked? "He had Katy's eyes."

Woody nodded. "In the old dreams, did he look like himself all the time?"

"No." I thought about it. "Sometimes he looked like other people."

"So he could have been messing with you," Woody pointed out.

"Oh, I guarantee he was messing with me," I said, "but I think it was a test. To see if I could hurt him in the little boy's body."

"And?"

"I failed," I admitted. "I couldn't do it. I mean, I knew it was Twist and that it was really just a dream, but I had this fireball all ready to go and then, meh, I couldn't do it."

"Fireball?" Woody raised his eyebrows.

"It was a dream," I said. "I knew it was a dream. Back when he was haunting my nightmares, I learned I could do stuff that wasn't possible in the real world, so after seeing Spook make fire in his hands, I figured I'd fireball Twist's ass."

"Humor me." Woody rose and moved closer. "How'd you make fireballs?"

"It was a dream," I pointed out.

"I get that." He paced a bit. "So he attacks me in my nightmares, it'd be nice to have an idea how to charbroil him."

So what had I done? I closed my eyes and raised a fist into the air.

"I made a fist and just. . . brought up all my anger at that son-of-a-bitch." Which was never hard to do these days. I squeezed the fist. "I sent all the anger into my hand, and. . . foom."

Foom!

"*No jodas!*" Woody shouted.

Furniture scraped and something crashed to the floor.

I opened my eyes.

My hand was on fire.

"My hand is on fire!" I waved it fast and the flames died. "Holy-shit-holy-shit-holy-shit."

I held my hand as far away from me as I could.

It hadn't burned me.

Woody pressed flat against the door.

We sort of stared at my hand breathing loudly, but it didn't burst into flames again.

"You saw that, right?" I asked.

"No shit. I didn't almost wet your jockeys because your fist is so impressive." He moved around behind me where he could get a closer look at my hand, but my where body would block him should my hand suddenly burst into flame. "Do it again."

"What?" I couldn't take my eyes off my own hand. "Are you insane?"

"Did it hurt?" he asked.

"No, but. . . Jesus. My hand was on fire."

Woody nudged my shoulder. "Do it again."

I closed my hand in a fist. The anger. I didn't know if I could call it up like before, but I remembered what it had felt like flowing out from my core and into my hand. I found that same spot and closed my eyes. I pushed it into my hand, but gentler.

Foom.

"Wow." Woody grabbed my shoulder.

The fire surrounded my closed fist as if I was the wick of a candle. I opened my fingers, and the fire curled into a ball in the rounded cage.

"*Ese*, that is the coolest thing I have ever seen." He pressed against my back as he reached one hand toward the flames. "Can you feel it at all?"

"Not a bit," I said.

"It's hot." Woody's hand neared the fire. Light flickered on his bare arm. "That's as close as I can get."

"Really?" I asked.

"Please don't start the bed on fire to test out how hot it is," he said. "And you just, like, send your anger into your hand?"

Woody curled his outstretched hand into a fist, and I felt him quiver a little bit in effort. He made a sort of grunty sound as if trying to send his anger into his own hand then he relaxed. His hand opened to warm itself on the fire in mine.

"I must not have the firestarter gene," he said. "You've never done this before?"

I shook my head, mesmerized by the flickering light.

As I relaxed, it fizzled and died.

"Aw, man," Woody said.

Then a wave of exhaustion hit me as if I'd just danced every heat for an entire week-end comp in two minutes. My legs buckled.

"Uh-oh." Woody caught me before I fell and helped me sit on my bunk. He kept an arm around me while I dropped my head into my hands.

"All magic comes with a price," he said.

"Huh?" I forced the stars out of my vision.

"That's what Stereo says," Woody explained. "You can't just miracle fire from thin air. The energy comes from somewhere. From the look of it, this is you paying for the light show."

"That's what Stereo says?" I repeated with innuendo.

"She's hot," Woody said easily. "You listen to what a girl has to say, she's much more likely to put out."

"Kenny's into Stereo," I muttered.

"Oh, *Jesus*," Woody said. "Didn't know. Never mind."

I couldn't sit up. Woody helped me stretch out flat on the bed. He even pulled the blanket over me.

"Stereo hates you," Woody said.

"Tell that to Kenny's dick." I clutched the blanket to my chin. "Did I really make fire in my hand?"

"Sure did." Woody patted my shoulder. "You okay?"

"Fine," I lied. I'd never been so exhausted in my entire life. But fire? I'd made fire. That meant I'd done magic, right? "Look, don't tell anyone."

"Why not?" Woody bounced up and down on the balls of his feet. "This is fantastic!"

"Maybe it is," I said. "Maybe it's not. Please let me talk to Spook about it first before saying anything to anyone and no subtle hints or jokes or anything. Please, *ese*." He deserved the truth. "The truth is that until everything at Bitter Sweets I didn't even believe in magic. This kinda freaks me out. Please let me get my head around it before everyone swarms me and expects me to show them what I can do. This price. . . if a little fire wipes me out like this, what good is magic?"

"You can light birthday cakes." Woody patted my leg. "Just so you know. . . I'll keep it to myself, but the reason it's so freaking cool is. . . well, since this started, all this magic was something other people did. And for the most part, did *to* us. You know? We had to go find Spook to do it for us, like it could never happen to one of us." He squeezed my leg. "But this means it's not just out there. It's in one of us, you know, it's like part of the family now." He turned to sit with his hands between his knees. "I sound like a *pendejo*."

"Dude, I get it." I nudged his hip with an elbow. "But can I just pass out now and get excited about it in the morning?"

"Hai." He patted my leg again and moved off the bed. "*Noches.*"

Chapter Next

Lucky hovered at the edge of the mats. The strange surfer maître d' sparred with Gunner. They used plain bamboo staves and even with practice equipment, Nicci's excellence shone.

Gunner fought like a street thug. Well, like a street thug from a tiny town in south Texas, a punk with no training who'd managed to create a reign of terror on kids in the neighboring towns but who'd get wiped out in a second from a real street kid out of Houston.

If Gunner hadn't had his first-string buddies, Lucky thought with a tinge of pride, Ethan would've handed him his ass on a platter.

Nicci seemed to feed Gunner knowledge, leading him into moves, forcing him to repeat blocks so his muscles would learn them. It was fun to watch a good teacher at work. It'd been a while.

And Lucky had to admit he liked being back in Austin. The city had an energy, a rhythm. Despite all the horror that had forced him to drag his son away, Lucky had missed the place.

Nicci swept Gunner's legs, and the punk landed hard on his back with a grunt. Sweet. Lucky approved. The teacher held the staff close to his chest and bowed, then turned to Lucky.

"Mr. Fox?" Nicci's surprise at seeing him there seemed quite fake. He tossed the bamboo to Gunner, who wasn't paying attention and took it in the head. "Put those away, moody sociopath dude. I'll be back in a minute to kick your ass again."

He jogged over to Lucky and stopped quite close, leaning in with an obvious conspiratorial intent. "Hey there, gay boxing dude. I'm. . . Nicodemus." He held out a hand. "But you can call me Nicci."

Was he shaking hands with Bill or Ted? "Hey Nicci. You look good out there."

He looked pretty good up close, too. Mid-twenties? And his shining torso wasn't big but shredded as shit. He had the kind of physique that came more from hours and years of fight training rather than from pushing metal, as Gunner had called it.

"I hear good things about your teaching of things like boxing and grappling and such like." Nicci nodded back at Gunner, who, surprisingly, had put the equipment away and then faded over to a heavy bag to kill time.

Oh. . . damn. Lucky couldn't stop the cringe. The kid was pathetic when he tried to look like a boxer. Lucky really wanted to arrange a one-on-one for him and Ethan.

"Thing is, the moody sociopath dude is salvageable," Nicci said, drawing Lucky's complete attention. "He can go either way. He'll never be a pillar of salt, but with the right person smacking him upside the head the good way he just might avoid being a rapist and a murderer." Nicci shrugged. "Preventing another supervillain sounds like a check in the good things column."

Lucky waited for more. Why say all this to him?

Nicci shrugged, lifted his hands and shook his head in a way that told Lucky his reasoning should be obvious.

Oh, hell no. Not just no, he-e-e-e-el-l no!

Nicci winked and jogged back to Gunner. "Dude, guess what! Mr. Fox is going to teach us how to box. I am totally kick ass with any weapon you can ever find but I know balls and all about boxing. This dude, like, makes champions."

Gunner grimaced.

Lucky had seen the look on hundreds of faces. Teenage punks who'd scored wins against younger and weaker kids. Or the teenage punks who assumed a gay man couldn't teach them anything about fighting. In this case, Gunner wore the added petulance built of the fact that he'd beaten the snot out of Lucky's kid, so how could the dad know so much?

Nicci looked back at Lucky and shrugged with half a smile.

Okay fine. But he was damn well going to enjoy teaching this kid a lesson.

He grabbed a pair of gloves and threw them at Gunner, who missed one and scrabbled after it in apparent surprise. Sliding into a second pair of gloves, Lucky walked out into the middle of the floor onto a square mat. It wasn't a ring but it was close enough. Sure, they should use tapes but screw it, Lucky wouldn't get hurt, and he didn't much care if Gunner sprained a wrist.

"Let's go, kid," he said. "Show me how I have nothing to teach you, and we both get to walk away telling Nicci that we gave it a shot."

Nicci helped Gunner into the gloves then the kid sort of danced toward Lucky. So many jokes, so little time.

"So what pussy rules do boxers have?" Gunner asked.

"Don't step out of the ring."

"What happens if I do?" The vast certainty on Gunner's face amused Lucky.

"You step out of the ring," Lucky said, "it means you're a pussy. You want rules, play board games. Let's fight."

Gunner grinned and came at Lucky full throttle.

Lucky stayed on the defensive at first, leading the kid on, checking out his moves, his balance, his strength. He had good instincts but everything else was for shit.

When Lucky had enough info for a week's worth of training sessions, he started to bear down on the kid, pushing him harder, forcing him to think faster.

Gunner ended up in a corner in a matter of seconds.

Lucky decided he was done, so he tapped the kid hard.

The sociopath dropped like a stone.

The funny thing was, a year ago, knocking someone out would've sent Lucky into a panic. With the son of a bitch who'd made a hacky sack out of Ethan's balls? Not even a twinge of guilt. Besides which, with a kid like Gunner, Lucky had absolutely no other way to get his respect.

Lucky stripped off the gloves and dropped them on the floor beside

Gunner's unconscious form. "Do me a favor," Lucky said to Nicci, "let him wake up there on his own and leave the gloves."

Nicci winked. He dropped a towel over Gunner's shoulders. "Gay boxing dude!" he exclaimed apropos of nothing. "Teach me heavy bag drills, please. I was serious what I said about not knowing boxing. I would be honored to have your teaching."

Lucky slammed a fist into an open palm and bowed. "I would be honored to give you the teaching."

They spent about ten minutes on the drills before Gunner woke up. He jumped to his feet from horizontal, and Lucky understood his instincts. Abusive parents. The kid watched Lucky teach Nicci, and the questions Nicci asked had to be for Gunner's benefit. The kid had tons of respect for the weapon specialist, so when Nicci showed that kind of deference to Lucky, the kid would likely follow suit.

"You're sure this kid is salvageable?" Lucky whispered to Nicci. "I don't want to teach him stuff he'll use to hurt other kids the way he hurt my son."

Nicci pulled Lucky into a clinch, speaking directly into Lucky's ear. "You tell me I'm wrong, Mr. Fox, we toss him out and let Twist deal with him."

Let the lessons begin.

Retro held the door for Ginger then followed her into the club. Wow! It was the coolest place on the planet, totally from an episode of *Hemlock Grove*.

A guy painted blue from his head to his waist and covered in puzzle piece shapes smiled and held up a hand. "You need to be at least eighteen, you delicious morsel."

On the dance floor—what the hell? Half a dozen dancers slithered all over each other, and none of them wore more than a G-string!

"Pretty busy for this early in the morning," Ginger said.

Thank goodness. Retro couldn't talk.

"Pretty vanilla for the club," Jigsaw said, looking them up and down.

"We're here to see the manager," she said. "I'm with Dance Monkey. I need to work out a couple of details for the show."

Jigsaw stared at Retro, who pulled his eyes away from the almost naked dancers. "I'm with the dance crew."

Jigsaw made a face. "I don't remember seeing you with them."

Ginger grabbed Retro's arm and squeezed. "He was too young for the regular visit," she said. "He came along with me to see the place before he performs here. We didn't realize you'd be open for business."

"Mm-hm." Jigsaw played with his belly-button ring and wandered away.

Retro couldn't get enough of the floor show.

"How can I help you?" someone asked from behind, like half a second after Jigsaw left.

Retro spun.

Blond guy. Kinda built from the arms and chest straining against the red and black velvet vest he wore. Top hat and guy-liner. Would Retro ever be able to pull off a look like that?

"I'm Billy." The man extended a hand that Ginger shook.

"I noticed my friend Kenny Valentino's car in the lot," she said.

Wait. She had? And wait, she was friends with Kenny?

Billy held her hand. "They left the cars here after the fiasco," he said. "They went with Spook, and he called later to say they'd pick up the cars after the show." He studied her. "You know Twist." He raised an eyebrow. "Biblically."

She yanked her hand away.

"Our friends are in danger," Retro said, ignoring the comment since he didn't understand what the Bible had to do with anything. "Were they here? Are they safe? We need to find someone who can help."

Ginger elbowed him.

"What?" Retro asked. "If a dude in a top hat who manages a club where a guy like Jigsaw works can't handle the truth, then no one can." He met Billy's bemused gaze. "We need all the help we can get."

"Ethan?" Quiet voice. Didn't know who. "Ethan?" A hand on my shoulder shook me gently.

"No school today," I mumbled into my pillow and pulled the blanket over my head.

"We still have practice, bro." Corey. Being nice and not yanking the sheets off me.

Shit! "Who's dead?" I shouted, jumping to a sitting position that collided my forehead with Corey's. Bam! Ouch! I dropped back onto the pillow. Pretty stars.

"Bro, no one's dead." He took a step away rubbing his forehead.

"Then why'd you wake me up nicely?" I sat up.

"The whole scaring the crap out of you thing isn't really funny anymore."

He had a point. I threw the blanket away and dropped my feet to the floor. Owie head.

No clock. "What time is it?" I asked.

"Around ten." He sat on the end of my bed. "Woody was pretty sure you needed some extra sleep." And it seemed pretty obvious Corey wanted to know why.

I pushed to my feet. Yesterday's sweats. Clean shirt and socks. A change of clean clothes for after the morning practice.

"So. . . how'd you sleep?" he asked.

I took a deep breath. I actually felt rested.

"Pretty well, I think, once I fell asleep." I touched the charm at my neck.

"So it works?" he asked.

I shrugged. "No bad dreams."

He looked at me, wanting to know what was going on.

"Please tell me they have coffee." I shouldered my duffle and headed for the door.

"Bro, seriously?" He rose to his feet, but I could tell he didn't want to go out the door until I spilled the reason Woody had insisted they allow me to sleep.

Deep breath. "Please Corey," I said quietly. "I just want to get moving. Nothing bad happened. I just have a lot to think about. I just want to drink coffee and dance."

He stared at me a moment. "Can I catch *you* up on the way? We've been awake a couple of hours already."

Which likely meant Total Drama Morning without me there to chaperone. Ugh.

"As long as you're leading me to coffee, you can catch me up all you want."

"Oh, there's coffee all right." He led the way into the hall.

"The way you say that makes me suspicious," I said.

"Apparently, Nicci doesn't get out a lot," he said quietly. "And they don't get a lot of house guests, so he kinda went a bit overboard on the hospitality committee."

We rounded the corner and the smell of freshly baked pastry woke up my stomach. Fresh coffee beat up the pastry aroma and told it to wait until after practice.

Holy crap. A bar had been set up outside the gym, and Nicci smiled behind it in a fresh tuxedo print t-shirt and Bermuda shorts. How many different tuxedo shirts existed?

"Good morning dance leader dude," he said with a huge grin. "Can I interest you in a freshly made omelet?" He gestured at a grill and choice selection of meats and vegetables.

Corey nudged me. Okay, post-douchebag response. I glanced at the spread and saw that it had gone mostly untouched. I pretended it was Corey back there. Someone I wouldn't want to hurt.

"You know what, Nicci? Keep the griddle warm until after practice." I grabbed a coffee mug and headed for the tureen. And yes, it was silver. "Dancers can't eat much before practice or we puke. But I bet we devour this entire spread after our morning workout."

His face lit up. "Oh wow, dude, I wondered why everyone kept sneaking past." He started covering everything. "I thought maybe I just, you know, had inhospitable food laid out."

They had caramel macchiato creamer. Heaven.

"Dude, it looks amazing. Thank you." I looked him square in the eye and saw how much my kind words had meant to him. Wow. Did he ever get out? "Seriously, Nicci. Thanks for everything. You and Spook saved our lives and opened your. . . home?"

"Clubhouse," he said very definitively.

"So thanks."

Big thumbs up.

I sucked java and moved to the doorway. "Catch me up." I did the quick scan.

Kenny, Lizard and Mike worked on a laptop at a sound system in one corner. From the snatches of music, they were working on the mashup.

Wait. "Mike?"

Corey nodded. "He wants to help, so they're teaching him how to tap screens for practice."

Wow cool. If he'd needed more points in the okay-to-marry-my-dad column he'd just filled them up.

"Jem got here about an hour ago," Corey said.

She stretched on mats with Trudy, Cosita and Katy, the last of which was a bit surprising since she'd just given birth.

"Jem's on board with the mashup?" I asked.

"Yep. Total pro, bro." Corey attached himself to my shoulder. "She likes the cross-publicity angle and got her hands on the separate tracks for a song about being a demon or a dragon or something spooky like that, so it totally goes with the feel of the Dance Monkey stuff."

Awesome.

"One problem." He sighed.

Damn. "Yes?" Sip, sip.

He nodded his chin at the other side of the room where Spook sat at a table with Ephraim and Stereo. What the? Arts and crafts time?

Oh. They were likely making anti-magic charms or something.

"Stereo and Jem are twice as good as Trudy," he said very quietly.

Holy shit.

He nodded. "I think Jem's better than you when it comes to hip hop and jazz."

Damn. "And Katy hasn't danced much in nine months and she just pushed a baby out a day ago."

I couldn't imagine what kind of friction the new dancers would cause. Hadn't even thought about Stereo as a dancer, but she'd grown up in Houston where they had kick ass dance programs.

"Weird thing on the Katy front," Corey said. "I've helped birth dozens of cows and horses and goats. I've never seen anything bounce back the way Katy has. And a person? It has to be magic or something."

Well, that made sense. After all we'd seen, a postpartum pick-me-up wasn't much of stretch. Speaking of which, neither were Katy's splits. Wow, she'd lost major flexibility and put on weight, too.

Don't get me wrong, boi-i-ing just looking at her, but in her mind? I had no idea the kinds of insecurities swimming around her post-natal brain.

And, yeah. My pulse raced just to look at her.

Damn it.

Movement in the far corner of the gym caught my attention.

Dad had Gunner in gloves, teaching him pad drills.

"Holy fuck."

"Give me a second to—" Corey said.

But I held up a hand. Glancing at Corey, I noticed that while he'd put on a fresh shirt, he'd been sweating. His wrists still had marks from tape.

So Dad had realized that since Gunner's parents had died, he might be in a place for rehabilitation. We might could break the cycle of violence.

"No need," I said. "Go finish your workout with them. I can see what Dad's doing, and if it works the world will be minus one crazy sociopath."

Corey's eyes opened wide. "Bro, you're psychic."

I laughed. "I'll go talk—"

Wait. Was I psychic? I mean, I had flamey hands, who knew what else I could do?

"What?" Corey asked.

I shook my head. "I promise to tell you today, bro, but I need to get my head around all this magic shit, okay?"

He didn't look okay. Maybe I *should* have made sure I was in the room with him and Kenny. They both seemed so far away.

I dropped a hand on his shoulder. "I don't have the right words to tell you what's going on, Corey. I mean that. I don't understand any of this. As soon as I talk to Spook and he tells me what's happening, I will come directly to you. I promise."

Corey still had some demons from when I didn't always tell him stuff because I underestimated him. He seemed to believe me, though. He nodded and trotted off to Dad and Gunner, which were two proper nouns I'd never expected to put into a sentence together.

I caught Dad's eye and he nodded hello.

I tilted my head at the girls stretching on the mats.

Dad nodded to tell me he knew what I was doing.

Huh. That wasn't psychic, was it? That was just Dad stuff, which wasn't magic, was it?

Ugh.

I headed to the mats and dropped down near Jem, offering a hand. "Ethan Fox."

She took the hand and smiled. "I am Jem." The accent was so thick on those three words that I pretty much assumed I'd heard the extent of her English.

"So how's it going?" I asked the rest of the group.

"So far so good," Katy said. "The boys are almost done with the mash-up. As soon as we know which parts of each song we're using, Jem and Stereo are going to choreograph Jem's sections, and Trudy and I are going to pull out material from what we used for the Dance Monkey phrases." She smiled. "I'm hoping you can help with the guy stuff and some of the sequences. It was nine months ago for me, and I'll need a refresher."

Just like that. So not the drama. She sounded like the Katy I'd met that first day in Dumass. Direct and humble and totally lacking in the horrible insecurities that'd poisoned everything at the camp.

Her brow furrowed. "That okay?"

"Yeah, yeah," I said quickly, folding over in a stretch to make sure my sweats weren't tenting. Deep breath. "That sounds great."

Trudy leaned closer. "We have a favor to ask." She glanced at the sound system. "We're not sure what to do with Kenny. We don't know what he can do with the bullet-in-the-leg issue, and we don't want to hurt his feelings by oversimplifying his part."

"I don't remember anything about the leads in the swing," Katy said. "Can you find a way to go over it with him to see how much we can push him safely?"

And not one word about whether keeping him in the routine would hurt the publicity.

They all stared at me.

"Yeah, yeah," I blurted. "I'll talk to him right away and figure it out."

"Figure what out?" Kenny asked, sliding to his knees beside me.

The girls jumped.

I leapt to my feet and pulled Kenny up.

He actually winced. Damn it.

"I need you to help me figure out what parts of the dudes' routine we can pull into the mashup." I threw an arm around him and directed him away.

"Mashup's ready, ladies," he tossed over a shoulder. "You can get started as soon as you like it."

"I'm sure it's great, K-pop," Katy called out. She winced. "I mean, Kenny. Sorry."

"No worries." He turned to follow me to the middle of the floor. "I actually kind of miss K-pop."

"I will call you whatever you ask," I said, dropping cross-legged in the middle of the floor and dragging him with me by the front of his shirt.

"So what are we really talking about?" he asked, reminding me that psychic powers didn't always require magic.

My entire body relaxed. I could say whatever needed saying to Kenny, and even if I said it bone-head stupid, he'd get it. I was so lucky to have a friend like that.

"Can I just sit here a minute and watch everyone?" I asked.

He smiled and nodded. See, he was glad we could do that, too.

Deep breath.

"Okay," I said. "We need to see what your leg can handle, and the girls don't know how to figure that out. My first question is do you want to be in the routine or do you want to work the system?"

He startled a bit then leaned back on his hands with a smile. "I want to do both, but I know I can't. The truth is, I'd be a bigger help backstage and with where things are going, that would look better on the resume."

"But you really want to share the stage with Jem," I said, "and the very idea has you boning in your jeans."

He sprang forward and grabbed my leg. "Oh my God, bro, you have no idea." He laughed and sat back. "I am such a little kid."

"What is it with us that we all worry about that so much?" I asked. "After all we've been through, aren't we all allowed some little kid time?"

He took a deep breath. "So then I'm not sure what I can do. I don't want to mess things up for the folks who're chasing their rising stars."

I glanced over at the girls. Jem worked with Katy, helping her stretch.

"I don't think that matters anymore," I said. "I really think all that drama is over. I mean, seriously, how can any of that even register now?" I turned to Kenny. "They want you to dance. Me, too, but it's up to you."

He glanced at the girls. "I really want to dance, bro. This may be my last chance at something big like this. I mean, I'll keep dancing, but off in college? It'll be back to little recitals and shows, and don't get me wrong, I'll be the guy *running* the Broadway shows and that's what I really want, but after this, I'll need to focus on the tech side if I want to go anywhere."

It made sense. But. . .

Deep breath. Because Kenny's leg issue was my fault. He'd taken a bullet because Twist had wanted me to suffer. I'd worked through a lot of that guilt and knew that it helped no one at all.

But. . . well, truth?

Watching my friends working on routines and learning how to fight and, God help us all, how to make magic charms, the fact that I could make fire in my hands abruptly stopped being scary and turned into something kind of cool. Something that might mean my friends could stop taking bullets.

"I need to show you something," I dragged him to his feet and headed for the locker room.

"If it's your dick, I've already seen it," he joked.

"This is way bigger than my dick."

He snorted.

I stopped. "Please pretend I never said that."

"Said what?"

Once we stood safely in the showering area where nothing was flammable, I planted him on one wall and moved out to the middle of the tiled floor.

Curiosity filled his face.

I held up a hand and closed the fist. Didn't know if the fist was necessary, but I didn't want to mess things up with a change. Although I kept my eyes open to see if I could.

Foom.

"Holy fuck!" He danced a step or two forward. "Do you have any idea how jealous I am right now?"

I held up my other hand. Could I do both?

Foom.

"Dude. I hate you." His voice was a controlled but excited whisper, as if he could tell I didn't want to make this newfound ability public knowledge.

I shook out both hands and the fire evaporated.

Kenny ran up to me and grabbed my hands. "Not even warm."

"I don't feel it at all," I said, "but Woody tried to touch it and said it was hot."

A wave of tiredness hit me, and I staggered a step.

"Are you okay?" Kenny grabbed my arm.

"I'm fine." It wasn't nearly as bad as it had been the night before. "It takes a lot of energy, I think."

"So as much as I want to see it again," he said. "You shouldn't show off before practice."

Whoa. I hadn't meant to show off.

He squeezed my arm. "Not what I meant. Sorry. What did Corey say?"

"Corey was there before coffee," I said. "I didn't even tell him about it."

Kenny winced. "That's going to sting a little."

What the hell? "He woke me out of the soundest sleep I've had in weeks," I said. "Please tell me he'll give me some slack."

He sort of nodded and shrugged. "Spook?"

"He's my first choice," I said. "I need to find out what he makes of all this. I mean, I wasn't going to say a word to anyone until I talked to him, but I just. . . I just had to tell you."

He squeezed my hands and turned them one way and another.

"I'm glad to hear that." The words echoed on the tile. Spook stepped around the corner, hands in pockets. "I was a little worried last night when you didn't tell me immediately."

"Wait," I said. "You told us the cameras were off."

"They are," he verified, "but you think you can cast a spell in this building without a dozen alarms going off in my room when I thought we had no magic wielders here?"

"You said you were going to test us for it," Kenny said.

Spook shrugged. "Just in case. The chances were infinitesimal." He met my gaze. "Or so I thought."

"But if magic users are rare. . ." Was Kenny's brain in overdrive? "The law of averages would say that since Ethan has magic, no one else should."

Spook moved closer and glanced from me to Kenny. "I see why you two are tight. You both like to think." He settled very close. "Magic doesn't follow the laws of math or physics. For some reason, mages tend to grow in clumps, usually in threes. Since Ethan is mage born, the chances of finding another in his hometown skyrocket."

Hometown? That's right. I'd been born in Dumass, no matter how much I tried to pretend otherwise.

Oh, also: Holy. fucking. shit. "So you're saying I'm what you talked about? A natural born mage?"

Spook smiled. "You made fire jump out of your hands without a single solitary lesson, and you have to ask?"

Wow. Just wow.

"How'd you figure it out?" he asked.

"After I saw you do it, I tried it in my dream last night to fight Twist." I stared at my hands. "Woody wanted me to tell him how I'd done it in the nightmare so maybe he could use it if Twist hijacked *his* dreams. When I showed him how I did it in my dream, my hand lit up."

"Yowsa," Kenny muttered.

"Show me," Spook insisted.

I hesitated. "It really tires me out. We have a lot to do today."

He laughed. "All you need to do is refuel at Nicci's buffet, and you'll be fine."

"All I need to do magic is eat?" It seemed too simple.

"For fire," Spook explained. "It's just an intense calorie burn. Sleep or food fixes it."

He made it all sound so normal. But. . . shit.

I could do magic!

I lifted a hand, fingers open in a round cage. The flames leapt to life with almost no effort now.

Spook moved close, staring at my hand with just one eye and then the other. He pulled out his cell phone and seemed to record me.

"Jesus," I whispered, "please don't put this on YouTube."

"I'm not taping," he explained. "It's amazing the apps you can find online if you know where to look." He held the cell to read it. "Okay," he said at last. "Kill it."

I shook the hand out.

Oh crap, that had been longer. My legs buckled.

Kenny helped but I still ended up on my knees.

"Sorry about that," Spook said. He touched the back of my head and all the exhaustion vanished instantly.

Wow. Cool!

Kenny and I rose to our feet.

Spook regarded me in silence a long time. "Ethan Fox," he said at last, "your life just became a *lot* more complicated."

Chapter Fourteen

Twist fed the chickens. Another motherfucking farm in the middle of nowhere.

Whee.

He clenched a fist and a chicken gurgled. He opened the hand and it exploded in a rain of blood and feathers. It was the most exciting thing to do on the lame-ass farm while he waited for his balls to drop and his dick to grow big enough to start fucking Mary again.

Although, he'd make sure to avoid her rituals this time.

Ten years old. He was, for all intents and purposes, ten years old.

"Come on, Mr. Bunny." He waved a hand. "I need to get rid of the evidence."

Mr. Bunny hopped along as Twist wandered back to the outdoor shower, stripped and washed the blood off his skin. Mary had a fetish for those damn chickens. He needed to keep his occasional explosions a secret.

He couldn't get used to the little boy body. Although, if the base line on his dick were any indication, at least he'd traded up. He rinsed, dried off and pulled on a spare pair of bibs.

He'd watched all the Chucky movies several times now.

They made so much more sense, this time around.

"You're bored again, aren't you?" Her voice just grated. If he couldn't fuck her, what use was she?

He crossed his arms. "Gee, Mary, I don't know why I'd be bored. No one to kill. I won't be capable of fucking for half a decade. Yeah. Life's a party."

She cracked her knuckles. "We could skip past all this boredom and run the risk that you end up with a mouse-sized dick. That's fine by me."

"Whatever," Twist said. "At least let me eat you out. I don't need gonads for that."

She laughed out loud. "That's disgusting. You're a child."

He glanced down at his waist. "Maybe if I tell a lie, it'll grow."

She covered her eyes and laughed, leaving him there. Bitch.

He hated that she treated him like a child. He might be in a pint-sized body, but his magic flourished more powerfully than ever. So did his lust for vengeance. So many people needed to die.

Mary included, but hopefully *after* he'd had lots of sex with her. Despite her vindictive evil nature, she was, hands down, the best lay he'd ever experienced.

Damn it. His little Johnson didn't even twitch at the thought.

Okay. Done with it.

He grabbed the desert witch's book and stomped out to the barn. Mary kept whining about how dangerous it would be to fast forward to adulthood. She hadn't been born with magic and this body was chock full of the shit. He could do so much more than she'd ever dreamed possible.

"Let's go, Mr. Bunny. We'll teach that witch to treat me like a little kid."

"5-6-7-8!"

I pulled Katy to the middle of the floor, spun her twice and dipped her. She felt so good in my arms, damn it.

Oops. I had to help her out of the dip, and she needed a second to adjust, but, hell, she'd spend nine months with her center in constant flux.

Apparently, Spook's magic had worked wonders to speed up her healing process and she was, at least physically, close to perfect health.

The crew moved easily through the swing sequences. Other than Katy, everyone had just danced them a couple of weeks ago.

But everything seemed a little weird with all the friends missing.

Ephraim danced with Lizard, of course, as Katy had danced with Whiskey, but they mostly used material Ephraim already knew.

Practice mode helped so much, just dancing and working out the parts and not thinking or feeling much of anything, just smiling and pretending we weren't in mortal danger. Having Katy in my arms, though, reminded me just how much I still loved her and wanted her, after everything.

The changes I'd noticed the day before? Not a fluke. *She'd* suggested Ephraim should dance with Lizard. She'd also asked if she could partner with me because she'd be the weakest link and needed help to get her dance legs back.

That whole honesty thing? Still wow sexy.

Damn it.

Everything had happened nine months ago for her, and she'd been through so much. Maybe it was time to just forget the past. Maybe.

Stereo picked up Mono's part in about ten seconds, which really highlighted her intense ability, and once we all had the swing stuff back in our feet, we jumped into the new material for Jem's music, which lived somewhere between K-pop and dubstep.

During a short water break, I watched Dad's workout with Gunner. How was *that* going? Having the sociopath in the same room would've wrecked me a few weeks ago, but he'd saved my life. More importantly, he'd saved Dad's life when I couldn't pull the trigger. He'd saved us all, and I had to cut him some slack for that.

And back to work.

Jem had an interesting way of communicating since she didn't speak English. For one section, she took Trudy and Cosita by the hand and led them downstage, planting them and sliding between them. She pulled the three together into a Korean sandwich and did body rolls that got all three girls undulating together.

Guys hooted.

She moved away and pressed the two girls together by the shoulders. "Hai?"

"Oh, hella hai." Trudy pressed close to Cosita.

Jem nodded then took me and Kenny downstage and planted us on either side. When she started her body rolls, she pressed back into my hips seductively and smiled over her shoulder. Yipes!

She took Kenny's hand and spun herself out from between us, repositioning in front of Kenny. She pulled his arms around her and backed him into me, so now she and I sandwiched Kenny for the body rolls.

Everyone hooted. What the heck. I threw an arm over Kenny's shoulder as we rolled our hips. Ha! He likely didn't even know I was behind him while he pressed up against one of his favorite singers.

She smoked to the hot, and I hoped Kenny had on his big boy shorts. Although, from the look on her face, she might not mind his enthusiasm in loose boxers.

She pulled away. "Hai?"

Kenny blushed.

I nodded.

She separated the rest of the dancers behind us with hand motions then held up one finger. Her raised eyebrows seemed to ask if everyone knew they would be offstage for only a moment. They all nodded a lot.

She glanced at Mike behind the sound equipment.

"From the top of your song?" he asked.

She nodded then gently motioned for Kenny and me to move offstage. She led Trudy and Cosita to the other side and held one hand down toward the floor to hold them there.

She cued the music.

The swing played for a few phrases then morphed into a dubstep bridge.

Kenny, of course, had made magic with the mashup.

Jem pulled up and strode to the middle of the floor as the lyrics started.

Holy bejeweled flying fuck! Instantaneous transformation.

From a quiet, almost mousy girl, she transformed into a feral lioness of a woman. She ticked and popped for a second then waved Trudy and

Cosita on. They ran into place and hit the body rolls at the exact moment auto-tune rolled Jem's voice through a two-octave slide. The singer threw one arm over Trudy in front and grabbed Cosita's ass behind.

Her eyes flicked to the side ever so subtly, and I tugged Kenny's shirt.

He startled but followed. "Bro, you are so glad you're behind me for this."

Ha!

Jem hit her spot between us the exact moment the vocal slide hit a second time.

Sure enough, she grabbed my ass as we rolled. Nice.

Kenny offered his hand and, now that he knew his role, helped her spin. She nailed at least ten before planting her hand on Kenny's chest and pushing him back into me for the Kenny sandwich and, sure enough, he even grabbed my ass. Not as nice as Jem's grab but cute.

When Jem stepped away, the vocals cut out abruptly.

Holy crap! She'd been singing live?

From the look of shock on Mike's face, he hadn't used any effects, likely didn't even know how to do so. That entire vocal slide had been Jem.

No one moved.

Jem seemed to notice all the buggy eyes and checked her outfit for wardrobe malfunctions. "Hai?"

Everybody applauded.

"I'm singing with her?" Lizard asked, his face a mask of terror. He'd been lip-synching to a prerecorded version so he could focus on his dance steps. "I suck so much."

Jem smiled a huge, friendly smile and walked over to him. "No sucking," she said and kissed his forehead. "Very cute boy. Good sing." She held a hand to Stereo who moved center.

"After the intro, we all run into place," Stereo said.

And Kenny had been right. Stereo wasn't warm to me or anything, but the anger and hatred seemed softer since the night she'd shown up at his doorstep and found out about my biological parents.

While Jem took a minute to show everyone else their positions, Kenny turned to me and dropped his head onto my shoulder, pounding my chest lightly with a fist. "I totally boned up behind her, bro. At once the best moment of my life and the worst. You think she noticed?"

"I've seen that monster," I teased. "She noticed."

He snorted and pushed me away. "I am *so* glad you were behind me."

"You and me both."

A nun. Billy had sent Retro to see a nun.

Wait. Hadn't he seen her in Dumass after the studio got torched? Had to be her. How many nuns in a dress from three centuries ago could there be?

"Billy told me why he sent you," Sister Liberata said, waving Retro and Ginger onto a plaid sofa. "It already happened."

"What? What happened?" Retro sat forward.

"The witch who contacted you—Mary—she released Katy Montez," the nun said. "That's why the witch wanted to find your friends. To give her to them."

"Katy's back?" Retro asked. "For real?"

"As far as we can tell," she said. "Your friends are with Morrison James, and they're someplace safe."

"Seriously? I wish people would please stop telling me that," Retro said. "What about us? We aren't very safe, are we?"

Sister Liberata crossed her arms. "As long as you're with me you are."

"Is that so?" A little kid stood in the doorway to the living room.

Sister Liberata just about did a backflip, she moved so quickly. Her hands shot up and she spouted nonsense words.

The kid held his hands behind his back calm as could be while electricity sparked between the nun's upraised hands. The lightning spun into a vortex and the vortex whirled into a black void.

If Retro had ever doubted the existence of black holes, he'd just been convinced they could be as real as magic.

The boy raised one hand and flicked it at the nun. Silvery dust flew from his fingers, grew into a bright sparkling cloud and swarmed Sister Liberata.

She froze in place as it touched her. The black swirling hole between her upstretched arms grew as Retro and Ginger clutched each other and pressed themselves into the couch.

"You know, bitch," the boy said as he moved closer to her. "There were some notes scribbled on the edges of your friend's book that didn't make sense at first. But when I realized what she needed to take her husband from a little boy into a man. . . and who had it, everything became crystal clear."

He moved closer to the couch.

The black hole continued to grow. It consumed parts of the nun's arms but she didn't cry out. Maybe she couldn't. Maybe the swirling silver dust kept her from screaming.

"Hello again, redhead," the boy said. "I'd fuck you for old time's sake, but, well. . ." He glanced down at himself. "That's why I'm here." He turned back to the nun. "To see a lady about a pocket watch."

Retro finally put the pieces together. The boy had to be Twist somehow... or controlled by Twist.

"Was she so old," Twist asked, "she had to write it all down? Or is that a witch thing? You're so convinced no one can beat you you never realize how stupid it is to write down the password to your friend's house, the location of her secret stash and everything necessary to make the theft."

The black hole covered the nun's arms completely. Lightning played around its edges before sucking down into the void.

"When I was a cop, I used to laugh at movies where the perps left their plans and blueprints lying on a table for the police to sneak in and find." He held up both hands in mock excitement. "What? They're digging a hole from the parking garage directly into the vault? Well then, we can catch them in the act."

He chuckled darkly, knelt on the floor and twitched a rug out of the way. Running a hand over the dusty floorboards, he muttered in some weird language.

With a pop, a perfect wooden square lifted out of the floor and slid to one side.

"Of course, I can't count the number of folks who off a husband or a wife because they find a diary." He reached into the hole and pulled out an old shoebox. "It's like they want to get caught."

He sat cross-legged in the middle of the floor with the shoebox in his lap. He ran a hand over it and glanced up at Retro. "If you ever have the chance to cheat on your girlfriend," Twist said, "don't write down the details anywhere."

Retro thought about Stacey Williams. Would she be his girlfriend? Would he ever have a chance to find out if he'd cheat on someone?

Ginger felt real and solid in his arms. She shivered.

He'd never cheat on a girl like her.

Twist glanced into the hole in the floor then nodded. "At least you didn't hide everything in one place like Delilah."

Above him, the darkness hid half the nun from view now. The lightning flashed brighter and faster and the silver dust swirled around it. If Twist left her like that, would the vortex swallow them all?

Twist opened the box, drew out a silver pocket watch and dropped the box into the hole. He rose smoothly to his feet and sauntered close to Retro and Ginger. He smiled.

Retro prayed his bladder didn't give out again.

"Please don't kill us," Ginger said.

Twist glared at her.

The swirling darkness completely enveloped Sister Liberata.

Silver dust swarmed the vortex.

Without a word, the boy who was Twist snapped his fingers.

The silver dust dropped out of the air as if shot.

Sister Liberata's scream shattered every piece of glass in the room.

The darkness expanded like an explosion. It sucked Retro off the couch, Ginger still in his arms. It yanked the couch into the vortex as well.

And the walls.

And the floor.

Pissing himself was the least of Retro's worries.

Spook called a break around two and promised us fish tacos from Beto's, which we'd never had a chance to try because we'd raced back to Dumass.

First, he wanted to say a few things. Oddly enough, no one tried to duck out, not even Gunner.

"I want to mix the other training with the dance this afternoon," Spook said when everyone had settled on the floor or a bench or whatever. "Y'all said you want to learn to fight. Well, Nicci is ready to show you how to hold a sword and a dagger."

The surfer dude looked completely different bare chested and holding the most ginormous sword I'd ever seen. The dude was shredded, and I swear he was bigger than he'd been standing behind the breakfast buffet.

"Why not guns?" Gunner asked. Of course.

Murmurs of somewhat surprised agreement followed.

"Guns and magic are a dangerous combination," Spook said.

Gunner snorted. "Worked well enough last time I met the little prick."

"Because he wanted you to shoot him."

The murmuring ceased. Surprisingly, Gunner shut up, too.

"At the time," Spook said, "I suspect Twist and Mary were on the outs. He decided it was safer to get himself killed and come back as a spirit than let her send his soul directly to the worst pit of Hell imaginable. He'd worked out how to come back mostly the same."

"That's a real thing?" Trudy asked. "Hell?"

"It is." Spook moved closer. "But not like you're thinking. It's not the kind of place sinners are sent for being naughty. It's an alternate dimension of its own, and soul-stealing demons and whatnot live there, but you don't get sent there by God when you die."

"Where do you go?" Tango asked.

"I wouldn't know." Spook shrugged. "I only deal with the spirits who don't want to find out." He gestured at Nicci. "The point is, guns are dangerous in crowded areas with lots of your friends circling the bad guy. Knives, daggers and swords are easier to use if you end up stuck close in."

"What if you can't get in close?" Woody asked.

"If you're so far away that only a gun can do the job," Spook said, "then you run in the other God damn direction." He opened his arms. "Look, I'm not training you to go into battle or anything like that. This is what to do if you're attacked. If someone grabs you from behind, you'd much rather have a knife in your boot than a gun in your belt."

He pointed at Dad. "Mr. Fox will teach grappling and boxing." He laid a hand on his own chest. "I'm going to help with charms and whatnot. We'll rotate every so often to keep it interesting."

"Wait a minute," Stereo said. "You were going to test us for magic."

Spook glanced at me.

Stellar. Was I about to be shoved out of the broom closet?

"As far as I can tell only one of you has any latent ability," he said, fixing his gaze on me. "But I'm open to checking anyone who feels that ol' black magic in their blood."

"One of us?" Stereo said. "Who?"

Spook raised an eyebrow at me. "Might as well get it over with, stud, telling everybody one by one is already tedious."

Deep breath. Fine. I'd been put on the spot a million times in my dance career.

At least I had pants on this time.

"Fox?" Stereo's voice came out as a pissed off whine. "*Fox* has magic?"

I raised a hand. Foom. It seemed so damn easy now.

Gasps and laughter and muttering.

For the hell of it, I tried to toss the fireball into my other hand.

Cool. I tossed it back and forth a few times.

Applause.

I shook out my hand

"Un-fucking-believable," Stereo moaned, and I really wanted to rub it in her face for wishing death on Dad, but I hadn't decided if this magic stuff was a good thing yet. And Kenny was truly smitten, boners for Jem notwithstanding. I'd noticed how often he watched Stereo. My friend had it bad.

The crowd gathered. Dad, Mike, Corey, Kenny and Trudy moved in with questions and comments. Gunner and Stereo hung back, obviously not liking the new development. Ephraim, Lizard, Katy and Cosita hung back, also looking unhappy, but more like unhappy scared than unhappy pissed. Woody hung back looking all blasé about it.

Dad and Corey each snagged a hand and examined it. Thank God that kind of attention was normal for me.

"The quick version," Spook said, thankfully taking the ball on this one. "Ethan discovered this trick by accident late last night. It's the only thing he can do and do not ask him for a repeat performance because it drains him dead. Do not try to come up with other party tricks for him because something as simple as trying to make a snowball will most likely kill him." He took a breath. "The moment his magic manifested, I used my own voodoo powers on the rest of you and I'm pretty sure no one else in the group is packing heat, as it were. Most latent mages manifest shortly after first discovering that magic is a real thing."

He focused on Stereo. "So I'm sorry, Stereo, but I doubt you're a natural. Don't get your tattoos in a twirl though, neither was Mary and she is the strongest witch I have met. Trust me, folks. This discovery is most likely a popcorn kernel in his teeth rather than a new toy."

Uh-huh, all well and good. However. . .

"Making a snowball could kill me?" I asked, sort of focused on that revelation. "And you're just telling me now?"

"Because I trusted you wouldn't try anything stupid until we had a chance to work together." He crossed his arms. "Okay, folks, tacos stay outside the gym and yes we have beef as well for those of you who prefer to kill farm animals."

Most of the gang filtered through the doors.

Dad dropped a hand on my shoulder. "So you're a flamer now?"

Of course, he'd be the one.

"Well, I figured with two middle-aged anti-queens in the family, someone had to keep up appearances."

He smiled, but the hesitation showed up, too. It worried him.

Of course, it did. It worried me.

Corey wore that kicked puppy look.

"When you woke me up this morning," I told him, "I hoped it'd been part of the dream. I didn't know if it was real."

"Totally." He nodded and made a reassuring face. "Don't even worry about it."

What a bad liar. He was hurt. Could he tell I'd mentioned it to Kenny? Most likely. So, what, the two of them were the only ones who could keep secrets now? Chit.

Mike hovered. Of course.

"As soon as I even know what this is, Mike," I said. "I'll make a beeline for the family's counselor if I need to."

"I guess I'll start googling," he said. Dad took his arm and led him to the taco buffet which had replaced the breakfast bar. Yay for Dad knowing when I needed time to process.

Trudy and Katy sat on a balance beam eating and shooting not-so-subtle glances my way.

My stomach growled.

A plate of fish tacos and black beans appeared in front of me. Not magic. Kenny.

"Eat up, hai?" He took a bite of his own. "I have a feeling it's going to be a long day."

Indubitably.

Wow! Best fish taco ever! I found Woody where he stood just outside the gym. When he met my gaze, I raised my taco to him in salute.

He grinned around a mouthful. "I told you, *ese*."

Nicci herded us out to the hall with his badass sword.

Oh yeah, no food in the gym.

"Stereo." Kenny chased her down the hall into the clubhouse lobby.

She didn't slow down, and her hands hit the front door.

"Please don't go," he begged.

She stopped, her hands on the door release, but she didn't turn around. "Please don't tell me what a great guy he is and how I should be happy that at least someone has magic in this pathetic group of tourists."

Kenny shoved his hands into his armpits. They wouldn't stop

shaking. "I'm not going to say anything like that. I just don't want you to go. You'll get hurt."

She turned to him, one hand still on the door, tears flowing down her face.

It broke Kenny's heart, and he moved closer. He even reached out, but did she want that? Would it matter to her?

"All my life, I've wanted what he has," she said. "I've studied magic for years, learning all I could, but I never. . . I never did anything real."

"You're good with tarot cards," Kenny said. She'd done a reading for him and Corey back when they'd been keeping their search a secret from Ethan.

She shook her head. "Tarot cards are chance and intuition." She met Kenny's eyes. "All my studying and I never really believed it. I never even thought anything like that. . ." She waved an arm. "Fireballs? Hell, that's Harry Potter stuff right there." She moved away from the door. "And *he* gets it? *Him*? Okay, I get the poor orphan boy and all that, but would any of this be happening to the rest of us if he'd just stayed away from Dumass, Texas?"

Kenny stood his ground, but he was so afraid of her reaction to what he had to say next. "Twist was stalking Katy long before Ethan showed up."

Stereo made a face, but she kept silent.

"I saw his hard drive, Stereo." Kenny had to swallow, remembering some of the sick shit on it. "He was on the road to Psychopathia long before Ethan fell for Katy, and that's all he did. Ethan fell in love with a pretty girl. And for that he was beaten one step from death, kidnapped by Twist and shot. All because of Katy." Kenny took a deep breath. "And he didn't even want to go to the camp. He'd already had all that fame and he didn't want it anymore. *We* talked him into going. And he only went because he knew we'd never make it work without him."

He stepped closer. He really wanted to take her hand but was afraid she'd just yank it away. "And you keep saying how people near him get hurt. . . they die. But do you know why? Do you?"

She shook her head, tears still dribbling down her cheeks.

"Because when someone is hurt or in danger, Ethan Fox runs straight *for* them to try to help," Kenny said. "You saw it in Bitter Sweets. He was the first one to follow Spook when that portal thing opened. He doesn't run away to save himself." He sucked in a breath. "When Twist shot me, Ethan covered me with his body to protect me. Someone else would've run away."

"Is that why you like him so much?" she asked, stepping closer. "Because he's brave?"

Kenny reached for her hand. She let him take it and even returned the squeeze.

"I like him so much," Kenny said, "because he was the first person who ever liked my hair." And it was the truth, but it was also kind of a joke.

She smiled. Good. She reached up with her free hand. "I like your hair, too." She ran a hand through it. "But I like it better standing straight up."

Kenny's heart pounded.

Her hand found his neck and stayed there. She smiled.

"Your pulse is racing," she said. "Did I do that?"

Kenny pulled her closer and kissed her before his brain tried to think of something clever to say.

She kissed him back.

He reached for her hair with his free hand, tried to run his fingers through it, but the spikes almost sliced him open.

She chuckled into his mouth, then laughed, pulling back a little, but her hand stayed on his neck. "One of the challenges of living life with perfect hair."

Kenny shrugged. "I can always find somewhere else to put my hands." Was that funny or creepy?

She raised an eyebrow. . . then smiled. . . and pulled him down to kiss her again.

"Foxtrot!" Trudy's call stopped me. She ran to catch me up then snaked an arm through mine and kept me moving. "How's it going, attention whore?"

We kept walking.

"You okay?" I asked. "What's wrong?"

She made a whole series of faces to show her disgust. "What makes you think something's wrong?"

"Well," I said, "unless something pisses you off, you pretty much keep to Cosita's side."

She made yet another face.

"Just sayin'."

She tugged me through the swinging door into the lobby and released my arm. "I wanted to check with you to make sure *you're* okay." She wandered to the counter. "I mean, a lot of shit has happened, right?" She looked away. "I know you have your boyfriends and all, but I just. . . I just wanted to make sure you know I'm your friend, too." She leaned against the counter. "We're friends, right?"

"What? Of course."

She nodded as if she hadn't been certain. Really? What the hell?

"Look, ever since you and Cosita made it official," I told her, "You've been kinda umbilical."

She scowled. Then she smiled. "She fucks better than anyone I've ever met."

I worked to avoid the grimace of TMI. "Which is why I've kind of left it alone."

She sighed. "And you? This has to be weird for you. . . especially with Katy."

"On so many levels." I settled beside her.

"She won't talk to me, you know," she said abruptly. "I tried to ask about all that shit with her family. . ." She cringed and turned to face the counter, both hands on it as if it held her up. "She just says it happened nine months ago and won't talk about it." She sucked in a deep breath. She looked at me. "I watched her mom explode two days ago and she won't talk about it because. . ."

And *that's* why she was here talking to me. "Because why?"

"She talks about Adam," Trudy said, "about the baby. For her that was. . ." She shook her head. "Shit, that was just yesterday for her. *Christos*, this is so fucked up."

I. . . what should I do? I put an arm around her. She allowed it.

"She will always be my best friend, Foxtrot," she said. "And I love her to fucking death, but I watched her mom explode two days ago and she won't talk about it."

I held her tighter.

"I don't even know how to tell you what happened," she whispered while I held her. "But then, you've seen it."

"Not like that," I said with a squeeze.

"You tripped over Whiskey's burning corpse," she reminded me. "What the fuck? How is this different?"

Wow. I had.

Wow.

Shit.

"Why does it seem worse when someone else tells it?" I asked.

She chuckled. "Because you don't want to believe it's real."

I pulled her to the serviceable but not very comfortable couch. "So tell me," I said. "Tell me everything that happened."

She huddled in my arms, her chin at my chest. "Do you know what you're asking?"

I stroked her hair. "Yep."

Corey missed Theresa. It was weird. Right after his mom had died, he couldn't even be in the same room with her without crying, now it hurt to be away from her for one day. The hardest part was not knowing how long he'd be stuck in the clubhouse. She'd offered to go into hiding with him, but Spook had said the same thing he'd said about Jimmy Russo: why put her in the line of fire when she was perfectly safe?

They were only allowed to call or text using a couple of Spook's phones in a certain room that also had the only laptop they could use for the internet. Like Twist would be able to hack into the satellite towers or something.

Like Twist would be able to harness magic and terrorize them all.

Bummer.

Ethan was off doing magic stuff with Spook. Kenny was busy flirting with Stereo. Woody was totally trying to get into Jem's dance tights. Ephraim and Lizard were most likely off making out somewhere. Mike was messing with the sound system with F-bomb.

Corey wandered out of the gym, grabbed a taco and headed toward the lobby. Maybe Gunner was hanging out there. He wasn't really allowed to mix and mingle with the gang, but F-bomb was working with him a lot, which was awesome. The respect he showed the big guy was kind of surprising, but F-bomb knew his shit and anyone who wanted his mad skills had to give him the R.

Yep. Gunner played video games on a huge monitor Corey hadn't noticed before. Now that he knew his old buddy was a violent sociopath, Gunner looked different. A lot of the shit he'd always said made sense now, a lot of the things Corey had heard and blown off, well, he couldn't ignore it anymore just because they were family.

Corey didn't have a lot of family left.

"You gonna stand there staring like a bitch?" Gunner didn't even look up, just kept killing robots.

"I don't know that game." Corey moved into the room. "What platform?"

"Not even sure." When he got into a game, he totally focused. He'd been the same way on the field. Focused. He'd had to find a way to go out of his head while his parents beat on him. Damn. How had Corey never seen that before?

Okay. Video games. Corey understood video games. He just needed a controller.

No gaming console anywhere near the TV. Corey looked behind it. Nope. In fact. . . "Bro, this thing isn't even plugged into the wall. How is it on?"

Gunner didn't glance up. "Because magic. Duh."

Magic. Corey'd thought the whole magic thing was kinda cool at first but not so much anymore. It seemed a lot of trouble and not a lot of help.

"I'd let you jump in, but I only got the one controller." Gunner leaned to one side while running along the wall of a space station. A team of giant, armor-plated fleas chased him through a ship that looked more like a sewer pipe.

"No worries." Corey plunked himself down on the couch, but something dug into his hip. A controller? "I thought you just had the one."

"I did." Gunner looked up at the camera in the corner. "Thanks, Nicci." He glanced at Corey for the first time. "Because magic. Duh."

The game was cool. Cooperative mode. There didn't seem to be a way for the players to fight each other. They just killed the giant bugs and robots. Oh, and creepy, white teddy bears with huge teeth. Maybe it was therapy for Gunner, not being able to attack the other players.

"I'm sorry about your mom," Gunner said while they shot up a boss. "I should've got there sooner." Blam, blam. "I mean, I should've. . ."

"No way, bro." Corey dropped his controller and grabbed Gunner's. "You want to talk about my mom, you look me in the eye when you do it."

Gunner's mouth quirked into that half smile he wore when he was about to say something shitty.

"I'm not asking you to hug it out or let me cry on your shoulder," Corey insisted. "But if we're going to talk about my mom, you will fucking respect her."

Gunner didn't mouth off. He nodded, broke eye contact and looked at the screen, which cut to black.

Sweet. "Thanks, Nicci," Corey said to the air.

Gunner looked down at his hands. "I was there. . . when it happened. I could've stopped it, could've taken out the little gay Jew."

"Ephraim," Corey said. "His name's Ephraim."

Gunner looked into Corey's eyes with his eyebrows knit. "Whatever."

"His name is Ephraim," Corey insisted, "and he didn't kill my mom. He was just, like, the weapon or something. The thing Twist used. It wasn't his fault." He took a deep breath to calm down. "It wasn't your fault either."

Gunner looked down at his hands and nodded. "It was," he whispered. "I knew shit was going down, but I didn't figure it out. I was just watching you and looking for my chance to whack the little blond prick."

Wait a minute. Who? "Ethan? You were going to shoot Ethan?"

Gunner shrugged. "Him, Twist. . . both. I wasn't sure." He looked up. "You say you want the truth these days." He shrugged. "That's the truth, so fine, I'm an asshole. I was going to kill your new bestie, I don't know, maybe. So go back to your new friends and leave the little *sociopath* to his video game. It's all I got left."

He stared at his feet.

That was more than Corey had ever heard from Gunner's mouth all in one go, unless it was about football, cars or sex. . . or drinking. He dropped a controller in Gunner's lap, settled back and hit start on his own controller. The ship reappeared and Corey gunned down fleas.

Gunner stared at him a few seconds then picked up his own controller and his avatar appeared beside Corey's.

"Go left," Corey said. "I'll go right."

"On it."

Chapter Fifteen

"You stole this from the set of *Supernatural*, didn't you?" I stopped at the edge of some kind of magic circle painted on the floor. "Freakin' stellar."

The room was black, walls, floor and ceiling. All kinds of symbols decorated the walls in white, yellow and blue. No red. Huh, guess that's stereotyping. The circle had a ring of symbols around the edge of it and a pentacle or pentagram, five-pointed star thingy in the middle.

Wow. That symbol was like the pink triangle for my new people and I didn't even know its name.

Spook stood behind a table, altar thingy that had a bunch of witchy stuff on it. Stereo would have known what every item did. She probably owned them all.

Then there was me. The Ken doll who hadn't even believed in all this until a couple of days ago.

Dad stood near the door with his I'm-not-going-to-let-you-know-what-I'm-thinking face firmly in place. Uh-oh. Was all this too much for him? I mean, how did either of us even have a point of reference?

"So what do we do?" I asked.

"So you step into the circle," Spook said. "I cast a spell and the circle on the floor glows brighter the more magic you have in you."

"A thaumometer," I muttered.

"Oh my God, you're an even bigger geek than me," Spook said.

"Thauma-whatsit?" Dad asked moving closer.

"Never mind." I shifted around the circle closer to Spook. "Obscure fantasy novel reference."

Spook waved me into the circle.

"Do I need to wear a special costume or something?" When I crossed the line into the circle a whole lot of nothing happened.

"You can always strip naked if you want." Spook moved things around on the table.

What the shit? "Will that help?"

"No." He looked up with a smile. "But I always give the same answer in case it's someone like Stereo. That way there's no hesitation in my voice so she's more likely to buy it."

Nice.

"That work?"

He went back to his magicky things. "No."

Oh. Poor guy.

"Is there anything I can do?" Dad asked. I could tell he hated this almost as much as sitting in the doctor's office waiting to see if my wrist was broken. Probably worse. Dad knew exactly how to handle a broken wrist.

"Nope." Spook moved away from the table and poured some kind of oil on the floor along the line of symbols around me. "I know this is bizarre for you guys. You've both seen shit in the past few days, but now that it's you, well, that's different." He looked up at Dad. "Just pretend I'm giving your boy his annual physical or something. This is that uninteresting."

Dad met my eyes. "Don't worry. I'll look the other way when it's time to turn your head and cough."

Ew. But joking was a good thing.

We all lapsed into silence while Spook worked his circle.

"Here we go." He clapped once then held his palms apart. "*Lorem ipsum dolor sit amet.*"

The circle on the floor ignited with a soft white glow.

Huh. That was it? No flashes of lightning or giant flames?

Did that mean I was, like, mystically challenged?

Spooks hands dropped to his side.

"Those words you said," Dad said. "What language is that?"

Spook held one finger up to his lips. "Shhhh." He gave me his full attention. "Now I want you to call up the fire. That will start the reading."

Oh, so the dull white was baseline. Well, then maybe I didn't suck so much.

Jesus, I didn't even know if I wanted magic and already I felt inadequate.

I held up a hand and the fire jumped to life.

Dad crossed his arms. Damn it, what was running through his head?

The lines turned golden, a faint yellow.

"Hm," said Spook, apparently unimpressed and unsurprised.

Foosh!

The shape flared purple, somehow dark and bright at the same time.

Then the colors flickered, flared and sort of separated into two distinct circles of symbols that shifted in and out of focus, like a 3D movie without the glasses.

My eyes watered and burned a little.

Spook sucked in a quick breath. His jaw, literally, dropped open. Not something I thought really happened.

"What?" Dad asked right away, a bloodhound when it came to unwelcome reactions from professionals examining me. "What's wrong?"

I rubbed my eyes and had to look up at the ceiling. My fire died but the circles around me kept up their colors.

"Are you okay, Ethan?" Dad demanded.

"I'm fine."

Spook moved closer and raised his hands again. His eyes flared yellow. He blinked and they turned purple. They shifted between the two, and the two circles of light shifted the same way.

They flickered between the two colors, slipped together and ended up a solid but fairly dim gold.

Gold seemed nice. Happy and, well, not demonic or anything. Right?

Spook clapped and the rings faded away. So did the light in his eyes.

"I apologize," he said. "My surprise was unprofessional, and it scared you. I'm truly sorry."

"What the hell does it mean?" Dad loomed over him.

The loom had little effect on Spook. "It means Ethan is rare," he said.

"It's neither good nor bad, it's just rare." He approached me, placed a hand on my shoulder and led me over to Dad, who, of course, grabbed my arms and examined me head to toe. "It's about as exciting as having a rare blood type," Spook continued. "It means some kinds of magic will be easy for you and some will be harder. It's like being gay." He waved at Dad. "It's not good or bad. It just is."

"I really don't like the analogy," Dad muttered. "Can we stick to blood type?"

What the hell?

My time to grab Dad's arms. "What is wrong?"

His face was so. . . blank but held there by brute force.

"Are you embarrassed about this?" I demanded. "Ashamed?"

His face went pale. "Christ, Ethan, no." He held my arms tighter. "I'm afraid for you. You heard what they said about the Cloaks. They don't allow knowledge of magic to get out. When it does, people disappear." He chewed his lip for a second. "Think about it, Ethan, you now have a secret that you can't tell people. They'll want to put you in a cage and study you. Some will want to burn you. Some will want to take advantage of you, and for your whole life, there's going to be this secret you need to keep." He took a deep breath. "All your life you've had to put up with shit because you have a gay dad, and now. . . I guess I'm getting a taste of what my parents went through. I have no problem with this, and I'm not afraid of you or. . . I just have so many questions, and I just don't want you to go through everything I did when I was your age."

I squeezed his arms one last time then moved away. I held up my hand.

Foom.

That tiny little fire meant most of the world would consider me a complete and total freak. People would hate me. Want to kill me. I looked up at Dad.

"You know," I murmured. "I never really got it." I shook the hand out because I already felt the drain. "I mean, I did the research. I watched the videos. But I never really understood what you went through growing up, why you left Dumass, how hard it had to be to go back." I stared at the hand where the fire had been. "I think I get it now."

He hugged me. Duh. Around his shoulder, I stared at my hand.

Spook smudged the room with sage after Ethan and Lucky left. The revelation from the magic meter had shaken him, but he hoped he'd covered well enough to keep Ethan in the dark until after the Twist situation had been handled.

A powerful presence tickled Spook's spine like a cleaver. He spun.

"We need to talk." Sister Liberata stood near the door, her habit in tatters, the shadows of many insectoid legs beneath.

Spook froze. The fact that her lower body needed an invite to a roach motel wasn't even interesting. The fact that she let him see it terrified him.

"What happened?" he asked.

"Two of Ethan's friends came to visit," she said, "then Twist attacked."

Another one of those coincidences Spook hated.

"He stole an artifact," she said.

The severity of the situation turned Spook's immobile blood to ice. A Cloak had come to him for help with a theft. How unimaginably powerful was this newbie thief?

"What did he get?" Spook asked. "And should I ask how he got it from you?"

She sighed and arranged her robes over her chitinous legs as best she could. "We spoke of my friend in the desert? He has her book, where he learned of the device my friend used to bring her husband from infancy to adulthood. He also learned the spell she'd used to immobilize me when *she* stole the artifact from me."

Joy. "What device?" Spook asked.

"A magical pocket watch," the nun said. "The man who created it used it for eternal youth. Every day, he'd wind it back twenty-four hours and the watch would remove that much age from his body."

"How does that help Twist?" Spook asked.

The nun didn't speak. Damn. She had no need. A watch that could turn back the hands of time could also spin them forward.

"You said your desert friend used it," Spook said. "I assume to bring her husband to adulthood."

The nun nodded.

"So why didn't you destroy the blasted thing?" he demanded.

She sighed. "Nothing like it has ever been made on this planet. Nothing likely will again."

And there was her hubris. She'd had a shiny toy, and she thought she was too powerful for anyone to take it from her. If Spook had a nickel for everyone with the same flaw. Oh, he did.

"So Twist has a pocket watch that he can simply wind forward and turn himself into an adult," Spook said. "Why does that merit a visit to me?"

She stared at him.

Drat. That meant it was really bad.

She folded her hands.

Double drat. Even worse.

"This item will allow him to become an adult, and. . ."

Spook hated when people said "and" and he heard the ellipses.

She sighed. "He took the pocket watch and prevented me from following," she admitted. "He also took a girl named Ginger and a boy named Thomas, I think the dancers call him Retro."

"Why?" Spook demanded.

"I don't know," she insisted. "I suspect he dances in an old-fashioned style."

Spook wanted to smack her, but she was a Cloak.

So. Twist had the ability to grow his avatar into adulthood and he'd kidnapped two of Ethan's friends. Fine. Sweet. Spook could still fix it. "Why did he take the innocents instead of just killing them?"

The nun sighed. "I cannot even imagine."

Triple drat.

The rest of the day pretty much blurred out. I worked most of it with Dad's group, which made some folks kind of mutter and stuff, but screw that, I'd just had a ton of bricks dropped on my head and boxing drills made a pure kind of sense to me.

According to Spook, my magic was limited enough to ignore it until we handled this thing with Twist one way or another. I had my little party trick and needed to keep it at that. If I tried to learn anything new right now, I'd never master it and would only end up screwing up badly.

That made sense. For newbie dancers, there's no point to learning anything new two weeks before a comp or a show. When the adrenaline hits, the last two weeks pretty much evaporate. In this world, I was a newbie.

I worked a series of pad drills with Corey and Kenny until my arms felt like lead and my sides hurt. Nice. I only stopped when Dad wrapped an arm around me from behind and pulled me away from the pads. "Enough."

Huh. The gym had emptied except for the four of us.

"Everyone else left half an hour ago," Dad told me. "Hit the showers, guys. There's sandwiches when you don't stink."

He wandered around picking up towels and stuff, which likely was Nicci's thing, but that kind of work relaxed the old man and he had a lot to make him tense.

Kenny reached for my gloves.

Holding out my hands, I watched his face. He'd believed in magic all along, and I'd been a douchebag. He would never criticize me for it.

"These stories your Papa Karela told you," I said. "Maybe the three of us should climb up on the roof later, and you can tell me some."

He smiled and nodded. "That'd be stellar." He handed over the gloves.

Corey pushed a duffle into my chest, and I shoved everything into it as we headed for the locker room. The place was deserted.

"Does it bother you?" I asked Kenny, wringing the sweat out of my clothes. I grabbed a towel, and we headed to the showers. "You're the one with the history and I never believed. . . and here I am with fiery hands."

My friends exchanged that knowing look I loved so much, but could I complain anymore? Hell, no.

Mmm. Cool, refreshing water. Showerhead massage for the cranky, sore shoulders.

Kenny would spill when he—

"I won't lie," he said. "It bugged me at first, but only because. . ."

"Because I was a douchebag before I saw it for myself." I tossed the shampoo to Corey.

"Yeah, because that." Kenny worked conditioner into his hair. "But while you were with Spook, Stereo pitched kind of a fit, and I don't want to be that guy."

"That must've been awkward," I said.

"We worked it out." A strange sort of smile played at the edges of his lips.

"So should I start making jokes about sleeping with the enemy?" I lathered my hair.

Kenny snorted. "Oh, bejezus, and here I was feeling all suave because I kissed her."

I immediately held up a fist for him to bump. "You are suave incarnate. Don't ever think otherwise."

He bumped the fist.

Corey remained strangely silent.

"Are you mad because I didn't tell you right away?" I felt guilty about that.

"Nah." He rinsed off then stood with his head back, eyes closed, letting the water run over him. "We're on opposite sides of the road. You have more friends than you've ever had in your life and I have less. You're running around trying to keep up with all of us and I feel kinda lonely without Theresa. . . and I still miss some of the guys on the team. I ain't mad atcha."

So all three of us let the water pour down, washing away the grime and stink and maybe just a little bit of the stress.

Kenny turned to the wall and let the water pour over his back, his hair a black and red curtain covering his face.

"Is it okay with y'all," I asked, "if I bunk up with you tonight?"

Corey grinned.

"Ha." Kenny laughed without looking up. "I win."

I smacked Corey's arm. "What, you had a bet on how long it would take for me to turn into a little girl?"

Corey opened his eyes. "Bro, if that makes you a little girl then I'm a fairy princess and Kenny's a little pony. The only reason we didn't ask you was the bet we made."

"Little pony?" Kenny shoved his hair out of the way.

Corey shrugged. "You know, like My Little Pony is totally girly and stuff."

"Don't be dissing the Bronies," Kenny said.

"Bronies?" I asked.

"Bros who like the Ponies."

Corey snorted and turned to him. "That's a thing?"

Kenny nodded sagely, our expert on all things animated.

Corey raised a hand. "I apologize to the Bronies."

Wow. At one point I'd been afraid that having two best friends would make them jealous of each other. Listening to the banter, I couldn't even be jealous myself. Maybe it was like having brothers. Sometimes you're closer to one. Sometimes to the other, but through it all, you're family and jealousy would be kind of stupid in the face of that.

"So I have an idea." Kenny's tone earned him my undivided attention. "We need to set a trap for Twist. He's in Adam, and we need to get that crystal into his body."

"Oh, that is totally my department," Corey said. "If he's still a little kid, I won't even need my special glove."

Ewww.

"Um. What?" Kenny asked.

I closed my eyes, having already heard about this.

"Bro, I do this stuff with cows all the time." Even with my eyes closed, I could picture him raising an arm and pretending to pull the glove up to his shoulder.

"According to Spook," I said before he could go into detail, "all we need to do is push the gem into his chest or his back and it'll magically go into his body."

"Oh, that's a lot easier than inserting it rectally," Corey said.

"I'm just going to assume you're right about that," Kenny said.

"So I'm thinking we need to do this show at Bitter Sweets as soon as we can." I opened my eyes.

Corey and Kenny did that look thing, but this time I could tell it was because they were glad we'd all landed on the same page. Finally, one step in the right direction.

"If we promo it right," Kenny said, "we'll piss him off and he'll have to show up, just like at the camp. He won't be able to resist."

Something about his tone. . . "Is that a guess, or did you find something on the almighty google?" I asked.

He scoffed. "With only one laptop for all of us, it's impossible to get any real net time." For Kenny, that was like being denied access to air. "But they have a library here." He whistled. "Bro, if you decide to embrace your inner Harry Potter, you need to investigate that room."

God love Kenny.

"What did you find out?" I asked.

He turned off the water, and Corey and I followed his lead. I considered seeing if they wanted to hit the pool, but Kenny would probably feel inhibited skinny dipping with cameras, even if Nicci was the only one watching.

"Twist is what they call the undead," Kenny told us while we toweled off. "No matter how different he thinks he is because of this kid's body, he still has one foot in the grave. That always, always, *always* creates a loop. The undead obsess. So if needing to respond to our advertising caused his death, it just might drag him back to us as well."

A clearing throat echoed against the tile. What the hell?

Spook. In his trench coat with his hands in his pockets looking none too thrilled.

You know what? I was done with it.

"Look, Rufus," I said, throwing my towel on the floor. "I know you think we're just a bunch of meddling kids, but I for one am tired of waiting for the cavalry to ride in to save us. We have an idea. It may be crazy and stupid, but at least we're trying to come up with a way to actually end this instead of just killing time with all this fake training."

Kenny pulled on his boxers.

Spook raised a fist in our direction.

My brothers held position.

I raised my own hand. Foom. Brighter than ever before.

Spook turned his fist palm up and opened his fingers.

A shiny chunk of amber rested in his palm.

"This is Adam's soul," he said. "If we *can* get it into his body, we have at least a small chance something good might happen."

I shook out the fire in my hand. "You changed your mind?" I grabbed my skivvies, slipped them on then took the crystal.

"No," Spook said. "I will not drag untrained civilians into a battle I can't possibly predict. But if you're going to do it anyway, I'd rather have you trusting my help than working behind my back. Please remember that. I'm a professional. I've been doing this longer than any of you have been alive."

So. What?

"I'm a lot older than I look," he said.

"So you keep saying," I pointed out, thinking about a 1961 yearbook I'd assumed was a hoax. "Wait… how did you know we were talking about this? Are there cameras in here after all?"

"Maybe he's psychic," Corey said.

"No." Spook said. "And yes, but I've learned to stay out of minds. Way too much stuff I do not want to know."

"So how'd you know what we were planning?" I demanded.

"I was just getting the hot tub ready." He pointed off to one side. "All this tile echoes." He crossed his arms. "But I can forego my soak. You want to lure Twist out and try this, let's make some serious plans."

Really? Wait. Something about his expression made me nervous.

"What changed?" I asked.

He raised an eyebrow.

"Earlier, you were all about damping down my magic," I said. "Our training is bullshit, and I can tell you don't expect this routine to be ready any time soon. What changed?"

He stared me down for a few seconds. "I can't keep you out of this anymore. I wanted to, to keep you guys safe, but my team is so far away I can't even conceive it and Sister Liberata. . ." He took a deep breath. "You're right, Ethan. Everything changed today. Can I please just be a guy with cocktails and a roof with an amazing view? I need to see if you can help me figure out how to keep everyone from dying." He gestured at us.

"The three of you. You're the heart of this crew. If you understand what's at stake, the others will follow your lead."

Corey scoffed. "Bro, you had me at cocktails."

The rooftop commanded an amazing view, two stories in the air on top of a hill, and the setting sun painted the sky a deep purple and pink. Lights from downtown Austin twinkled closer than I'd have thought for a super-secret clubhouse.

I couldn't quite place us, but we had to be southwest of downtown.

Damn, I'd missed that city. Music. Theater. Dance, my God I missed the dance festivals. A lump filled my throat.

Kenny bumped my shoulder, something red and clinking with ice in his extended hand.

"Hai." I took the cocktail, and he settled in beside me.

Corey took his spot on the other side. "Bro, I see why you miss this town so much."

Huh. So much for that lump.

"It does have its perks," Spook said. He drank deeply then refilled his glass from a shaker on the bar. "I had a visit from Sister Liberata. I have bad news and worse news."

Oh. shit.

Chapter Sixteen

Retro finished digging a line that bisected the creepy circle Twist had sketched in the dirt. A few feet away, Ginger worked hard on hers. Her hair had come undone and hung around her shoulders. Even sweaty and covered in dust and dirt, she was the prettiest girl Retro had ever seen. He trotted over to help her finish her work.

The hot sun beat down on them as if it were August instead of January. Who knew? Maybe it was.

Ginger looked up as Retro set his shovel to the hard, red clay, and she smiled.

His heart skipped a beat.

When they finished that line, Retro stepped away from the circle. Did it make any more sense from a wider perspective? The whole thing stretched about twenty feet across, with a collar of zigzagging lines like a maze. Inside that ring, a smaller ring of weird symbols had been burned into the dirt with, like, lasers or something that'd shot out of Twist's hands.

A star sat at each of four corners, with lines making a square around the whole thing.

Creepy.

Retro and Ginger had dug it throughout the afternoon. No water. No food. If there'd been any chance of seeing the next day, Retro would've been stoked at how many calories he'd burned off.

He shivered. He wouldn't live to see the next day. He knew it.

"What do you think it does?" Ginger asked.

"I have no idea," Retro said. "I'm afraid to even think about it."

She wiped an arm across her face. "Where do you suppose we are?"

"I have no idea." While Retro didn't have the world's best sense of time, the sun should not have crossed the sky nearly that quickly. "But I can guarantee that we're definitely not in Dumass anymore."

She smiled at him.

In an alternate universe, he'd already have kissed her.

The sound of an engine and a cloud of rising dirt captured his attention. A piece-of-shit Chevy Nova drove around the barn and parked near the other side of the circle. The engine died, and the boy with Twist inside stepped out.

"Good work, slobs." He waved a hand over the circle. The ground shimmered, and the rough lines and symbols perfected themselves instantly.

"If you could just do that, why have us dig it out in the first place?" Ginger demanded.

Retro winced. Was she about to die now?

But Twist laughed. "It's a magic thing. The sweat of your brow and all that. Makes it stronger."

"Wouldn't the sweat of your *own* brow be better?" she asked.

Retro nudged her.

"What?" she asked. "He cast a spell on me at that campground so he could have sex with me. I have a right to be mouthy."

"Be honest." Twist popped open the hood of the car. "You kinda wanted to have sex with me anyway."

Her fists clenched at her sides. "We'll never know, will we?"

Rage burned in Retro like nothing he'd ever felt. That. . . that asshole had forced her to have sex, and was. . . he had the balls to. . . damn it, what an asshole!

"*Etiam fallidis cere eamte.*" Twist waved a hand over the engine block. For a moment, the car glowed yellow.

The evil ten-year-old walked into the circle, pulling a metal stake out of a pocket. He stopped, held the stake up and threw it at the ground. "*Exerci.*" The stake planted itself halfway into the dirt. Twist tossed another one. "*Exerci.*" The stake buried itself into the ground in the trench Retro had dug.

Ginger gasped.

Retro looked up.

A silvery line drew itself in the dirt from the car like a snake.

Retro sniffed. His dad worked in a garage and something smelled like welding. Melted metal. The line of liquid metal snaked into the trench and spread throughout the maze Retro and Ginger had dug.

Twist drove two more stakes into the ground in the other half of the circle. What the heck?

"The cool thing about magic in the modern age," Twist said. "Shit like steel is a lot easier to come by. This spell is so much better with steel, isn't it, Mr. Bunny?"

Okay, that stuff freaked Retro. Every now and again Twist would talk to an invisible someone he called Mr. Bunny. What the heck was that?

The steel poured out of the engine block and wound its way into the trenches. As much as it creeped Retro completely, it looked pretty darn cool.

After a few minutes, the process ended and the whole. . . *thing*. . . the drawing had been filled with metal, which also encased the stakes Twist had driven into the ground.

"*Ubique nostrud id mel,*" Twist said.

The design glowed bright, hot orange for a moment, then cooled.

"Come here." Twist waved a hand and something grabbed the front of Retro's shirt, dragging him forward until he stood between two of the stakes. "Down boy." An invisible something pushed on his shoulder, forcing him to kneel.

Twist clicked a handcuff around Retro's wrist and secured the other cuff through holes in the stakes. Retro knelt in the circle, unable to pull himself free. Twist secured Retro's other wrist as well.

Then he repeated the process with Ginger.

So they would be part of a spell? That couldn't be good.

Retro looked across at Ginger.

Her face showed her own fear. "Kid?" she said. "If I had it to do again, we so would have made it together. You're a sweetie."

Somehow, that didn't help.

Twist moved out of the circle and unbuttoned his shirt. "I wonder how long it'll take for her to show up." He pulled off the shirt, kicked off his shoes and stripped naked. Leaving his clothes folded neatly in the dirt, he stepped into the center of the circle and held up the pocket watch he'd stolen from the nun.

Retro pulled against the cuffs, but he was going nowhere.

Twist muttered in that weird magicky language, closed his eyes and held his arms away from his body. Wind swirled the red, red dust.

Twist muttered some more and sparks like electricity skittered across the metal of the design. The wind swirled into a whirlwind and the sparks grew into lightning, grounding on the circle of metal.

"David!" a woman's voice shrieked. The woman who'd tricked Retro. The blonde. Mary. "What the hell are you doing?"

"I'm growing up," Twist shouted.

"I told you how dangerous this would be," Mary screamed.

"Because dangerous scares me so much, you stupid bitch!"

Oh damn. Was this going to get ugly? Although. . . if they fought, that could only help. Right?

Lights flickered around the metal circle. A column of light rose from it to the clouds above. The lightning grounded on Twist. His body convulsed.

Mary strode forward but couldn't cross the glowing circle of metal.

"That witch in the desert," Twist shouted over the howling wind. "She was a Cloak. She had a whole chapter on you."

Twist's head rocked back.

And he grew up.

"You have no idea what you're doing!" Mary shouted.

Twist screamed. His body grew taller, his muscles grew larger, hair sprouted where hair usually sprouted. He screamed again, high pitched and agonized. The sound cracked, warbled and then dropped an octave.

A huge bolt of lightning struck him.

Thunder crashed.

"Mother fucking hell!" Twist fell forward onto his hands and knees. Steam rose from his body. It was the steaming that scared Retro.

"Oh, wow. . ." Ginger breathed. "Fuck everything I ever knew."

Twist reached adulthood. Black hair. Dark skin. At least six feet tall. More.

Except, why had Retro felt nothing? If Twist needed him and Ginger for this spell to work, why had that entire growth sequence touched Retro not at all?

Twist rose to his full height. Whoa. New body off balance. He glanced down. Score! Nice package. Bigger. Every dude's best-case scenario.

Mary stood outside the circle, open-mouthed. Idiot.

He felt her attempts to penetrate his barriers and let them drop with a shudder so she'd think she'd breached his defenses.

He stopped the pocket watch but palmed it into a fist so she might not notice.

She hurried into the circle and seemed to have no idea what he planned. "I told you how dangerous it would be to do this," she whined, stopping so close he could smell her desire for his new body.

Fuck that.

He punched a hole into her abdomen.

"Oh?" She shuddered. "You've seen one too many episodes of *Once upon a Time* if you think you can steal my heart that easily."

Twist smirked. "Who said I was stealing anything?" He withdrew his hand and wiggled his bloody, empty fingers. "I was delivering a present." He took a step back, well, stumbled a step. This body was different. Taller. When he possessed someone, he used the body's memory of how it moved.

The clock inside Mary wound itself forward.

She laughed and stared down at her stomach. "You think a toy like this can age me enough to matter? Have you no idea how old I really am?"

Twist grinned. He knew exactly how old since he'd unraveled the desert witch's book. He staggered back a few steps, out of the circle.

"None of this fancy shit was to make me age," he said. "All I had to do was twitch the watch forward to make myself an adult."

Mary's face turned to panic.

Good. He'd nailed it. The circle had made a pretty picture for his aging spell, but it was there to ground the real spell, the one to steal Mary's magic and allow the pocket watch to age her into death.

Lightning raced through the maze. A brighter column of light leapt from the ground and raped the sky.

The runty Mexican screamed. Well, stealing his soul to suck away Mary's power would likely hurt.

The redhead shrieked.

She'd been a fun lay, but shit, Twist had needs.

Mary stood frozen by his magic.

Oh yeah.

Twist stepped forward. Light and darkness played festive games on the metal frame he'd made. It'd worked perfectly. She'd been so preoccupied with his aging spell, she'd never noticed that the complicated metal containment circle and the two sacrifices had been brought there to fucking kill her for as long as fucking mattered to Twist.

The circle glowed brightly. Beams of light connected Mary to the sacrifices, drawing her power away and shuttling it through the shackles and into the metal ring itself.

She aged into an old woman. Her skin blackened, turned papery and blew away. Her skeleton rattled and crumbled. As she changed, so did the sacrifices. Within moments, three piles of ash dotted the circle.

Fuck yeah! Twist stepped forward into the center of the violent ring. He held his left hand to the pile of ash on one side and a line of magic grounded him to the metal spike.

He held up his other hand to the pile of ash that had been Ginger and a stroke of energy connected him to her lifeline, as well.

Power poured into him.

"Mary mother of God!"

The power filled him.

Light and fire flared in the dark Texas night.

The lives he'd tethered to the circle blew out in a phantasmagorical explosion. And then they all sucked quickly into Twist's soul.

He gasped. Oh yeah. That felt nice.

"All right, Ethan Fox," he said. "You are so dead."

He stepped out of the circle. . . and fell on his face.

What the hell? These legs were so much longer. Twist pushed to hands and knees.

"All right, Ethan Fox," he repeated. "You are so dead. . . once I figure out how to make this body work without falling down."

Woody lay back in the hot tub and let the water wash away his tension and fatigue. If only there was some way to move into Spook's clubhouse permanently. Man, what a rough day. But at least in a good way. Every muscle in his body hurt from training with Nicci. That guy seemed like such a brainless *pendejo*, but Woody had come away knowing a hell of a lot more about how to swing a sword than he'd have guessed possible.

He also knew a thing or two about good looks getting a guy underestimated.

Some sort of club remix of Indian prayer chants played in the background. Not exactly Woody's thing but relaxing enough. He rolled his shoulders, let his feet slide apart and rested his head back on the handy headrest. If only he could talk Jem into joining him. *That* would be perfect.

Except that Kenny had a total hard-on for that hottie. And he was completely infatuated with Stereo, too. Hardly seemed fair that he got to call dibs on the only two heterosexual girls in the crib. Oh well, Kenny was sure to get laid at some point, and about time, too. Woody didn't need to be the one everyone wanted.

Voices echoed on the tile. One was a voice Woody would recognize anywhere, so it had to be Ephraim and Lizard. Sure enough, they trotted around the corner in swimsuits and t-shirts, with fluffy towels over their shoulders.

It was nice to see Effy smile like that, his arm around Lizard's waist. How far had they gotten? A room of their own, sure, but with Effy who could say what had gone down.

"Hey, *mijos.*" Woody sat up a bit. Just how awkward would this be?
Ephraim froze.

"Hey, Woody." Lizard dropped his towel and stripped off his shirt
then glanced back at Ephraim, who finally shook off his, surprise, but
stood there wringing his towel.

So. . . awkward it was then.

Lizard glanced from Woody to Ephraim and back.

Woody had no idea how to play it.

"So. . ." Lizard said, "I'm just going to go away for a while and let
y'all talk."

Smooth. Direct. Nice.

"Thanks, *ese.*" Woody sat all the way up and scooted back.

Lizard glanced at Ephraim as he left. "Thank me after y'all talk."

"Ass," Ephraim muttered but seemed almost amused.

"And a nice one it is." Lizard slid back into his shirt as he disappeared
around the corner.

So. Back to awkward.

"At least get in, *mijo,*" Woody suggested. "Otherwise it just feels like
the opening of gay porn."

Ephraim almost smiled, dropped his towel on a bench and climbed
awkwardly into the tub. The fact that he hadn't even taken off his shirt
didn't mean anything. That was just Effy.

"I like him." Woody figured small talk was a good place to start. "Y'all
fuck yet?"

Ephraim rolled his eyes. "Not everyone is a total horndog like you."

"So. . . no." Woody grinned. "I figured."

Ephraim crossed his arms. "Why, because I'm a little kid?" Only Effy
could sit in a hot tub looking like he had a stick up his ass.

Woody lay back again. Just because Ephraim was a stress case, didn't
mean he had to be.

"No, *mijo,* but if you'd actually *had* a stick up your ass," he said once
he was comfortable, "you wouldn't be sitting there with your usual
metaphor."

Ephraim smirked. "Okay, that was a good one."

"Not bad for the straight man."

Effy sat back in his best impersonation of relaxation. So the ice breaker part of the conversation had paid off.

"Look, Sam. . ." Ephraim folded his hands under the water. He shook his head. "All I have is *I'm sorry*, and that seems painfully inadequate."

Yeah. Vulnerability had never been Effy's strong suit. Well, not so much for Woody.

"I knew you were gay back in junior high when you tried to convince me that two bros hanging out watching straight porn and whacking off wasn't queer."

Effy chuckled. "What about that, exactly, gave it away?"

"How pissed off you got when it didn't work."

The smile vanished. Effy had gotten pissed off a lot over the years. He looked down at the water.

Yeah, Woody was going to have to do most of the work here. Well, that was kind of his thing, which they'd get to eventually. "I realized you were in love with me about a year ago." He settled back and brought his knees up when he started to slide under the water.

"Okay, maybe I had a crush on you, but not. . ." Effy's eyes stayed down. "In *love*."

"I walked to your place drunk as shit and you let me crash," Woody said. "I stripped naked and passed out in your bed."

"Is this because I crashed in my own damn bed when you were there?" But his cheeks burned red and not just from the hot tub.

Woody shook his head. "We'd crashed together before, that wasn't it." He leaned forward now. He really wanted Effy to understand. "You didn't touch me, I mean, we bumped shoulders and shit, but I passed out naked in bed with you, and you didn't once convince yourself a little grope wouldn't matter because I was passed out drunk. That's like, ninety percent of all gay porn and you didn't touch me." He sat back. "That's love. You kept me safe, even from yourself."

Ephraim sat there, as if unable to speak, which was the first time Woody had ever accomplished that.

"How do you know I didn't touch you?" Effy asked at last. "You passed out."

"Not at first," Woody admitted. "I faked it because I didn't want to answer a million questions about whoever I banged that night. When you climbed in with me, I was kinda nervous at first, I mean, ninety per cent of all gay porn, right?" He shrugged. "After a while, when nothing happened, I knew I could trust you." He crossed his ankles and put his hands behind his head. "And that's how I know you haven't fucked Lizard yet. You love him. It's not just sex, so you'll take things one at a time even in your own room because you, my friend, are a gentleman. . . even if you are a little bitch once in a while."

Ephraim shook his head. "And you are unbelievable." He sat back, but was he really relaxing?

Woody laughed and opened his arms wide. "It's a guy's locker room, *mijo*. Do you need the t-shirt? I've seen you naked a thousand times in gym class."

Effy blushed but he did climb out of the t-shirt, which was funny to watch because it was wet and didn't seem to want to leave the safety of his torso. "You realize. . ." he struggled to get the shirt over his head. "This is part of that ninety percent, too."

Woody laughed and splashed him.

"Do you understand why I'm such a little bitch?" He spread the t-shirt carefully on the side of the hot tub.

"You tell me." Woody saw no point in making it easy.

Ephraim leaned back, arms across his chest. Well, one step at a time.

"When we were kids," Effy said, "you were this gangly, awkward geek with zits and no chest who had asthma and got stoked over a chemistry set."

Woody grinned. "Rather like my best friend."

Effy unfolded his arms to take a little bow. "Then puberty hit you like a fucking hottie bomb, and you ditched the chemistry set and found girls. . ." He grimaced. "Like every girl in over a hundred square miles." He waved a hand at Woody. "And you had this amazing body."

"The body I worked damn hard for," Woody said. "Some of it was the genes, but I worked out every damn day."

"And that was all time you used to spend with me." Effy shrugged.

"How many times did I invite you?"

Effy scoffed and splashed him. "Because I'm the kind of guy who's going to spend all his time in a gym."

"See, that's the problem right there, Effy." He sat forward again.

"You didn't want anything to change. You wanted me to stay exactly like you, but I changed, and I don't just mean the hottie bomb. I *like* working out. It makes me feel good. I wanted to share that with you, that endorphin rush that makes a guy feel powerful, brave. I never once invited you because I felt sorry for you or because I was embarrassed that you were little. I invited you because I wanted to hang out with my best friend doing this new thing I loved."

Ephraim's face pinched up.

"And don't ask why I never said that to you before, because I did," Woody told him. "A thousand times."

Annoyance flashed across his face then faded. "So why'd you put up with me if I was such a little bitch?"

"You're my best friend, *mijo*. Have been as long as I can remember. And all the girls. . ." Okay, how to say the rest? "The big reason I'm always chasing girls is that for years, I was that awkward, scrawny guy the girls never noticed. Once they did? Damn, it was like having a new toy I wanted to play with because I kept expecting it to end. I kept expecting the girls to stop noticing." He frowned. "To be honest, I think I finally get that the hottie bomb hit. I'm not even sure I need the girls so much now. I see you and Lizard." He nodded. "Mr. Fox and Dr. Mike. Trudy and Cosita. I'd like something like that."

Effy's brow raised an inch.

Woody splashed him. "With a girl." He sighed. "The thing is, even with all those girls, there was something you had that they didn't, and I don't mean a dick."

After a moment's thought, Ephraim shook his head. "What?"

"My heart."

Effy's eyes grew wide and watered up. Then his whole face changed. Shaking his head, he rolled his eyes and snorted.

"I had you there!" Woody clapped his hands. "I *had* you!"

"You complete and total ass!" Ephraim kicked out in Woody's general direction. "And here I thought the dumb, pretty boy thing was just an act."

It was. Folks didn't like someone to be hot *and* smart. They got pissed off and jealous. Woody had done the smart, awkward thing most of his life. He'd decided a few years ago to try the hot, stupid side of it. It did get him laid.

"Every time you didn't call back," Ephraim said, "every time you showed up late or ditched me, I was certain it was the last time I'd ever see you, that you'd finally decided your new friends were cooler than me and you'd ditch me along with the chemistry set."

"New friends?" Woody slid around closer to Ephraim. "There were girls I had sex with and guys I work out with, but none of them are my friends. I may be all hot now and people like to hang out with me, but none of them wants to be my friend." He waved a hand. "Well, except the other guys on the dance team, though that's just since you and Lizard met, so it's not really germane to the conversation."

Ephraim laughed. "Germane? See, you're a closet intellectual, you ass."

Good, Woody still had a few surprises left. "I even fooled *you* with the dumb shit pretty boy thing?" He snaked an arm around Ephraim's shoulders and squeezed him.

Effy hugged him but didn't try to hang on when Woody moved away. Good sign.

"Okay, I have to ask." Ephraim stared him in the eyes now. "The porn site. Was that part of realizing you were hot and never got any attention as a kid?"

Woody shook his head. "Not even a little. The porn site was because God gave me a big dick, and I realized I could make serious coin whacking off online. I wanted a way to get out from under my parents."

"Isn't that what college is for?"

"Where do you think they're going to let me go to college?" Woody asked. "UT? They're not going to pay for any place I want to go. They're set on Baylor." Which was one of the most conservative colleges in the state.

"And financial aid is impossible when your parents make money." Ephraim sat back. "Hell of a way to make the dough, though."

Woody shrugged. "Not everyone is hung up on the naked thing, *mijo*. We all have bodies. We all get naked at least a couple of times a day. We all like to see naked people. Deep down inside, most of us like to be seen naked."

"I'm going to stop you there." Ephraim shook his head. "Not everyone is built like you."

Woody shrugged. "Did I ever wear a suit in the tank in your back forty? I never cared. Even before the muscles."

"True." Effy laughed. "My mom's face the last time she brought us Cokes." He snickered. "I have never seen her speechless before or since."

That'd been hysterical. It'd also been the last time they'd had Cokes brought out to them, so it hadn't been all good.

"I would've died of embarrassment if I'd been naked." Effy blew air through his lips.

And that was his own mom. "I guess we aren't all built the same," Woody said, "inside *or* out."

Chapter Seventeen

I stared at the sky and wished I could see a satellite.

Kenny followed my gaze then quickly looked at Spook. "So I've been googling on the one laptop we're allowed to use and this place doesn't exist on any satellites. How do you do that? They say it's just trees."

Spook didn't say a word, just wandered over to the other side of the building. A-a-a-and a parking lot. Overgrown. He waved a hand and Bessie Junior appeared along with the other cars.

We all jumped.

He waved the hand again and the cars shimmered from view.

"Will I be able to do shit like that?" I asked. The ol' flamey hand trick already seemed pretty feeble.

Spook sipped his drink. "I'm not certain. It's always hard to predict how magic will go. It rarely follows a logical path." He led us over to a patio set and sat. Five chairs circled a fire pit. "Care to do the honors?" He waved his drink from me to the logs.

Wow. Was my fire more than a light show?

I transferred my drink to my left hand.

Foom. Nope. That would never get old.

I threw it at the pit and, sure enough, the flame leapt from my hand and landed in the middle of the metal brazier. Fire blazed merrily.

"That will never get old," Corey said with a grin.

Indeed.

"Here's the thing, guys," Spook said after a moment. "There's no way I can let you lure Twist and Mary to Bitter Sweets. You saw what they did to the dance studio. It'd be the same thing with three hundred people inside."

He was right. "But we can't just sit here and wait."

"I know," he said, crossing an ankle over a knee. "That's why I invited you guys up here, to try to come up with a plan that can work."

"Shouldn't we have F-bomb, too?" Corey asked.

Spook raised an eyebrow over his cocktail.

"My dad," I explained.

Spook's bemusement dropped off his face like a stone. "No. In all likelihood, any chance worth exploring will be dangerous for Ethan. His father won't even let us entertain it."

True. Preaching to the choir on that one.

"Could we lure them here?" Corey asked.

Spook nodded. "Possibly. I could lower the defenses a little, let them see a crack."

"Mary's too smart for that," I contradicted. "Twist might jump at it, but from what I've heard I don't think she'd fall for it."

"Maybe we could trick them into going out to my farm?" Corey poured himself a second drink. "You could set up some kind of magical trap. There's no one for miles."

Kenny snapped his fingers. "Hey, what about that soul cage thing. Do both souls have to be in the same body? Could you throw the two of them into the circle together. . ."

"And they'd battle it out to see who could escape," Corey finished.

"That's nice thinking." Spook watched them over his drink.

I studied him. I could see he'd already discounted the idea but was letting us work through things on our own. Good teaching skills for such a little moody guy.

"It wouldn't work," I said.

Corey deflated.

"It's a great idea," I told him quickly. "But we just did that. They'll expect it."

"Keep going," Spook said. "It's called brainstorming. No idea is too outlandish or bizarre."

We talked and we drank. After the second cocktail, the ideas did indeed veer into the more outlandish.

The door to the roof opened and shut.

"Hey, battle planning dudes." Nicci wandered over. "May I partake in your rooftop shenanigans?" All he had on were the loose, gauzy pants he wore when teaching weapons.

"Seems a might breezy for the outfit," I said.

"I'm hot blooded." He shrugged.

"Do you mind?" Spook asked us.

We did not, so Nicci poured himself a drink and climbed into the last chair. He sat on the back with his feet on the cushion, yanking his pants up over his knees as if they were shorts. What kind of story must he have?

"Could Ethan Freddy Krueger him?" Kenny asked abruptly.

"Meaning?" Spook looked intrigued.

"Is there a way for him to take the actual soul cage into a dream and shove it into Twist's actual body?"

Wow. Could that work?

"It's an impressive thought," Spook said after a moment. "I didn't think you guys would come up with that."

"Lots of Anime," Kenny said quietly, as if embarrassed.

If that could work, we might have a real chance at eliminating at least one threat. "Is it possible?"

"Possible, yes." Spook exchanged a glance with Nicci, who sort of shrugged.

"But?" I leaned forward.

"Well, it's not the kind of thing I do a lot," Spook said. "It's dark magic. Blood magic. Since we have Katy, the body's mother, and his uncle Lizard, I might be able to. . ."

Oh, shit. Uncle Lizard. I hadn't even thought about that. That kid had had a bad month. At least he had Ephraim and a private room.

"Why black magic?" Kenny asked.

"Because I don't know a lot of *nice* people who plan to mind rape someone and then shove an object into their chest," Spook explained. "It's not really a typical good fairy kind of plan."

"Oh, come on," I said, "all four of our fairies are good and they'd approve of this plan, especially Uncle Lizard, and he's likely the nicest fairy in the bunch."

Nicci snorted his drink.

Spook raised both eyebrows. "Jesus, did you really just call them that?"

I scoffed. "Gay dad, fuck off. Okay, so doing this makes us bad guys. Fine. Are there any practical downsides?"

Spook swirled his drink. "Well, if we want to create a conduit for you to physically interact with Twist, then Twist has just as much opportunity to attack you and have it really hit. Even if the soul cage works, its effects likely won't be instantaneous. The moment Twist realizes that you can touch him, he'll probably blow you into atoms."

Blown into atoms seemed a less than stellar result.

We stared into the fire.

"Do you begin to understand why I want to wait for my team?" Spook said quietly. "If I thought we had that kind of time that's exactly what we'd do, but with the pocket watch in Twist's hands we might have a window of opportunity. It'll take him time to get used to the changes after he grows the body into an adult. In all likelihood the spell will exhaust him, too. That kind of magic takes a lot of power, and he may need a few days to recuperate, but then. . . well, then he may be more powerful than ever."

"Okay," I said. "All of our options suck. The one with the least possibility for massive death and destruction is me attacking him in my sleep."

Corey punched my arm. "Bro, we can't let you sacrifice yourself."

"Then tell me a better plan." I finished off my drink.

Nicci hopped down from his perch and refilled us.

"Maybe we just haven't thought of it." Kenny declined a third drink.

I did not. "Until we do, we should move forward with this one."

Nicci met my eyes as he poured. From the look on his face, he and Spook had known all along where we'd likely end up. The surfer seemed impressed that I'd go along with it.

What other choice did I have?

"No one other than Stereo is going to let you do this." Corey sucked down half his drink before Nicci could move. He held it out for a top off.

"Which is why we aren't going to tell anyone," I said. "Anyone."

"I don't keep secrets well," Corey pointed out.

"You didn't spill about Bessie Junior," I reminded him. "When it matters you can keep your mouth shut. And this matters. A lot."

He obviously didn't like it. Neither did Kenny.

Neither did I, for what it was worth.

"So what do we tell the others?" Kenny asked.

"We go with my original thought," Spook said. "They'll think we're taking time to perfect the routine."

"How do you get blood from Katy and Lizard without them knowing why?" I asked.

"Leave that up to me." Spook rose and nodded for Nicci to follow.

"Why did you really want to talk?" I asked, staying in my chair. "This is the plan you knew we'd end up with, so why even pretend to get our input?"

"It wasn't pretend." The way he looked at me, I knew it was important to him that I believed him. "I sincerely hoped y'all would help me come up with an idea that didn't suck so much."

"When do we go?" I asked.

"We go tomorrow." He nodded at Nicci again, but the normally carefree dude kept his perch.

"I could go with," he said, his voice much deeper than usual and, once again, had he just bulked up when I wasn't looking?

Spook sighed. So, they'd obviously already had this conversation and Spook had hoped to get Nicci off the roof before he could bring it up.

"I can go with," Nicci said to me directly. "I can watch your back and possibly provide a distraction to let you get close enough for the crystal. There's even a tiny chance I might be able to distract him long enough for you to wake up before he vaporizes you."

Wow. It seemed like a huge risk for him, but that's what these guys did, right?

Why hadn't Spook mentioned it already?

"Wait one damn second." Kenny rose and advanced on Spook. "If you can send him, you can send us, too."

Corey rose beside Kenny, determination written across his face.

Ah. So that's why Spook hadn't mentioned it. Perhaps he'd planned to offer Nicci's services when my friends weren't around.

Nicci laughed, but it sounded more like a growl. The change in demeanor astonished me. "No offense brave little dudes," he said in an amazingly deep voice that Darth Vader craved, "but you'd just trip over each other and make it worse." He grinned. Were his teeth kinda pointy all of a sudden? "This is what I do."

His eyes smoldered dark red.

So-o-o there was that then.

Needless to say, neither of my friends objected further.

Nicci hopped down from his perch and patted my shoulder. I swear to God he'd shrunk again. Damn my eyes! It's amazing how much attitude can change a man's appearance.

"Thanks, Nicci."

He followed Spook toward the door, backing away and flashing me a hang loose sign.

"Until tomorrow then," Spook said.

Once the three of us were alone, Kenny turned to me. "I'm sorry we couldn't find a better plan."

"With Nicci I might could survive," I said.

"This plan sucks," Corey said.

"Still waiting for a better one," I said.

"Bro." He frowned.

"I'm sorry." I gathered the glasses and brought them to the bar. "I don't really know how to avoid being a douchebag under the circumstances. I missed the counseling session on how to be Mr. Cool when getting ready to throw myself into a dream world to attack the vengeful spirit of a murderer trapped in the body of my ex-girlfriend's little bastard."

Shit. I leaned against the bar and hung my head.

"Sorry, Adam," I muttered. "I shouldn't have called you that."

Two hands dropped onto my back. I could tell whose was whose by the weight of each.

"Please don't say anything." I didn't move. "Anything you're going to say, I already know. And I need to just do this and not think about it too much. Twice now, someone has saved my ass when Twist wanted me dead. This time it's up to me."

I turned to face my friends and the hands dropped away.

"I was just going to ask you to move so I can get at that bottle of vodka." Corey quirked half a smile.

I snorted, grabbed the bottle and handed it to him. "I'm gonna hit the pool, guys."

"I'm in." Kenny rubbed his hands together.

"That's cool, but just this once, I can use the time on my own." I crossed my arms. "I'll bunk with y'all tonight, though, right?"

Kenny nodded, his mouth pressed in a tight line. He had to be so afraid for me.

Corey, too.

Before either of them could speak, I nodded and left them together on the roof.

They'd have to get used to helping each other through shit like this without me.

Just sayin'.

Hitting the bag felt real, solid. Gunner could just pound on it and pound on it until all the C4 drained out of his system. That's what he called the need to jump up and down on someone's face. It was like an explosive in his veins, and if he didn't drain it out, he'd fucking explode.

It was the C4 that made him beat up the weak kids. It was the C4 that made him fuck girls he didn't like or even know, when the only girl he wanted. . .

No. He pounded harder, faster. He stopped working the drills Mr. Fox had given him and just pounded the bag. He wouldn't think about her, about her fingers on his stomach, about her lips on his neck.

He hit the bag as hard as he could. "Argh!" He slammed it again and his wrist flared in pain. Whatever.

But he stopped. The gay shrink had told him to stop when it hurt, to. . . say hello to the pain or some such shit. Acknowledge. He'd said to acknowledge the pain.

Fuck. It really hurt, too. So what was the point if it just made it hurt worse? He shook out his arms. The gay shrink was on the other side of the floor working staff drills with Nicci.

Dr. Lopez. His name was Dr. Lopez. He'd already sent a memo to the state saying Gunner couldn't have killed his parents. He also told them he was in protective custody and apparently the little Mexican. . . Spook, apparently Spook had a way to forge the documents so it looked like the FBI had him.

Damn, those papers had looked real and they meant that Gunner just might not live the rest of his life behind bars. Although that hadn't been all that different from home. Regular beatings from the inner-city kids who knew their shit. Although they had nothing on Gunner's old man when it came to inflicting pain.

Dr. Lopez dropped the bamboo again. He was working on a spin drill and as soon as he turned his back to Nicci, he lost his shit.

Gunner tore off the gloves, trotted over and picked up a bamboo staff. "Dr. Lopez, I'll do it on the other side so you can still see when you turn away from Nicci."

Breathing heavy, the doc bent over to pick up his staff. "Thanks."

They set up for the exercise and ran it.

Dr. Lopez dropped his staff again.

"Dude." Gunner stood with his back to the doc and held the staff straight out in his left hand.

In the mirror, he saw that the doc just stared.

"Dude." He shook the staff, and Dr. Lopez hurried to match his stance.

Gunner passed the staff across his chest and switched hands at the sternum then extended the staff out to the right. He shifted the staff back and forth a few times like that then glanced over a shoulder. "That's all it is, yo." He did the same thing one more time then turned the staff after the hand off. "Don't start to turn it until it's in the right."

The doc tried it in place then nodded. "Let's do it."

Alrighty then.

The doc nailed it that time.

When Gunner leaned on his staff, Nicci grinned at him.

"What?" Oh shit, were they going to make a big freaking deal about it?

"That was a nice piece of teaching, not-so-grumpy, not-so-sociopath dude." Nicci made a hang loose sign.

Gunner scoffed. Why'd Nicci have to say anything? Now he just felt stupid.

"He still fights like a fag." Gunner stalked away and dropped the staff on the pile.

Damn it. He stopped.

Dr. Lopez had done so much for him when he didn't owe Gunner a God damned thing.

Gunner sucked in a few deep breaths to get the red out of his eyes. "Congrats," he said without turning. "I hear you and the big guy are engaged or some shit. So, congrats."

He went back to the bag and just wailed on it without the gloves. That shit Nicci had said. Why'd he say that?

"It's called a compliment."

Gunner jumped and spun, both fists up.

Nicci stood less than a foot away. How the fuck did he do that?

"When someone compliments you," the surfer ninja said without a trace of the beach in his voice, "you say thank you."

"What—" Gunner's knuckles had already started bleeding from hitting the bag without gloves. He shook out his hands. "Thanks."

Nicci nodded and walked away.

Chapter Eighteen

What did it say about me that water always made everything better? I stroked quickly to the middle of the pool and surfaced with a gasp. Pretty lights danced at the edge of my vision, so good thing the water only came up to my chest. The drinks had been fairly weak, but I had a bit of a buzz going on. Unless that was just, you know, all the unbelievable shit in my life.

A throat cleared behind me.

Yikes! I spun.

Jem stroked toward me from the diving well. "Sorry if I startled you," she said with a very cultured British accent. Wait. She knew English? She stopped several feet away. "I find it easier to keep to myself and just do the job if no one knows I speak English." She smiled. "As sweet as boys like Kenny can be, they are so much less distracted if they assume there's no point in hitting on me. Plus, I know he likes Stereo, despite his fanboy infatuation."

She moved closer.

"Uh. . . I'm kind of naked," I told her. "I thought I was alone."

She smiled. "Sorry. I must have been underwater when you announced yourself."

Sure, although that would've been a long time underwater. I'd called out several times.

"Is being naked a problem?" she asked. "I certainly hope not."

I glanced down. Oh!

"I understand you plan on undertaking quite the heroic task." She stood there unselfconsciously in water that only barely covered her breasts.

Could I manage to pull off unselfconscious?

Even soaking wet and without makeup, she was stunning. She wore more her performance persona and less her practice meekness.

"I hadn't really thought of it that way," I said. "There's just stuff that needs to get done and no one else to do it."

Her eyes hypnotized me. Brown with flecks of gold that glittered in the lights under the water. "That's what all heroes seem to say. . . right before they get eaten."

"To be honest, I'm trying not to think about it."

She inched closer and seemed to sniff me. "If you like, I could help you not think about it." Her hand touched my arm, and a spark made me jump. "We could even go back to pretending I don't speak English."

She caressed my arm, inched forward and raised her lips closer to mine.

I shouldn't. I didn't know anything about this girl, except that she was beautiful and had an amazing body and a sexy accent.

You know what? Fuck it.

I took her face in both hands and kissed her.

Her lips parted and her tongue lashed mine.

Wow, sexy.

Why the hell should I play the gentleman? What had it gotten me so far? If I was going to die tomorrow, I might as well make merry tonight.

Her hands grabbed my shoulders and pulled me closer.

"Stop!" Spook's voice shouted loud and angry as it rattled across the tile.

It scared the piss out of me, and I jumped back like a little kid caught with his hand in the cookie jar. But you know what? I wasn't a little kid. Not anymore.

"We're consenting adults, Spook. What's your damage?" Lights flared from the anger and the blood flow toward the little head.

Jem crossed her arms.

"Did you tell him?" Spook asked her, ice in his voice.

She set her jaw petulantly.

"Tell me what?" I asked. Did she have a boyfriend? Was the I part of Jem-N-I a husband?

"Then I think you're done here." Spook held a towel out.

Without a word, she made her way to the ladder.

"Wait a second." I followed her. "We can go back to the not-speaking-English, then you can't tell me whatever it is. . . Spook. What the hell, dude? I could fucking die tomorrow."

I stayed in the water as she reached the ladder. If I followed, I had no way to talk her back into the pool.

She pulled herself out, sparkling water drizzling like molten glass over perfect skin, her ass bunching and stretching, her boobs small and pert as she took the towel from him and covered up all that naked loveliness that she'd planned to let me enjoy.

"What the hell, Spook?" I muttered. "I could fucking *die* tomorrow."

"You should have told him," Spook said as she passed.

She turned to him, showing me her profile, hatred in her eyes. . . and she hissed. Seriously, *hissed*. Her mouth opened way too much and a snake's tongue flashed out and licked him!

Fangs! She had fangs.

And her eyes flared dark red with vertical slits. They nearly doubled in size.

Her skin rippled and turned a soft golden with faint black lines.

She raised her hands and displayed foot long black claws. She shook her head and her hair fanned out behind her like a crown or the thing lizards have that fans out behind them that I don't know—

"Fuck me!" I shrieked. I'd almost made it with that? What was it? "What the hell are you?"

She jumped and turned to me, instantly the girl she'd been before. She met my eyes and must have seen the horror there. All the anger at Spook drained out of her face, replaced by embarrassment and hurt.

She ran away.

"She should have told you she's not human," Spook said.

I climbed out of the pool, all potential wood embarrassment gone. "What the fuck was that?"

"She." He spoke very quietly now. "What the fuck is *she*. She is a person, she's just not human."

I stared at the swinging door. "If she's not human how can she be a person?" I glanced at him. "Jesus, dude, thanks for that save."

His eyes narrowed, looking kinda pissed. He held out a towel.

I took it and dried off.

"Have you not figured out that *I'm* not human?" he said. "Neither is Nicci. Few of my friends are. The nun. Billy." He made a face. "No, actually, Billy *is* human. I keep forgetting."

"Wait, what?" I wrapped the towel around my waist and backed away. "What the hell are you then?"

"Interesting place for this conversation." He met my gaze evenly. "Do you realize how many people react exactly the same way about your father when they find out he's gay? Men who've been in the locker room with him get sick to their stomach. Your father is not a man who looks gay, so the men he sees naked have no way of knowing. How violated do you suppose—?"

"That's—"

"Different?" And no, he didn't smile.

Well, it was completely different, wasn't it? Dad wasn't some kind of freaky monster.

But I'd seen it happen. Guys in the locker room. Guys after rolling with him on the mats.

In their eyes, he *was* a monster.

"No. It's exactly the same." I sighed and ran my hands over my face. I forced myself a step closer. "Look. I'm sorry. I've never met a. . . non-human person before."

"Not that you knew about anyway." Now he did smile. "And we prefer the term Unknown American."

"Okay, okay, enough with the minority subtext." Wow dizzy. It sucks when the booze runs out of your system and the night isn't over yet. I sat on a bench. "I'm an asshat. I get it. But gay men aren't dangerous. The worst they'll do is rearrange the furniture or tell you to match your leathers."

Spook sat beside me. He said nothing.

"Okay. That's not what those other people think," I admitted. Deep breath. "So my only experience with non-humans is Twist and Mary." I ran my hands through my hair. "Not all non-human people are evil? I mean, okay, I guess that makes sense, but the only two I've met want to kill me, so at least cut me a little slack." Wait a minute. "Am I still human? Does the magic mean I'm an. . . Unknown American?"

He shook his head. "Still human."

"Okay, thank God." I rolled my eyes. *Fuck*. I did it again."

He chuckled. "Actually, you've made the transition remarkably quickly." He stared at the water.

"Transition?"

He turned to look at me. "From fearing and hating us all to wanting to learn enough to rid yourself of your fear and hatred."

Okay, his point? What was he? Was it visible? Would he turn into a werewolf?

Please God not a vampire. Vampires were lame.

"Us, you said." I turned my whole body to him hoping to let him know I wasn't afraid of him. "What. . . who. . . shit, I don't even know the polite questions to ask."

"What am I?" He raised an eyebrow.

"Yes. How do I ask that?"

He furrowed his eyebrows. "So, what are you?" He relaxed and sat back, crossing his ankles.

"And?"

He unbuttoned his shirt, revealing a rather skinny chest and a tattoo of a circle and arrows over his heart. He took my hand and placed it on his sternum. And no, I didn't in any way want to pull away and scream. I felt completely at ease.

"Christ, you're cold." And he didn't have a heartbeat.

Not cold. Room temperature. Which was worse.

Seriously. No heartbeat.

I yanked my hand away.

Could I get just one week off from the life lessons? Please?

"Sorry." I replaced my hand over his unbeating heart. "Room temperature skin feels kinda. . ."

"Dead?"

"Yeah. Dead."

"I'm a zombie." He said it as if telling me he was Hispanic.

So there I sat with my hand on a zombie's chest.

"If I take my hand away," I asked, "can it please be more because I feel a little weird sitting here in a towel with my hand on your chest rather than because you're a zombie?"

Yeah. Not a sentence I ever thought would come out of my mouth in this lifetime.

Spook lifted my hand from his chest. "I actually dated Mary. In 1961."

"In Kaukauna, Wisconsin?"

"Yes. There." Of course he knew we'd found the yearbook. "I didn't know what she was, that she was a three-hundred-year-old witch who wanted to suck the life and magic out of me. When she did so, she also ripped my body to shreds and left me there held in a magic stasis so I would linger for at least a few days with my guts spread out on an altar. A man found me, one of the good guys. He put me back together and used his magic to keep my body from decay. He just wanted to give me a chance to say goodbye to my family before Mary's spell wore off and I died. He didn't realize at the time that he'd turned a corpse into a zombie."

"That's not like the *Walking Dead.*"

He buttoned up his shirt. "Different kind of zombie. Voodoo zombie, I guess you'd call me. I don't know if the *Walking Dead* kind of zombies exist. I've never met any. So no, I don't eat brains. No, I don't decay and yes, I'm dead." He raised a finger. "My body is anyway."

"Do you have a soul?" I asked.

Huh. So that's how I made him speechless.

"Was that rude?" I asked quickly. "I'm sorry. With all this talk about taking Adam's soul out of his body and stuffing Twist in, and Kenny said all undead things—people, undead *people* go hinky." I poked his arm. "You don't seem hinky."

He laughed. "Can I play that back for the rest of my team to hear?"

Oh yeah. Surveillance. Whatever. I didn't care if Nicci had seen me naked.

"I have a soul," he said. He kicked off his shoes and pulled off his socks. "My soul never died, just my body, which is about the best I've come up with to explain why I never went hinky like the undead usually do. Kenny was right about that. He's very smart, that one." He rolled up his pants and moved down to dangle his feet in the water. "Mary's magic binds my soul to the lifeless body. My friend's magic keeps me walking around and shooting off my mouth."

"Your life is very complicated." I sat beside him and dangled my feet, too.

"You have no idea."

"When I first made my hand go foom. . ." If I said it quietly, maybe I could unsay it if I needed. "I thought it meant I was evil. The only magic I'd seen was evil, and there's so much crap in movies. And on the web. It terrified me, thinking I was evil all this time and never knew it." I chuckled. "Is that stupid or what?"

"After Mary turned me," he said almost as quietly, "my parents realized I didn't have a pulse and they thought I had to be a demon or something possessing the body of their son. My dad chased me down the street with a crowbar. My brother Ross had to beat me up a few times before I believed him when he said I wasn't evil."

"I like the sound of this brother," I said. "I'd like to meet him."

"I'm afraid he died recently."

Ah hell. He'd said something about a bomb in his head, right?

He splashed the water with his feet.

He missed his friends. He missed his brother. I didn't need magic to figure that out. And I was someone who could be a new friend. It's one of those things I could just tell. We kinda clicked. And now he had to send me off to die.

How much did that suck? For both of us.

Splash. Splash.

"So. . . Do you swim?" I asked, cocking my head to one side. "Or, I don't know, will you. . ."

He snorted. "Oh my God, no. Pieces of me will not fall off in the pool and yes, I like to swim."

So I pushed him in.

No more talking. No more thinking.

Splash. Splash.

Duffle bag over one shoulder and my towel clutched against wardrobe malfunction, I headed to Kenny and Corey's room, still a bit damp and with my clothes shoved into my duffle because I'd hung out with Spook longer than I'd planned and the guys might be worried.

Katy's door stood open, but I bee-lined past it, not eager to deal with anything like emotions. I just wanted to hang with my bros and talk about video games.

"Foxtrot?" Katy called.

The best laid plans.

I stopped. "Hey there."

She leaned in the doorway and smiled. "Always playing with the boys."

I thought about commenting on my luck with girls but decided against it. Instead, I gave her time to say what she wanted.

She poked a thumb at the room behind her. "Would you come in?"

My heart beat a little faster. Probably not a good idea.

So I followed her in.

Cinnamon. My heart raced.

She closed the door and leaned against it.

She was breathing fast, quick and light.

Me, too.

So we could talk through all the bullshit and have a heartfelt conversation and maybe get into an argument.

Or I could just pretend I didn't speak English.

I dropped the duffle bag onto the floor and she met me in the middle of the room.

When we'd danced together earlier, her body had held so many memories.

The way her hands undid my towel and explored held so much promise.

But she'd just given birth, like—

"Don't ask," she said. "Spook's magic fixed everything perfectly. That's not an excuse."

I pulled her blouse over her head.

"No excuses this time."

Damn. No purple bra.

Well, the fact that she wasn't wearing a bra at all made up for it.

We dropped onto the bed.

Fortunately, she'd remembered that I wasn't an armadillo.

Afterward, we lay tangled together, sweaty and content. Her heart pounded against my side, and we took a deep breath at the exact same time. We laughed.

"I'm sorry about—"

She pressed a finger to my lips then kissed me lightly.

Okay. She was right. Not the time to talk about that.

"Foxtrot," she said between kisses. "What do I need to do to keep you from wanting to talk about anything?"

Hmm? "Well, I can recall one way that got me to shut up."

She growled hungrily and climbed aboard with a throaty chuckle.

When I woke up, several hours had passed. She was a warm, solid presence against my side, and she felt a lot like home.

Her eyes opened.

"Hey there," I said.

She smiled and rubbed a hand across my stomach.

Hmmm.

"How you doing?" I asked.

She smirked and rubbed lower.

Hmmmmmm.

Except.

"Seriously, Katy," I asked as gently as I could. "How are you doing?"

She rolled onto her back. "You and Trudy," she said. "Everyone here." She pulled the sheet up over her chest. "How do any of you think I'm doing?" She looked at me. "And just how do you think talking about any of it is going to make it better?"

Wow. I mean, she'd never been a big talker, but getting shut down like that didn't feel so good.

Her hand went to work between my legs, and she turned to face me again. "We might be dead tomorrow, Foxtrot," she said, sliding a hand behind my neck and drawing me to her. "I don't even know why Mary left me alive in the first place."

I knew. She'd been sent back to us so we'd know about Adam. So he'd be a person and not just Twist's new body. So we'd have a harder time killing him.

And Mary was right. About me anyway.

But who knew if I'd ever have Katy like this again?

Even if I survived.

Her hands grew a bit more insistent as she kissed me. "Would you rather spend the time talking about a past that can't be changed or making new memories for today?"

What the hell. Yay for the new memories.

Twist was bored.

He'd blown up all the farm animals. The farmer's wife on the next place over was far too unimaginative, even under mental influence. Once Twist had test driven his new body half a dozen times with her, he'd grown bored of her and blown her up, too. And her husband. The new body was nice. Big. Muscly.

Bored. Bored. Bored.

He jogged the perimeter of the farm with Mr. Bunny. Sex was easy since it didn't really require tons of mobility, but he wanted to be in top shape when he wiped Fox and all his little friends from the planet. The aging spell had grown the body into a pretty strong machine with an eight pack and everything, but he needed to make sure he knew how it worked. He'd kept Mary's time-speed-up spell going until just that morning so he'd had a couple of weeks to gather his strength.

He also had to get better control over his power. That'd been part of the reason for blowing up the animals, to test spells.

Well, that and blowing shit up was so much fun.

Mary had warned him about do-gooders and Cloaks. Well, the one Cloak he'd met hadn't been so tough since he'd had the desert witch's book, and Mary had given him all the information he needed for that do-gooder Spook.

A Hummer raised a trail of dust on a road in the distance.

Twist stopped to watch for a few seconds then glanced down at Mr. Bunny. "What do think? Do I have the aim yet?"

Mr. Bunny twitched his nose.

"All right then." Twist rubbed his hands together. "*Mea ignota verear constituam.*"

He lifted one bare foot.

The magic gathered throughout his body. He felt it tingle in his core.

Wait for it. Wait for it.

"Die!" He stomped his foot as hard as he could.

In the distance, a ten-foot spike of rock shoot out of the ground and pierced the truck, lifting it from the ground. Boom! It exploded.

"He shoots, he scores!" Twist made fake cheering noises. "The crowd goes wild."

Mr. Bunny zoomed circles around him then settled beside Twist.

After a moment, nothing but black smoke drifted into the air from the Hummer.

"Bored." Spook headed back to the farmhouse, scratching his chest. He didn't miss chest hair. Not one bit. "Bored, bored, bored."

Chapter Nineteen

By the time I left Katy's room, morning had arrived. The air in the hallway felt chilly considering the sweat that covered my body and soaked my hair. And I had several new memories that'd kind of surprised me.

I dashed a couple of doors down to the room I shared with Woody. Thank God he was gone. I wasn't really in the mood for hearing the shit.

I dropped my towel on the floor and grabbed a washcloth by the sink to scrub up in the room. Most likely everyone had already eaten breakfast and I needed to hurry. Big day, big day.

No idea what we'd be doing, so I pulled on jeans, a t-shirt and chucks.

The door opened and Woody entered with a bucket of shower supplies and wearing a full-length fuzzy bathrobe he'd obviously stolen from the locker room. "And where did you spend the night, young man?"

"Dude, can we avoid the teasing this morning?" I put gel in my hair and washed my hands.

"Oh wow, *ese*." He chuckled and dropped his bucket in the closet. "I just figured you'd spent the night with your boyfriends—"

"Woody!" Damn it. Too tired for jokes.

"What the heck? They call themselves that." He pretended to address someone. "Ethan? He's with his other boyfriend watching lame videos." He pretended to address someone on the other side. "Ethan? He's with his other boyfriend hitting the lame punching bag." He turned to me and shrugged.

I dropped onto a bed. "Sorry." Deep breath. "I've been saying that a lot recently. But it's true."

"You need to talk?" he asked.

Meh. More talking.

Except.

I chuckled. "Katy's the one person I really want to talk to, and she calls me a lesbian and just wants to have sex."

"I feel your pain, bro." He said it with such seriousness, pounding a fist against his chest.

"I'm an ass," I said. "I know." Deep breath.

Woody and I might not be as tight, but he probably knew a bit more about girls. . . women. "So before, when we fooled around. Afterward, we'd talk about stuff, and just, you know. . ."

"Cuddle?"

Seriously? I shook my head.

"I am not giving you shit, *ese*." He sat on the bed across from me. "*Lo entiendo.*"

"Really? You get it?"

He got this older brother look on his face. "Are you looking for me to say something here or are you just talking?"

Good question. Nope. Nothing to say. I gestured for him to go ahead.

"You love her, right?"

Did I? "I think so," I said. "Thought so. I mean, when I was there in her arms again, I felt like everything was right with the world, and not just the sex, but just being there with her felt right."

"We'll call that love," he said. "And I've seen the way she looks at you when you aren't looking. She loves you, too."

"Yeah?"

"I'd bet the condo on it." He leaned forward. "But here's the thing, back then, when the two of you basked in the afterglow snuggling, who really did the talking?"

Both of us, right? I mean, I didn't do all the talking, did I?

"I tease you about your boyfriends, but the fact is I remember that night at the camp where y'all rambled on for half an hour about *Modern*

Family versus *Modern World*." He raised a hand. "Not judging, even though I was really glad for the booze that night." He closed the robe a little tighter across his chest. "I just don't think Katy's built that way. Shit, Trudy complains that Katy won't talk about the day her mother died and Trudy was there with her."

He leaned back and crossed his ankles. "As much as you love her, Ethan, I don't think you really *know* the girl at all. Especially now. Especially after all the shit you've both gone through." Another shrug. "If you want something to work with her, you need to accept the fact that you are starting at ground zero trying to learn about her and expressing herself is likely not something she really wants to do right now."

"But why not?" I mean, with all the shit she'd been through, why wouldn't she want to talk to someone?

"*Ese*, that girl is wound up so tight, if she tries to tap into that giant knot of shit, she'll probably lose it completely." His face turned sad. "And I mean really lose it, like pretty white coat that ties in the back lose it." He waved a hand. "*En verdad?* A little time with you exercising the demons was probably the best thing for that girl last night."

Okay, I couldn't stop myself. "It was more than a little time." I think I actually blushed. "And this morning, too."

He barked a laugh and clapped. "I thought this room smelled like sex and candy. You need a shower, *ese*." Then his face turned deadly serious and that hand came back up. "And I don't care how much your *Teen Wolf* side tells you you need it, I am *not* hugging it out with you right now."

When I reached the gym, hail, hail the gang was all there, most of them at the breakfast bar. Kenny met me with a cup of steaming hot caffeine goodness and a smirk. So yay and damn all at once.

"Bro, I am so sorry for not showing up." I dropped a hand on his shoulder even before taking the coffee that was gently reciting my name like a mantra.

He held up the mug. "From the way Katy is actually smiling this morning," he said quietly, "I can assume it was for a good cause."

Thank God he wasn't mad, but Corey? I glanced around and drank.

"While you probably don't want to serenade him with the details, I expect he's fine, too." Kenny picked up his own mug and sipped. "He has Theresa back home."

Thank God for Theresa.

"So. . ." He dropped an arm around my shoulders and led me past the food, which I didn't want until later anyway. "You finally found a condom?"

I almost horked coffee. Okay, this was Kenny. "I found three."

He palmed my face and pushed me away. "I could hate you if. . ."

Yeah, never has an ellipsis born so many portents of disaster.

I circled his waist with an arm. "So we're good?" I squeezed.

"Hai."

Katy worked with the other girls in the middle of the floor. She looked up and met my eyes. She smiled. Dare I say she glowed?

I winked.

Trudy punched her hard in the arm, but Katy met my eyes again for a second and winked, too.

They went back to doing girl stuff.

Fine. All that lived in the file named Later.

"Ethan?" Kenny had his I'm-really-your-best-friend face in full force. "At some point, I do want the details and not just the graphic ones. You're good?"

What was I? You know what? If nothing else, I'd just been fantastically laid. "Yeah, I'm good."

"Hai."

"So what's going on?" I asked.

He pointed. "Spook, Nicci and Jem are trying to get the dance ball programmed, or whatever you call it. Spelled? Magicked?"

The three of them worked in the middle of the floor with a big white ball on a stick. In normal, fluorescent lighting, the magic whatsit didn't look all that interesting.

"Apparently, the way we want to flow into and out of the spell is complicated," Kenny explained.

Speaking of complicated, Jem met my eyes then pointedly turned away.

Damn.

I'd been mean to her.

I lifted my mug to Kenny. "Dude, you know I love you, but I need to talk to Jem."

He laughed. "You know she doesn't speak a word of English."

Oh. Ooops. "Well, you know what I mean. I want to double check some choreo, and I want her to pantomime it for me."

"Whatevs." He joined Mike and Lizard at the sound station.

When I made my way to the middle of the floor, three pairs of eyes met mine.

Jem looked away.

"Nicci," Spook said, "come over here and help me do this thing with the thing I told you about."

Nicci muttered but followed.

Nice.

"I'm here to apologize," I said quietly, "but can you pretend to show me some choreo so no one finds out you know English?"

She considered me for a long moment then slowly started moving through something I already had down pat. Nice.

"I am so sorry about last night," I said, following her movements. "I was a rude asshole and I'm sorry. I'd never seen anything so. . ."

She seemed keenly interested in the word I would choose.

"Magical."

She smiled.

"And I freaked out." I shrugged while dancing. "If it helps any, I did the same thing when I first made fire in my own hand."

She laughed and fell out of the choreo for a moment. She smiled and made certain her back was to everyone and that the mirrors wouldn't betray her secret. I saw her eyes do all that.

"It was as much my fault as yours," she admitted. "I should have told you, and the way you found out, when you were intoxicated and all the blood was flowing away from your brain, you were bound to be shocked."

So the part about the blood flow made me blush a bit.

She glanced at me out of the corner of her eyes. "It seems you're more inclined to your own species anyway."

"What? Does everyone know?" That would actually embarrass me.

She shook her head. "Dragons have a very keen sense of smell."

Dragon? Really?

Wait, smell? I dropped out of the choreo and took a few steps away. I really wanted that damn shower.

She repeated the move I'd missed. She repeated it again.

I jumped back into the groove.

"Dragon?" I said.

"We can shift shapes," she said. "Korean dragons are not the same as the cruel brutes that King Arthur killed off in Europe all those years ago."

Wait. That happened?

Oh. Because skepticism was really my thing these days.

I thought back to the beginning of the transformation I'd witnessed. Huh. Dragon. I couldn't tell if it was ultimately cool or totally creepy that I'd almost banged a dragon.

I pulled out of the choreo. "Again, I'm sorry." I glanced across the floor. Kenny was popping and locking with some amazing moves, but he kept stealing glimpses of Stereo and smiling, so. . . "And if you're still looking for someone to play with, Woody's bigger than me."

She chuckled and covered her mouth with a hand.

"Not something I'd admit about many guys." But Woody would definitely enjoy the fact that she was a dragon.

And I really needed a shower. After a quick bow, I trotted off with fist bumps to Woody and Ephraim as I passed. They seemed better.

And there was Dad, heading me off at the pass. Damn. I'd hoped to avoid seeing him until it was too late to change plans.

"Hey there, son," he said as I bumped through the locker room door.

"Hey, Dad." I dropped my duffle on a bench. "Can this not be an awkward conversation? Please?"

"So. . . Katy?" he asked, which was awkward, too, but a great way for me to avoid the conversation I didn't want.

"I have no idea, Dad." Hot water. Nice. Shit, forgot my shampoo. . . but it sailed through the air into my waiting hand. Go Dad.

"That's fair." He dropped his arms on the hip wall between the showers and the lockers. "So what's the real plan for Twist?"

Fu-u-u-ck!

"What? We're just. . ."

"Bullshit," Dad said. "You can't lie to me."

He was right. He was like a ninja wizard. Dad magic?

So I told him the plan while showering. At just the right moment my favorite conditioner, which I'd also forgotten to pack, appeared out of nowhere.

He let me finish my shower in silence. After I'd dried off and pulled on sweats, I couldn't take it anymore. "So when do you tell me I'm not going to do any of this?"

He dropped his hands on my shoulders. "Sit. Straddle."

So I straddled the bench facing away from him, and his hands worked on the knots in my shoulders. Jesus fish, that felt good. Dad didn't have a license as a pro but his back rubs and massages were the best ever. My whole spine turned to jelly.

"At some point, all dads need to let their sons go off into the world and make their own decisions." Whatever. As long as he kept working out my shoulders and arms. "A year ago, your biggest stress was what happened when your ridiculously expensive haircuts went wrong."

I wanted to disagree, but he was right.

"And suddenly, here you are in mortal danger." He moved to sit in front of me so he could work out my arms. "I know it's the same as parents whose kids go off to war, or folks in the Middle East who live in fear for their lives every day, but to go from my son the ballroom dancer to my son the guy who's going to attack an evil powerful witch? I really thought I'd have a bit more time to adjust."

The arm massage stopped, and he grabbed me in a tight embrace.

"All I ask is you let me be there when you do it." He kissed my head. "I know I can't do more than hold your hand when you're asleep, but if that's all I get then that's what I want."

Holy crap. "You aren't going to try to stop me?"

"Would it work?"

"No."

He cupped my cheek in one meaty hand. "Then why waste my breath?"

And that scared me more than anything. That Dad would let me go through with it.

That meant it was real.

I was really going to do it.

I was going to try to kill Twist.

A shiver raced down my spine, and I pulled on a t-shirt.

But was I scared? Truly, actually scared?

Who the hell had time for that?

"I have one question," Dad asked.

Considering how much he wasn't objecting to the plan, I had to allow it.

"What happens when they attack us here?" he asked.

I shook my head. "We went over that last night. There's no way they'd attack us here."

He squeezed my shoulder. "My entire adult life has been spent in fight strategy."

He was right. I nodded.

"I have an idea, if you're willing to entertain it." He patted the shoulder. "But we'll need Kenny and Corey on board." His eyes actually twinkled. "And you shouldn't tell Spook."

As if by magic, my two best friends appeared from around the corner. "How did. . ."

"I took liberties." Dad shrugged. "This is the best place to avoid surveillance."

Gunner jumped to his feet at the knock on his door. He snatched up his jeans, but no one barged in. What the hell? Ding, dong, ditch? He slipped into his jeans and pulled on a t-shirt, then opened the door to see—

Mr. Fox?

"Hey, Gunner." He stood there. Was he waiting for an invitation or something? What the hell? "Can I come in and talk to you a second?" He *was* waiting for an invitation. Weird. He raised an eyebrow.

"Oh, yeah. Sorry." Gunner jumped out of the way. "People don't normally. . ." wait for the invite, but that sounded gay. "What do you need? Am I late for something?"

Room inspection? But no, he didn't even look around at Gunner's stuff, just stopped in the middle of the room and folded his arms.

"I have a job for you." He always met Gunner's eyes so steady, it was kind of freaky.

"Time for me to start earning my keep cleaning the toilets?"

"Nothing like that," Mr. Fox said. "You know the gist of the trouble we're in, right?"

Gunner shrugged. "Fucking Twist is back as a ghost and found himself a bitch—" Shit, he wasn't used to giving a shit what anyone thought about him. "A girlfriend with even stronger mojo than him. We're pretty much screwed if we leave here."

"Close enough. There's one more thing, though. He's found a way to steal Katy's son, to. . ." He shrugged. "I don't really get how this works either, but he's in this Adam kid now, and it's likely he found a way to make the kid a grown up. You hear about that?"

Gunner nodded. One more dude Katy had messed up.

Mr. Fox pulled a gun out of the back of his pants.

What the shit? Gunner backed up with his hands in the air, stumbled against the bed and sat down hard. Was he finally going to do Gunner for beating on his son?

Fox held the gun by the barrel. "Relax, Gunner. If I wanted to kill you, you think I'd need this?"

As much as Gunner hated the idea, it was true. And he'd panicked like a little girl, damn it. He pushed to his feet. "So why you have a piece?" He crossed his arms. You could do a lot of damage pistol whipping someone without firing a shot.

"It's for you." Fox held the gun out, grip first.

Gunner reached for it.

Fox pulled it back. "If you agree to help out with Twist."

Gunner shrugged. "Already killed him once."

Mr. Fox seemed nervous all of a sudden. "I don't like asking this of you, but everyone else keeps talking about Katy's son, about Adam. But you. . ."

And suddenly it made sense. "But I'm a sociopath who won't care about a little kid." Damn it, why did it suck so much to know what the big fag really thought?

Fox scoffed, though. "It's nothing like that."

"No?" Gunner stepped into his face. "Then why aren't you handing that piece over to your kid, to Mr. Hero?"

"Ethan has his own job," Mr. Fox said. "So do Kenny and Corey. I'm trying to cover all my bases, and, outside Spook and most likely Nicci, you're the best shot in the building."

Gunner backed up a step. Mr. Fox was including *him* in some big plan? *Gunner*? But he'd fuck it up. He always fucked up. He shook his head.

"I don't know when we're going to get hit," Mr. Fox said, "but Spook has a plan to send Ethan into Twist's dreams to kill him. If it doesn't work, he'll storm the castle with a vengeance." He held the gun out again. "I need someone I trust to see Twist, to know that even if it looks like Katy's boy all grown up, that thing in him will kill every last one of us in here if it isn't put down."

Gunner took the gun.

"If Spook's plan does work," Mr. Fox added, "then Mary'll be the one after us."

Gunner cocked it. Checked the clip. It was fully loaded, so he snapped it back into place and sighted at the fire alarm on the wall. Seemed true. He dropped the gun to his side and met Mr. Fox's gaze. "Who knows that you just handed me a loaded gun?"

"You do."

And no one else?

"These witches are psychic," Mr. Fox said. "The more people who know the plan, the more likely Twist is to find out."

Gunner shoved the gun into the back of his pants. "We ain't supposed to lie, Mr. Fox, or is that just a rule for the sociopath?"

Mr. Fox crossed his arms. "If Mike or Spook. . . Hell, anyone out there finds out I gave you that gun, I am in a world of trouble." He sort of grimaced. "Mike would most likely dump me."

That was the truth. And Mr. Fox trusted him that much? He could hardly believe it.

"Why don't you hate me?" Gunner asked.

"You seem to be trying," Mr. Fox said. "You really seem to be trying. And to be honest, even if I did hate you, we're not in a situation where I can let that matter. My boy is walking into a whole world of danger and there's not a damn thing I can do to protect him or stop him."

"This dream thing," Gunner asked, "it can kill. . . Ethan?"

"Even if it works, there's a good chance Ethan goes down with Twist, yes."

Gunner yanked the gun out of his pants and looked it over. So Mr. Fox was doing this, putting a gun in the hands of the one guy everyone agreed was no good, to protect his son. He was risking everything for his kid. Gunner couldn't wrap his head around that, no matter how hard he tried. Is that what being a dad was *supposed* to be?

He sighted the gun on the wall again. "You think this'll actually hurt Twist?"

Fox shrugged. "It might just turn him back into a ghost and with Adam out of the way, no one will hesitate to end Twist by any means necessary."

They were all so big into honesty? "Why not do it yourself?" Gunner asked. "You must know how to shoot a gun. You really want me to believe this isn't just because I'm already a murderer, and you figure I won't give a shit about blowing someone away?"

"I'm a murderer, too, son," Mr. Fox said.

Oh yeah. Gunner had forgotten about that.

"Do you give a shit about blowing someone away?" Mr. Fox asked.

Did he? Not in this case, not really. "But aren't you supposed to be helping me overcome my evil ways?"

"Right now, you could sit in this room whacking off to your heart's content and leave the rest of us to die," Fox said. "Or you can step up and try to save people who don't give a shit about you, because they matter to someone who does. Maybe I'm lying to myself but that sounds like a step in the right direction."

Gunner smiled. "Anything to save your boy, right, Mr. Fox?" He put the gun away again.

"There are two reasons I don't do this myself." Fox moved around Gunner to the door. "One is that you're a better shot. I'm sure of it. The second is that those people see *me* haul out that pistol and blow that kid away, they'll freak out and Twist gets extra time to regroup." He stopped at Gunner's shoulder.

Please God, don't let him hug him or pat his shoulder or something gay like that.

"It's not because I think you're a sociopath," Mr. Fox said. "It's because everyone else does, and I happen to think they're wrong."

He left. No hug, thank God. Although a pat on the shoulder might not have been so bad.

Christ, was *he* turning gay now?

Kenny knocked on Stereo's door, his hand shaking so much the sound was almost a rattle. He took a deep breath but didn't feel any calmer. What if she laughed at him? What if she thought he was pathetic? More frightening, what if she said yes?

The door opened. Stereo smiled. That was a good sign.

"Can I. . . can I talk to you a minute?" he asked, his voice barely more than a whisper.

Her brow furrowed, and she moved aside so he could enter the room. "Are you okay?" she asked.

"Yeah. Fine." His voice cracked.

She took his hands. "Christ, Kenny, you're shaking. What's wrong?"

"I'm just a little n-nervous," he said. All right, he had to get it under control.

"Come here," she said, leading him to the bed. "Sit down. Talk to me."

"I really like you," he blurted out.

She smiled. "I like you, too."

Well, so did Corey but that wasn't the point, was it?

"I mean, I *like* like you," he said. "A lot."

She squeezed his hands. "Kenny, you don't need to be nervous about that. I *like* like you, too. I'd have thought the make-out session told you that."

"And I think you're really pretty." Holy Naruto, where was this coming from?

Her brow furrowed again. "Okay, would you just tell me what's going on? That's a little creepy when you say it like that."

Kenny sucked in a deep, ragged breath. "There's this plan we have," he said. "A way that just might work to get rid of Twist, but if anything goes south, I'll likely end up dead."

Wow, saying it out loud made it even scarier.

"Who's we?" she asked.

"Me. Ethan. Corey. But the plan is his dad's, and it makes a lot of sense."

And it did, if Kenny didn't freeze at the last second and ruin everything.

"Did you want to tell me about the plan?" she asked. "To see what I think?"

"That's not why I'm here." Kenny squeezed her hand and rubbed it with his other hand. "I'm here because. . ." But the words wouldn't come out. "Because. . ."

What if she laughed? He was such a damn little kid. Someone like Woody wouldn't even be shaking unless he thought it would get him sympathy points. Of course, Woody wouldn't be here trying to ask this particular question either.

"Kenny? Because why?"

Damn, his mind always wandered. He focused on her eyes. They were so deep. Everything about her was deep, and kind of dark, and so much more mature than him. And seriously freaking hot.

"I wanted to ask you something," he whispered.

She took both of his hands. "Ask me anything you want. The worst I can do is say no."

Or laugh at him.

"If this plan goes south," he said again, trying for momentum. "If it goes wrong, I could end up dead. . ." Okay he couldn't say it looking into her eyes. He looked at the floor. "And I don't want to die a virgin."

Oh God, when he said it out loud like that, he sounded like the most pathetic piece of crap on the planet. His body shook so hard it hurt. Wait for the laughter. Wait for it.

"Kenny."

Wait for the laughter.

"Kenny," she said quietly. Her hand touched his chin, lifted it. "Look at me."

He looked up.

God, she was so amazing. Every time he looked at her his chest hurt. She didn't laugh. She caressed his cheek. She smiled.

She leaned forward and kissed him gently then pulled back.

Was this going to be the kind and polite let down then, instead of the cruel laughing rejection?

She patted his hand and rose.

What, was she just going to walk away and leave him there?

"I'm sorry," he blurted, jumping to his feet. "I'm just kind of scared and a total dork about this stuff. I shouldn't have asked. . . I shouldn't have said. . ."

"Kenny," she said. "Hush." She looked at him with one eyebrow raised. "I just thought I should probably lock the door."

Chapter Twenty

Using the dance ball created complications. We could only use it when the whole crew danced the same moves, so we had to learn how to slide into and out of its control. None of the partnered swing could be magicked because leads and follows danced different parts.

Spook and Nicci demonstrated. Nicci ran through martial arts kata because that was his thing. Spook stepped in behind him and gently moved his limbs the way I'd seen sparkly fairy dust move my friends in Bitter Sweets.

"At times, you'll feel a suggestion like this." Spook moved Nicci's arms then rotated his torso. "And sometimes, you'll be on your own." He released Nicci and let him do his own thing.

"In the end," Spook said facing us, "you can always pull out of the dance ball choreo. It's all voluntary. We made this one much softer than the traditional sets at the club."

He glanced my way, as if remembering my nearly dislocated shoulder. "In the club, they need to be fairly strong to help the know-nothings. With you guys, we can use a lot more finesse." He patted the glowing orb. "Who wants to go viral?"

We all set up for the first run through.

Wow. We sucked.

The swing went well enough, but as soon as the dance balls kicked in, everyone stumbled. Of course, I wasn't in the least distracted by the beautiful girl with whom I'd just had sex for the first three times and had no idea where the future lay. Nope. No distraction there.

Okay. We set up for another run through. I caught Spook by an arm. "Any chance we can up the control of the spell? My friends are all free thinkers. They'll fight it on choreo they actually know, try to do it themselves."

He grimaced. "They'll have to really concentrate then to make the spell release for the. . . other stuff, whatever you're calling it."

"Let's try that," I said. "Let's go for having to work to release the spell."

Spook raised his hands in the air and waved them around as if he just didn't care then he nodded at me.

"5-6-7-8!"

The music jumped in and we hit the swing like pros. No worries there. Thirty seconds of pure genius and the music changed, hit a dubstep beat. We all breathed deeply to let the spell control our bodies.

Rose petals fell from the ceiling like a soft, velvety rain.

What the hell? Who would've planned that?

No one. Not any of us.

Fuck me senseless.

I tried to pull out of the choreo, but the gentle nudge of the dance ball had turned into a vicelike grip.

Smoke poured from the center of the floor, smelling of cinnamon.

No! God damn it, no! Not so soon!

A tall, dark figure rose out of the smoke. Hispanic. Built like a god in black leather pants and nothing else, he reached out to the dance ball. Black lightning arced from his fingers to the sphere then jumped from the sphere to each of us. No matter that I wanted to jump out of the way, I had to keep dancing.

When it hit me, I swear to God I felt my soul try to leave my body.

Such pain. Everyone screamed.

And the roof exploded. Boom! Blew completely off the building.

The guy, it had to be Twist, he held a hand out to Spook who flew into the air and slammed into the wall, cracking the cinder blocks. Twist held out his other hand and Nicci crashed into another wall.

Dad? He and Mike slammed into each other then fell behind the sound equipment.

For a moment, Nicci broke free. He dropped to the floor and charged with a roar. His skin turned red and enormous horns grew out of his head.

His bare chest scintillated ruby and black, and fire exploded from his eyes. His hair billowed black behind him and he grew at least six inches taller and God alone knew how much broader across.

He screamed and his black, angry teeth had been filed into points. Holy flying fuck! This was the surfer dude who didn't much like wearing pants?

Then blue fire hit him. It surrounded Nicci, picked him up and glued him to the wall.

And the music danced us all.

I couldn't stop, moved through the choreo like a freaking puppet.

Dad had been right. As usual.

Twist strode to the middle of the floor like a rock star. "Spook, you piece of rotten flesh, let's start with you!"

Spook's shirt ripped from his body. A blood red line drew itself from his hairline to his belt. . . and parted. The skin on either side of his sternum slowly ripped away, revealing the bare muscle beneath.

"Oh no," Spook said with far more blasé attitude than I'd have imagined possible, "not again."

"No one fucks the women I fuck," Twist shouted.

"I bet Mary would have something to say about that," Spook said.

"She's not here is she?" He gazed up at Spook.

"I gathered." Spooks blasé attitude while his flesh crawled away from his bones amazed me. "If she were here, I'd be naked and not just shirtless."

"Yeah," Twist said. "I've seen enough dudes' junk to last a lifetime." He pointed up at the crucifix Spook on the wall. "Mary won't be making an appearance. I killed the bitch, which was more than you could do, you limp-dicked little asshole."

Spook's face, as bloody and muscle-hewn as it was, found a way to blanch. "You. . . killed her?" Something in his voice told me just how screwed we had to be.

"Took all her power, too!" He turned a circle with his arms out. "Does it suit me?"

Jem strode forward. She hadn't been included in the dance ball since she had to keep control to sing. She barreled down on Twist, raising her arms, which turned into wings.

Her neck stretched forward, she leapt into the air. . .

. . .and became a dragon. A real-and-for-true dragon. Her long sinuous body rattled with golden scales. Her wings beat the air with a vengeance—

Then Twist raised his hands.

A yellow glow enveloped the dragon.

Twist brought his fists together and she flustered in midair.

He pulled his fists apart and the dragon spilt in two.

Orange blood poured out of her middle as he cast aside both halves of her body like so much garbage. They dropped from the air and landed in opposite corners of the gym.

Holy shit, we were so screwed.

I kept dancing because I had no choice.

He stepped up to Katy and she stopped.

"Hello there. . . *mami.*"

She stood still, hands down, face pallid.

"If you'd have just come away with me in the first place," he said. "None of this would've happened."

"No, you piece of shit!" I screamed. I fought the spell.

Spin, down, up, hit, hit.

He cupped her cheek in one hand, staring over her shoulder at me.

She twisted her face away from his. Tears ran down her cheeks.

That was her boy. All grown up, he was her boy.

And his soul was in my pocket.

"Tango, Tango, Tango." He forced her to meet his eyes. "If only you'd been reasonable. If only you'd left Dumass with me. All this could have been avoided. You're still beautiful. As beautiful as you were the first day I saw you. Do you know how old you were when I first saw you?"

Lock, pop, hold and go. Damn it! If Twist kept talking, if he'd just babble on until the next swing bridge when the spell would let go then I could kill his sorry ass.

Just another few measures. Less than half a minute.

"You know," he said. "Once upon a time, you were the only girl I wanted. I thought you'd fix everything bad in my life, that you'd be the only girl I'd ever want."

She closed her eyes as he stroked her short, short hair. Then she opened them again, as if she just couldn't keep her eyes off her son, no matter who lived in his body.

God, just like Dad. No. Don't even look in that direction. Looking would just draw attention

"Now I've had dozens of women," Twist said.

I fought the spell.

Wait. Could I—

Fuck! My shoulder popped. Dislocated?

Ignore it. Keep going. I'd do it. Had to!

"I've had more sex in the past few years than I expected to have in my lifetime." He kissed her. He cupped her cheeks in both hands.

I struggled against the spell. Ugh! Would I dislocate the other shoulder? Didn't matter.

"And you know what?" Twist asked. "There's still a part of me that wants you. That thinks you might still be enough for me." He looked down at himself. "But in this body? That'd be sick and wrong, *mami*."

He grabbed her head at the chin and crown.

And twisted. Sharply.

Her eyes focused on me, wide and full of tears.

I could save her, damn it! I could!

Except her head was the wrong way round now.

Then her eyes went blank.

Dead.

No tengo Tango.

Gunshots rang out.

Gunner stalked across the floor, arm straight out at Twist.

Blam, blam, blam, blam!

But the bullets froze in midair a foot from Twist, who turned and smiled at Gunner. "Fool me once shame on me," he raised a hand. "Fool me twice? No fucking way." He pushed the hand toward Gunner, and the bullets flared yellow and shot back across the floor.

Hit square in the chest, Gunner flew at least five feet, landed in a heap and lay still.

But I felt a crack, the tiniest crack in Twist's control. Stopping bullets took energy.

I pulled at it. I poured all the anger and hatred against it. I yanked everything I had out of my soul and poured it into my limbs.

A switch in my brain flipped, and my entire body burst into flame. I wrenched myself out of the choreography, jumped Twist like a blazing lamprey and held on.

His eyes opened wide and he froze. "That's not possible."

It bought me two seconds to pull the amber out of my pocket, grab his hair and force his head back, exposing his chest. I slammed the soul cage into his ribs.

It burned hot and painful in my hand. Fine. Let it kill me.

"What the shit?" Twist wrestled against my grip "That actually hurts, you little prick."

All the dancers dropped free of the spell.

In less than an instant, Corey jumped him. He grabbed Twist, punched him like a hundred times in half a second, then put him in an arm bar, twisted the arm and kicked into it with one knee. The arm broke soundly.

Twist screamed

Yeah, baby.

Corey spun him around so he faced Kenny, who appeared out of nowhere.

He grabbed Twist's hair and planted a pistol under his chin.

Blam!

Blam, blam!

Corey threw the body to the ground.

Kenny popped two more rounds into his chest.

Just like Dad had planned. It'd worked.

It'd actually fucking worked!

Twist didn't move.

Spook dropped to the floor, leaving a Rorschach of dark blood on the wall.

I caught Corey's eye. He nodded.

So did Kenny.

Ouch. My shoulder hurt like hell.

I tried to take a deep breath. . .

But Twist grabbed me by the neck. How the hell had he risen so fast? I couldn't breathe.

Corey and Kenny lifted from the floor, holding their own necks. Choking.

"All right, you worthless spit," Twist said. "I'm done playing with you. Now you just die."

He held me a foot from the floor by my neck as if Cory's broken bone and Kenny's bullets meant squat.

"You!" he screamed. "You die *now!*"

I was so fucked. Which was fine if it saved my friends.

The lights lit up in my peripheral vision.

Then something changed.

Twist's grip loosened. His scowl softened.

For a second, he stared deeply into my eyes, tilting his head one way and the other. Tears welled up, and he set me on my feet, stroked my neck as if he wanted to wipe away the damage.

For one second, his hand on my neck felt kind.

Then he recoiled in horror. "What the fuck was that?"

It was Adam. Deep inside, Adam didn't want to hurt me.

"No, no, no, no, no. . ." Twist shouted. "This is my body now. *Mine,* God damn it!" He pounded his own chest. "I worked for years for this. Years! You had it for two weeks, you fucking seed."

He spun on the spot, sweeping his arms.

A massive circle of fire built up around him and exploded out in a sphere.

Everyone ducked and covered, but it passed harmlessly over us and dissipated at the edges of the room.

"No! Fucking *no!*" Twist glared at me with hatred burning red in his eyes. "All right, Fox, you win this round, but I'll find a way to get this fucking fetus out of me and send it to the deepest pit of Hell itself where it can join its bitch of a mother. And, when I do? Each and every God damn one of you will die!"

He shrieked so loudly half of the lights exploded.

The sparks swirled around him, and he vanished.

Corey fell to Tango's side. Oh hell, he'd lost so much already.

I felt. . . nothing. Everyone and everything moved a million miles away, unable to touch me.

Kenny talked at me, and I knew it should matter, but I couldn't get the words to make sense.

Nicci, back to long-haired hippy dude, scooped Gunner into his arms and ran off with his bullet-riddled body. Had his attack been the distraction I'd needed to break free? Regardless, it'd been a ballsy, selfless move.

I knelt beside Spook, who sat leaning against the wall in a puddle of blood. I could see his ribcage. I shouldn't be able to see that sort of thing, should I? I watched the muscles in his eyes move as he looked at me. Could I do anything to help him?

He grabbed my hand. "First of all, I never in a million years would have predicted that Twist could steal Mary's power. I've fought her more than once. The amount of power he has now? I couldn't even begin to calculate it." He squeezed my hand and nodded for me to help him to his feet. "This was a colossal failure."

"Are we dead?" I asked, pulling with my good arm.

"Most definitely." The tattoo on his chest, visible in the muscles, glowed bright golden, and his skin crawled back into place and began to knit itself together.

"Second of all. . ." He turned me around and popped my shoulder back into place. "What the cheese was that quarterback sneak you did that almost got all three of you killed?"

"If he'd been the guy you told us he was," I said. "It would've worked."

He held my gaze then nodded. "I'll give you that."

Corey stood with Katy cradled in his arms like a baby.

Dad knelt beside Mike holding a wadded-up shirt against Mike's head. His eyes met mine.

"I'm fine," I said. "Go wherever Nicci took Gunner. Get Mike fixed. I'm fine."

I bet Dad had never once felt torn like that before today.

"Go," I insisted, then looked away before I lost it.

Everyone else seemed alive.

Except for the large, golden dragon in two pieces.

And Tango.

A lump grew in my throat, and I looked up.

At the sky.

"Your roof's gone." I laughed.

"And so is your last chance to handle this your way," a woman said. The nun. Sister Liberata. "If you don't get this miscreant under control, we'll do it for you."

"It's fine," Spook said. "We'll handle it. Now that I know what we're dealing with, I have a plan."

"You'd better." She looked at the destruction around us.

"Why don't you just handle him now?" Kenny stalked into her face. "If you can wipe a city off the map, can't you wipe one Godforsaken lunatic off the globe?"

"No." Her eyes softened. "Because it's too easy for us to do so."

"What the hell does that even mean?" Kenny demanded.

"We could wipe Twist off the globe, yes, but where do we stop?" She pointed at Spook. "There have been a number of times I've wanted to wipe him off the globe, but he's also saved the entire planet on more than one occasion." She lowered her arm and fixed me with a rather unfriendly stare. "And Ethan Fox. . . bad things happen around you, Ethan Fox, far above the national average. To one way of thinking, I might be doing everyone you know a favor by simply wiping you out here and now."

It was what Stereo had said. People who touched me died.

Both of the women I'd touched last night proved her point.

Nope. I didn't feel any of it, though. It was all too much to feel. I guess maybe I understood Katy, at last. After a certain point, there was just way too much to feel.

Liberata stared at Kenny. "But I don't end him because even I answer to a higher authority. We don't shoot the criminals before they commit the crime. We just pick up the pieces after they do."

"On the one hand, sure, that makes sense." Kenny didn't back down in the least from her glare. "On the other, it also sounds like a justification. Like a prime directive for non-interference that lets you walk away from something like this. . ." He waved a hand. "And still sleep at night."

She smiled. "I assure you Kenny Valentino. I do not sleep well at night."

She walked away and faded into the shadows.

Weeping surrounded me. I blocked it out and turned to Spook. "Do you really have a new plan?"

"Hell no." He crossed his arms as if not thrilled with playing leader with no shirt. "I just didn't want her to cut her losses and wipe Austin from the globe."

"Like, the entire city?" Woody asked.

"If that's what it takes to contain the damage?" He looked us over. "Yes."

"What about your team?" Woody asked. "You haven't heard from them?"

He looked up at the sky. "If *that* didn't bring them back immediately, for all I know they're dead." His face showed just how much it had cost him to admit that. "We need to leave. Someplace less populated. . . where no one can get hurt but us."

"I have the place," Corey said quietly.

"Where?" Spook asked.

"The place where all this started, where my mom shot him the first time." His voice was so quiet. "Back in Dumass. My farm."

Some damn thing beeped loud enough that Gunner couldn't sleep. Fucking alarm? He'd find it and smash it. He opened his eyes. Bright fucking lights.

"What the hell?" He blinked to focus. Hospital bed but the room was open to the night sky. He tried to sit up, but a strong hand held him down.

"Whoa there, beat to shit dude." Nicci stood over him. "You're safe." He shrugged. "For now." The big goofball wore hospital scrubs covered in blood with his hair pulled back in a bun. "You took a bunch of metal to the chest, but I think we got most of it."

We? Gunner looked around. Some red-headed dude stood by a sink washing up. He was covered in more blood than Nicci.

"All that red was in me?" Gunner asked.

"It most certainly was." Nicci released Gunner's arm and took a step back. "We weren't sure you had enough left to, you know, live."

Clouds boiled past overhead. "What happened to the roof?"

"Tcha." Nicci looked up. "Evil dude took the roof off the clubhouse. Made saving your life a lot harder to do."

"What happened to Spook's healing magic?"

The redhead moved closer. "What healing magic? He can maybe jumpstart a heart, but that's just an electrical charge. He can't—"

Nicci nudged him. "And this is Pete. He helped me dig all the bullets out of you."

"He looks more like a cop than a doctor."

Nicci laughed and the cop scowled.

"Nailed it." Nicci laughed. "But he saved your life so don't hold his lame job against him."

Pete crossed his arms. "I'll have you know—"

Nicci nudged him again. "And then you'll have him *know,* too."

Pete scowled more. Seemed like his face was one permanent scowl. He walked away.

Nicci bent over Gunner. "And what do we say when total strangers save our damn lives, even if they are cops?"

Seriously? Life lessons in a hospital bed. Fine. "Thank you, Officer Pete, for saving my damn life."

The cop turned, nodded once then went back to washing up. Under the scrubs, he wore a black uniform. Absolute cop clothes.

Wait a minute, the last thing Gunner remembered Twist had everyone strung up like piñatas.

"Everyone else?" Gunner asked. "Mr. Fox?"

"Mr. Fox is fine." Nicci crossed his arms and lost the surfer attitude. "You saw what happened to Katy. She's gone. So is the singing dragon chick. Ethan got the soul cage into Twist, and the kid's spirit slowed him down enough he split. No other casualties."

Katy. Dead. That sucked. For so many reasons.

"How's Corey?" Gunner tried to sit up, but Nicci held him down again. "He's gotta be wrecked. I need to—" Pain shot through his entire body. "Fuck." He lay back.

"You need to lay here awhile." Nicci looked up. "The explosion took out our best equipment so it'll be awhile before we can move you."

"What if Twist comes back?" Not that Gunner was all that afraid of that asshat or of death.

"Hopefully he thinks you're dead. A-a-nd. . ." He smiled and bobbed his head up and down a lot. "My guess is after the last little smack down from the Three Stooges, he's not that pissed off at you anymore, shot-up grumpy dude."

Gunner chuckled. Of all the God damn things. The Stooges? He closed his eyes. All of a sudden, he felt dead tired. "What happened to sociopath dude?"

"Sociopath dudes don't let themselves get filled full of metal trying to save their friends, shot-up grumpy dude."

"Pft. Friends?" He started to drift. "Maybe Corey." And maybe Mr. Fox. . . and, well, Nicci was still right here. "And you."

But the rest of them? Meh, they could suck it.

Part III

How does a story actually end without the main character dying?

Chapter Twenty-one

"Kenny? Kenny wait up." Stereo called.

Kenny's pulse jumped. One foot on the bottom step of Corey's porch, he closed his eyes and ran through a thousand different things she might want to say. Their time together had been. . . amazing, probably the most amazing thing that'd ever happened in the history of the universe. And now would he have to go back to being that guy who just wanted her?

"Hey." She stopped on the opposite side of the same step.

"Hey." He made himself look at her.

Her brow furrowed then her eyes opened wide. "Oh Jesus, I'm so sorry." She grabbed his arm and dragged him up the steps to the porch swing. "You must be exhausted." She pulled him onto the swing and wouldn't let go of his hand. . . not that he wished she would.

She stared into his eyes but what was she trying to see? Would she think the whole thing had been a trick?

"So. . . um, I didn't die after all."

Her eyes scanned his face, then she sucked in a little gasp. "Oh my God, Kenny." She wrapped her arms around him and held on tight, her cheek pressed to his. "We all could've died. Are you afraid I only. . . that the only reason we made love was because you thought you were going to die?" She scooted back and held his arms. "While that does win the award for the most original—and at the same time factually accurate—pickup line ever, I already wanted you."

The hell she said? "Really? But. . ."

She went back to holding his hand. "But I'm so worldly and beautiful, and you're kind of geeky and awkward?"

Kenny ran that through his head. "Actually, yeah, exactly like that." He lifted the hand she held in her own and looked at their union. "I mean, I know you said you, you know, *like* me. . . but. . ."

She kissed the back of his hand. "Okay, the whole shy and self-deprecating thing is cute and will remain so for at least another day or two but you seriously need to get over it." She leaned close to his ear and whispered. "If I dragged you off to the barn and blew you would it help you overcome the lack of confidence?"

Boing! "It sure might be worth trying." He smiled.

She chuckled and nudged him.

Holy crap, she really liked him! She was willing to have sex with him again even.

He looked down at the porch. Okay. Okay, he could get used to that.

He kissed her hand. "That was the most amazing thing ever. Was it. . . I mean. . ." Was there any way for him to find out if he'd been any good without. . . nope. He shook his head. "Ignore that. It was wonderful. That's all that matters."

She wouldn't want to run out to the barn with him if he'd been terrible.

"That's better." She squeezed his hand. "And I. . . I really wanted to talk about something else." She looked nervous for a second. Then she shook it off. "What you did back there. That's what you meant, why you thought you weren't going to survive, the way you attacked Twist."

He nodded and shrugged. "Yeah, but it was all three of us. . . and Mr. Fox planned it."

"No." She shook his hand. "Do not discount what you did. I was there. Spook was ripped apart at the seams. Nicci turned into that huge demon thing and got tossed around like a rag doll anyway. And Jem? I have no idea how to process that. Even Gunner's pistol couldn't touch him." She shook her head, eyes wide. "And you jumped right on top of him. . . you didn't hesitate. It was amazing."

His cheeks burned. "Ethan and Corey. . ."

"Ethan had magic and Corey's a freaking linebacker. He's trained to attack, but you. . ."

Kenny deflated a little. "I'm the geeky one. . ."

She squeezed his hand again. "Okay, I was wrong, the self-deprecating thing's already boring. You're the intel guy. You're the Watchtower. You're Oracle. That's your thing, and then suddenly you had this gun shoved up in his chin. You just grabbed him like you hadn't even thought about how dead you'd be if he snatched that gun out of your hand and ripped every ounce of skin off your body and made rubber bands out of your muscles."

She was right. Kenny really *hadn't* thought about that.

Oh hell, what had he been thinking?

He jumped off the swing and barely made it to the railing before puking his guts onto the lantana. Suave.

Her hand rubbed his back. "Sorry. I spout off a lot without thinking."

Kenny wiped his mouth and stood up. "Don't apologize. There really wasn't time to think about it. I mean, we had no idea it would happen that soon." He smiled. "And you know the Watchtower and Oracle?"

She smiled. "I may know jack-all about manga, but I read comic books." She grimaced. "Not the New 52. That's just shit."

Hands down the sexiest girl on the planet.

Kenny glanced over at the barn.

Stereo tapped his chin. "Not until you brush your teeth."

"What does bad breath have to do with giving me a blow job?" He tried the innocent face.

She punched his arm.

"What? You offered." Was that funny or stupid?

She slid her arm into his and dragged him toward the front door. "The reason I found you was I wanted you to know something." She stopped him at the door. "When you did that, when you attacked Twist and the three of you, well, and I guess Gunner, too, when you scared him off, two things ran through my mind. The first was that you were right what you said about Ethan."

She took both of Kenny's hands. "He was the first one there. None of us could break free in time to save Katy. There was nothing any of us could do, but he was the first one to put himself in the line of fire for the rest of us. It's not that people who touch him get hurt, it's that he's the first one there to try to save them." She squeezed Kenny's hands and smiled. "The second thing I wanted to tell you was that when you jumped in, I couldn't stop thinking, wow, this guy just jumped a supervillain to save us all." She kissed his cheek. "I'm so damn proud of you, Kenny Valentino. I just want you to know that."

Wow. Okay, hard to say which was better, the amazing sex or the huge ego stroke she'd just given him. Hm… maybe he needed to compare.

He leaned in for a kiss, but she stopped him with a finger across his lips. "Not 'til you brush," she said. "I'm serious." She slipped through the door, leaving him there in a cloud of ego and testosterone.

Ethan appeared on his way out, so Kenny stepped aside.

"Wow, do you have a boner, Casanova." Ethan walked past without slowing.

"Bro!" Kenny spun around and adjusted.

"Seriously? At least you have pants on this time." He tromped down the steps.

Kenny raced after him. "Ethan."

Ethan stopped and turned.

"You never told anyone about, you know, what you saw at the camp?" It's not that what happened before he'd met Stereo should matter, but what did he know about girls? He didn't want it to get around to her before he'd had a chance to discuss it.

Ethan winced. "Dude, not even my dad."

Okay, good. Would she even care about something like that? Would she think it was cute?

Ethan glanced from Kenny to the door and back again. He studied Kenny's face.

"What?" Kenny rubbed at his mouth. "Is there something on my face?"

"There is, you dog." Ethan looked up at the front door. "It's called a smile."

Kenny rolled his eyes and grinned, his face turning hot. "Geesh, a guy can't smile, you know, after. . ." After people had died. He should not be so happy. He was evil.

Ethan grabbed him in a rough hug and tapped his side a couple of times. "Get the smiles where you can, my friend."

Kenny jabbed back but hoped Ethan wouldn't take into some kind of roughhousing boxing thing that Kenny wouldn't know how to defend. But no. Ethan just released him.

He stood there staring at Kenny with a grin of his own.

"What?" Kenny asked.

Ethan crossed his arms. "You're going to make me ask?"

Wha-at?! How did he know? Did he know?

Ethan barked a laugh, grabbed him in one last quick hug and kissed the side of his head in that cool way he had that always made Kenny feel like part of the family because Mr. Fox did the same thing with Ethan all the time.

"Was it everything you could've hoped for?" Ethan asked.

"It was." And it really had been. Fun, hot, kind of funny at times.

"I am so sincerely happy for you, brother." Ethan said with a smile, then turned and walked off toward one of the outbuildings. "Can I get a hand with some equipment? Spook has some stuff we can do to keep Twist from killing off the rest of us, and we need paint sprayers."

Kenny couldn't move. It hit him like a two-by-four to the frontal lobe. Katy had died. Just a few hours ago, Ethan had been basking in the afterglow from marathon insane sex with the girl he'd thought was dead to him forever. And now she was. . .

How the hell was he even standing?

Kenny ran to catch up and grabbed Ethan's arm.

Ethan turned to him, his face completely blank now.

"How are you even standing?" Kenny wouldn't let go the arm.

Ethan's jaw set and he returned Kenny's clasp. All of a sudden, it was like some kind of Roman soldier hold. "When this is over," he said quietly. "I expect you to get me falling down, puking, pissing and shitting myself drunk. And I will have whatever reaction you think I should. But until Twist is gone forever, please don't ask me that again."

He shook Kenny's arm.

"Yeah. Right." Kenny squeezed Ethan's bicep.

Ethan returned the pressure, his eyes boring directly into Kenny's. "I once won state with a broken leg and swollen appendix. I was twelve."

Something in his face, in the diamond hard glint in his eyes. He needed Kenny to understand why he couldn't talk about it until they ended Twist. He seemed desperate for it.

So Kenny released the arm and headed for the shed. "Let's go win state."

Hello, Twist666. I may have an answer for you.

About fucking time. *Lay it on me, Whiteisforbitches.*

Twist had been searching message boards for hours and keeping his inner child quiet took a lot of energy. Fortunately, drinking beer seemed to distract him. Where was the blonde whose laptop he was using? He wanted another beer.

Just to make sure: you were a self-cognizant ghost who found a way to strip the soul from a fetus, implanted yourself, were born naturally then sped up the aging process with a magical item. A pocket watch, I believe. Now the original soul has been re-implanted and you want to "make it go away."

Well, you know, Bob. . .

Lol. Just making sure. The details are important.

Yeah. Yeah. What you said.

The bar told Twist that Whiteisforbitches was typing. Then it paused.

Sorry, appeared on the screen after a while. *Checking some sources. The problem is the original soul has priority. You can possess the body and shove the soul aside as in a typical spectral possession, but no matter how tightly your soul was knit into the very fabric of the host body the original soul has a deeper root. For you to own the body, as opposed to merely possessing it, you have to eject the soul another way. The original "soul cage" you described will assume you're the invader. Sorry.* ☹

Blah, blah, blah. . . that had taken too long. Now he *really* needed another beer. He snapped his fingers, and the blonde hurried into the room.

"Get me a beer," he told her.

Sorry, Twist typed, *I was busy being annoyed that you haven't given me any actual help.*

Because your situation is so general that the proper spell will just be laying around. You don't want my help go to Wikipedia.

Fine, fine. *Do you have an option other than the soul cage?*

I think so, but I need to know what RPG platform you're using so I get you the right one.

RPG? What the hell was that? Royal Privileged Ghosts?

RPG?

Role playing game, newb. Sounds like you're playing on a bitching complex platform where the tiniest mistake could wipe out the spell.

Game? You think this is a fucking game?

Sorry to break character, princess, but going to the message boards pretty much says you're okay with that.

Twist pounded on the keyboard. He slammed the laptop shut and pounded on the case.

He threw it across the floor and blasted it with lightning.

A fucking game!

A ball of purple plasma formed around him and exploded outward, blowing the house and everything in it to splinters. The energy drained out of him and the brat took control of his legs for a second. He stumbled and fell to his hands and knees in a five-foot-deep crater.

Well, all the rage had evaporated, anyway.

See? Mary had been convinced he had anger management issues. All he had to do was blow off a little steam and, presto, instant zen calm.

He wrenched control of his legs and rose to his feet.

He stepped over the smoking skeleton of the blonde and headed to his car.

Damn it. He'd blown all the beer to foam and the nearest store was miles away.

Well, the next farm over was bound to have beer. He was in Texas, after all.

But time was running out. All the magic he'd poured into the brat's body made it the most powerful vessel around. If he wanted to keep it, he had to find a way to get rid of the annoying parasite.

He opened the trunk and pulled out his gun belt, sliding his weapon out of its holster.

You know. . . maybe it was better to just go with what he knew.

My sprayer ran out as I met Kenny coming the other way. We joined his red line to mine and killed the equipment. Others with similar sprayers were spaced around the house and barn, completely circling Corey's place.

It was something to do. A way to keep moving and not think too much, not feel too much, especially when there was definitely way too much to feel. A way not to wonder how I hadn't heard the sound of Katy's neck cracking, not to see the spout of golden blood that'd shot out of Jem's body. A way not to deal with the fact that Gunner, the sociopath who'd once tried to kill me, lay somewhere with enough bullets in his body to drop a horse because Dad had asked him to try and save me.

Yeah, Dad had told me about that conversation.

Yet another thing to avoid feeling.

"Once upon a time," Spook said, taking the sprayers and tossing them into the back of a pickup, "we just circled everything with rock salt and herbs, but this shit can't get blown away by a pissed off ghost."

The stuff in the sprayers was a combination of salt, holy water, other anti-magic stuff and latex paint that made for a much more durable barrier than what the Winchester boys used.

The rest of the paint crew converged on our spot: Dad, Woody, Ephraim and Lizard from one direction, Trudy, Cosita and Stereo from the other. It was good to have a task to keep us busy, although I wished like hell we were making some kind of anti-Twist bomb instead of just setting up defenses yet again.

They'd worked so well before.

"There's no reason to make it any easier for him," Spook said as if reading my mind.

Wait. Was he reading my mind?

"No one needs to be psychic to read you, Ethan," Trudy said. "You wear every little thought on your perfect Ken doll face."

Well, not all of them.

Trudy lost her smile, so maybe she'd been right after all.

I looked into the bed of the pickup. "So what else can we do? You have a ghost killing sprayer too?"

No one made a Ghostbusters' joke.

"Not without killing Adam as well," Spook said.

"That needs to be an option," Dad said.

Hard to tell what everyone thought about that, but lots of muttering happened.

"Come on, people," Trudy added. "Tell me any of you believes that if he's the casualty who actually ends all this, we shouldn't take the shot."

"I agree," I said quickly. "Gunner had the right idea." I glanced at Dad, who didn't react.

Trudy nodded.

"I'd prefer it if we make sure that a kill shot takes Twist with it." Spook closed the back of the pickup and brushed his hands. "Just shooting the body in the head may leave Twist free to wreak more and more havoc. We saw how well it worked out for our resident sociopath."

"Don't call him that," I snapped, surprising even myself.

Spook raised an eyebrow.

"Okay, he is a sociopath, maybe, still. . ." I floundered. "But he's trying to change, and if we keep calling him that, even as a joke, we're just making it harder." I exchanged a glance with Corey. "Anything we can do to keep him from hurting someone else is a good thing."

Corey nodded.

"Point taken." Spook strode closer to the red circle. "Now that Mary is out of the picture, any restraint on Twist's part is unlikely. Which means the Cloaks are as much of a danger as Twist."

I strode to the edge of the red circle.

Spook raised a hand. "*Erant civibus oporteat at has.*"

An orange sparkle spread up from the ground. It rose into the air and swept away in both directions, following the line we'd painted. A wall of orange glitter curved and met in the air at the top of a dome, then simply melted away.

Spook stepped back. "Ethan, do the honors."

I raised a hand. Foom. The fireball hit an invisible wall and spread out across it, leaving a faint blue glow hanging in the air for a few seconds.

"Yeah, but Twist is a helluva lot stronger than that," Dad said.

"If nothing else," Spook said, "it should slow him down."

"And now we're on the outside." Trudy stopped with her toes at the line.

Spook stepped across. "It only works on magic. I can step through because I cast the spell. It won't stop Ethan as long as he's not actively casting magic."

"What if Twist is forced out of Adam's body and then possesses one of us?" I asked.

Spook smiled. "You have a knack for this kind of thinking." He gestured everyone inside the magic circle, which was also not a thing I'd have imagined myself ever thinking. "If Twist ends up disembodied again, he will, by definition, be repelled."

"We hope," Woody murmured.

"Does anyone know how much food we have?" Spook asked.

"Coupla days," Dad said. "Longer if we eat cow chow."

"I doubt it'll come to that." Spook stared at the house. "Twist doesn't seem to have great patience or time. If Adam is fighting him, he's in a hurry to beat that clock. If he's won against Adam, he'll be in a hurry anyway, to get his revenge. No matter how much he tries to deny it, he's nothing more than a glorified vengeful spirit."

"With all the patience of a rabid cat in heat," Woody added.

Bam! A gunshot.

Woody spun and fell.

What the hell?

More shots.

Spook's head snapped back, and he dropped like a plank.

Everyone screamed and fell to the ground, but I couldn't tell who'd been hit and who was ducking and covering.

"I don't need magic to kill you, you little shit!" Twist stood right there on the other side of the line with the same damn gun he'd used to shoot me the first time. "Fuck your magic dome!"

Bam! Bam!

Trudy screamed again.

Adam had kept Spook from strangling me. He was probably fighting him with magic while he shot at us. But would a baby understand guns?

Would he know to stop Twist or would he think it was just a complex version of peek-a-boo.

I couldn't take the chance.

Spook lay on his back. His eyes stared blankly at the sky.

No one else would die, and no way in hell would I wait for someone else to save me this time. I jumped to my feet and sprinted right at Twist, directing all my anger and pants-pissing fear into one outstretched hand.

The fact that Dad hadn't already rushed Twist meant he'd been hit.

And that was as much time as I wasted on that thought.

"You can't hit me," I screamed. "*You-can't-hit-me-you-can't-hit-me!*"

And he didn't, even though he fired round after round directly at me.

Each bullet reached a spot directly in front of me then burst into flame and vanished.

Every shot sucked energy.

"Why won't you die?!" Twist kept plugging away, his eyes wide. Anger and shock seemed at war there. He screamed and kept on shooting.

I jumped him in a flying tackle.

He dropped the gun and we rolled in the dirt.

I let him pin me.

Let his hands find my throat.

Let him shove his face so close I could smell his breath.

"You will die!" he screamed.

"Your name is Adam," I said, barely a whisper because of the hands squeezing the life out of me. "I know you're in there, and your name is Adam."

"No!" Twist screamed. He jumped off me as if pulled away by taut strings.

Someone headed in our direction.

"Leave him alone!" I shrieked, waving my hand to keep everyone back, my voice cracking and sliding like a grackle. "Don't hurt Adam. He's just a little kid."

Twist staggered and a wave of energy blasted out from him, knocking us all down. He spun in a circle and a huge black cape spread out behind him, fluttered a moment then snapped back inside.

"We won't hurt you, Adam," I shouted. "We want to help you."

Twist raised a hand and a gusher of pure white light hit me full in the chest. It lifted me from the ground and pounded me against the invisible barrier that surrounded the farm. It lifted me and slammed me again. All the air rushed out of my lungs.

A third hit and darkness flitted at the edges of my sight.

"No bad man!" Twist shouted in a completely different voice and the light changed. From a crushing hold, it became a soft embrace. It lowered me to the ground.

The cape blew up above Twist, split in two and flashed ten feet in either direction, before snapping back into Adam's body.

He staggered forward, lifted a foot and stomped it hard against the ground.

The gravel under my feet trembled.

Oh shit. Time to die.

Nothing, so I jumped and rolled.

A five-foot, pointy spike of rock thrust into the air where I had stood.

"Fight him, Adam!" I shouted as I leapt to my feet. "That body is yours!"

Black ribbons unfurled from Adam, flapped wildly then wrapped around him. They slithered around and around his limbs like insane serpents, then blasted out in a fan before wrapping him again.

"Get inside the barrier!" Spook shouted.

Wait? How was he alive?

Oh. Zombie. Never mind.

"Everyone," he shouted. "Now! If Adam gets rid of him, he'll want a new vessel to possess."

"What about Adam?" I shouted.

Black liquid fire blew out above Adam like an enormous inverse candle flame. He stood there, hands in fists, feet wide apart, a look of, well, constipation actually, on his face.

"At least duck!" Spook shouted, and I hit the dirt.

A blast of pure white light, just like the one that had nailed me to the barrier, slashed the air above me. It hit the black ribbon of Twist's ghost, or spirit or whatever, and completely severed it from Adam's body.

Two horrible screams ripped the night so loud, I got dizzy.

But I caught Adam before he hit the ground.

I half-dragged, half-carried him toward the barrier.

Spook met me just as the big guy I carried brought me to the dirt.

And then all of a sudden the dirt changed under my feet.

I looked around.

We lay inside the barrier. Adam had me kind of pinned.

The black oily ribbon battered the shield, but it only created a light show of momentary blue spots. It coalesced on the ground, a silvery version of Twist's original form.

A glowing rabbit hopped over and stood at his feet.

Really? Ghost rabbit?

Twist pounded his fist on the barrier. "I'll get in there." He pointed at Adam. "Mine!" His mouth opened huge and his whole face grew to accommodate it. Fangs dripped black oil. "MINE!"

In a whirlwind of black, oily smoke, he vanished.

I passed out.

Chapter Twenty-two

I came to and sat up abruptly, only to be forced back down by the pretty lights.

"Whoa there, Tex," Corey said, holding me down. "You're safe in your room at my house"

My room? His house?

Oh, so we'd decided to give me the room next to his that I'd used when I—

Twist! What the hell?

"Bro, chill." He held me down. "Twist took off, we're picking up the pieces."

"Help me sit up," I asked. It seemed more likely to work than trying to brush him off.

Crap my throat hurt.

He helped me up.

"Who's dead?" I asked.

Please don't let it be Dad.

"No one died. Chill."

Deep breath. Okay, no one was dead. Good step one.

"How's my dad?"

Corey's face turned pale.

I swung my legs off the bed. Fully dressed. Good.

He grabbed me again. "He's in surgery, bro. You can't see him."

"What the fuck? Surgery? Where?"

"It's a small town, and I have shitloads of money now," he said. "I called Dr. Cherkasky and told him we needed doctors out here and that a blank check would be waiting to pay for it all." He mellowed a little. "Your Dad and Ephraim, bro. They're pretty bad."

"I saw Woody get hit."

He shook his head. "Shoulder. No big deal." He sat on the bed beside me. "We live in a world now where a shoulder hit that could mean losing the use of his arm is not a big deal."

"As long as it's not the hand he uses to make money." The words fell out of my mouth before I could stop them.

Corey snorted.

Shit. Anything to keep our sanity, I guess.

I teetered at the edge of a cliff.

"My dad," I asked. "How bad is it?"

He wouldn't look at me. "Bad."

"How bad?"

"Punctured lung," he said. "Internal bleeding. Shit's ripped up, bro."

Human beings were so God damned fragile.

He was still alive, and we had magic. "How's Spook?"

Corey scoffed. "He took a slug to the head and shook it off." Another scoff. "The living should be so lucky."

"He has magic," I said. "He fixed Tango when she first came back."

But she was dead now.

Corey's eyes clouded. "He did that with things at the clubhouse that went kaput when the second story blew off."

Fuck.

"How long was I out?" I asked.

He glanced at the clock. "An hour."

I rose and only kept my feet because of Corey's arm around my waist.

"Effy?" I asked.

"Worse than your Dad. Slug to the head." He helped me out of the room. "There was so much damn blood. He's in surgery, too."

Wow. That was a lot of surgeons.

"Yeah, I know. Thank God I have a buttload of money and nobody else to spend it on." He paused us outside his room. "Look, I know this is absolute zero on your I-give-a-shit-o-meter, but Adam's been asking to see you."

"Me? By name?"

"When he woke up he started spazzing out, saying, 'Fox Bastard. Please. The Fox Bastard.'" He adjusted his grip around my waist. "I can't even imagine what it was like with Twist inside his head."

Or how long he'd been there for that matter, considering Mary's time shift thing.

"Okay," I said, trying to hobble. "Let's do it."

"Seriously?"

"If Dad's in surgery, it gives me something to do."

Hobble, hobble, hobble.

Adam sat staring out the window. He glanced up as we entered then jumped to his feet, his face concerned. He wore an old pair of Corey's bibs.

"He tore out of Twist's clothes almost immediately," Corey whispered, "and really seems to like the bibs."

Adam walked over and reached out to me, but Corey stopped him with a hand on his chest. Adam looked down then stared deeply into Corey's eyes. He glanced at the window. At the bed. Back at Corey.

"My mother spent much time here," he said quietly. "You made her happy here." He glanced at the bed. "Very happy."

Corey pulled away. "What the hell?"

Adam took the opportunity to wrap his fingers around my neck. "I hurt you again, Fox Bastard. I hurt you." My neck grew warm. Hot.

Damn hot!

I broke away and Corey had to snatch at me to keep me on my feet.

Adam held up his hands. "I'm sorry. I scared you. I'm sorry." He backed up several steps.

But my neck. It didn't hurt at all.

I snatched at Corey. "My neck. Is it bruised?"

"Holy shit. No. It's completely healed."

Adam sat heavily onto the bed, tears jumping into his eyes. "I'm sorry."

I dropped onto one knee, all pain and exhaustion forgotten. "Adam. I'm sorry. You startled me. Thank you for healing my neck." I touched his knees.

"I hurt you." He stared down. "I'm sorry."

"No," I said. "It wasn't you. It was the bad man. He did this to me."

Adam nodded. "Motherfucking asshole." He glanced up at Corey. "That's what the big retard calls him."

Oh shit.

Corey clamped down on my shoulder before I could speak.

"I know that's what the bad man called me, Adam," Corey said as calmly as could be. "But I'd like you to call me Corey."

Adam nodded. "Corey."

"Adam?" I asked, not wanting to gloss over the moment, but, yeah, I kinda did. "What you did to fix my neck, is that something you can do for other people?"

He nodded innocently. "Some."

Please God, let it be enough.

I had a million questions. How did he have magic? How did someone who was a two-week-old fetus in amber a day ago have this kind of vocabulary and ability to communicate? Why didn't he need diapers?

Because magic. Fuck you.

The three of us navigated the maze of a mansion to the waiting room for the improvised surgery.

"Is anyone watching for Twist?" I asked quietly, since everyone I knew was in the waiting room.

"Spook says he has it handled," Corey said. "I was afraid to ask."

Amen, brother.

We beelined for the surgery, and I deflected any and all questions with a finesse born of years in the spotlight. "No time to explain. Lives to save."

We pushed through.

"Keep everyone out, Corey."

He nodded and released me.

Adrenaline held me up. Also, since Adam had healed my throat, the rest of me felt better, too.

Alarms sounded. I knew that sound. It was a bad sound.

"He's coding again," someone shouted. "Get the paddles back over here."

I froze. Coding meant dead. Again made it worse.

I grabbed a strap of Adam's bibs. "Please. Don't let him die."

His eyes searched mine.

He nodded.

I released him, and he sailed into the array of doctors and nurses in the makeshift surgery.

"What are you doing in here?" someone asked, blocking the way.

I sprang forward. "Let him through, God damn it!" I shouted as loudly as humanly possible and it worked. They jumped and hesitated.

Adam snuck past and latched onto the gaping hole in my father's chest.

I saw Dad's heart. It wasn't beating.

That right there was his fucking heart. Right there. His heart.

Still. Not beating.

And those were his lungs. Not moving.

A sparkly golden glow enveloped Adam's arms. It spread over my father's chest.

People cursed and hurried away. More alarms.

Ephraim lay on the other side of the room.

"Keep Effy alive!" I shouted. "Either this works or it doesn't!"

As they rushed to help Effy, I made it to Adam's side.

"Can you fix him?" I asked.

He didn't answer. His brow knit in concentration. How the hell did he even know what was inside a human body?

"The bad man has seen inside many, many people," Adam said. "He was very good at keeping people alive for a long time."

Jesus shit. He had Twist's memories?

The exposed heart in my dad's chest twitched.

I snuffed and had to swallow. Twice. My vision blurred.

The heart twitched again then took up a steady beat. The lungs expanded and contracted.

Blood poured over Adam's hands. So much blood.

Adam's entire body glowed with gold fairy dust.

So did Dad's.

Adam brushed behind Dad's back, around his sides and across the front of his chest. Everything closed up, neat and clean, if bloody.

Adam massaged the massive muscles until all signs of open-heart surgery and bullet holes vanished. The monitors showed a steady, even heartbeat.

The golden glow faded.

Adam smiled and stepped away.

I threw myself over Dad's chest. Almost lost it

"Hey, miracle man," someone shouted. "Got one more in you?"

Ephraim. In trouble.

I grabbed Dad's hand in both of mine and turned to the second table. Oh, God. Effy looked so pale.

Adam hurried over and the doctors stepped aside. One for the history books.

Adam cupped Effy's shattered skull. He dropped his forehead all the way down until it touched the bloody, broken face. The glow came up.

Then it faded.

Adam kissed Ephraim's forehead. "He isn't here anymore." He looked at Dr. Cherkasky. "I'm sorry. He was gone before you arrived. This is just his meat."

The doctor pulled back a fist, but I let go of Dad to grab the doctor's arm.

"He doesn't know," I said. "He doesn't understand. He tried."

Ephraim was the doctor's nephew.

Someone led Dr. Cherkasky away.

Adam watched him go. "Am I bad?"

I swallowed another lump. "No, Adam. You did your best." I pushed through the doctors already gathering around Dad and took his hand again. "You did something miraculous."

"Ethan?" Oh fuck, Dad's voice almost destroyed all my barriers. I almost completely lost it. I mean, tie me with a bow behind my back lost it, but Dad was alive. I had better than most of my friends. I'd lost less. I had to keep it together.

"Hey, Dad."

"Did we win?" he asked, squeezing my hand.

I squeezed back. "You and me, Dad. We won. We grabbed the brass ring and don't let anyone tell you different."

He smiled and closed his eyes. "Differently."

Oh hell. That one almost wrecked me.

Woody ran over to Corey. "What the hell, *ese*? Why's the weirdo in there with Ethan?"

The big arms crossed over Corey's chest told Woody he wouldn't be allowed into that room, but doubt flickered across the stern face. Corey leaned close and draped an arm around Woody's shoulders. "He's some kind of healer."

Gracias a Dios! "So they'll be okay, then, right?"

"Bro." Worry filled Corey's face. "He healed a few bruises. . . what happened to Effy—"

"Shut up." Woody pulled away. He stared at the door. "There's a magic healer in there." They'd made Katy all right. "He'll fix it."

Except Katy had died.

The lump permanently lodged in Woody's throat threatened to bounce out of his mouth.

"He has to be okay," Woody whispered. "He has to."

The thing is, even with all those girls, there was something you had that they didn't, and I don't mean a dick.

Woody sniffled. No. Effy had to be all right. He was the only one Woody had left in the whole wide world. It just. . . it just wouldn't be fair.

Someone shouted inside the surgery.

The door flew open and banged against the wall.

Dr. Cherkasky rushed out, and the way Dr. Olmos held his shoulders looked like Effy's uncle was being forcibly removed.

"Let's take it outside," Olmos said.

Cherkasky's face. . .

It was like someone punched Woody in the chest. Hard.

He couldn't breathe.

He grabbed the doctor's arm. "How's Effy?" The words trickled out like a weak stutter.

Cherkasky didn't speak.

"I'm sorry, Woody." Olmos removed Woody's hand. "He didn't make it." He hurried Effy's uncle out of the house.

He didn't make it.

The words made no sense.

Didn't make what?

He wasn't in arts and crafts class.

"No." Woody turned to the surgery door, but Corey clamped down on his arm.

He jerked away. "No!" he shouted as loudly as he could.

It wasn't true.

He pushed through into the surgery.

Everyone inside turned to look at him.

Where was the bustle? Where were the panic and shouting he saw on TV doctor shows? Why were they all standing—?

One bed. . . a white sheet covered someone. Over his head. A huge red stain soaking through the sheet that must have just been laid over his face.

So much blood.

Why was the sheet over his face?

From the other bed, Mr. Fox stared at Woody.

Ethan held his hand.

The weirdo. Katy's grownup boy. Adam. He stood in the middle of the room. He took a step toward Woody.

"Fix him," Woody said firmly.

Adam's eyes opened wider.

"Fix him!" Woody pointed. "Now."

Ethan left his father's side, but Woody raised a hand to stop him.

"No. He fixed your dad. He can fix Effy."

A ball of snot threatened to hurl itself out of Woody's chest.

"Fix him!"

But Adam just shook his stupid head. "I can't."

Woody shook his head, too. "You fixed *him*." He pointed at Mr. Fox.

"It's not the same, Sam," Ethan said quietly.

"Don't call me that," Woody said just as quietly. "Effy calls me that. Only Effy gets to call me that."

The blot of red kept growing on the bright, white sheet.

"Only Effy."

No.

No.

His eyes burned. Someone punched him in the chest again.

"No."

Corey's big, stupid arm curled around Woody's shoulders.

He recoiled from the arm. "Don't fucking touch me!" It was Effy's job to comfort him, to hug him like the little brother he'd always been.

That's what Effy did.

"Woody." No idea who said it. Didn't matter.

"No." He fled the surgery. They wouldn't fix Effy.

Corey tried to grab his arm.

"Don't touch me!" He yanked the arm free, dashed full tilt through the room.

A table hit his knee.

He had to get outside. He couldn't breathe inside the house.

A lamp crashed to the floor.

He hit the patio door, slid it out of the way, ran out into the night.

Twist.

He'd killed Effy. Killed him. He'd ended the best of them. The innocent one. The smart one. The best of everything.

Dead.

Gone.

No. It wasn't fair. It didn't make sense.

Not Effy.

Woody ran.

If he ran fast enough, he'd outrun the pain. The fear.

Because now he was utterly alone.

No!

"Twist!" It came out a scream Woody didn't recognize as his own voice. "I'm going to end you, you undead motherfucker!"

He ran faster. It was something he could do.

He could find Twist.

Twist would find him.

There. A faintly glowing line.

He stepped over it.

"Come on, Twist, you chickenshit!" Woody didn't know what he'd do to the ghost, but he had to face him. He'd think of— "Twist!"

Hands on his arms.

"No!" He tugged against them, but Corey held on tight this time. "I'm going to end that bastard," Woody shouted.

Corey didn't speak, just held on and dragged him back.

The angry scream that leapt out of Woody's throat burned and scratched, but it kept the pain at bay.

For about one second.

. . there was something you had that they didn't. . .

Gone.

Dead and gone.

And only evil came back from the dead.

Woody's legs went out from under him. "No." He dropped to the ground and pounded it with both fists. "God damn you, Twist! God damn you to the deepest pit of Hell!" He struck the grass as if it were Twist's stupid face.

Corey's big arms encircled him.

No. That was Effy's job.

But Effy was gone.

No.

Dead.

No.

Effy was gone.

Forever.

Woody couldn't hold the pain away anymore.

He screamed again.

And again.

One advantage to being a ghost was the whole invisibility thing.

Twist watched the little girls cry and scream.

Wah. Wah. Wah.

Poor dead gay Jew.

But Big Fox had survived.

Huh.

Corey dragged the crybaby toward the house.

And there in the dirt where they'd scuffled. . . a break in the line.

Perfect.

"Gunner?" It was little Fox's voice. Damn it.

Gunner opened his eyes. . . what the shit? Twist in Katy's kid! Was Fox here to finish him off?

"It's not Twist," Fox said. "His name is Adam. It's not Twist."

"I get that a lot." The guy who wasn't Twist shrugged. Sounded just like a little kid.

Fox held Gunner's shoulder, holding him down. Fox. Touching Gunner.

"You're touching me." Gunner just stared at the hand.

Fox yanked away. "I didn't mean. . ."

Meh. Gunner had just been surprised that Fox would touch him. "Whatever." Let him think what he wanted.

Nicci stepped up to the other side of the bed, so Gunner was safe anyway.

"Why are you here?" Gunner asked.

"Twist shot you up pretty bad," Fox said, like it was news to Gunner somehow. "Adam can fix you. He fixed my dad."

"Your dad?" Gunner hadn't heard anything about Mr. Fox getting hurt.

"He's fine. Adam fixed him." Fox looked all surprised as if Gunner couldn't possibly care. Asshole.

"He's a standup guy, your dad, even if he's. . ." Gunner caught Nicci's glare.

"Even if he's a fag?" Fox acted smug like he was so much better than Gunner.

"Even if he's the guy who raised a douchebag like you," Gunner lied. "You call your own dad a fag? Kinda proves my point."

Nicci nodded and grinned.

Fox looked confused.

Cool on both counts.

"Can I fix him now?" Adam looked fully grown, but he sure sounded like a little kid. "You can make fun of each other later."

Nicci moved closer. "Go ahead freaky baby soul dude." He stared hard at Gunner. "He's the real thing. You can trust him."

Gunner nodded. What exactly would he do?

Adam moved close, and Fox took the hint and sat in a chair on the other side of the room.

"I need to touch you to do this," Adam said.

"Just say yes," Nicci suggested before Gunner could threaten to beat the shit out of Adam if he tried anything.

Gunner shrugged it off. "Yeah. Whatever. Nicci had his hands inside my guts to pull out the bullets. No big deal."

"I shouldn't need to put my hands in your guts." Adam pressed one hand over a bullet hole in Gunner's chest and the other over Gunner's stomach. Kinda awkward but whatever.

Gunner closed his eyes and started to just go away from it. But wait. . . "Keep your damn back turned Fox." He didn't want that fag checking him out if the sheet—damn it. Whatever. He didn't want Fox to see him.

"Not even interested," Fox said. "Playing Clumsy Ninja."

"Um. . ." Adam's hands lifted.

Gunner opened his eyes. Nothing had changed. Ah hell, Gunner didn't even get the magic healing? Typical.

"Spook is trying to teach me how to be discreet with. . . seriously personal shit not everyone needs to know." He met Gunner's eyes. "He was annoyed with me for pointing out that since he doesn't have a beating heart to pump his blood he must not be able to—"

"Your point?" Nicci asked.

Adam's eyes opened wide.

Chuckling hurt Gunner. A lot, but Fox didn't react so he must have ear buds in or something.

"I have a question to ask Gunner, and he might not want anyone to hear it." Adam looked at Nicci and the surf ninja startled and took a step away.

Gunner grabbed his arm. "Stay." Who knew what the freakshow was going to ask?

Nicci nodded and settled in. Gunner yanked his hand away, but he really wanted Nicci's opinion on any damn question he might hear.

Adam rested his hands on the bed railing. "Would you like to be able to make babies or do you like shooting blanks?" He asked it as if he wanted to know Gunner's favorite flavor of ice cream. When Gunner didn't reply right away, Adam continued. "Something very bad happened to your baby making parts. I can't tell what it was. But I can fix it if you like."

"Okay, okay. Shut up. Jesus." What kind of question was that to ask? And with Nicci right there?

Nicci scowled. Gunner had asked him to stay. Whatever.

Gunner closed his eyes and lay back. He'd known. His asshole parents had juiced his balls with electricity too many times. He'd always figured what the hell, one less stress in life. What right did he have being a dad? He'd just mess up the kid's life the way his dad had.

Like father like son, right?

A lump filled Gunner's chest. He thought about Mr. Fox. With a dad like that, maybe Gunner wouldn't have turned out. . . maybe he'd be different. He opened his eyes.

Fox sat on a stool with headphones in, playing his lame video game.

Gunner glanced at Nicci, who nodded as if he knew exactly what Gunner was thinking.

"Hey, Fox!" Gunner called out.

Fox looked over and pulled a bud out of one ear. "That was fast."

"Come here. I got a question for you." Why the hell was he asking Fox?

Fox trotted over. "Sup?"

Okay, just ask him quick before he changed his mind. "You think I'd make a good dad?"

Fox scowled. "Hell, no. You have to ask?" He glanced from face to face. "What the hell?"

Gunner closed his eyes. "You know what? Never mind. Stupid question. Go back to your game."

Fox crossed his arms. "So I'm guessing you asked that wrong. What do you really want to know?"

Why was he even doing this? Why put himself through this? He should just tell Adam to heal the gunshots and leave the rest of it.

He opened his eyes. "My folks ruined my junk, so I can't have kids. Magic man here says he can fix it." He leveled Fox with his strongest stare. That douche needed to know how important this was. "So I always assumed that was for the best because I'm the world's biggest waste of skin. But now. . . now I met your dad, and I think. . . I think maybe. . ." Once again, why was he doing this? "Maybe it would be cool to try to be like that. . . to be a dad, and if next year I'm still just a stupid juvy, I can always snip it back."

Fox stared at him a long time. "I have no idea which part of this freaks me out more." He looked up at Nicci. "You told my dad he's salvageable. That somewhere in there is someone who doesn't need to end up in and out of jail his whole life." He leaned on the rail. "You still think that?"

Nicci nodded.

"And does that extend to procreating and imposing himself on the world as a parent?" Fox stared at Nicci.

Nicci looked down at Gunner, who'd never once in his life seen that look on someone's face directed at him. Didn't even know what it meant. Then Nicci looked back up at Fox with, like, nothing in his face.

"My dad worshipped a demon and sold my soul to it," Nicci said, "leaving me as a slave forever. When I managed to crawl my way out of Hell, permanently changed into a demon myself, he was mad at me for pissing off his god." He shrugged. "What do I know from good parenting? Not everyone can be Lucky Fox."

Fox's eyes opened wide. He turned to Gunner, who shrugged. He'd had no idea about the surf ninja's past. They'd just talked about weapons and fighting.

Fox hung his head. "The worst part is that's not even the weirdest thing I've heard this week." He met Gunner's eyes. "Okay, I'm almost there. Answer me this: Twist was wandering around doing witchcraft all the way back to the beginning. When you assaulted me, was he in control or was that you? It's something I can't get out of my head."

"That was me," Gunner said without hesitating. It was a question he'd asked himself a hundred times. "Twist was in my head, sure. He gave me some kind of potion in a beer, I think, but, hell, I'd have beat the shit out of you anyway for what you did to Corey."

Fox stood up straighter. "Why do feel like you owe Corey so much. What's the damned truth between y'all? Answer me that, and I'll know whether I think you can ever be a father without completely fucking up one more life."

Gunner swallowed. Shit. Why *that*? Why did he want that answer? No. He couldn't tell him that, not him. Gunner lay back. Who cared what Fox thought anyway? Who wanted kids anyway?

"That's what I thought," Fox said with his smug voice. "All your talk about how much you respect my dad but it's just bullshit, isn't it?"

He still thought Gunner was queer for Corey? Really?

Gunner opened his eyes. "I fucked Katy."

Fox's face went completely blank. He took a step back.

Wow, first time Gunner had ever seen that douchebag unable to speak.

"Wait, you mean. . ." He moved forward again, his face turning red in anger.

"I didn't force her, you asshole." Gunner tried to sit up, but it hurt way too much. "I've done a lot of bad shit in my life, but I never once forced a girl to do something she didn't want. Not once."

Yeah, that set Fox back on his high-heeled dance shoes.

"You can't tell Corey," Gunner begged. "I gave you your damn answer, but you can't ever tell him."

"But. . ."

But she was a popular, pretty girl and Gunner was redneck trash.

"We were drunk. At a pool party. Corey was out of town. Everyone went off somewhere and all of a sudden it was just the two of us in a hot tub without a lot of clothes on." It was both the best memory of his life and the absolute worst. "It was just once, and I don't use the booze to make excuses. I did what I did and. . ." His throat caught. Oh hell, not in front of Fox. He wiped his face just in case. "Corey is the only person on this planet I give a shit about, and I fucked his girlfriend behind his back because I'm exactly the low piece of shit everyone says I am." He forced himself to look Fox in the eye.

"You were in love with her." Fox said it like it was the absolute most impossible thing he'd ever heard. "You were in love with her, too. The whole time."

The moment Corey had started dating her, Gunner had tried to push it all aside. But that night, in the hot tub, their feet had touched, and she hadn't pulled away in disgust. And so he touched her knee and she didn't pull away. So he kissed her. . . and she'd kissed him back.

"So there it is, Fox. And I know what you're thinking. You're thinking someone who would do something like that to a guy who was like his God damned brother should never be a dad."

"No." Fox's voice wasn't much more than a whisper. "That's not what I'm thinking at all." He leaned on the railing again, looking about a million years old. "You should tell him. Maybe not today, but you should tell him. He'll forgive you. Because that's the kind of guy he is. He forgave me for stealing her from him completely. He'll forgive you for one night." He met Gunner's eyes. "But not if you keep it from him now. That he won't forgive."

Fox pushed away from the bed. "That attack you did, with the gun. I'm not sure, but that may have been the difference between saving lives and Twist killing us all."

"Still afraid of being the hero?" Gunner asked. "I saw you moving before I fired a shot."

Black circles hung around Fox's eyes. "What say we share the spotlight? And Kenny and Corey. They bought time for Adam."

"We're all just a bunch of God damn heroes, I guess." Gunner lay back and closed his eyes. He still didn't have an answer to his question. Oh well. Might as well leave things as they were.

"Oh, wait." Fox dug into his jacket and pulled out something wrapped in plastic. He tossed it to Gunner. "From Corey. He says get well soon."

Three Stooges boxers bounced on the bed. Gunner turned the sob into a cough so no one would know. Fucking Corey, with his fucking presents and shit. Always. . .

Gunner coughed again.

Fox dropped a hand on Adam's shoulder. "Go ahead and fix him if he really wants it. I'll just need to make sure Dad keeps coaching him for, like, the rest of his life." He walked to the door.

Nicci took Gunner's hand but Gunner pulled it away, well, tried to pull it away. "Fag, let go." He pulled again. "Let go. I'm not like those fags. I don't want all that shit." Shit, he wasn't supposed to talk like that anymore. He'd never fucking learn.

Nicci squeezed harder, so hard it hurt. What the hell?

"Is it okay if it hurts?" Nicci asked. "Can I hold your damn hand, grumpy dude, if I hurt you?"

Corey's present slipped and fell to the floor. Damn it! Gunner reached for it. He felt his guts tearing up, but fuck it, Corey had given something to him, and he'd let it fall. He lunged for the package, had to. . . he had to show more respect to someone like Corey.

Fuck, that hurt his guts.

Nicci's hands grabbed his shoulders and forced him back.

"I dropped his God damn present!" Gunner shouted. "I fucking dropped it."

Nicci held him down, pressed him flat on the bed and Gunner couldn't move, couldn't stop him. He bucked against him, but there was no fighting it, just like a little kid, a bad little kid and any second now, the belt would start in or the paddle or the straps or the water or. . . or the pillow over his face.

"I'm sorry," he shouted. "I'm sorry I dropped it! It was an accident!"

But accidents didn't matter. Only good boys had accidents. Everything Gunner did came out of his sin, out of his evil, out of everything in him that was evil and wrong and horrible. And only the pain, only the whip and the burning fire would fix him. Nothing else.

"I'm sorry!" he screamed. If he screamed it loud enough maybe someone would hear. Maybe they'd hear how sorry he was, and they'd stop hurting him. "I'm sorry!"

He screamed. . . and he screamed. . . and he screamed.

Seizures convulsed Gunner's entire body. It was the scariest thing I had ever seen in my entire life and that's saying a lot. That son of a bitch, that sociopath screaming and crying like a baby and then just, what? He shuddered and seized and puked.

And the shit he'd shouted. I mean, I'd known his parents had abused him, but Jesus. It was like he thought Nicci was going to kill him for letting the God damn underwear hit the floor. That had been his life?

Nicci rolled him to one side so his puke wouldn't drown him.

Adam grabbed him with both hands and the glow started.

Gunner collapsed, just fell still like a puppet with its strings cut.

Thank God.

Nicci wiped off his face, checked his mouth and rolled him onto his back, pulling the sheet all the way up to his chin after noticing me.

Adam slid his hands under the sheet onto Gunner's abdomen. "He ripped himself apart again. Worse than before." He looked up at Nicci. "He had bad parents. Very bad parents."

"Yeah, freaky baby dude," Nicci sighed, wiping the back of a bloody hand over his own face. "He had really bad parents." He tucked the sheet in around Gunner's shoulders. "You got this?"

"I got this, fighter demon nurse dude." Adam frowned. "I don't think I have the hang of the nickname thing."

"But you got the healing thing down." Nicci headed in my direction. "And that's awesome."

We just sort of stared at each other a while.

"Say it," he said at last.

"I had no idea," I said. "I mean, I had an idea."

Nicci looked over a shoulder at Gunner. "But until you see it for yourself, there's just no believing is there?"

"I. . ." I tore my eyes away from Gunner. "Can I go over there?"

Nicci nodded.

I picked up the boxers, tucked them under Gunner's arm. "Can you. . . can you make sure he sees these right away when he wakes up?"

Adam nodded but didn't look up or open his eyes for that matter. He pulled the sheet down to Gunner's sternum and the gold dust floated and played in the moving air.

His chest had been ripped apart. It was a miracle he hadn't died immediately.

"What's the difference?" I asked.

Nicci appeared at my side.

"What's the difference between someone like Twist. . .?" What was I even saying? "Why do I actually care about Gunner now, but I just want Twist ended forever? What's the difference?"

"Gunner wants to be saved," Nicci said quietly but quickly. "No matter how much he protests and calls me a fag for things like this." He patted Gunner's shoulder. "He wants it. He hated you because you had what he wanted, and I don't mean Katy. I mean friends. A father who really truly loves you and isn't afraid to show it even when it embarrasses you."

"It will never, ever embarrass me again," I promised. "But what about Twist's parents, or mom or whatever? Maybe he had it just as rough."

Nicci shrugged. "Maybe even worse, but at a certain point we all have to take responsibility for our own shit. And Twist? He enjoys it, hurting people."

"So does Gunner," I pointed out. "At least he did. Who knows now?"

"Gunner liked the rush he got from feeling powerful," Nicci said. "That's close, but not quite the same. Twist? He just likes the sound people make when they scream." He shrugged. "But who the hell am I to say? I'm just a surf ninja with a skin condition once in a while."

Wait a minute. The surfer had left the building a while ago, hadn't he?

"Dude!" He gave me a big hang loose sign then settled down again. "You tell me why you care about Gunner all of a sudden."

"Why?" I leaned over and held Gunner's hand, which I would never tell him I'd done if I lived to be a thousand. "Because of the way he feels about Corey. The way he feels about Katy, which is something I will need a fifth of vodka to wrap my head around. And because, if he'd had my dad and I'd had his parents maybe I'd be him and he'd be me."

Nicci patted my shoulder. "Lesson learned."

I glanced at my shoulder. Blood. "You realize you just stained the only clean shirt I have right now?"

He laughed, hugged me tight with both arms. "And now the whole thing is stained, Vanity Fair dude." He released me, patted my chest then moved off to the sink."

I held Gunner's hand a while longer.

Chapter Twenty-three

Dad slept peacefully. I leaned in the doorway to his room, arms crossed, listening to the sound of his breath. I was so fortunate to still have him after everything. Mike sat beside the bed, holding his hand.

I left them there in peace.

We'd lost Effy, Jem and Tango. As far as we could tell, Ginger and Retro had died as well. They'd last been seen sucked into a black hole at the nun's house. Spook suspected they'd been used to help Twist steal Mary's power and kill her. Too bad the good guys couldn't slaughter innocents to kill the bad guys.

No. I didn't mean that.

I thought about Gunner. Who the hell was I to say who the bad guys were anymore?

Twist. Twist was a God damned evil thing. That was certain and I hung onto that one thought while I walked past the rooms.

Trudy sobbed in the room she shared with Cosita.

Corey muttered and rolled from side to side in his sleep.

Kenny lay with his back to the door, but I knew from the sound of his breath that he was awake. Stereo had curled up at his chest, with her face tucked under his chin. Chances were, he stayed awake just so he could remember that moment with her.

Woody and Lizard lay on their own beds, but in the same room, tranked out of their minds. With all they'd lost, Mike wondered who'd be the first to try to jump off the highest thing he could find.

We'd all lost so much. And there we were curled up at Corey's house, licking our wounds and trying not to go insane while a vengeful ghost regained his strength to attack again and kill more of the people I loved.

Deep breath.

It had to end. Somehow.

I loved these people. All of them, and I saw exactly how fortunate I was to still have each and every one of them in my life. Nothing and no one would hurt one more of them. Not if I had anything to say about it.

I ended up out back by Corey's pool, staring up at a sky full of stars. Normally, in almost any other situation, I'd have wished one of my friends would follow me, would help me figure out what the hell to do.

Not tonight. Tonight, I just wanted to be alone so I could pretend that none of it touched me, so I could figure out what to do to protect the people I had left and to put down the insane thing that wanted them all dead. As I'd said to Kenny, today I just needed to get shit done.

If by some damn miracle I lived after Twist had been put down? Well, then I'd deal with how it all felt.

"That's one of the things that makes you unique." Sister Liberata. Behind me. I recognized the voice and didn't bother to turn. "While everyone else cringes in fear and waits for the inevitable, you're out here trying to figure out what to do next."

"So what should I do next?" I turned to her.

She raised an eyebrow.

"I get the whole we must not interfere thing as much as I hate it." I hoped I wouldn't piss her off too much. "But if you're here tonight, you're here to help, so save me all the bullshit, and let's just dance."

She smiled, reached under her black robes and pulled out an enormous dagger. "You are an anomaly, Ethan Fox." The dagger glinted.

"No riddles," I said. "I have no patience. Tell me outright what you mean to say or just kill me if that pisses you off."

She raised that eyebrow and held out the dagger. "It's Lucifer's dagger. Forged for the war when he was cast out of heaven."

So. . . wow. Badass blade then.

"Twist is a ghost," I said. "This will kill a ghost?"

She looked down at me from her considerable height. "There are few weapons in this universe that can destroy a thing utterly, that can rip the soul apart and prevent it from ever reconstituting in any way whatsoever." She nodded at the blade. "This is such a weapon."

So. . . wow. Badass blade.

"It cannot cut a disembodied spirit," she told me. "It needs flesh to do its work."

"So Twist needs to possess someone?" I asked.

"Do you doubt that is his plan?"

I didn't. "Okay, cool. Badass blade and all. How do I get him to come back here so I can do this?"

She smiled. "This spell will prove more enticing than he will be able to ignore." She tossed a crumpled-up piece of paper.

I caught it. "What does that mean in English?" Stupid witches. Spanglish was easier to decipher.

"It means that if you cast this spell outside the barrier, Twist will have no choice but to appear." She turned to go.

"Wait," I said again. "Giving this to me has to violate a million creepy Cloak laws."

She stared at me. "Even the Cloaks answer to a higher authority."

"You keep saying shit like that. What does it even mean?" I demanded. "Spook knows more than me about everything, and he doesn't know what that means."

She stared at me. She took a deep breath. "Have you ever asked yourself, Ethan Fox, why you weren't asleep in your parents' apartment when that fire consumed them?"

Santa on a crack whore's sled! I'd asked myself that question a million times but had been too afraid to figure out the answer.

"I give you a dagger to defeat your current enemy," she said. "It's more than I do for ninety-nine percent of the human race. If you do this thing, all your remaining friends will live. Perhaps you could just be grateful and do something with the blade."

Smoke consumed her and she was gone.

So. . . I walked out through the gate and around the house.

The red line was visible even in the dark as a faint glowy shimmer.

Creepy.

Said the guy holding Lucifer's dagger.

Yep. There was the line. On the other side of it I could call Twist to me and have done with it.

Yep. All I had to do was step over that line.

Deep breath.

I stepped over the line.

What if I needed eye of newt or some such shit?

Damn it. Newb.

I unrumpled the paper.

Blank. Seriously? What the hell?

"Hey there, Fox," a familiar voice said.

Oh. I got it.

Wait. He stood behind me, inside the ring.

I turned. Dad? The voice was wrong. And why'd he call me Fox?

"You really thought that stupid little barrier would keep me out?" Twist's voice said from Dad's mouth. "Me?"

He'd taken Dad.

I hadn't thought that far ahead, hadn't really thought at all. If Twist needed to be in the flesh, then someone had to die with him. I mean, totally utterly die gone forever.

Not Dad.

He smiled, but all wrong. It wasn't Dad's smile.

My fist tightened on the one weapon we had that would destroy Twist utterly, but it would take Dad with it.

I couldn't do that.

Not Dad.

I'd almost lost him just a few hours ago.

Not again. Not for real. Not forever.

Twist glanced down. "Oooh, big scary knife." He waved his hands. "What is it, some kind of magic dagger?" He pulled Dad's shirt off over his head and held his arms out. "Go ahead you wuss, give me your best shot."

I pulled the dagger up and over my head, the way Nicci had shown me, switching my grip so the blade pointed at Dad.

"Go ahead!" Twist shouted.

If I killed Dad, then everyone else would be safe. No one else would die by this freak's hand. Ever.

"Do it!" he screamed.

But I couldn't. Not Dad. I couldn't kill my father.

No. Not ever.

Twist relaxed and chuckled. I doubt he knew what the dagger was. I'm sure he thought he'd be immune, that I'd end up killing Dad and he could just float free. He was completely at my mercy.

The blade twitched in my hand as I fought with myself.

Twist smiled. "I have an idea." He closed his eyes.

Then Dad opened them. I knew it the same way I'd known when Adam looked out at me in the clubhouse. They say the eyes are the windows to the soul. I knew in that moment they were right.

"Will it work?" Dad asked so calmly.

I nodded. My eyes blurred with tears.

"Really work? Everyone will be safe?"

I nodded. "Lucifer's dagger." My air sniffled out of my mouth.

I saw in his eyes that he understood, that Twist was too damn arrogant to think a simple dagger could end him. That this was my only fucking option.

"Do it, son," he said. "You know there's no other way. I love you."

He held my eyes in his.

My hand shook. "I. . . can't. . ." I adjusted my grip, held the knife up again.

I don't know how long I stood there staring into my dad's eyes, shaking, crying, snot dripping down my face.

Apparently, it was too long for Twist.

A spark jumped in Dad's eyes.

"You want something done right," Twist said with Dad's mouth, "you damn well have to do it yourself." And he jumped out.

The black oily smoke hovered between us then slammed into me.

"There's always another way," I said, all the tears gone. "I love you, too, Dad."

I plunged the dagger into my chest all the way to the hilt before Twist could take control.

Dad cried out and caught me as I fell.

Twist screamed in my mind.

He screamed and screamed and screamed.

And it hurt. Jesus Christ how it hurt. I think I screamed, too.

Then everything started to go dark. I looked up into Dad's face, but he was blurry. . . so blurry, like looking up at a 3D movie without the glasses.

Then everything faded to black.

I guess I died.

Lucky caught Ethan before he hit the ground. That huge dagger had pierced his boy all the way through. From the look of it, it'd gone right through his sternum and spine. How was that even possible?

"Ethan!" Lucky shouted. "Oh God, Ethan."

What had the boy been thinking? How could he make that decision for Lucky? *He* was the father; it was *his* job to die for his son not the other way around.

So much blood. Lucky had never seen so much blood. It was like Ethan's body was racing to empty as fast as possible, and if he pulled the dagger out, it'd be even worse. Had it gone right through his heart?

"What've you done, you stupid, stupid kid?" Spook stood over Lucky, staring down.

"Can you. . ." Lucky couldn't make his voice work right. "Can you fix him? Please tell me you can fix him."

Then Adam appeared on the ground beside Lucky. "Fox Bastard?" He grabbed the hilt of the dagger.

"Wait!" Lucky snatched at Adam's hand. It started to glow.

"I can't fix him with a giant knife sticking through him." He pulled it out.

Blood gushed from Lucky's son in a torrent. Lucky pressed his hands to the wound, trying to stop the flow of blood. The sobs returned.

Dear God, he couldn't stop the blood.

Adam moved Lucky's hands away and replaced them with his own. His hands glowed. Ethan's chest glowed.

Spook's hands took Lucky's arms. "Give him a little room."

"No." He grabbed Ethan's hand. "I'm not moving."

"Okay, okay." Spook sat beside Lucky and held one shoulder. "Can you tell me what happened? It might help us save your son."

"It was that big fucking dagger," Lucky mumbled.

"How did the dagger get all the way through your son?"

Did he think Lucky had done it? "It wasn't me. Twist took me. He brought me out here. Ethan was waiting."

"Wait. Ethan was waiting for you?" Spook's voice grew dark.

Lucky nodded. "For Twist."

Blood still flowed from Ethan's chest, but less. Was that a good thing or bad?

"Ethan had the dagger," Lucky said, "called it Lucifer's dagger."

"Deep fried drat!" Spook grabbed the discarded weapon. "How did it end up in Ethan?"

Lucky told him while Adam sat so still, pouring what looked like gold dust into Ethan's chest.

No one spoke for a while.

Spook moved away and Mike took his place, held Lucky with both arms, and Lucky leaned against Mike's shoulder, but he wouldn't take his eyes off Ethan. Ethan was always the most beautiful thing Lucky had ever seen. "He shoved a dagger into his own chest to save us."

Mike's hold tightened. It was the first time anyone had been there to help Lucky when Ethan was hurt. For eighteen years of broken bones and concussions, Lucky had been alone. Having those arms around him felt strange.

Mike kissed his head. He seemed to know that Lucky didn't want him to say anything, that he just wanted him there. It was hard to believe someone knew him like that.

"Please don't die," Lucky muttered.

Spook knelt close to Adam and whispered in his ear.

"What?" Lucky demanded.

"Nothing," Spook lied.

A father always knew that kind of lie. "Don't think I won't kick your ass."

Spook held up a hand. "I asked if Ethan was in there."

"Why?"

"When you were close to death," Spook explained calmly, "Adam could tell that your soul was still in your body. He also. . ." He looked around then shrugged. "He knew that Ephraim was already gone.'"

"So what?" Lucky demanded. "What does that have to do with Ethan?"

Spook held up the blade. "Lucifer's dagger was forged specifically to destroy a living soul completely and utterly. It's the darkest magic imaginable. So if Ethan stabbed himself with it to kill Twist, it's likely that the blade erased Ethan's soul as well."

Lucky trembled. Even with Adam there to fix Ethan's body, his soul might have been blown out of existence? What did that even mean?

"Adam?" Spook laid a hand on the young man's arm.

Adam looked at Ethan with one eye, his head cocked to the side. He switched eyes.

"Well?" Spook prompted.

Adam switched eyes again. "*Someone's* in there."

"Twist?" Spook said quickly, raising a hand.

Adam shook his head. "No. Bad man's gone."

Spook's hand lowered.

"Adam?" Lucky asked, working so damn hard not to grab him and shake him. "What the hell do you mean? Is Ethan in there, or isn't he?"

"He is and he isn't." Adam shrugged then looked back down at Ethan. "I don't understand it, but I think it's worth fixing him." He looked up at Lucky. "I don't know everything. I'm only a couple of weeks old, you big gay bastard."

The way he said it, like it was just a name and had no invective at all, Lucky couldn't be offended. "Lucky," he said. "My name's Lucky."

Adam smiled. "I like that name. Now, can I get back to fixing your son? His spine got cut in half, and I'd guess he'll want to use his legs."

Oh God.

"How does someone sever his own spine?" Mike asked.

"God damn magic," Lucky muttered.

"Magic might be the only thing that keeps your son with us," Spook said.

Lucky glared at him for a long time. "If Ethan pulls through this, I may change my mind, but I haven't seen magic do much good, and I've seen far too many good people die, too many lives ruined."

"Mr. Fox. . ." Spook waited until Lucky met his eyes. "Ethan has magic."

What could Lucky say to that? He'd love his son no matter what he did or who he was, but if he chose to pursue magic? To make it his life? Well, he'd love his son no matter what he decided, but a father didn't need to approve of every choice his son made. He just needed to love him.

Chapter Twenty-four

A voice talking, but so far away. Something about batting averages and strikeouts. Baseball stats? Oh yeah. I'd died. Apparently, Hell for me was the sports' report.

"Dad," I muttered, "I'm not in enough pain as it is? You have to read sports to me?"

"Ethan?" Paper rattled and he grabbed my hand. A chair fell over. "Are you in there?"

I opened my eyes. Shit, that hurt. Everything hurt. Worse than getting worked over by the first string.

"You look like shit," I said.

It was true. His eyes were all blood shot, and he hadn't shaved in days. Days?

"How long was I out?"

"Days," he said. "I don't know how many." And then he lost it.

Just. . . lost it, sobbing and kissing my hand, my arm.

I closed my eyes and waited for it to subside. Not that it embarrassed me or anything. I totally understood. It just hurt too much to keep my eyes open, and I wanted to give him whatever time he needed.

His sobbing finally subsided.

"Why were you reading that to me?" I asked.

"It's all Corey had laying around. I just wanted you to hear the sound of my voice. . . in case it brought you back."

"Brought me back?"

"Well, you stabbed yourself with a dagger meant to destroy your soul forever," Dad said far too matter-of-factly. "We weren't certain you were still in there. When you didn't die right away, we were a little afraid something demonic might have ridden the blade back into you.

"Wow. We live in a world where you can say that and not be making a huge joke." I tried sitting up.

Dad jumped to help. "Jesus, Ethan, you shoved a massive dagger through your gut. Maybe you should take it easy."

Jesus shit that hurt, but I made it to sitting as long as I leaned against the pillows. "See, that's another one of those sentences that shouldn't be real. I don't feel like someone who had an enormous dagger shoved through his gut."

I lifted the blanket. Barely a mark. "Whoa. How am I not a piñata?"

"Adam." Dad sat beside me, resuming his clutch of my hand. "Did his magic thing on you. Jesus, son, I've never seen that much blood ever, and Spook was afraid that when you woke up, it might not be you."

That didn't sound good. "Who might I be?"

"Some demon," he said, "or just a mindless zombie."

I winced. "I hope you didn't say it that way to Spook."

"What? Why?"

Heh. "Long story for another day."

He lifted my hand and kissed it again. Feel free to mock. You're jealous.

He explained everything that'd happened after I, well, I kinda died, but I kinda didn't. I couldn't imagine what it'd been like for him. To see me healed of a wound like that but then not knowing if I was gone anyway.

"Help me up." I needed to see my friends. I needed to see them still alive.

"Not a good idea," Dad said but helped me swing my legs to the floor. "Despite the healing spell, you still lost most of your blood."

"My spine was severed, Dad," I said. "I need to see if my legs work."

"Then let me do this my way, in case they don't." He stood between my legs and hugged me around the chest. He'd had guys at the gym in wheelchairs, so he knew the right way to do a lift.

He brought me to my feet then slowly released the pressure, passing the baton to me. When I was on my own, he backed a step away.

I stepped forward. No problem. I marched in place. Easy peasy.

He grabbed me in a full body hug.

Then I remembered that I'd seen his lifeless heart and unmoving lungs exposed in his open chest, and I squeezed him back with all the strength I had, which wasn't actually as much as I'd have liked Dad to believe.

"Is he gone?" I whispered. "Is Twist really gone?"

"That's what Spook says. Him and Sister Liberata both."

"She's here?" Nope, still not letting go.

"She was, briefly. Just long enough to get the dagger from Spook." Dad chuckled. "He was pissed when she wouldn't let him keep it."

"She gave it to *me,* anyway," I said, finally leaning back against the bed. "If anyone got to keep it, it'd be me."

Dad frowned. "Now that this is all over, you wouldn't need it."

I crossed my arms. "Dad, I'll believe this is over ten years from now when my wife is popping out the first of your grandchildren and flying monkeys don't swoop down out of the sky to kidnap the little bean."

He smirked.

Yeah, no reason to make him deal with the fact that I planned to find out every damn thing about magic that I could.

"Help me dress?" I asked. "I know you love helping your wittle boy get dressed."

"Okay, once was a nice bit of nostalgia. . ." He grabbed a pile of clothes on a chair. "But you can seriously stop needing my help, and I'll be all right with it."

"Well, I don't want to walk out there naked and scare the lesbians." Wow, I really did need the help, too. One leg, then the other. Commando was fine and who needed socks?

"I hope to Liberace that you're careful who you say that stuff in front of." He tried to help me with the t-shirt.

"Gay dad." I waved him away. "Automatic get out of jail free card for having to put up with all those stories at the gym, stories that no son should ever have been forced to hear."

He laughed and ruffled my hair.

See, I used the jokes to trick him into thinking I felt a hell of a lot better than I did. Truth was, almost every movement brought up lights in the edges of my vision.

Music videos played on the TV in the living room, but no one really watched them. Everyone seemed sort of camped out, staring at a wall.

Kenny sprawled on the couch with his feet on an ottoman, Stereo curled up on his chest. Man, just seeing him with her brought a lump to my throat. That's why I'd been willing to kill myself to end Twist. So I'd see shit like that from Heaven. . . or wherever.

Corey sat on the other end of the couch with Theresa snuggled up to him, too.

Trudy had an arm around Cosita at the patio doors.

Ditto and ditto.

Mike stood at the bar behind Woody, rubbing his shoulders absently. God. Poor Woody. I would do everything in my power to make sure he moved in with us. The rest of them had girls to help out. Woody had no one. Well, he'd have me.

"Where's Lizard?" I whispered to Dad.

"His parents showed up yesterday to take him home."

I needed to check on him soon.

So everyone had just sort of hung out, waiting to see if a dagger had sucked my soul off to infinity and beyond. Wow. A lump filled my throat, a lump of love for everyone there and regret for the people we hadn't been able to save.

For Tango. . .

"Yay, your soul wasn't sucked into the infinite void!" Adam walked into the room wearing Corey's bibs, barefoot and eating pie out of the dish with a spoon. "And I didn't wire your legs backward either, so that's good." He shoveled pie into his mouth. "I wasn't sure."

Everyone looked over. Their faces flooded with relief, joy, all that good stuff.

They swarmed me.

Corey cried. So did Kenny.

Adam ate his pie and stood a few feet away, grinning. Then he stepped beside me and gently moved Kenny away a bit. "I need to see." He lifted the back of my shirt, sort of looked from the pie to my back.

I offered a hand for the pie dish.

He smiled and handed it over. "Don't eat any, please. I need the sugar." He placed a hand on my back and rubbed my spine from the base of my skull down to my coccyx, his touch gentle and warm. His eyes shifted, as if he saw something, maybe even saw with his hand as it traveled up and down my spine.

He released my shirt and held out a hand for the pie. "Thank you. You should have some, too. You need the sugar."

Then he walked over to the couch and sat down, staring at the music videos with rapt attention.

I exchanged curious glances with my friends. "So, Adam?" I asked.

"Uh-huh?" He shoveled pie, his eyes glued to the screen.

"Am I okay, then?"

"Uh-huh," he said around a mouthful of food. "The cancer you would've had is all gone, too."

"Cancer?"

"A few years from now." He waved the spoon. "All gone." He glanced down. "Like my pie." He sighed then gave his complete focus to the screen again.

"Glad to see you up and around." Spook appeared from I knew not where. He wore a trench coat and I recognized Corey's fedora. Nice. And yet. . . He seemed so formal again. All business.

"Did you hear from your team?" I asked.

He smiled. "I did. Thank you for asking. I had a text shortly after you ended Twist." He rolled his eyes. "I send a million messages and get a single text. 'Don't be such a little girl. Did you break the clubhouse?'"

Yep, he had definitely assumed the detached investigator mode.

Gunner wandered in behind Spook and seemed to want a corner to hide in.

The temperature in the room dropped when my entourage noticed him.

Stuff that. I broke away and stomped over.

His eyes narrowed and he backed up a step before I caught him, grabbed him with both arms and hugged him. His whole body went stiff, and he held his arms out at his sides.

"I know," I said. "I'm a fag. I'm just glad to see you up and around, too."

When I released him, he jabbed me in the ribs.

Woody and Trudy moved forward, but it hadn't hurt at all.

Playful?

"Mr. Fox, you let your son talk about your people like that?" He jabbed a thumb toward the patio door. "You want I should take him outside and beat his ass?"

While everyone, Corey included, sort of stared open-mouthed, Dad waved off the suggestion. "Not today, son. If he doesn't learn his lesson pretty soon, he's all yours."

"Bar's open," I told Gunner, backing away.

He nodded and headed that way.

Water glistened in Corey's eyes and Kenny's face evinced utter and complete confusion as they welcomed me back into the huddle.

"What you did—" Spook's professional face pissed me off after everything we'd been through.

"I did what I did because it was the only way to do it," I insisted," the only way I could end him once and for all without killing my dad which I was not going to do because fuck you."

"Down, killer." Spook adjusted his coat.

Dad ruffled my hair. Nope, nothing would embarrass me ever again.

"I get it," Spook said. "My guess is anyone in this room would have done the exact same thing had he or she been handed the dagger." He glanced at Gunner. "Absolutely everyone. Although. . . I'm not sure it would've worked for me. The magic binding my soul to this plane is pretty strong, too."

So, what do you say to that?

"You're immortal?" Kenny asked, answering my question.

Spook shrugged. "Immortal just means no one's figured out a way to kill me yet."

"So we're safe?" I asked. "Well and truly safe? Twist is gone forever, and the Cloaks are off our backs?"

"Yes, and yes." The vague pout reminded me of Spook's confrontation with the nun.

"And Mary?"

He shrugged. "Hard to say with that one, although if anyone was going to end her for good, it would've been Twist. Bit of luck there, really." He shook his head. "If she does come back, she has no beef with you. I may have to dance with her from time to time, but I'd guess you're safe."

"I ended Twist." Surely that could piss her off.

"Twist was someone to steal power from," he said. "Like me. I imagine I've not seen the last of her, but you're most likely fine."

"Most likely?"

"If I say one hundred percent, she will jump up from behind the bar."

Everyone looked at the bar.

Nothing jumped out of it.

Deep breath.

Adam sang along with the TV, loudly and badly.

"What about Adam?" I asked.

"I have a home for him," Spook said. "People will take care of him and will understand what he's been through."

"How is he?"

"It's hard to say. He's an infant in a full-grown body." We watched as he rose and started dancing with the video. Also, badly. "There's a lot of magic involved that I don't quite understand yet. I think there's residual memory from Twist, like the magic he knows and the names he has for all of us. That may fade in time."

For Adam's sake, I hoped so.

"It's best for him and all of you if you trust that I will take care of him."

"So it's really over?" I asked one last time. "Well and truly over. For real?"

"I'm even riding off into the sunset now that you're awake." His face turned a little more solemn. A little more detached. He looked us over, bunched together like puppies. Rather than splitting back up into couples, we held together like one big family.

"Contrary to what you're feeling right now, you're most likely going to feel nothing but pain with each other." From the tone, it was a speech he'd given a million times. "You've gone through so much and most of the time, when people go through this, especially people who were close before it happened, within a few weeks you won't even be able to sit in the same room with each other. Don't let that happen. You can't tell anyone else what *really* happened. If you do, the Cloaks will hunt you down and drive you insane to discredit you. They will watch you for years, and the people in this room are the only people on the planet who understand."

"What happened to the doctors who were here?" Corey asked.

"They have no memory of it," Spook said. "The scary lawyer can help you donate money to them anonymously if you want."

I raised an eyebrow.

"While I was in there holding your hand," Dad whispered in my ear. "Saundra confronted Spook and offered to sue him for reckless endangerment."

Ha.

"She was more frightening than the nun." But Spook smiled. "I'm going to hire her as soon as I get back to Austin." He lost the smile. "Don't let go of each other and make sure you get drunk and weep in each other's arms once in a while. I've been through this speech hundreds of times and the people who do what I say are still alive and, within reason, if not happy, then content. Those who decide they know better are, without exception, dead, institutionalized or living in a gutter."

Kenny drew me close and kissed the side of my head. "You know what, Spook? I think I can promise you that we will follow your advice."

"Especially on the drinking together thing," Corey added, punching my shoulder.

Amen, brothers, amen.

Gunner appeared at my side with something red in a tumbler. "I hope this is girly enough for you."

"Bro. . ." Corey made an apology face to me.

I took the drink. "You forgot the little umbrella."

He smacked himself in the forehead and laughed. "It's always something with you metros." He looked me in the eye. "I heard what you did, how you ended that ghost." He nodded. "I guess I'm glad I was smart enough to have my buddies with me when we took you down."

I returned his nod then turned to face my friends. . . the rest of my friends, I guess.

My family. I turned to face my family and I raised my glass.

Chapter Twenty-five

The barn door slid open with a faint rumble, but not much more.

Woody had expected a barn to be, well, more barnlike. Old. Smelly. Every door with its own private screech. He raised an electric lantern he'd found in a utility room. Apparently, this building held the feed: straw, or maybe it was hay, and bags of what Ethan called cow chow. The building was only a couple of years old and Corey's maintenance staff obviously took their work seriously. The place gleamed.

The animals must have lived in a different part of the building. *Gracias a Dios.* Woody had made up his mind to sleep out in the barn but had really worried it would reek of cow shit. Or horse shit. Shit, at any rate, had dominated his fears.

A faint scent of grease and oil emanated from Bessie, who stood near one wall in all her shining glory. Man, the way Corey maintained that tractor, you'd think she was a formula one race car. She shone like a mofo.

Okay. A pile of loose hay lay beside about a hundred bales. Good enough.

He dropped a sleeping bag onto the hay with a blanket and two pillows. No God damn way he was going to sleep one more night in the house where Effie had died. Spook had assured him that Effie's spirit wasn't there. He must have moved on or whatever the hell. At any rate, his ghost wasn't haunting the place.

As if that mattered. The few nights Woody had tried to sleep there, he'd dreamed of that white sheet with a flower of red growing across it. He'd seen the bullet hit Effie's head and splatter his brains to the winds.

Nope. Not going to try to sleep in that house ever again.

Which sucked. Where the hell else could he go? Corey had been so insistent that Woody needed to think of this place as his home. *Mierda*, he'd almost balled like a little kid at that. And Corey had seen him cry too much already. Hell, they'd all cried too much already.

So screw it. He'd sleep in the barn. The rest was fine. He could chill in the house, shower there, eat there. He'd just camp out in the barn at night. It was a hell of a lot better than sleeping in his car and waiting for the new Dumass cops to shine a flashlight through the window. With everything the town had endured, the cops didn't give a lot of leeway anymore.

He set the lantern on the floor, kicked off his shoes and stripped down. Everyone else had already gone to bed. Woody had waited so no one would know he'd headed out to the barn. He didn't want the argument and figured after he survived his first night, no one would give him shit.

He spread the bag and climbed in. The extra blanket seemed like overkill since the place was heated. Who knew? He hunkered into a comfortable position, smacking his pillows a few times to make them just so.

Huh. Who'd have guessed a pile of straw could be so comfortable? Well, if it was good enough for the baby Jesus. . .

The door slid open.

What the hell? Woody jumped to his feet in a fighter's stance he'd learned from Nicci, the dude who'd sprouted giant horns and demon red skin. Wow. That was normal life now.

Ethan slipped into the space carrying a bag, a couple of pillows and a blanket. He slid the door shut.

What the hell? "I don't need a fucking babysitter," Woody insisted.

Ethan stopped, his eyes wide. "I don't want to wake up my Dad again, screaming in the middle of the night. With you and me, I figure it's a fifty-fifty shot which one of us does that these days, so I thought you'd be cool if I crashed here with you. But I can go. . ."

Mierda. Woody needed to let go of his baggage where this one was concerned. "No. Stop." He hurried to Ethan and grabbed him tight.

Ethan dropped the stuff he'd been carrying, and Woody held him close. "I'm so sorry. I'm the douchebag this time, *ese*. I didn't think."

Ethan's arms closed around him. "And if I had been out here to babysit you," Ethan muttered, "that should be okay, too, you piece of shit."

Woody shut his eyes tight. "You're right. I'm sorry."

God, everything in life seemed so different, now. People actually cared about him. It was so damn hard to keep up.

Ethan gathered up the blanket, and Woody grabbed the sleeping bag while Ethan recovered his pillows.

"Welcome to my nest," Woody said. "This seems the most comfortable spot."

"At least it doesn't smell like cow shit, hai?" Ethan dropped his stuff near Woody's.

"No kidding." He watched his friend spread out his things. "How'd you even know I was here?"

Ethan snorted. "With everyone else coupled up, I was hiding on the porch hoping Corey and Theresa would take the night off, if you know what I mean."

Yeah. The walls of the rich folks' house were not as thick as one would hope. Woody dropped into the nest and crawled into his sleeping bag.

"I saw you come out here and decided you were brilliant." Ethan stripped down and dropped his clothes in a pile. Huh. Hanes? What had happened to the designer stuff?

"You really don't mind the company?" Ethan hunkered down and punched his pillows a few times.

"Reminds me of the camp." Woody settled in.

"Lindy-ho-ho."

Woody lay on his side to watch Ethan. "God, that seems like so long ago."

"It was what, three weeks? A month?" Ethan lay on his back with his hands behind his head. "Jesus, I met you four months ago?"

Woody chuckled. "I don't even know."

Ethan chuckled, too. "I've had friends I knew for years I didn't care about as much as I care about you, *ese*."

Woody sort of chuckled and shook his head.

"What?" Ethan's face reddened. "Is it stupid when I use my bad Spanglish?"

"Not at all." Woody hugged a pillow closer. "It's cute. But saying stuff like that. . . about your feelings for me. . . that's why people like you. I mean... I mean, Effy and I would say shit like that, but I just figured that was 'cause he was gay and had a crush on me for so long. I didn't. . ." Shit. Would Ethan understand what he wanted to say? "Please don't laugh at me for this, or think I'm going for pity, but I don't remember the last time my own dad hugged me the way you do. Or told me he loves me." He tried to use his old man's voice. "Men don't do that, Woody." He rolled over and gave Ethan his back. No reason to make a big deal out of it. "People like you, Ethan Fox, because you actually tell us how you feel."

Ethan had nothing to say to that. Good. Woody wanted to sleep. And who knew, maybe having a friend out here watching his back, maybe Woody would actually sleep for a change.

The hay crinkled and stuff while Ethan settled in.

Woody turned down the light. But not off. Never off. Never again.

Ethan's screams tore a gaping hole in the silence of the night. Woody only needed one second to recognize the voice from that first night in the clubhouse. He threw the blanket to one side, turned up the light and grabbed his friend where he sat staring ahead, screaming again.

Ethan tried to push him away.

"Ethan, it's me, Woody. You're okay. You're. . ." He had to pin him to the floor to stop his struggling. "You're awake now." Thank God Woody had learned some sweet moves from Mr. Fox and Nicci.

Ethan stopped struggling. Air wheezed into and out of his lungs under Woody's body.

"My dad," Ethan muttered. "I need to make sure he's all right."

"You told me you don't want to wake up your dad, Ethan. You're out here so you don't wake up your dad. He's fine."

As Ethan's body relaxed a bit, changed from taut as a military bedsheet to more like a panther ready to spring, Woody switched from holding him down to just holding him. "It's over, Ethan. He's dead. She's dead. Fuck, all the bad guys are dead. It was just a dream."

Ethan relaxed more, and his arms switched from pressing against Woody to clutching him desperately. "They're so fucking real, Sam. It's like it happened all over again. . . but. . . this time. . ." He shook his head. He didn't need to say the words for Woody to know that in his nightmare he'd stabbed his dad with the big fucking dagger this time.

Woody pressed Ethan's head to his chest and stroked his hair. "Shhh."

They lay like that for a few seconds.

"I'm okay, now," Ethan said, but his voice quavered.

"No, you're not, and I'm staying right here tonight, so you might as well get comfortable."

He stiffened for just one second, as if he might protest.

"I never wake up screaming when I'm in bed with someone," Woody admitted.

Then Ethan relaxed, really relaxed, against Woody's side. He snickered. "So that's the real reason you sex up all the girls."

Woody tried to laugh. He really did. "Nah, I just like the sex."

It had been meant to be funny. No way to tell if that worked.

He turned down the light so they could sleep, but he didn't turn it off.

Lucky Fox stood in the open door to the barn. He'd slid it open during the fourth scream but had stopped in the smallish crack. Woody held Ethan down, and from the look of it, he'd paid attention in the grappling classes at the clubhouse.

Every muscle in Lucky's body wound tight as a spring, ready to rush over and hold his boy while he cried. But then. . .

"My dad," Ethan muttered. "I need to make sure he's all right."

"You told me you don't want to wake up your dad, Ethan," Woody insisted. "You're out here so you don't wake up your dad. He's fine."

And then Woody just held the boy, held him to comfort him.

So Lucky watched from the open doorway. His son wasn't alone in the world anymore. And Lucky needed to let his son's other friends take care of him.

Maybe he and his boy had been too close all those years alone. Maybe they'd been alone all those years because they were too close.

The boys snuggled together and dimmed the lights.

Man, times had changed. Two boys would never have cuddled up like that twenty years ago.

Or maybe that was just Lucky, maybe he'd always been afraid someone would figure it out. Maybe he'd been afraid he'd pop a boner in the middle of the night. Because all teenage boys didn't do that every night.

He sighed.

And maybe they curled up like puppies because after a month of horrible violence, death and destruction, they didn't care about all that shit, and they were smart enough to know they needed the comfort.

A hand touched Lucky's arm right on cue.

Mike. Drawing him away from the doorway. Lucky allowed it and left the door where it was. Corey could afford the extra electricity to heat the space with the door open.

Lucky followed Mike about halfway back to the house, where they turned to each other and latched on.

"He has someone tonight," Mike said. "And so do you."

Lucky nodded. And that was new, too. He'd never had someone who'd take care of him before. It took getting used to, but Lucky liked it. He hugged Mike closer, noticed the stiches and fuzz where Nicci had shaved Mike to clean the head wound and apply the stiches. Lucky kissed Mike near the spot.

"And what are you trying not to think about?" Mike asked.

Lucky smiled. It was a common question with his fiancé the shrink. "That my boy has the same magic that almost killed us all." He stared at the moon. "What the hell does that even mean?"

Mike squeezed, his arms barely able to reach around Lucky's chest.

On the front porch, Theresa squeezed the railing with both hands, watching the two middle-aged men who held one another under a cold, stark moonlight.

Ethan's screams had pulled her out of a shallow slumber.

She hadn't seen any of the things the others had, but she believed them. Ethan had made fire with one hand to show her that magic was true, so it would be a real thing to her and not just something she believed on faith.

So it was real. Every horrifying moment had happened, and the scars left on every soul involved would mean many, many sleepless—

Footsteps.

Theresa spun.

Stereo padded across the porch to her.

Theresa slowly let out the breath she'd sucked in.

Stereo settled at the railing.

"He must be all right," Theresa said. "His dad never went into the barn. Just another nightmare." She sighed. "Just."

"Woody's in there with him."

How many nights would Ethan wake up screaming?

"You know," Theresa said, "when I first met Ethan Fox, he seemed like such an insufferable ego. And the way he treated Corey." She shook her head. "I had no idea why Corey would be friends with someone so unthinkingly cruel."

The two older men held each other silently in the moonlight.

"But he changed," Theresa continued. It was nice to tell someone what she'd thought. She'd never admit to Corey how much she'd detested Ethan in the beginning. But Stereo would understand. "He took the time to understand Corey. He even tried to help him tune Bessie one time and laughed at himself when he almost destroyed the engine. And while Corey tried to explain it all again, he patiently listened without comprehending a single thing Corey said."

Theresa sighed. "He has that focus. When he's with someone, he gives them his undivided, one hundred percent attention. I think that's what draws people to him. That focus, that attentiveness is something we all crave."

Beside her, Stereo shook her head. "He shoved. a giant dagger. through his own spine. to save us all." She glanced at Theresa. "What more do you need?" She moved away, heading toward the door. "It must suck sometimes, being the smartest human being on the planet."

Theresa shook her head and looked out at the men, who'd started to move toward the house. "You have no idea," she whispered. Yes, Ethan's act of heroics gave him a free pass in most eyes now, but the point was that he'd proven himself to Theresa already. That was important. Well, to her anyway.

She followed Stereo into the house. The men likely wouldn't enjoy knowing their private moment hadn't been so private.

Inside, Kenny stood in the foyer in his superhero boxer briefs, scratching his head and mussing his hair even more than sleep had. "When I woke up, you were gone."

Stereo put her arm around him and turned him back to the hall that lead to the bedrooms. "Everything's okay, sweetie," she said. "I just thought I'd get some fresh air. Sorry if I scared you."

"Hey, Theresa," Kenny said over one shoulder as they disappeared down the hall.

Kenny had been so shy a few months ago. Theresa had never seen him without a shirt, even on the few occasions he'd gone to the community pool. He'd always kept his eyes on the floor, too, except when he danced.

They'd all changed so much.

Theresa headed down the same hall but slipped into the first door on the right. Corey's room.

He lay sprawled on his stomach with the sheets twisted around his legs. That hadn't taken long. In the dim light from the open window, she could see the subtle movements of his sleeping. Were he and Kenny so accustomed to screams in the night that they no longer noticed? Or were the boys just better sleepers?

Boys. Girls.

Theresa had stayed in Corey's house, sharing Corey's bed and his room, for a few days now. He'd even asked her to live there with him, like it was normal for two seniors in high school to suddenly move in together. And what about Stereo and Kenny? Would she move in?

Even more than the flame Ethan had used to prove magic was real, the fact that Corey and his friends were so blasé about things that would have freaked them out a month ago convinced Theresa of their adventures together.

Of course, Mr. Fox and the boys would move in together. None of them had good homes, and Corey shouldn't live out here by himself. He wouldn't do well alone. And they'd all lived together in the cabins at the camp, and at the place they called the clubhouse.

She shook her head. No. She'd need to gather her things and go home in the morning. She loved Corey, but she wasn't ready to live with anyone but her parents. She hated to admit it, but she wanted to enjoy the last few months of her childhood before graduation. She wanted to wake up to the smell of her mom's famous pancakes. She wanted to know that her laundry would wash itself magically every weekend while she studied at the library.

Corey and his friends. . . her friends, perhaps, too. . . They may have had their childhoods ripped away by everything they'd experienced, but Theresa wasn't ready to let go of hers just yet.

Corey would understand. He always did.

I woke up with a nice, warm body pressed against mine. I rubbed her chest. No boobs.

Whoops! That's right, I hadn't fallen asleep in the afterglow. I shifted a bit to extricate myself from Woody's limbs.

"Morning." Woody didn't move much.

"Sorry," I muttered. "I forgot it was you."

Woody chuckled and continued to not move. "Dude, it's chilly in here. No apologies necessary."

Chilly? The barn door stood open about a foot. Just enough for an overprotective father to peek in during the night.

I settled back, dropping my head onto Woody's chest. "That would be because my dad heard me last night and came to check."

"I figured." Woody's heart rate sped up a bit. "I mean, if this makes *you* uncomfortable. . ."

"Nah." I dropped an arm across Woody's chest. "I may as well admit that when the nightmares started, I spent a number of nights curled up with Dad like I was still a little kid." I closed my eyes. "It actually feels kinda nice. Safe." An image of Dad with Lucifer's dagger in his chest flashed across my mind. I shivered. "After all the shit we've been through, I think we all deserve whatever comfort we can give each other."

"Amen."

"Knock, knock," Dad called from outside.

I opened my eyes. "You can come in, Dad. It's not like I'm having sex with anyone in here."

Woody chuckled. "How did he know the exact minute you'd wake up?"

"Dad magic. He's spooky."

Dad crouched beside the nest.

"I'm not moving today," I said. "Nothing can induce me to leave this bed. . . pallet. . ." I glanced at the straw. "Nest."

"Mike and I made pancakes, sausages, eggs and pretty much everything else Nicci had for us that first morning." He grinned. "And coffee."

Which he had not brought out with him.

My stomach growled. "You are an evil, evil man." I opened my eyes wide, then, just in case puppy dog might work. "Dad. . .?"

He laughed. "Don't even try it. I am not bringing you breakfast in bed today." He ruffled Woody's hair. "Thanks for taking care of Ethan last night." He rose.

With a sigh, I drew myself away from Woody's side and sat up, pulling the blanket away before it tangled in my legs.

Woody sat up, too.

"And you both need pants," Dad insisted.

"Argh." I let my head hang back. "Pants are for suckers."

Woody chuckled.

"The girls will be leaving for their respective homes today," Dad told us. "When it's all boys again, fell free to run around naked for all I care, but as long as there are ladies in the house, I expect you to act like gentlemen. . . at least outside your respective bedrooms."

And there was Dad logic. He wouldn't interfere with the guys' sex lives, but God forbid the girls see us in our underwear. Whatever.

"Plus Saundra's here."

"Saundra?" I pushed to my feet and looked around for jeans. "That's cool. I never did find out why she wanted to see me."

Woody slipped his jeans on.

Where were mine?

Dad held them out. Oh. Cool.

Something in Dad's face, though.

"Am I not going to like this?" I asked.

Dad shook his head. "Everything's fine. With everything going on. . ." He sighed. Hm. That meant I would not like what she had to say. It also meant I would not get a sneak preview no matter how much I cajoled.

Dad turned to Woody. "She's also here to chat with you, Woody."

"Me?" He sort of paused mid-sock and ended up hopping on one foot.

This part I knew. Dad and I had discussed it earlier.

He dropped a hand on Woody's shoulder. "You already know Corey wants you to live out here with us."

Woody finished with the sock but let the t-shirt dangle in one hand. "Mm-hm."

"There's no easy way to say this," Dad began, "but it seems like your parents are trying to actually, legally disinherit you. I think you already know that."

Woody nodded, his jaw set in stone.

"It's complicated because you're a minor, but they're also trying to have you remanded to the state as a danger to yourself or others."

Woody's jaw fell open. "What the fuck?" He flinched. "Sorry, Mr. Fox. But. . . they can't do that. Can they? I'm not, like, insane or anything."

Dad's hand tightened on the shoulder. "Slow down, son. We're not going to let any of that happen. I just want you to know what's going on. Saundra's going to fight all this with you. She's countersuing, or something like that, for negligence, and. . ." He sighed. "It's all so damn complicated, but the upshot is you might need to have them legally removed as your parents, prove they are unfit in order to avoid detention."

"Removed?" Woody made a long series of scoffing sounds. "Which makes me a ward of the state, and I go into a string of foster homes instead." He'd obviously already thought through some of this.

Dad shook his head. "Not if I adopt you."

Woody gasped. Like real and for true gasped.

Wow. I hadn't expected Dad to drop it on him quite like that.

Woody looked from Dad to me.

"I know I'm a total douchebag and you might hate this," I admitted, "but I think it'd be cool to have a brother after all these years."

Woody shook his head in silence. His eyes sort of sparkled with water. "Wow," he said at last. "But. . . my parents hate me."

"Woody—" Dad started.

"No." Woody shook his head. "They do. They must. They're embarrassed by me and. . ." He looked up into Dad's eyes. "There's no way you can afford to fight them. They're loaded."

"Corey has ten times the money your parents have, and Saundra will do this pro bono." Dad glanced at me for some reason. "Besides which, other resources might be coming into play."

Huh?

"But I can't. . ." Woody looked from me to Dad. "Why? I mean, I'm just some stupid punk kid who messed up his life jacking off online. Why would you. . . You've only known me a couple of months."

I could handle that one. "And last night I woke you up in the middle of the night, and your very first reaction was to grab me and hold me and protect me." I shook my head. "Jesus, Woody, it's not like I don't already consider you a brother. This is just a formality to keep your parents from messing with your life until you turn eighteen."

Woody stared at me. A single tear fell down his cheek. "Shit." He wiped it away, but a few more trickled out. He wiped his face with the t-shirt. "Shit. I'm sorry."

"No reason to apologize, son." Dad ruffled his hair.

Woody sniffed loudly in surprise. Tears flowed out of his eyes now. He swallowed really hard, and his voice, when he spoke, was little more than a murmur. "When you say that, it's like you mean it. I mean, my dad. . . I don't think. . . I don't think he's ever called me that." He wiped his face with the shirt again. "I'm sorry. I just. . ." He hiccoughed. He shook his head.

"What's really wrong, son?" Dad asked, his dad magic obviously telling him what ran through Woody's mind.

Woody wiped his face again, staring down at the floor. "What kind of piece of shit kid sucks so much his own parents hate him?" He snuffled. "I should've been the one shot in the head, not Effy."

Holy shit.

I couldn't breathe.

Dad wrapped his arms around Woody. "This is not your fault, Woody. Your parents. . ."

With everything else that had happened, all the violence and terror, Woody carried that around with him the entire time? Jesus shit.

"Your parents fucking suck, Woody," I said, moving closer. Dad opened an arm to let me in. My jeans still dangled from one hand. Whatever. I dropped them so I could wrap my arms around Woody and Dad.

What the hell to say?

"It breaks my heart that Ephraim died," I said. "And if I could take his place, I'd do it in a heartbeat. But I'm also glad as hell that you're still alive." I squeezed Woody. "Fuck your parents," I said. "Let us be your family."

After that, none of us spoke for a while.

We just held Woody while he cried it out.

Chapter Twenty-six

I tromped up the steps to Corey's house. It was a sweet place, but would I even live there long enough for it ever to feel like home? Home meant memories, and not the kind I associated with this place.

Although. . .

Kenny leaned against a post, arms and ankles crossed. He held out a cup of coffee, my old mug, the "I was a world champion ballroom dancer. . ." mug. So Dad had brought it over. Nice.

I took the mug, sucked down a mouthful, then hooked a hand around Kenny's neck and pulled him close so I could kiss the side of my friend's head. "You realize you make me wish I was gay, don't you?"

Kenny held his silence. Hm.

"You okay?"

Kenny startled, then rolled his eyes. "Stereo took off to go stay with her folks. I'm just pining like an idiot who doesn't know how good he has it."

"Take the good where you can get it," I said and passed into the house.

Saundra stood in the foyer with dreadlocks and a peacock-colored kaftan. She managed to hug me tight without spilling a drop of my coffee. "I am so glad to see you on your feet again." She released me and cuffed my head. "You gave me a scare, you little bastard. I don't scare easily."

Indeed, she did not.

"Sorry, Saundra."

She held my face with both hands and stared into my eyes.

She did that rather a long time.

"So it's really you in there?" she asked at last.

"Dad buys it."

She nodded and released me then took my hand. She led me into the house and down the hall to my room.

She stopped. She turned to me. "Finish that cup."

I chugged the coffee.

Saundra nodded, took the cup and held it up. "Kenny, love, be a dear and refill this for him toot sweet."

"Yes, ma'am." Kenny took the mug and held out a second.

Saundra smiled. "And you make me glad I'm straight, if possibly a bit too old." She waved Ethan to take the offered mug.

Oh boy. A two coffee meeting.

What the hell could be going on?

Kenny opened his eyes a bit and did a shrugging, head shaking thing that told me he had no idea why she needed to see me.

Joy.

Well, she still had my hand and led me into the room beside Corey's that had been officially labeled mine. Literally. Corey had handwritten a sign with my name on it and taped it to the door.

Inside Saundra moved to the desk in one corner and settled against it facing me.

Almost by instinct, I closed the door and leaned there. "So what's up?"

"First of all, how are you really holding up?"

I sighed. "I'm hanging in."

"Last time I saw you, you'd recently had an enormous dagger shoved through your spine," she said. "No ill effects?"

"Did you meet Adam?"

She nodded.

"Damn miracle worker, that one." I turned a circle, hands in the air. "I feel fine."

She smiled, but it wavered for a millionth of a second. Long enough to read her thoughts. If only Adam had been able to work a few more miracles.

If only. . .

"Show me your party trick, please." She crossed her arms.

I held up one hand and the flames leapt to life so easily. Something as insane as magic and it had become as easy as breathing. I snapped my fingers and the flame spun out.

Saundra nodded. "That's not why I'm here, but it's part of the discussion."

"Why are you here?" Ethan asked.

She removed the wig, unzipped the kaftan and slipped out of it. Under the costume she wore her normal close-cropped hair, jeans, a white Oxford and a dark blue blazer. One version of her "professional attire." She dropped the costume onto the bed, resettled against the desk and regarded me with her professional face.

The woman was Dad's best friend. They'd known each other long before she'd become one of the scariest lawyers in Texas, and she'd always made a strong point of separating her friendly visits with her professional ones. The costume changes helped.

She held up a folder. "You just came into a rather sizeable chunk of change."

Wait. What? "I have no idea what you mean." Nope. Not even moving to take the papers until she explained.

She lowered the folder. This was her as my lawyer saying things Dad's best friend did not want to say. It was obvious. "Your biological parents' tragic death created a rather large sum of money," she explained. "Their own father had recently died with a sizeable insurance policy and a modest estate. They immediately rolled that into a trust for their—as of then— unborn son. Also, for reasons of their own, they invested in rather sizeable life insurance policies."

I couldn't stop myself from interrupting. "Okay, right, but that all went to diapers and formula before Dad had a decent job."

Saundra's face pinched. "None of the fire detectors in your biological parent's apartment building sounded an alarm. The company was declared criminally negligent and a sizeable settlement kept the litigation out of court."

"Right," I insisted. "I know. Diapers."

"As you developed your reputation in the dance world," she

continued, "a number of video productions, personal appearances and innumerable coaching sessions were paid to you as well."

"Which went to pay for my own coaching, travel and costumes," I insisted. "That's what Dad always told me."

She raised an eyebrow. "He lied."

What. the. fuck?

"He put every penny you earned into the trust and paid for the coaching with his own money." She shrugged. "He knew you wanted to pay your own way with the dancing. He disagreed."

The information swirled in my head.

We had money.

We'd always had money.

We'd lost everything and gone through hell, almost literally, while some kind of trust fund gathered interest?

"What the fuck!" I shouted.

A wave. . . a literal wave of energy rippled out of my body and flowed to the walls of the room, carrying dirty clothes and papers and anything light enough with it. It hit the walls with a resounding thump.

Holy shit! What the hell was that? I could do that, too? All that stuff had flown through the air as if I'd used the Force or something.

Saundra didn't react. Not at first. Then she pulled her phone from a pocket. She tapped the screen and held it to one ear. "Voicemail," she muttered, then rose a few inches. "Hello, Mr. James. This is Saundra Delecroix. Apparently, Mr. Fox also has telekinetic ability that manifests with emotional outbursts. I'm going to recommend anger management training with Dr. Lopez but suggest you arrange a visit as soon as possible. Any further destructive activity will be therefore considered negligence on your part and billed accordingly." She tapped the phone.

"You need to understand what this did to your father." She shoved the phone into a pocket. "I've known him since he was your age. I've seen him drunk, stupid and nearly anything else I'd ever thought possible." She shook her head. "When I got here after they'd pulled that dagger from your chest?" She shook her head again. "I know you think your father is invincible. I've heard you call him Conan the Dadbarian." Again with the head shake. "But that? What the hell could he do to protect you from that? From a soul sucking dagger made by Lucifer himself."

She dropped the folder on the desk. "Everything he did since the day he stole you away from your Aunt, and I hope to Christ he told you that story?"

I nodded. How the hell could I do anything else?

She nodded. "Everything he's done has been to be worthy of you. To be worthy of the trust Karl and Megan placed in him. A gay man entrusted with the care of a baby? No one back then bought it. The battles he fought were unreal. But this battle? How could he fight this battle? A battle against something Lucifer made? Lu-ci-fer." She sighed. "He frightened me, Ethan. Me." She waited a second. "Me."

It sank in.

"If you hadn't come back," she said, "if he'd let that horrible evil take you away?" She stared into my eyes. "You need to know this for many reasons, Ethan, but I seriously contemplated having your father committed. He was that out of control. Wouldn't eat. Wouldn't leave your side. I was terrified that if you didn't pull out, he'd commit suicide from guilt over letting that happen to you."

Wow. Dad the invulnerable. Suicidal. How was that even possible?

"After the accident last year," she said. "He was not completely rational." She sighed. "I admit I did not agree with his decision to keep the trust from you, but he knew you better than I." She quirked half a smile. "We were uncertain how you would react, what you would do with the money. He assumed you would survive your three-month exile into Dumass, Texas and then use the money to resume your prior life in Austin. It would be three months, which, at the time, seemed like nothing. He was afraid you would borrow against the trust to fix his conflicts, which would not have worked. His trials created a money pit that would have sucked every single penny out of your trust and left you as destitute as he was."

"And you?" I had to know.

She smiled. "Ethan, I am more impressed with the young man you have become in a few short months than I can express."

"But then," I pursued. "What did you think I'd do with the money?"

"I thought you'd buy the house out of bankruptcy," she said, "and blow the rest on costumes and coaching." She shrugged. "Or other such bullshit. I was afraid that you'd disown your father."

Wow. Had I been so fucking shallow?

"Do you not remember your arguments?" she asked.

I did. What would I have done?

No way to say.

"That was then," I insisted. "But I'd never have disowned Dad."

She raised an eyebrow.

"No. Never." I moved closer. "It's important you believe that. Please. No matter how fucked up things got. I never stopped loving him."

She regarded me under one very arched eyebrow. After a moment, she nodded. "Then please do not judge him for the decisions he made in that same bad time."

I sucked in a deep breath.

"He is very afraid you will hold it against him," she told me.

Wow. "How much money are we talking about?"

She rifled through the folder, held out a single sheet of paper.

I took it.

One number stood out. $753,435.45.

"Holy fuck!"

Three quarters of a million dollars.

"After taxes," Saundra added.

Lucky Fox waited at the end of the hall down which Saundra had taken his son. How would Ethan react? The money in the trust would have fixed everything from one point of view. Which meant every damn bad thing that had happened in the last few months was Lucky's fault.

Would Ethan see it that way? Would he. . .?

The door to Ethan's room opened.

Lucky held his breath.

Ethan. He stepped out of the room, then saw Lucky. Without a moment's hesitation, the boy rushed to Lucky and threw his arms around his waist. "I will always fucking love you," the boy said. "Even when you do the stupidest shit on the planet." He kissed Lucky's cheek. "And everything you did makes total sense, even if it pisses me off." He squeezed as tight as he could. "I love you. Stop worrying about that. Never worry about that."

Thank God. Lucky hugged his son and looked at Saundra over his shoulder. She winked.

Thank god. After all the hideous bullshit they'd survived, thank God Lucky wouldn't lose his son over his own stupidity.

"I don't know if I say this enough," the boy continued, "but I am the luckiest damn guy on the planet to have you for a dad. And if we do this adoption with Woody, then that'll make two of us, and you can bet your ass Corey wishes he was still seventeen. Shit, Dad, every one of my friends has told me how jealous they are." He pulled enough away to look Lucky in the eyes. "Saundra reminded me of the crap Auntie Mac said to you back then, and you need to let go of it. It was all crap. You are the best Dad any kid ever had ever." He looked away for a second. "And I think you need to talk to Auntie Mac, too. I think it's different now. I know she was a total bitch to you back then, but after all the shit we've gone through. . . I think maybe you need to give her a second chance." His eyes were so damn wise. "We all deserve second chances."

Lucky's throat closed so tightly, he couldn't speak at first. He nodded. Then he grabbed Ethan again. "And so, my wise young man, did you figure all that out before or after you threw shit around the room in a childish snit?"

Ethan stiffened a bit in Lucky's arms. "Yeah. About that. . . It was kind of an accident."

In the doorway, Saundra's face went blank. Well, it would be blank as far as anyone else was concerned. Lucky saw the way her eyes pinched ever so slightly.

Dear God, what now?

A foghorn broke the quiet Texas morning.

"A foghorn?" I pulled out of Dad's arms, happy for the strange distracting noise.

I headed to the front of the house and out onto the porch.

Two huge semis hauling what looked like the two halves of a double-wide had pulled into the parking lot in front of Corey's house and now rumbled their way around the house. Corey stood in the lot waving them on with his hat.

I pounded down the steps and across the gravel. "What did you buy now?"

"Ethan!" Corey opened his arms and engulfed me. "Good morning. I hear you slept like shit out in the barn, so I bought you and Woody a house."

"A house?" I pulled out of Corey's grasp to watch the second semi disappear around the corner.

"Yep." Corey followed the trucks. "Impulse buy. You do remember that I now have shitloads of money?" His boots crunched on the gravel before they hit the grass.

"You can't just buy me a house." I jogged to keep up with my friend's long stride.

"Actually, I can." Corey held one strap of his bibs as he walked. "Shitloads of money remember? And I really bought it for me." He stopped to open the patio gate. "I don't want you to go back to the city, Ethan. None of you. If I need to buy you a separate place to crash to keep you out here? Whatever it costs." He gestured me through the gate, then followed. "Besides, I may end up out there myself. All the memories kinda get mixed up in my head in the main house."

He stomped onto the back porch, then turned to lean against the railing.

I joined him.

Beyond the amazing patio and paisley-shaped pool with waterfall, past the pool house with both indoor and outdoor showers and a fully stocked bar, a crew of folks directed the semis. The cargo was hard to see, really, all wrapped up in plywood. Why was a double-wide all wrapped up?

"Well, what's it going to look like?" I asked. If I could handle my new powers of the Force without shrieking like a little girl, I could be cool about a new crash pad special-delivered to the backyard. "And why right there? It kinda blocks the view."

Corey scoffed and played with his phone. "There's still plenty of view, and there's no way any house I buy is not going to have this pool and bar right there. Besides. . ." He held out the phone. "It has a rooftop patio, so the view is actually *muy bueno*-er."

"Holy shit." The image on the phone looked like no double-wide I'd ever seen. Largely built of glass and steel and concrete, which explained the plywood wrapping, it was a tiny version of a California cliffside mansion. "That's a prefab?"

"I know, right?" Corey held the phone to his own face. "Modern technology is awesome."

"What the heck is that?" Kenny hit the railing at my side, staring out at the construction site.

"Our new clubhouse," Corey declared as Woody hit the rail on Kenny's other side. "I got the idea at Spook's place." He grinned. "Including the rooftop patio." He looked up at the clear Texas sky. "I mean, why the hell doesn't the main house have one? We have, like, a million times more stars out here."

"Tell me you didn't buy an entire house because I have sleep issues, *ese*," Woody asked, a little breathless.

"First of all, fuck you if I did." He glanced pointedly over one shoulder, as if checking whether anyone might be listening from an open doorway. "And B, I know Ethan's Dad is *muy* very *mucho* against the whole magic thing." He nudged my shoulder with his own. "I also know there is no way in hell we're not going to find out everything we can about the shit." He grinned. "So I figure we need our own clubhouse where we can work on stuff without him noticing."

I chuckled. Dad would figure it out anyway, but it was a nice gesture.

"So is this a he-man woman-haters club," a girl's voice said behind us, "or can a chick join you holy hell what the fuck is that?"

Stereo hit the railing beside Woody.

Kenny smiled so much his face almost shattered, and I could tell he'd used every ounce of reserve to avoid plowing through Woody to hug her.

"It's our new clubhouse," I said. "And we should vote. All right he-men. Girls allowed?"

Every one of us raised a hand. "Girl's allowed," we chorused.

"Hai!" Kenny added. He showed her a quizzical face.

She shrugged. "I forgot my laptop."

Kenny winked at her.

"I'll need to see a hot babe in a bikini once in a while," Woody said, "to make up for the sausage fest my life is about to become."

"I need to wear a swimsuit?" Stereo asked.

After a very pregnant pause, during which absolutely no one glanced at Kenny to see his reaction, Corey cleared his throat. "Bikinis optional."

"As long as Dad's not around," I clarified.

A loud shushing sound drew everyone's gaze back to the construction site.

"Don't you need, like, water hookups and stuff?" Woody asked.

Corey waved a hand. "Abracadabra." He grinned. "My magic is called moola. They'll take care of it."

Wow. At least it gave everyone a reason to smile for a few minutes. That alone had to be worth every penny to Corey. But still. . .

"So. . ." I waited until all eyes pointed at me. "We're all hooked into this supernatural stuff, are we?"

Kenny laughed. "We just found out that fireballs are real."

"And magic lightning and interdimensional portals," Stereo added. "And witches and ghosts."

"It's going to be hard as hell to go back to classes next week as it is," Kenny continued. "There's no way I can just live my life as if none of this happened."

Corey nodded at the clubhouse with his chin. "This way we all have a place to hang out and study it together." He lost the smile. "Knowing the bad shit out there, too." He shook his head. "I want to know more about that. About how the hell there's so much out there no one really knows about."

Yeah. That had to be the Cloaks. How the hell *did* they keep it all hush hush? How close had Dumass, Texas really come to being completely wiped off the planet?

What was out there? Really?

"The story never ends, does it?" Kenny spoke so softly, like he was almost embarrassed. "I mean, if Spook and the nun are right, this part of it is over. *That* story closes. Hai? But it's never really going to be *over*. We're going to keep looking. And that'll most likely lead us into some other hornet's nest we're too stupid to leave alone." He shrugged. "Hopefully we can at least get a break for a few days."

The silence lasted ten seconds, then Woody burst out laughing, and it was so good to hear that. He grabbed Kenny around the neck and hugged him with one arm. "So I guess you must be the smart one who thinks too much." He released Kenny and looked down the line. "That makes me the pretty one, Ethan the blond leader guy, and Corey the funny one with the helmet." He turned to Stereo. "So you must be either the spunky kid sister, or the hot studio exec in charge of us all." He held out a hand. "No wait, the smart one has the freaky weird one for a girlfriend. Perfect!"

Huh?

Stereo dropped her face into her hands. "You did not just turn us into a bad Disney sitcom."

"Oh, yes I did." Woody grinned. "Na na, na-na, naa-a-a," he sang, and I got it. Ha!

"Na na na-na, naaa-a-a," the guys all chorused while Stereo made gagging sounds.

Lucky stood inside the patio doors with Mike on one side and Saundra on the other.

How the hell could those kids go looking for it? Knowing what they knew and before they'd even buried the dead. How the hell could they already make plans to go looking for that kind of trouble?

"The magic is in him, Lucky." Mike spoke quietly. Hopefully the kids wouldn't realize they were eavesdropping. "You heard what he did with Saundra. If he pretends it's not there, he could end up hurting himself. Or someone else."

Lucky shook his head. "Then while they're trying to find new ways to fucking get themselves killed, I'll just have to do my own research and find a way to rip all that fucking magic right out of him once and for all. There is no fucking way I'm going to let my boy, hell, any of my boys throw themselves in front of that fucking bus again and again and again. Fuck *that* shit."

They stood in silence a moment.

"At least now," Saundra said in her African queen impersonation, "we all know where Ethan got his damn filthy mouth."

"And I'm still waiting for the maniacal cackle," Mike added. "You realize that was a textbook supervillain speech?"

Lucky sighed and let his chin drop onto his chest. "Fuck you both."

Six Months Later

Ethan Fox poured cranberry juice over ice at the bar near the pool. His closest friends had gathered for his dads' wedding party. How long would it take to get used to the apostrophe after the S instead of before it?

They'd had the actual service and reception a day earlier at Trudy's dance studio, the rebuilt Esmerelda's, but Ethan had insisted on a party out at the ranch for close friends.

For people who knew the Unknown.

Spook had been right. The world had turned into a place divided between those who knew about the supernatural and those who did not. When Ethan had been a world champion ballroom dancer, the world had been divided between those who danced and those who did not. Perhaps he'd live his whole life in worlds split that way. Perhaps everyone did.

"Can I have one of those?" Saundra Delacroix leaned against the bar with a hand extended. As far as Ethan could tell, she was her real self and not one of her amazing personas. No wig, a white Oxford and skinny jeans she managed to work, despite the fact she was his dads' age.

There was that apostrophe placement again.

"It's just cranberry, Ms. D." He offered her a glass.

"Mm-hm." She sipped and smiled. "And you're sure no one will pour something into their glasses?"

Ethan raised three fingers. "I promise no one will add a drop of anything to these glasses, except more cranberry." And, as far as it went, he spoke the truth.

She stared at him while she took another sip.

"At least while you're still here," he admitted, "and everyone has a room for the night, so no one is driving." He waved at the sparkling glass and steel clubhouse at one end of the pool.

"Carry on," she said.

"Saundra?" Ethan leaned closer. "Can I ask a favor?"

"For my second favorite client?" she asked. "Anything that doesn't end up with a body in a trunk."

"My brother's birthday is almost here," Ethan said, still getting used to the idea that where Woody was concerned, the word was literal. "Any chance you have an agent and a photographer as clients I could pay to set him up with the world's best modeling portfolio?"

She glanced across at the Mexican god in swim trunks with the water all aglisten.

"I'll make some calls." She winked.

Stellar. Ethan carried a tray of drinks around the bar.

Trudy and Cosita lounged in chaises near the bar.

Ethan bent at the waist and held the tray where no one else could see it. "Drinks, *chicas*?" He lifted a cup and held it out to Trudy. "*Domine ex.*"

Glitter sparkled in the juice.

She smiled and took the glass.

He repeated the spell for Cosita.

"If Daddy Lucky sees that. . ." Trudy drew a finger across her throat and made one of her famous noises.

Cosita tapped their glasses together. "*Gracias.*"

Ethan's phone buzzed in his shorts.

Front door is locked. Should we come around? The text was from Spook.

Stellar. Ethan hadn't been sure he'd attend. *On my way*

"Spook's here," he whispered to Trudy.

She raised an eyebrow, glanced at Ethan's dads where they bickered over music at the stereo system near the waterfall. She winked. "On it." She held a hand out to Cosita. "Time to distract the gay men."

Cosita frowned, glanced down at a swimming suit that concealed very little of her curvaceous body. She shrugged, took Trudy's hand and patted Ethan's cheek as they moved off.

Nice.

He stopped at Kenny's side and slid an arm around his shoulders, waiting for him to finish the story he told Stereo.

". . .and Ethan was standing there the entire time," he said.

"The entire time?" she asked, laughing loudly.

"Not the entire time." Ethan felt nearly certain which story Kenny had finally told her. "There are still a few things about him you know that I, hopefully, never find out."

"Hai and amen." Kenny laughed and reached for a drink.

"Uh-uh." Ethan smacked his hand away. He picked up a drink, spelled it, passed it to Kenny then picked one up for Stereo.

"Uh-uh," she mimicked and picked up her own. "*Domine ex.*" Her brow furrowed in concentration. She sighed. "Abracadabra." The glass sparkled, and she smiled and sipped. "I have no idea why that's the only word that works for me." She dipped a quick curtsy.

Kenny held her close and kissed her. "Now you see why I'm bewitched."

Stellar. After Ethan had pretty much offered up his life for everyone, Stereo ended her vendetta and the two of them frequently researched magic spells together in the new clubhouse. Kenny joyfully scoured the net for them both. He didn't have the knack for spellcasting, but he was a wizard with the almighty Google.

Ethan tightened his arm around Kenny and leaned close to his ear. "They're here. Give me five minutes."

Kenny nodded. They'd made plans to help Ethan wheedle important info from Spook. In some ways, this entire party had been arranged for that very reason, although Ethan's dads had no idea.

Yeah. His first dad still had issues with Ethan's magical "lifestyle choices."

Ethan continued the circuit.

Woody, Gunner and Lizard hung out by the diving board inventing some sort of game. Lizard had brought his new beau, Johnny, which had made everyone, especially Woody, rather uncomfortable at first. Once Lizard had told them Johnny was a werewolf, interest had peaked because everyone could tease him about lacrosse and the body hair he obviously shaved.

Ethan gave his brother a drink. "I talked to Saundra. She's going to go through her contact list."

Woody's eyes opened wide, and both hands planted themselves on Ethan's shoulders.

"No promises, *ese*," Ethan warned.

Woody patted Ethan's chest and took the drink, raising the glass in a toast.

"I need to you keep her busy while I grill Spook for info," Ethan reminded him.

Woody's gaze rested on Trudy and Cosita, who had cornered Ethan's dads. He glanced at Saundra, who headed in the same direction, then opened his eyes wide into pretty, simple mode. "We'll keep her from telling your dads why Trudy's suddenly so interested in Abba." He grabbed Gunner—who seemed overdressed in jeans and a t-shirt—around the neck.

Ethan offered Gunner a drink. They exchanged a nod then Ethan handed the last of his drinks to Lizard and Johnny.

"What's our job?" Lizard asked, leaning close.

Ethan leaned in closer and smirked. "Don't you dare let my Dads find out I spelled those drinks." He ruffled Lizard's hair. "Thanks for the backup, guys, but I think the team has this one."

Lizard grabbed him. "Thanks for the invite."

Ethan hugged him back. Time to make sure Lizard understood the situation. "You have an open invite, Lizard. And bring Johnny whenever you like." He glanced around at the misbegotten weirdoes surrounding Corey's pool. "You have been officially adopted into the family, God help you, and I expect you to visit often." He squeezed them both. "But I have an investigator to hustle, and precious little time to do it before Dad breaks my balls."

Lizard laughed and raised his glass.

Ethan nodded, abandoned the empty tray on a table and wound his way into the house.

Corey and Auntie Mac argued in the kitchen. Somewhere in all the mayhem, she and Dad had decided to like each other again, and she loved cooking in the ranch's enormous kitchen.

"And who exactly is it who owns a restaurant?" Auntie Mac towered over Corey, but that didn't seem to be the reason he backed down.

"Sorry, ma'am," Corey said. "I'm sure you know how much rum goes into the punch better than—Ethan!" He obviously welcomed any diversion possible.

"Company calls," Ethan said.

Corey's eyes narrowed. "I'll make sure the welcome wagon is set."

Ethan's aunt ruffled his hair as he passed. "Go get 'em, tiger."

He nodded and made his way to the front door. Opened it.

Spook stood there in his trench coat and fedora. Adam stood beside him, his hands in his pockets, his eyes so much like Tango's they made Ethan's heart ache even after six months.

"I am so glad you could make it," Ethan said.

Spook held back, his professional persona obviously in place in spite of the fact it was a wedding party. No huge surprise. He'd been increasingly distant and ridiculously hard to contact since his usual team had returned. He nodded then gestured. "Adam, this is—"

"Ethan Fox," Adam said. "I remember you."

"You do?" Spook seemed surprised. "He's lost a lot of the memories from before he had control, and those first days are kind of a blur."

Adam touched Ethan's chest. "The first time I opened my eyes, you were there."

"Wow." Ethan remembered the moment, too.

"And I fixed your spine." Adam smiled. "Looks like it's still working."

Ethan danced a couple of easy moves. "Like a charm."

Adam grinned. "You knew my mother and father?"

Ethan remembered the frequent non sequiturs. "I. . . yes, I did."

"And you know about. . . about what I am?"

"About who you are," Ethan corrected. "Yes, I do."

Spook nodded and smiled.

"Will you tell me stories about my parents?" Adam asked.

"I. . . yes. Sure." Ethan touched his arm. What had Adam gone through, trying to figure out how to live a normal life? Ethan sighed. His own journey wouldn't really be so much different, would it? He'd hoped it was something he and Adam might share, but Spook had all but severed ties—

The door opened. "Bro, what are you doing out here?" Kenny called, dripping wet. "Oh. Spook! Adam! You came for the party. Y'all are awesome." He tagged Adam's arm.

Adam grinned. "Fake Asian! Hello. You taught me swing."

"I did!" Kenny grinned. "I remember how much you like pie. You want cake?"

"Cake?" His interest literally rolled off him in waves, like heat over summer asphalt.

How did Spook keep that under the radar? He grabbed Kenny's arm. "Make sure you find him a suit. He spends way too much time in the pool swimming laps with Nicci."

Kenny laughed. "Stat."

Ethan opened the door for them. "Y'all go ahead while I annoy Spook."

Kenny corralled Adam into the house and left Ethan with Spook, who settled into a comfortable but respectable pose.

Damn. Was he that far gone? Ethan hoped he could get things back to the friendship they'd started at the clubhouse. "Adam looks good."

"He is. Very good." Spook wandered to the porch swing and sat on it.

Ethan followed. "How. . . how old is he?"

"I'm not sure," Spook said. He pushed the swing back and forth with his feet. "But I assume you didn't hold me back to talk about Adam."

"No." Ethan stood firmly in front of the swing.

"So. . ."

Well, time to shit or get off the pot.

"Why didn't Lucifer's dagger end me forever?" Ethan demanded.

"What?" Spook's face crinkled in confusion, then he laughed it off. "Of all the rancid garbage that happened last winter, *that's* what you obsessed on?"

Ethan sat beside his friend. "And that's your pathetic attempt to trick me into thinking it doesn't matter. But it's not just the dagger. I did some experimenting. A lot of spells don't work on me."

Spook rolled his eyes. "Drat." He glanced at the door then shook his head. "Kenny coming out here wasn't a coincidence at all. You planned it."

"I noticed you as soon as you hit the boundary around the house about half a mile away," Ethan said. "I can tell any time magic hits it." Hopefully, knowing how far Ethan had progressed would convince Spook to cooperate.

Spook laughed some more. "Ah Ethan, are you going to be the one in a million?"

"One in a million?"

"Nearly all the people I save go back to the real world and either pretend the Unknown doesn't exist or they try to ignore it as best they can." Spook pushed the swing so they'd move back and forth. "It makes seeing me again horribly painful."

Oh. Did that explain why he'd pulled away?

"One in a million," he continued, "they have to know more. They have to understand it. They have to get it to make sense."

"Then two in a million," Ethan said, pushing the swing. "Me and Kenny both." Of course, Stereo had already been interested long before. Then there was Woody, Corey and, of all people, Gunner. "Well, several in a million. You don't need to stay away from us, Spook. It doesn't hurt us."

Spook's eyes widened, then he relaxed into the swing. "I'm sorry you saw it that way. That isn't why. . ." They swung a few times. "I've been staying away more because something's looming on the horizon. Part of my absence is simply that I've been very busy. Part of it. . . a lot of it is I want to make sure you don't get tied into my world right now." He held up a hand. "And I know you'd all be perfectly willing to jump in, but trust me when I tell you this is beyond you right now." He sighed. "It might even be beyond my team. So ask me your questions, and I promise to answer them as truthfully as I can."

Ethan processed the information. "Why does magic get fucked up around me?" he asked at last.

"It's not all magic," Spook said. "Just spells that depend on you to be in a certain place at a certain time, to be right there where you are. You don't register to them the way most of us do."

"Why not?" Ethan asked.

"I'm not entirely sure." Spook kicked his feet like a kid. "Remember the magic test? The thaumometer?"

Ethan nodded.

"Remember the way the circle split in two?" He shrugged. "In some ways you're both here. . . and not here. It's the only reason Lucifer's dagger didn't end you permanently. I don't really get it."

"Don't work me like a client," Ethan demanded.

"Am I?" Spook asked.

Ethan stared at him a long time. "No," he admitted. "You aren't." Apparently, much of this was beyond Spook's understanding as well. Damn.

"All right." Spook patted Ethan's knee. "What *can* I tell you no one should ever know about himself? You're the reason the Cloaks didn't blow Dumass off the map after Twist created a spectacle of the town."

"Me?" The idea seemed ridiculous.

"Yes," Spook insisted. "Sister Liberata wanted to level Dumass, but she couldn't because you were here." He shrugged. "Someone told her not to, and it pissed her off. The only thing I could get from her was that she answers to a higher authority, whatever the heck that means."

"She said the same thing to me," Ethan admitted, "but aren't the Cloaks the highest authority there is?"

Spook raised an eyebrow.

"I've been researching," Ethan said.

Spook shook his head. "I've been digging, too, and I'm coming up empty. I have a friend who knows more, but he won't share and trying to force info out of him is pointless and bad for my health." He reached out and almost touched Ethan's arm. He dropped the hand in his lap. "You're a mystery, Ethan Fox, a mystery I have yet to solve and that, my friend, woes me greatly."

Ethan stared at the wooden slats. "Something the nun said to me. . . when she gave me the dagger." He steeled himself. "She asked me if I'd ever wondered why I wasn't in the apartment when my parents died."

The rocking stopped.

Spook went pale. Which said a lot.

"What?" Ethan asked.

Spook just stared.

"We were friends, damn it." Ethan touched Spook's shoulder. "I wasn't just a client. I know you have your regular team back, but we were friends, weren't we? What the hell did you just figure out?"

Spook slumped a little and his face relaxed. "I'm sorry. One in a million, remember?" He rose from the swing, removed the hat and pulled the jacket off, too. He dropped them on the swing and unbuttoned his shirt. "Unprofessional enough for you?"

Ethan liked it much better.

"How much have you adjusted to the magic?" Spook asked.

Ethan held up a hand. A miniature tornado appeared above it then a glass filled with ice, vodka and cranberry. He handed the glass to Spook. "Corey mixed it for you."

Spook took the glass with a wry grin. He sipped. Then he sighed and shook his head. "*Etiam partem temel.*" The glass sparkled brighter than when Ethan turned cranberry juice to booze.

"No blood flow," Spook said. "So alcohol doesn't work on me without an assist." He raised the glass. "Thanks. I'll teach you that one some time." He drank. "You've heard the many worlds theory? Every choice we make creates parallel timelines, one where we turned left and one where we turned right?"

Ethan nodded.

"I could be wrong," Spook said, "but from what Sister Liberata said to you and from what I divined from the magic test, you're from a timeline when someone turned right, whereas this is the timeline where we all turned left."

Ethan couldn't even process that.

Spook sighed. He shook his head and drank. "I think that in this timeline, an Ethan Fox died with his parents. And someone brought you, another Ethan Fox from another timeline, to take his place. For some reason, it seems rather important that an Ethan Fox exists in this dimension. You're him now."

Ethan heard the words, but they didn't connect, not in any realistic manner.

He ran them through his head again.

No, no, no, no, no. . . that sort of thing couldn't be true.

"But my Auntie Mac was babysitting," Ethan insisted, doubting his own words. "*She* had me when my parents died."

Spook shrugged. "You might need to have a talk with your Auntie Mac."

Bam! The door banged open, and Ethan jumped a foot in the air.

Dripping wet and in an old pair of Ethan's trunks, Adam hurried to Spook. "Um, excuse me. The girl named Stereo told me I should go fuck myself." His face contorted into an expression of obvious confusion. "I'm not sure what she means, but I figured I ought to ask if it's okay first. Can I?" He glanced from Ethan to Spook. "Is it fun?"

Spook nabbed his jacket and hat. "I think we should chaperone."

Ethan grabbed his arm. "Wait. All this about me. It's the truth?"

Spook slipped off his shirt. "I'm not honestly sure, Ethan. It's part of the reason I'm here. I want to help you figure things out. We *are* friends."

Good. Friends like Spook were hard to come by, which said a lot coming from Ethan.

"So, can I go fuck myself?" Adam asked.

"Do you have any idea what that means?" Spook asked.

"I think it has something to do with penises and vaginas. . ." He frowned. "Except I don't have a vagina." A huge smile lit his face. "But I couldn't find the cake, and it seemed like maybe the next best thing? I like cake."

Ethan barked a laugh. With that expression of interested confusion, Adam looked exactly like Whiskey. Ethan couldn't help himself, he threw his arms around the strange young man and hugged him close. "Tell you what, let's get you some cake because I am willing to bet Stereo was making a joke." At least, that's what he'd tell her to say. "I'm certain we can get Woody to show you some cool diving games. Almost as much fun."

Adam hugged Ethan tightly. "Woody. Heh, heh. His name means penis."

Ethan snorted. "Yeah, you're going to fit right in with the rest of the family." He took a deep breath. Okay, he shoved the bizarre revelation into the "to be dissected later" file.

He released Adam and turned to Spook. "Without you, all of us would've died. I'm going to bet a lot of people just count the corpses and lay the bodies at your feet." He moved closer. "Without you, this wedding wouldn't have happened. I wouldn't have my Dad." Ethan thought about what he'd just learned. "My real dad. No matter what I find out about any of this other crap, Dad's my dad. He always will be, and you made his wedding possible." He closed the space and clutched Spook in a tight hug. "Thank you."

After a second, Spook's arms closed around Ethan. "You're welcome."

"Son?" Speak of the devil as the screen door squealed. "Oh, hey Spook. Adam. Glad you could make it."

"Lucky!" Adam grabbed Dad in a hug, too, apparently not wanting to be left out. "I can't see your heart or lungs anymore, but they seem to work okay."

Dad stroked Adam's back. "I never really had a chance to thank you for that, so thank you."

"You're welcome," Adam said. "I was promised cake."

"I bet I can help you find it," Spook said. He turned to Ethan with a raised eyebrow. "Should I ask for a pair of shorts or can I just jump in the pool with my boxers?"

Ethan and his dad exchanged a glance.

"Go for the boxers," they both said.

Spook led Adam into the house.

Before his dad could say a word, Ethan hugged him tightly. "I know you're out here to prevent me from connecting to Spook, but please let me say something before you regale me with the dangers of magic for the hundredth time."

A couple of grackles argued on the fence.

Ethan watched them from the porch railing.

His dad settled beside him and waited.

"Remember that first trip to the cemetery when we moved here?" Ethan asked. Less than a year ago, but it felt like a lifetime. "That was the first time I'd ever felt like an orphan. Standing at those graves, I realized I'd never in my life felt like an orphan because I've always had you. But after the accident, I was truly afraid I'd lost you forever."

The grackles bickered a moment longer, then flew off.

"Our family has grown considerably since then," Ethan said, "but if

I ever lost you for real, none of the rest would matter. You have to know that. Please, please, please don't ever make me feel like an orphan again. I know how much you hate magic, Dad. But please don't ever let your fears take you away from me again."

A big hand rested on Ethan's shoulder. "I'm sorry that I ever made you feel that way, son. I promise never to do it again." He squeezed Ethan's shoulder. "Although I only came out here to ground you for serving magically enhanced cocktails to all your underage friends."

Ethan snorted. "I am such a drama queen." He sighed. "Okay, fine. I'm grounded, but only until the next time I need to save Dumass from horrible, undead evil."

Dad kissed the top of his head. "It's a deal."

The End

Postscript

Sister Liberata hated the White Room, a vast expanse of pale nothing that extended infinitely in every direction. Even down. Although her feet stood on something solid, to her eyes nothing kept her from falling into the infinite void. Despite everything she'd seen over the centuries, this place still disturbed her tremendously.

"Liberata." The unnamed man's voice drew her attention. He stood where he always stood: a couple of feet away in an old-fashioned three-piece suit and a leather top hat that contrasted sharply with the decidedly contemporary black braids that fell over his shoulders and the dark round glasses that made him seem like a Beatles fan.

"Do you have it?" he asked.

"Of course." She held up the golden chunk of amber.

He smiled and extended his hand. "And you're sure the soul didn't die with the body before you removed it?" She hated his self-satisfied smirk. Why did he never tell her his name or show her his eyes?

"The amber would be black if the soul had perished," she explained. "By the time the body expired, the soul lay in my palm." She withdrew the soul cage. "Why this one? With the dozens Twist killed and the hundreds of lives ruined. . . why save this one?" She held the crystal up where it reflected the light of the infinite void. "What makes this one so significant?"

He smiled. "In the great scheme of things, we're all fairly insignificant, aren't we?"

"No." She scrutinized the amber crystal. "Not all of us."

The fact that they protected certain lives at all cost proved those few had to be valuable beyond calculation. Leaving Dumass, Texas intact and protecting Ethan Fox had carried enormous risks. And this soul, too? In such close proximity? What could it mean?

The man pulled the glasses from his face and casually deposited them into his vest pocket. His eyes glowed with a golden radiance that would have been lost in the general light of the White Room if his skin had not been so very, very dark. "You know why I don't tell you more."

Because if the wrong people managed to extract the information from her in any way, the fate of the entire universe might be compromised. She knew the stakes.

"And yet, think about how much more effective I could be if I knew why you had me do the things I do." She held the crystal out again, accepting the reveal of his eyes as the conciliatory gesture it had to be.

He took the amber. "You are already as effective as any agent we have." He pocketed the soul. "The world is a safer place because of you."

"World?" Surely, she didn't seem so gullible.

He smiled. "Worlds." He patted the pocket with the soul cage. "Many worlds."

Liberata placed her hands on her hips. "Why not just rip some version of this kid from another dimension the way you usually do? What makes this *particular* Ephraim Miller so important?"

The man frowned and his eyes flared. "You know better than to use names. Even here."

And he vanished.

"You use mine all the time," she muttered before closing her eyes and escaping the damnable place.

Interstitial
Step 3.5 in the Tango Triptych

Notes on the Special Edition

The following stories are a bridge between the *Tango Triptych* and Ethan's inclusion to the *Tales of Mystery and* Woe series. The first crossover book, *Witches Grow in Threes,* picks up shortly after "Interstitial." Ethan and some of his friends from *Tango* try to rebuild lives while also attempting to fill the very large shoes left by Spook's team. *And* they fight giant armor-plated fleas.

Originally, "Interstitial" was a series of notes filling the gap between novels in my own mind. I started *Witches* sometime after *No Tengo Tango,* and I needed to figure out how the characters got from point A to point B. The more of these notes I wrote, the more I realized my readers might want to see the journey, too. These stories are an experiment. They aren't fully edited and vetted. This gives the reader a glimpse into the process of writing, an idea of how my mind works before the words have been wrangled into submission. As with all the "Special Edition" stories, they aren't particularly action packed. Instead, they flesh out the characters and relationships a bit. These young men have temporarily ended up in a sort of off the road group home for wayward men.

A note on all the drinking. Every story about investigators who deal with unholy crap includes a lot of drinking. Frankly, who can blame them? In this case, the characters end up realizing the negative consequences and clean up their act. The problem with a long story arc about addiction and recovery is that in the beginning, the addiction will seem glorified. I hope that these stories aren't triggering for anyone and that my readers will follow through until the end of the new series to see how the plotline develops.

Mmmm. Coffee. Best thing on the planet besides sex.

Not that Ethan had had a lot of sex in the last couple of months.

Well, not that he'd had any. The last girl he'd had sex with had died a horrible death at the hands of a vengeful spirit, and the only other girl he'd seen naked had turned out to be a dragon who'd also died at the hands of the same vengeful spirit.

On the same day.

So. . . coffee. Mmmmm. . .

"Morning, brother." Woody's sleepy voice preceded the plaid bathrobe he wore. It was funny. They were literally brothers since Dad had adopted Woody. They both liked saying it.

"Back atcha, brother."

Woody walked right at Ethan and opened his arms.

Nice. He'd been a little uncomfortable with all the affection at first.

Plaid flannel wrapped around Ethan, who hugged back, but. . . somehow Woody's action felt distinctly un-huglike.

The clink of glass and gurgle of liquid explained things.

"You know I'm all about the good morning hug, *ese*. . . but this is all about the *covfefe*." He relaxed into Ethan while adding cream, then drew away. He sipped. "Hot, hot, hot."

After a lifetime of pretty much no one in his daily life other than Dad, Ethan loved having roommates. These guys were so much more real friends than people he'd known in the dance world for over a decade. Well, they'd gone through hell together.

Woody drank his coffee.

How would he react to Ethan's proposal?

"You're thinking things." Woody regarded him over his mug. He sipped. "Stop it." Even with wrinkles across his face from the odd corduroy pillow he kept and his hair a ratty mess, Woody could still be a Gucci model. He frowned, shook his head, and palmed Ethan's face. "No thinky. Too early. Stop thinky."

Ethan pulled away, but he liked the casual affection. Was he about to kill all that?

Woody sighed with exaggeration. He waved his coffee cup at the dinette set. "Sit." He led the way. "Talk."

Damn. How did he know. . .? One day Ethan would learn how to hide his emotions.

They sat across from each other over the rustic wood table in the kitchen nook that had three glass walls overlooking a swimming pool that more closely resembled a natural pond with waterfall. Yeah. They'd both come up in the world.

Woody followed Ethan's gaze. "*Ese*, seriously. I'm getting worried."

Ethan pulled the check from his shirt pocket and slid it across the table. Was nine in the morning too early to add Irish crème to his coffee?

Woody slid the check closer. Lifted it.

"Fifty thousand dollars." Woody met Ethan's gaze over the paper. "We playing Monopoly tonight?"

Ethan shook his head.

"What the fuck is this?" And there was the anger Dr. Mike had told him to expect.

Fuck it. Ethan rose and crossed to the bar. "Kenny gets one, too." He brought the Irish crème to the table and poured a generous portion in his mug, offered it to Woody who waved him on.

Why the hell would anyone be mad about money? But Dr. Mike had warned him.

Woody sipped the coffee, then scoffed and shook his head in disgust. He moved to the bar and grabbed Whiskey which he added to his own mug. He offered it to Ethan with a raised eyebrow.

Ethan waved him on. In for an inch. . .

"You're my brother, *ese*. For real." Ethan sipped his spiked coffee, sort of glad that Woody had offered him a hit. "And not just because Dad adopted you. You, Corey, Kenny: you're my God damned family."

Woody held up the check and wiggled it. His raised eyebrows asked for more.

"Your parents were loaded," Ethan said. "You made tons off the website they stole from you."

He waved the check. "Not like this."

"I lucked into money," Ethan tried. "So did Corey—"

"Lucked?" He sucked his coffee. "You both lost your parents."

"So did you."

Well, it shut him up.

"So did Kenny, when it comes down to it."

Woody sipped.

"Look, none of us can have normal lives, anymore." Ethan pointed at the check. "That means my brother doesn't need to worry about where he's going to get his next meal, not—"

"I'm not worried about my next meal." He dropped the check on the table. "God gave me an enormous dick to make all the money I need." He rose. "I don't need your charity. And thanks for having faith that I can take care of myself."

Damn it. "That's not what this is about."

"No?" He finished his coffee. "Then what is it about?" He sipped, but his mug was empty. The way he fidgeted, he'd obviously wanted to make a grand exit, but he took the time to refill his mug with coffee, Irish Cream and whiskey.

It gave Ethan an extra minute. "It's about the fact that none of us is going to be able to get normal jobs and live normal lives, and why make life harder than it needs to be?"

Woody spun around. Whoa!

"Because maybe I can take care of myself," Woody spat, "and maybe I don't want to owe. . ." He huffed. He drank. "Fuck you and your money."

He stormed out of the bungalow.

A minute later, the outdoor shower turned on.

Maybe Ethan wanted a second drink, too.

What the almighty fuck? Having a new brother was usually cool and stuff, but what the almighty fuck? Woody had lived through the whole experience of family "taking care of him." And what had that meant? It

had meant towing the line and obeying the fucked-up rules and when he
didn't, when he'd disappointed his parents, what had happened? Not
only had they yanked the financial umbilical, they'd kicked him out of
the house, disowned him and. . . AND managed to steal all his hard-
earned money.

He scrubbed with the luffa and refused to chuckle at the pun.
Carajo.

A throat cleared nearby.

Dr. Mike.

Ugh.

Likely trying to play psychologist.

Well, he *was* a psychologist.

"Hi, Dr. Dad." Ha. That'd actually been a mistake, but it kind of
fit. Woody could let go of his annoyance enough to like the new nickname. "That's your new name."

Dr. Dad smiled. He held out a towel. "I'm probably better than
Ethan at explaining stuff."

Ugh. *Madre de Dios.* Woody turned off the water, took the towel
and went to work with it.

Dr. Dad held out the coffee. Did he know. . .?

His eyebrow raised. "Do I look stupid?"

No. He didn't. Woody sipped. He wrapped up in the robe
Ephraim had given him for Hanukah a few years back.

Dr. Dad waved at a bench.

Woody straddled it.

Dr. Dad sat opposite. "Are you going to let go of this supernatural
stuff?"

Woody scoffed. "Seriously? How can I? I found out that magic
and demons and ghosts are real. How do I pretend none of that exists?"

"Exactly." Dr. Dad pointed at Woody's mug.

Really? He handed it over.

Sip. Sip. Eyebrow raise. "You *mean* it these days."

Really? That was his take—

"That's the whole point, Sam."

Woody shuddered. Very few people got to call him Sam.

Dr. Dad startled. "Sorry. Woody."

Woody waved it off. "My bad. It's okay for you."

Another nod. "Ethan and Corey suddenly have shit-tons of money." Dr. Dad shrugged. "And you and Kenny don't. But y'all are family." He looked around. "I do all right, but nothing like this."

Well, Corey was worth millions.

"My bank account just grew, too."

Sure, but he'd married Lucky.

The other man held up a hand. "Lucky didn't inherit Ethan's money. Nor did he inherit Corey's. Those boys know all of us will want to help them figure out this whole witchcraft thing, and they know none of us will ever have normal lives again."

It was like he could read everyone's minds.

"This isn't charity," Dr. Dad said. "It's payback."

Woody scoffed. "What the fuck do they owe me for?"

His eyes grew so sad. "Ephraim."

Qué mierda?

"Ethan, at least, feels he's to blame for Ephraim's death. If Twist hadn't come after Ethan, Ephraim would be alive."

Well, that wasn't wrong.

And that made more sense than anything.

Of course, Ethan felt guilty. It's what he did.

Carajo. Woody sipped. Held the mug out to Dr. Dad.

He sipped.

Carajo.

Wait a minute. "Lucky adopted me before you and him tied the knot. Are you legally my dad?"

Dr. Dad stiffened. He set down the mug. He shook his head. "No. I'm not. . . not legally."

Woody grabbed his hand. "Legal doesn't matter. Right?"

Dr. Dad met Woody's gaze. His eyes got all watery and shit. His other hand found Woody's. "No, son. Legal doesn't matter at all."

He'd blown it. Ethan had hoped that setting Woody up with a... what the hell was it? A stipend? An allowance? Hm. Calling it that did make it less attractive. He'd hoped to ease Woody's mind. Nope. That dude had such messed-up parents who'd screwed him over that maybe he'd never trust anyone. Ethan hadn't seen a sign of his brother all day.

And then there he was.

Ethan sat in the hot tub with a drink at his side.

Woody approached and seemed not so hostile. Maybe?

"Hey, brother," Woody said.

Every muscle in Ethan's body relaxed. His use of that word had to mean he didn't hate Ethan.

Okay. Could he push it?

He raised a finger, then pointed it at the cocktail waiting at the side of the hot tub. "First you take that." He pointed at the water. "Then you climb in here." He raised the finger. "Then we talk."

Would it work to break the ice?

Woody smiled. Nice. He picked up the cocktail and sipped. He made an appreciative face. Extra nice.

A minute later he sat in the tub facing Ethan, the Cape Cod held up between them.

Stellar.

Ethan raised his glass as well.

Woody sipped the drink, then eased back. "I'm sorry. I talked to Dr. Dad."

Ethen snorted. Awesome!

Woody smiled. "Yeah. That's his name from now on."

Perfect.

Woody deflated. He leaned closer. "*Ese*, you know my parents, right?"

Ethan nodded.

"Please tell me that explains it all?"

It did. Ethan raised his glass again. "Cheers."

Woody raised his. "I'm really sorry."

"I get it." Sip. Sip. "You trusted them to take care of you, and they righteously screwed your pooch."

"Without lube." He sipped. "Okay… so we all have a bunch of money. Now what?"

That was the Twenty Thousand Dollar Question, as it were.

Might as well say it out loud. "I'm not going to college."

Woody sputtered his drink. "Straight-A-Boy said what?"

"I don't know. I might do something online, but this…" He raised the cocktail glass. "*Ad luntum de classio.*" A tiny whirlpool formed in the drink that grew into a spout lit by little sparkling lights. "I'm not going to learn about that in any college."

Light applause reached them from the deck. "Not unless we can find a real-world Hogwarts." Kenny moved into the light. "I hear we're all rich, now." He set his drink on a table and stripped off. "So what do we do next." He settled into the hot tub near Woody. "You were a dick about it, weren't you?"

Woody blushed.

Kenny chuckled. "Yeah, that's why Corey talked to me and Ethan got you." He chucked Woody's shoulder. "My parents aren't great, but they didn't completely screw my pooch without lube."

Well, of course, he'd overheard them.

"As far as next," Ethan said, "I say we all move to Austin."

Kenny nodded sagely. They'd already discussed this.

"I like the idea," Woody said. "More words?"

"I'll need to take a class or two to keep the dads off my back." He'd given it a lot of thought. "Plus, I'll be closer to Spook's group, so maybe I can get training."

"Me, too, on the training," Kenny added. "And Stereo three."

"You can give the modeling gig the ol' college try." Assuming he wanted that. "Or take classes or whatever." He pointed at the house. "Corey needs a business degree or something, and Saundra can help him with all the legalese."

"Plus Theresa will totes def want college," Woody said, "And UT is awesome."

Ethan nodded, but Theresa? Of all of them, she could do better than UT. "Juicy is rebuilding the studio, so she'll stay here, and Cosita is heading back to Mexico."

"What the what?" The boys were so cute when they said things at the same time.

Ethan nodded. "She wants to be a doctor." She was a smart girl, but not Theresa smart, and as a Mexican woman without a green card in a male-dominated world, she already had a couple of strikes against her.

"How's Trudy taking it?" Woody asked.

"She's not thrilled, obviously, but she gets it."

Woody sipped his drink. "I give the studio six months, then Trudy will hand it off to someone and end in Austin, or LA or someplace like that." He met Ethan's eyes. "I'm not sure about the modeling thing."

"Eight-pack said what?" Ethan almost choked on his drink.

"Don't get me wrong," Woody said, "I appreciate the help from Saundra and all, but I could make a lot more money with porn, and I really don't see those going hand in hand."

Which made sense. Hopefully, Kenny would field this one.

"You know I love to watch you fuck as much as the next straight guy," Kenny said. "And if you genuinely like doing the porn, then I'll keep filming… but you don't *need* to do it, anymore."

Woody's face fell a little flat.

Before he could get pissed again, Ethan jumped back in. "No, I did *not* give you that money to save your soul or some other self-righteous bullshit." Like Woody's parents would have done. "But if we all move to Austin, we'll have rent and shit, and this way we all have our *own* money, and if you want to go your own way, you can do that, too. I mean, if you're serious about a career in porn, you're better off in LA or something, right? And this way you can pick and choose what you do, or, hell, hire your own models and make your own videos with a better budget. You and Kenny both."

Woody's face relaxed.

"Corey and I just want everyone to have options," Ethan insisted. "After all the shit that went down, I know we all feel like the future was ripped out from under us."

Woody looked down into the swirling water.

Kenny dropped a hand on his shoulder.

Woody looked up. Met Kenny's gaze. Sort of almost smiled. Then his face pinched. "What about all the film stuff? Austin has a great film school."

"Ha." Kenny patted the shoulder and settled back. "They have a great film school that I'm not likely to get into at this point." He shrugged. "I really don't know, though. After finding about this whole Unknown world out there." He drank. "Nothing else really seems to matter to me." He glanced at the other guys in turn. "Except this new Bizarro World family."

Yeah, Ethan felt much the same.

"Ethan?"

The voice was unfamiliar. Maybe it would go away if he ignored it.

"Ethan?" A little louder, but like he was pretending to whisper.

"Who?" It was all Ethan could manage as the deep, deep comfort of his blanket coaxed him back to slumber. He squeezed his eyes shut hoping the voice would go away. Bad voice.

"Fox Bastard?"

Ah. Shit. Adam. That's right. He and Spook were visiting for the weekend. Ethan opened his eyes—

Holy Hell! Bright golden face glowing at him from a foot away.

The light filled the entire fucking room.

"Ahhhh!" Ethan's back hit the headboard, vaguely reminding him of a similar situation with Corey once upon a time. A fireball flared into his hand.

Adam dropped onto his butt, his eyes wide and staring. "Sorry! Sorry! Sorry!" He was, unsurprisingly, naked. Fortunately, as long as nobody's girlfriend was around, the ranch didn't have much of a dress code.

He also glowed from head to toe.

"What did I do?" Adam asked in that too low, too young voice of his, afraid and guilty all at once. "What's wrong? What'd I do?"

Ah, hell, the poor kid seemed terrified. "You're glowing." Ethan shook out the flaming hand and crawled out of bed to Adam's side. "You just startled me."

Adam stretched out his arms and regarded them. "I did that so I wouldn't scare you sneaking into your bedroom in the dark." He clutched his arms tightly to his sides. "It didn't work so well."

No. No, it hadn't. Ethan slouched against the wall. "What's up Adam?"

Adam shook his head. "Never mind. I'll go." He started to roll away from Ethan, who touched one arm.

"Don't."

The touch stopped the strange man-child. He looked at the hand on his arm, into Ethan's face.

"I'm not angry, Adam," Ethan said. "You just scared me."

Adam slouched. "I scare a lot of people."

Oh, damn, not the right thing to say to someone with Adam's vast power and lack of control. He likely scared everyone.

Adam looked into Ethan's eyes. "You're afraid of me?"

"Hell, no." Ethan opened his arms to Adam and beckoned him with both hands. "You startled me. Not the same thing. Come here."

Adam grinned and crawled into Ethan's arms, hugging him tightly like a toddler. "I like hugs."

After a moment, he relaxed against Ethan's side, crisis likely forgotten. "Will you swim with me?" Adam asked it as if swimming at whatever the hell o'clock in the morning were perfectly normal. Well, in all honesty, Ethan did more of that than the average guy.

"I'm sorry." Adam pulled away and he rose to his feet. "I should go. I... I miss Nicci."

Nicodemus the often-naked demon who was likely the reason for Adam's complete and utter lack of inhibition.

Ethan made a non-committal noise to slow him down. "It just takes me a minute to wake up." He pushed to his feet. It wasn't like he had to get up early in the morning.

Adam brightened. He also smiled a lot. "Are you sure?"

Feet. Legs. Oh yeah. That's how they worked. Ethan pushed up to vertical.

And yet Adam was at least two inches taller. How weird that someone only a year-and-a-half old was so tall.

"Lead the way, my intrepid friend." Ethan gestured past Adam at the hallway.

More with the big smile. "I like the words you use. What is

intrepid?"

"Bold, courageous."

Adam nodded a lot. "I am those things." He frowned. "Maestro says it a fault." He smiled. "I'm glad you think it's a good thing."

He turned and lead the way, the golden aura settling into something a bit more like a night light than a lighthouse beacon as they navigated the short distance from Ethan's room to the front door of the prefab bungalow he and Woody shared.

Once outside, Ethan hit the switch for the underwater pool lights, which would be more than enough. Adam took two more strides and dove smoothly into the water, his glow fading.

Ethan stripped out of his boxers and dove. When he surfaced, Adam stood in the waterfall, laughing and turning in circles. "Our pool doesn't have one of these."

He said the same thing every time he visited. When he smiled, he looked so much like Tango. Even after almost a year, that still tugged at Ethan's heart. But Adam was so… he was so much his own person, and he was so… good. Kind. Affectionate.

His mother would be so proud.

Adam waved Ethan closer with both hands. "You, too!"

So Ethan waded into the waist deep water toward the waterfall. When he was close enough, Adam held out his hands, waving them, and Ethan took them. They turned circles under the waterfall, Adam laughing and laughing.

With everything he'd been through, his joy was a miracle. He claimed that he'd forgotten everything that'd happened with "the bad man," but Ethan suspected the truth was more complicated than that.

Adam released Ethan's hands. "This is the best place ever!" His face somehow managed to smile even more. "Watch this!"

He lifted his hands toward the top of the waterfall, and the water— the water morphed into liquid light! Pink and yellow and orange like a watery sunrise pouring down over them.

And when it splashed into the pool below, it fractalized and spread out across the surface until a million splinters of light faded into the main body of water.

Ethan could barely breathe. He'd never in his life seen anything so amazing, and he'd seen a girl transform into a golden dragon.

And Adam laughed and laughed. "I'm glad you like it."

"How do you do that without getting exhausted?" Almost anything Ethan tried left him exhausted.

"Pretty lights don't take much," Adam explained. "It's all fake. Only real stuff wears me out, and even then, not so much."

And how would Spook explain *that* tidbit of information?

"I wish I had your training," Ethan admitted. He waved a hand.

The water nearby swirled into a whirlpool.

"That's about all I got. And it wears me out." He waved a hand to dispel the magic before it tired him.

"You're actually moving water," Adam said. "That's harder." He gazed up at the light show he'd created. The colors painted his skin.

"See? I wish I knew stuff like that." He ran a hand through the liquid light. It felt like water. "You're lucky to have people training you like this."

"Come live with us!" Adam grabbed Ethan's arms.

Ethan had wished a hundred times that he could. "Unfortunately, I have, like, a family for the first time in my life. I mean, Dad's always been great... but I have all these brothers, now, and a second dad." He held Adam's arms, too. "I'm hoping to move to Austin, though, so maybe Spook will train me, but..." But what? "But I have to think of my family."

The ubiquitous smile faded, as did the stellar light show. "I wish I had a family."

"What about Spook and his team?"

"They're a team." He shrugged. "Not a family. I mean, they're great. I love them all like what I think family feels like... but they..." He sort of slouched.

Ethan put his arms around Adam and pulled his head down onto his shoulder.

"See?" Adam muttered into Ethan's neck, encircling Ethan's shoulders with his arms. "That's what's different. I don't get so many hugs as when I'm with you."

And, in reality, he was less than a two-year-old living inside the body of a muscley adult who a lot of people would feel strange cuddling.

Hmmm…. Maybe all the training wasn't worth it for someone like Adam.

In a way, Ethan had been there for Adam's birth, not the physical birth of the body which had been Twist's property at the time, but the moment Ethan himself had returned Adam's soul, the moment when this magical child had first looked through his own eyes.

Adam remembered the moment, too.

"When I move to Austin," Ethan whispered. "I'll make sure you get as many hugs as I can manage."

Adam squeezed him tighter.

Wait a minute, who was in bed with Ethan? What had he…? Who had he…? Oh, yeah. Adam.

Ethan chuckled. In his unusual life, he woke up with dudes more often than any girl.

Adam sucked his thumb with his fingers curled around his nose.

After the swim, Ethan had known that Adam didn't really want to be alone. He'd never actually slept naked with another naked man curled up around him, but Adam, who Ethan would always remember from that first time their eyes met, was just a little kid who didn't understand why anyone would need to wear clothes to bed.

Ethan rubbed a hand over his eyes.

Someone cleared their throat.

Spook. In the doorway. "Sorry… This is creepy."

Really? "You obviously don't know my dad all that well." He climbed out of bed, careful not to wake Adam. Boxers. T-shirt in case it was chilly.

He led the way outside to the pool. The door to Woody's room was, as always, open, and if he were still asleep Ethan didn't want to wake him.

"Sorry about that," Spook said once they were outside.

"Why?" Ethan dropped into a chair and swung one leg over the arm.

"What?"

"Why apologize?" Ethan waved at the chair opposite. "Adam may look like a grown man, but he's a baby in most ways. Did you know he sucks his thumb?"

Spook paused mid-sit. "No. I…" He sat. "No. I didn't."

"You should."

"I know."

They stared at each other in silence a few moments.

Something was missing.

Something important.

Something vital.

"Holy fuck!" Ethan jumped up. "I don't have covfefe!"

"Covfefe?"

Ethan shrugged. "Coffee. It's a joke."

He waved Spook into the bungalow and padded over to his brother's door. Woody lay sprawled on his stomach, every limb splayed out in a different direction, sheet bunched around his waist. His brother. In spite of all the horrible shit that had happened in the last year, Ethan had exactly the family he'd always wanted without even knowing it. Was he evil for being just a tiny bit grateful?

He closed the door as quietly as possible. Alone time with Spook would be a good thing.

When he turned back to the kitchen, Spook already had coffee brewing.

Sweet.

Spook was kind enough to hold a comfortable silence until Ethan perched atop a stool at the breakfast bar with a steaming hot cup of coffee in both hands.

Sip. Ahhh….. Life.

"Any chance I can get some training today?" he asked.

"Absolutely." Spook glanced at the main house. "Do we need to go out to the back forty so Papa Lucky doesn't see us?"

Damn.

"Probably."

Spook sipped his own coffee, but his was likely for show and camaraderie. "You know I wish I could work with you more." He held up a hand. "Sorry. That sounded too professional." He sighed. "You know I wish I could work with you more." And the tone of voice changed everything.

"I know." Mmm, caffeine. "But you have a lot going on, and I'm hours away from Austin… but…"

"But?"

Ethan leaned closer. "We're talking about moving to Austin. I'd be closer. Maybe once in a while…"

Spook smiled. "I'd like that." Then his face changed, a sort of shadow passed over it. He started to lean away from Ethan but stopped. He leaned closer instead. After a moment's hesitation, he dropped a hand on Ethan's. "If things were different, I'd invite you all to live at the clubhouse. That place is huge."

"Really?" That would be amazing.

Spook released Ethan's hand and held up his own. "I'm sorry. I shouldn't even have said." He leaned back. "It's just not possible right now." He glanced as if someone might overhear them. "Look. I understand. When I met Maestro a year and a half ago—" He startled. "Jebus, is that all it was?" He shook his head. "Anyway, I begged him to train me, and I have learned more than in all the years since I died." He shook his head.

He sat back. "We stirred up a hornet's nest. A number of our enemies have banded together and are targeting us." He sipped his coffee. "That's how Ross died. Right under my nose. Someone put micro-explosives in his head and killed him with what any normal doctor would have called the world's unluckiest aneurism. They've targeted people everyone on my team cares about. I think we've kept Adam off the radar so far, but it also means he's pretty much stuck at the clubhouse all the time. We just can't risk putting a bullseye on anyone else right now. Not until we figure out who's doing this and stop them."

Wow. Just wow.

Spook smiled. "Welcome to the life." He frowned. "If you really do jump into this life… don't… don't stir up the hornets."

More wow.

"This is something you can't tell anyone," Spook said. "Not anyone. Not your dad. No one."

"What the hell?" Ethan sucked at keeping secrets. "Why tell me?"

"Adam knows you. He likes you and trusts you." He glanced around the kitchen. "You're the logical place for him to hide out for a few months while we track down our stalkers. And…"

He held up a key.

"What's this?"

"Nicci's insurance policy." He handed the key over. "You saw his demon form. He's cursed to the property… to the land under the clubhouse. He can't leave it. If… If the rest of us die… and we don't figure out how to remove the curse, we want someone to be able to visit him. To make sure he isn't alone. To maybe talk to someone like Liberata to see if she can find a way to release him."

"Why not go to her yourself, now?"

Spook shrugged. "Right now, Nicci doesn't want to owe her any favors. But… if worse comes to worst."

Ethan turned the key in his hand. Seemed pretty much like a normal key anyone might have made at Wal-Mart. "So… that's a key to the clubhouse?"

"It is," Spook said. "It works the physical lock and also opens all the magic cantrips and whatnot."

"Whatnot?" What might that even mean?

"Whatnot." So he wasn't going to elaborate.

Ethan placed the key on the bar. "How much danger are you really in?"

Spook met his gaze evenly. "I just handed you a key to the clubhouse. You are the only human being outside my team who has one of those. I'm also…" He paused and took a deep breath. "I'm also asking you to babysit Adam, someone who is potentially the most powerful mage this planet has seen since Merlin. Neither of those things would happen if we had a realistic shot at surviving this attack."

"Wow." Was he serious?

"Yeah." He nodded.

"Merlin was real?" Ethan asked.

Spook's face devolved into confusion, then he shook his head and chuckled. "And that's the takeaway."

"Not really," Ethan admitted. "Just trying to defuse the tension."

Spook smiled. "At least you didn't push me into the pool this time."

"I could. "

He lost the smile. "No. Sorry. Not today. I'm really not in the mood."

"No. Me neither." Mmmm, coffee. "Not really." He drank more coffee, not wanting to ask the next question. "So... you might actually die?"

"Might could."

"Didn't think you could. I mean, you're already dead."

"I thought the same thing for the same reason." He sighed. "The stakes are higher."

Ethan pushed away from the bar and around it. He grabbed Spook in a hug.

Spook slipped off his bar stool and hugged Ethan with equal conviction.

"I really hope you don't die," Ethan said.

"Me, too, Ethan. Me, too."

"They're dead!" Adam screamed. "They're dead! They're dead!"

Ethan awoke in an instant. Adam's outbursts weren't uncommon, but this had to be a nightmare of Herculean proportions.

Wait. Where was he? Oh yeah, they'd had a pizza party in the main house, so Ethan had crashed on the couch fully dressed.

He shifted onto the other couch, where Adam had fallen asleep watching a *Stranger Things* marathon, chuckling the whole time.

He pulled Adam close. "It's okay, Adam. It was a dream."

The TV played on in the background.

Kenny had passed out in a recliner. He rubbed sleep from his eyes and sat up. Yeah, people waking up screaming was kind of the new normal.

Dad and Dr. Dad stood nearby in their PJ's all concerned and stuff but had apparently accepted the fact that Ethan comforted Adam better than anyone.

"On the moon!" Adam shouted. "They explodicated on the moon!"

Wow, that was a weird dream even by Adam's standards. Ethan stroked Adam's hair. "It's okay, Adam, it was just a dream."

"Ethan." That was Dad in a less than patient voice. What the hell?

"On the moon." But Adam's voice was quieter, now. "They explodicated on the moon. Dead. Dead."

"Ethan!" And that was Dad's pay attention voice. Really? What the fucking hell?

"Just a minute, okay?"

"Look at the God damned TV, Ethan." And that was Dad's don't you dare ignore me voice.

Ethan looked at the God damned TV. And he listened.

"An explosion of unprecedented power shook the moon." The commentator seemed pretty freaked out. "Literally *shook* the moon. Originating on the dark side, we have no photos or video…"

Adam pointed at the screen. He shrieked.

Windows shattered.

So did the TV.

Ethan held Adam closer.

Adam wept.

Could he be right? Spook had talked about a hornet's nest they'd stirred up.

But the moon? The fucking *moon*?

"Could it…" Kenny dropped onto the couch beside Ethan. "I mean… how… the moon?"

"Because that would be the deal breaker?" Corey stood behind the couch.

Damn. Ethan held Adam.

Kenny dropped a hand onto Ethan's arm.

So did Corey.

"Who do you think is dead?" Dr. Dad asked.

Who indeed?

"Spook's team," Ethan said. "He knew this might be coming. He told me."

"What?" Kenny's hand squeezed all the tighter.

Their dads closed in as well.

"He told you this might happen, and you didn't share that?" Dad asked.

Ethan kissed Adam's head. "When someone like Spook tells me to keep a secret, I damn well keep it a secret."

Everyone seemed to understand. Even Dad.

"So what do we do?" Corey asked. "I mean, what'll the news make of it?"

Kenny worked his tablet. "They've laid down a smokescreen. Something about a satellite off course."

Of course. Ethan shifted Adam to Kenny, who easily took the big man into his lap.

"Because satellites are all the way up past the lunar orbit?" Woody's voice. He must have heard the commotion.

So they were all there.

Well, everyone but Stereo who'd suddenly moved to Houston with her parents and dumped Kenny. But that was an entirely different story.

Ethan moved to the bar. He tapped the side of it, and a little drawer opened.

His dads made noises of surprise.

His brothers did not.

Ethan held up the key Spook had given him a month earlier. "I think it's time for a road trip."

The clubhouse hadn't changed, at least on the outside. It was still a piece of shit, beige brick building with the windows boarded over. The parking lot had grown over with weeds.

"Hard to believe what's inside that thing," Corey said.

Amen to that.

Ethan glanced to his left. Kenny and Woody stood still as statues. They knew the reverence they needed to show this place.

To his right, Corey and Adam stood just as still. Corey glanced at

Adam, seemed to notice his fears and threw an arm around his shoulders. "You let us know if it's too much, big guy."

Adam nodded. "Thanks."

Ethan had the key, so he moved in first.

He slipped the key in the lock.

It turned.

The door opened.

And there was absolutely no fanfare at all, just the vague smell of sandalwood as Ethan passed into the foyer of the most incredible superhero clubhouse on the planet.

Lights turned on automatically.

Beige and olive green predominated.

The foyer was the same as it ever had been. Except for the silence.

"I miss the bossa nova," Kenny said.

And there it was. When they'd been there before, music had played through every corridor.

It had almost made the building seem alive.

Now? Nothing. Quiet. Dead.

Adam rushed forward, hurried behind the reception desk.

In moments, the *Boy from Impanema* sung by Astrud Gilberto filtered through the speakers.

He popped up from behind the counter. "Better?"

"Much better," Ethan said. "Thanks." He glanced around. "Nicci?" Maybe louder. "Nicci! Nicodemus!"

And nothing. No naked demon.

Ethan looked to Kenny who would likely have the best explanation, but he just shrugged. "Maybe they found a way to release him?"

It made as much sense as anything.

"Any way to figure out exactly what happened?" Ethan asked.

Kenny rushed around to take up a station beside Adam. He futzed with the computer there.

He futzed some more.

Everyone remained patient, against all odds. What the hell else could they do?

Kenny sighed. "Unless I can find a computer that hasn't been wiped, I'm empty."

"Wiped?" Ethan asked.

"Maestro would know a million times more about computers than Kenny," Adam said, then startled. "Sorry, Kenny. No offence."

Kenny harrumphed. "None taken. From what I've heard about the guy, I wish I could've learned from him."

Adam nodded. "He was very smart."

Understatement of the century that, from everything Spook had told Ethan about the guy.

"So now what?" Corey asked.

Indeed.

They wandered down corridors into the living quarters the entire dance team had occupied an entire lifetime ago, last year.

"Wait." That was Kenny. He pointed at a door. "Ethan Fox."

A label on the door had Ethan's name on it.

Kenny hurried to the next door. "Kenny Valentino."

Corey stopped at the door across from Ethan's. "Here's me."

Woody crossed to the door beside Corey's. "And me."

Adam sighed. "I'm in a different part of the building."

But Ethan found something that spoke differently. "I think you have a new room."

It was the room beside Ethan's on the other side from Kenny's.

He kept walking. "Trudy. Cosita. . . Stereo." Oops.

"And over here we have Jimmy Russo and…" Kenny chuckled, but it was forced. "And this one is labelled, 'The Dads.'"

Wow. They'd thought of everything.

Damn.

"Dude," that was Kenny again. "So they want us to take over?"

Ethan shrugged. How in the world would he know what they'd really wanted? Spook had given him a key to the castle, but other than that. . .

His phone vibrated.

Really? Who in the world…

"Saundra," he told the rest. A text. "I'm in the lobby of that fucking maze. I saw your car. Don't make me wait."

Shit. Saundra?

They high-tailed it to the lobby.

And there she stood, in a three-piece suit and tons of righteous indignation. As soon as they hit the space, she pulled up, which made her taller than everyone but Adam.

"Ethan," she said in her professional voice. She nodded at Woody, who was also one of her clients. "Sam." She sort of glanced at the rest. "Boys."

"What are *you* doing here?" Ethan asked.

She raised an eyebrow.

"Ma'am." Ethan amended.

Saundra glanced around the lobby. "How long have you been here?"

Ethan glanced at his phone. "About 20 minutes?"

Saundra nodded. "About the time you turned the key in the lock, I received a text." She held up the phone.

Hello Saundra. I don't care what you're doing right now; go the clubhouse right fucking now. The sender had been Maestro.

"So I did." She raised an eyebrow. Yeah. That meant he'd paid her a shit ton of money to generate such a prompt unquestioning response. "And this interesting document hit my phone when I arrived."

She held the cell out again.

Lots of words. Lots and lots of words.

"I'm sorry, Saundra," Ethan said. "Can you translate for me?"

She raised an eyebrow. "I can do better." She glanced at Kenny. "Bluetooth me?"

He worked on the computer behind the reception desk.

The TV in the lobby came to life.

"Ethan Fox." The man in the video was white, middle-aged, and not very remarkable. "I know a friend of yours." It had to be Maestro, Spook's mentor. "If you're viewing this video, I'm dead, which will likely surprise me as much as anyone else."

Well, he *had* thought he was immortal from what Spook had said.

"We're all dead." He frowned. "Spook, too. I know you were friends. I'm sorry." He waited a second or two. "The thing is, this building is special, and it needs a caretaker. If Nicci is still bound to the soil, he'll need friends. And Adam..." Another pause. "Adam most likely is better off with you than with me, anyway, from all I've heard about you."

Adam shifted away from the reception desk and Ethan met him, circled his waist with an arm and squeezed.

Adam smiled.

"I assume your lawyer is there with you," he said. "Saundra will take care of the paperwork, but I am leaving you, Ethan Fox, also known as Foxtrot, full ownership of the property known in familiar terms as the Clubhouse. It's yours to do with as you see fit." He grinned. "From what Spook has told me, you will do us proud."

And the video ended as every one of Ethan's friends gasped.

Fuck.

No, seriously: Fuck.

"It's mine?" Ethan muttered.

"It is," Saundra said. "So now you own a superhero clubhouse."

No matter what else he wanted to think, one idea permeated Ethan's entire being. "Yeah. Dad's going to birth a cow."

Saundra snorted. "An entire herd. And then he's going to kill me."

Ethan turned to her, trying his almighty best to stay connected to reality. "You realize that may actually be literal and not figurative."

She scoffed. "I am well aware, Ethan Fox, of the potential literary ramifications of my statement."

Gunner stood on Corey's porch, a place he'd been a million times, but somehow, he just couldn't push the fucking doorbell.

Do it! Fucking do it!

It was the shrink, the one the court had appointed as part of his probation, and he had all these ideas about atonement and making shit right.

Fuck. Make it right or go back to jail.

Fine.

Fine.

But all those... but everyone lived here, now. And he hadn't seen

Corey in months.

Hard to do from inside jail a hundred miles away.

Fine. Push the God damned button.

And there was that lame set of chimes.

The door slammed open.

Fox. In his damn boxer briefs and a t-shirt. His eyes opened wide. "You're not Lenny with pizza." He glanced down. "Lenny doesn't care..." He shook his head and moved forward... stopped. He extended a hand. "It's good to see you, Gunner. I mean it, but I'm not hugging you in my underwear."

Gunner scoffed. "No shit—" Not what he was supposed to say. He took the offered hand and shook it. "Good to see you, too." He grinned. "Although I don't know I needed to see so much of you."

Fox smiled and smacked Gunner's hand. "You just keep wishing."

Good. He could give him shit. That... had made the whole...

Fuck...

"Come on in," Fox moved out of the way. "What brings you out into the middle of nowhere?"

Corey. Who used to be Gunner's best friend but was now practically a stranger.

Damn it.

"Um..." Fuck. New manners. "I was hoping to see Corey."

The weird "duh" reaction Fox made helped, as if he realized that while he lived here now, Gunner used to be....

Had always been....

Fuck.....

"He's out in the barn throwing hay." Fox gestured. "I'm sure you know your way out there better than me."

Yeah. Nice try, douchebag.

Fuck. Chill. *Chill.*

Fox's face changed. Did he know he was being a dick?

"Look, Gunner..." He stepped forward, but thankfully didn't, like, try to hug him or anything. "I can't say this without sounding like a douchebag, but it's good to see you, and I know you're Corey's brother, long before I came to town. He has been fucking worried about you, but they wouldn't let him visit, and it.... It wrecked him. He tried, he *seriously* fucking tried to see you." He shook his head. "We all did, but I know Corey's the important one."

He finally shut up.

"You tried to visit me?"

His mouth hung open a while. Then, "I did. Don't read too much into it."

Nice. Snarky.

"I won't." Gunner turned to go out to the barn. He stopped. "Fox?"

"Uh-huh?"

"For a douchebag," Gunner said, "you're not so much of an asshole as most."

"Well, that just makes my entire week."

God damnit. He kept not being an asshole.

Whatever.

More issues.

Tromp, tromp, tromp.

Coery's usual gay-as-shit music poured out of the barn.

Damn it. Not the right words.

Every fucking thought in Gunner's head was wrong. Every word he said to his fucking shrink was corrected and sanitized.

He was such a complete fuck-up, why would Corey even listen to him?

Well, the shrink fuckin' insisted.

Because probation.

Fine.

Just fine.

Fine.

This was Corey. Gunner owed him.

Corey was in his zone. Pick up a bale, heft it, throw it. Repeat.

Gunner had seen it a million times, had been there to help him a million times, too.

This was different.

This was now.

Corey had new friends.

And that was cool. Shit changed.

The shrink had convinced Gunner changing shit was good.

Shit always changed.

That's how shit worked.

Fine.

When Corey was in the zone, only one thing touched him.

Gunner turned off the Bluetooth speaker.

As expected, the big goofball spun around with murder in his eyes.

Then everything changed.

"Gunner! Holy fuck!" Corey ran full tilt at him, engulfed him in his huge fucking arms and pulled him tight to his giant farmer's body.

Well, hell, that was just Corey's way. In some ways, he was just a big kid.

Gunner would never admit how wonderful the enthusiasm felt.

He'd worried, you know?

Had Corey moved past it all?

"I tried to visit you," he said in a voice that practically begged Gunner to believe him. "They wouldn't let me. You have to believe me."

A thousand instincts screamed at Gunner to make a joke out of it.

To insult Corey for being a little girl.

But no…. not anymore.

Fuck all that.

Gunner squeezed Corey back. "I heard, bro. I heard."

It was as much as he could do.

Corey held him at arm's length. "So what now?"

Wow. Could he have come up with a worse question? Gunner was on probation. His fucked-up parents' place was gone thanks to all the debt and bullshit.

Where would he go?

No. Not Corey's problem. Not why Gunner was there.

"Whaa—at?" He blew it off. "Not why I'm here."

A giant smile appeared on Corey's face. Nice. He bought it. "You came to help me throw hay!"

Well, not really, but sure.

With the usual grunt, Gunner took his place opposite Corey.

Grab. Lift. Throw.

Grab. Lift. Throw.

Huh. With not much to do but push metal for the last six months, whether hiding out or in jail, Gunner was big enough, now, he might throw these bales on his own.

But, nah, doing the work with Corey felt like old times. Every time he stayed over, he'd always helped with the chores. That was Corey's mom, likely doing her best to help her son's asshole friend turn out respectable. He'd never understood why Cory did chores at all. Couldn't the truck that brought the hay just dump it over there rather than over here, but he'd have been damned if he didn't show appreciation for all the weekends he'd been able to escape the insanity of his asshole parents.

"So why you here?" Corey asked at last.

Grab. Lift. Throw.

Start with the easy stuff. "I wanted to talk to you."

"Ha!" Corey rolled his eyes. "Don't be a douchebag."

What the fuck? The bale fell between them.

Corey's eyes went wide. "Oh shit. I'm the douchebag. Sorry." He leaned over the bale. "but c'mon, you used to tease me for my 'chick flick' moments, dude."

And he had. A lot. Damn it.

Corey smiled. "We've all changed a lot, bro." He lost the smile. "A lot."

Change was good, said the shrink.

Yeah. Not all change.

Corey hopped over the hay bale and sat on it on Gunner's side. "So what's the little girl want to talk about?"

Ha. Sure. He deserved that.

Corey patted the bale.

It was big enough for both of them, sure, but no. "I'm fine here."

Corey shrugged.

"Look, I have this shrink," Gunner said. "Who says I need to... to 'atone' for the shit I've done. So I have a couple of things I need to say.... And I want to start by..." Fuck. What was the word? Fuck it. Gunner pulled the rumpled note card out of his pocket. This was Corey. He'd understand cheat sheets. "'Express gratitude.' That means thank you." He looked up at Corey. "Bro, all those weekends you let me stay

here were about the only thing that kept me sane, or as close to it I'll
ever see. Anyway, thank you for that." He pointed at the bale of hay.
"Even for all the chores. It let me feel like I was giving you something,
you know, for getting me out of that hellhole."

Corey's face turned sad.

"What?"

Corey shrugged. "I'm sorry I never noticed we always stayed here.
I mean, I should've known—"

"Don't." Gunner laughed. "Bro, I did everything I could to hide
all that shit. This was my escape. I didn't want to talk about it. Didn't
want to think about it." How much should he say? "I was afraid that if I
told you, you'd say something to someone, but they were my parents,
bro. Sooner or later, I had to go back to them, and then… then it
would've been worse."

"They told you that?"

Gunner shrugged. "All the fucking time. They were my fucking
parents. I didn't…" What had the shrink said? Gunner glanced at the
card. It was so fucking confusing. "I know you're going to say that if
you'd known you could've taken me away, brought me here to live all the
time."

"Well, fuck yeah…"

Gunner waved at him. "Let me talk. This is hard."

Corey literally put his hands over his mouth.

Cool.

"I wouldn't have let you," Gunner said. "It's this thing my shrink
says, and he's right. I wasn't worth saving, not to me, I know you
disagree but let me talk."

Corey nodded, his stupid hands still over his mouth.

Argh! See? He just couldn't stop.

"I never would've believed it was possible to get out," Gunner
said. "I mean, they were my parents."

Corey's eyes got so sad.

"I know," Gunner said, "I know you would've done anything for
me, and that's why I'm saying thank you, but I want you to understand
you couldn't have changed anything. I wouldn't have let you. I didn't
want saving, I didn't think I deserved it."

He glanced at the card. Ok. That was is for part one.

Part two was going to fucking suck.

Corey sat there with his hands over his mouth. That wasn't going to stop, was it?

"You can take your hands down, now," Gunner said. "Thanks."

Corey dropped his hands. "I get that I couldn't have done anything, bro. I just... I just wish I could have. I mean, back then I had this perfect life and my best friend was going through hell. I wish I could have helped."

"I get that, shithead," Gunner told him. Calling Gunner his best friend meant more than it should. "That's why I'm here to say thank you."

Corey looked so sad. "You're welcome." Then his face changed; he smiled. "You might thank me for watching all those fucking *Three Stooges* movies with you."

Gunner scoffed so hard he almost choked. "Are you shitting me? I *hated* those fucking Stooges. I only watched them for your sake." He undid his fly to expose the Curly on his hip from the boxers Corey had brought him in the hospital.

Well, in the infirmary at the clubhouse. Whatever.

He did up the fly. "You mean you seriously hated them, too?"

Corey shook his head. "Maybe we should have talked more back then."

Yeah. Maybe they should have.

Shit.

"So.... You said there were a couple of things you had to say." Damn Corey and his touchy feeling seeing Gunner's emotions on his face.

Gunner ran his hands over his hair. Okay, this was the hard part, but the shrink had prepped him. He didn't need the card for this part.

He shoved it back in his pocket.

He took a step back and squared up. "Okay, this part is going to piss you off, and I want you to know.... I want you to know that if you need to punch me, you go ahead and punch me, and I won't stop you and I won't hit you back, okay?"

Okay. Okay. He'd been hit so many times, he wouldn't even feel it, and from Corey, more than anyone ever, he deserved it.

Okay. Okay. He might be about to lose the only person he'd ever cared about...

Wait. Corey was on his feet and moving forward.

Gunner took a step back.

"Don't fucking walk away." Corey gestured Gunner forward, then hugged him.

Oh, fuck... just....

"Corey..."

How the hell could he say it with the big goofball hugging him?

"I know you fucked Katy," Corey said. "I'm over it."

The fuck?

The FUCK?

Gunner pushed Corey away. "Did that fucking Fox Bastard—"

"Katy." Shock filled his face. "Wait a fucking minute." He shook his head a lot. "You told *Foxtrot* and not me?"

Okay... as usual, Gunner was the asshole.

He pushed past Corey and sat on the hay. "You knew?"

"I'm still lost on you told Ethan." Corey sat, too. "You fucking hate him."

Gunner shook his head. "I don't. Not anymore." He looked at Corey. "I did. I fucking did. When I beat the shit out of him. That was me... that..."

That was a fucking complicated story.

And it all rolled around the God damn underwear Gunner wore.

He rubbed his face with his hands. "It's complicated. Fuck. It's all so fucking complicated."

Something touched him! What the fuck?

Corey yanked back the hand he'd dropped on Gunner's arm, shock on his face.

Fuck. What the hell had to be on Gunner's face?

He relaxed. "I'm sorry. The shrink calls it shell shock. I just..." Fuck. "You can touch me if you want." It's what the shrink had told him to say when he freaked out like that.

The pressure of Corey's hand returned.

It was okay.

Why did he stop hating Fox?

"It was his dad," Gunner said. "his dad was the one who gave me the gun, the one I pretty much almost got myself killed with." Wait. That sounded wrong. "But that's not what I mean, I mean, he came to me and told me that stupid plan y'all had to take down Twist, and he gave me a gun… me… the guy who'd played kickball with his son's nuts, he gave me a gun and trusted me to do the right thing."

It had completely messed with Gunner's mind. After Mr. Fox had left his room, Gunner had stared at the gun for an hour, trying to figure out what it meant. "I figured a man loved his son so much he'd give me, *me*, a gun, a man like that had to be a good dad, and a good dad? Well, maybe if I'd had a good dad…" Fuck. Fucking throat closing up. "If I'd had a good dad, maybe I wouldn't be such a fuck up." He wiped his eyes. "Fucking hay allergies."

And Corey didn't laugh at the lie.

"And so I went to your practice," Gunner said. "I stood in the back of the room with a gun in the back of my pants while ya'll danced." Fuck. How could he tell anyone this, let alone Corey? "And then it happened. Rose petals fell from nowhere, and all that smoke? And then that guy came out of nowhere. I mean, I didn't know who the fuck it was. Right? I fucking killed Twist myself. Who the fuck was this Jim Morrison wannabe?" Fuck. Hold it together. "And then the fucking roof blew off. I mean, no one told me *that* would happen, and then Nicci turned into a fucking huge demon, and the Korean chick turned into a fucking dragon." Fuck! He could barely see. "A fucking dragon, I mean, what the fuck was I supposed to do? And then the dragon fucking split in two and her fucking blood flew everywhere. It covered me. I couldn't fucking see. I wiped it off with my shirt, but by then…"

By then Twist had found Katy.

"And I froze." It was the hardest thing he'd ever have to admit. "I mean… a fucking demon? A fucking Dragon, and Spook? Fucking Spook whatever the fuck he was, they all went down in a second, and all I had was a gun in the back of my pants. A gun?"

Seriously, what the fuck would a gun do?

"But Fox? Stupid pretty boy Fox?" It had stunned him. "I saw him fighting it. Heard his fucking shoulder pop like a turkey leg, saw it hit his face. But he didn't stop." Fuck. Gunner was blind. Fuck! He wiped his eyes. "I was frozen like a little bitch because I was afraid and fucking Ethan Fox fought against the magic that had killed a fucking dragon, and found a way to move.

"And then Twist touched her, touched Katy." That had done the trick, had forced Gunner into action. "But I was too late." The sound of her neck snapping filled half of his nightmares. "Fox found the strength to push through Twist's magic, and I froze."

Don't say it. Don't admit it!

"If I'd been that strong, I might have shot that mother fucker before he killed Katy."

Fuck!

"But I didn't. And she died."

Fuck! Gunner wiped his face. Fuck!

"So I can't hate Ethan Fox anymore." He wiped his face. "He was stronger than me."

The look on Corey's face. Fuck. He wanted a hug or some gay shit like that.

Fuck! Bad word! Would Gunner ever learn?

He stepped back. "I know you want a hug and shit. I can't." He shook his head. "I can't."

"Gunner." Corey's voice was so loud and forceful Gunner listened. He stood with hands clenched. "I've talked to Ethan a thousand times about that night. About what we could have done differently."

So... what?

"Nothing could have saved Katy," he said. "Nothing. Twist couldn't fuck her any more, since she was the mom to his body, so no one could have her either." He shook his head. "As far as he was concerned, she had to die." He waved a hand. "But what you did? Your distraction?" He shook his head. "None of us thinks Ethan could have completely broken free without you. So..." he swallowed. "You might not have saved Katy... but you helped save the rest of us."

Ha. Fuck. Ethan had said the same thing that day.... In the infirmary...

"We all saved the day, bro." Would Corey understand how important this was? "You jumped on top of a fucking thing that killed a dragon, a fucking *dragon*, and you jumped on him and broke his arm."

Fuck it.

"That's not what we're talking about." Get it together, Gunner. "But that's why I stopped hating that pretty boy." Fuck words! "Ethan. Why I stopped hating Ethan. He moved before I did."

Fuck. Would that make sense.

Corey nodded.

Okay. He seemed to understand.

And, fuck, the big goofball wanted a hug again.

Well, fine.

They hugged.

During the hug, Corey muttered in Gunner's ear. "Still not sure why you told him you fucked Katy instead of me. Just sayin'"

Gunner broke away. Ha. Seriously?

Well, from the look on Corey's face, he wanted to know, but he wasn't pissed.

Fine.

Fine.

Fuck. How even to explain it?

"So my rock star attack on Twist backfired, right?" Gunner admitted. "I got completely fucked up and am only alive because Adam fucking glued me back together."

Corey smiled. "Everyone should have an Adam."

From his mouth to God's ears.

"Well…" Fuck. How could he possibly explain what had happened?

Fuck.

Okay, they'd been friends since before either of them had had pubic hair. Could Gunner trust in that? "Can the deets materialize some other time? The thing is, I almost died. Ethan was there when I woke up right after that glowing weirdo yanked a dozen slugs out of my gut, and he answered some really important questions and shit."

Fuck!

"And the whole Katy thing came up, and I told him." Fuck! How lame!

But Corey settled back. He smiled.

"There's something about Ethan," Corey said. "He gets us all to tell him shit."

And Corey pounced on Gunner like a lamprey latching on.

"You know I love you, bro," he said, "even if it makes you weird when I say it."

He let go, thank God.

"And thank you for all of this." He grinned like an idiot. "I get it."

"Yeah, yeah, yeah... but now it's your turn. When did Katy tell you?"

How long had he known?

The grin faded. "At the Clubhouse. Somewhere in the middle of all the horrible shit going down, she pulled me away from training and we went out to the lobby."

Man, that lobby got a lot of traffic.

"For us, it'd just been a couple of weeks." He picked up a bale. Threw it. "She had nine months to think about shit, and not much else to do." He picked up a bale. Threw it. "I think she wanted to get it out to someone. So she told me." Pick up at bale. Throw it. "I was pissed at first, duh. But the more I thought about it..." He lifted his arms and dropped them. "She cheated on me with you, then dumped me for Ethan, then cheated on Ethan, too."

He sat. "It all says a lot more about Katy than any of us." He fidgeted with a piece of hay. "She's not the person I thought she was at the beginning." He smiled. "But with Theresa? It's all different. I mean, she's the smartest girl I ever... no, the smartest *person* I've ever met."

After the scary lawyer.

"Oh, yeah, after the scary lawyer," Corey said.

Sweet. Great minds and shit.

Corey looked into Gunner's eyes. "And she talks to me just like anyone would." He looked down. "With Katy... I didn't really know it then. But she treated me like I was dumb. We never much really talked about things." He shrugged. "Not that the sex wasn't good."

His lips curled into the world's smallest smile.

Gunner nudged him.

Corey rocked more than the nudge had done. "I'm glad you told me yourself."

He hadn't actually said the words, though, had he.

Corey chuckled. "You would've. I just bored out waiting for you to get up the guts." He pushed up to his feet. "Okay, so you got out the gratitude and the betrayal. Anything else you need to say, or can I restart my gay music and we can throw some hay?"

Ha! "Let's throw some hay… But let me try to do one on my own, okay?"

Lucky stood in the barn doorway watching two young men picking up bales of hay and throwing them into a stall. They sang along to disco that even Lucky thought was pretty "gay."

That dumb kid had managed to get arrested. After everything they'd been through, Lucky had had high hopes for Gunner, but shortly after the wedding, he knocked over a liquor store, already drunk, waving a gun around to steal a fucking bottle of rot gut.

The gun wasn't even real, and the store owner knew it, so he tackled Gunner and held him until the cops arrived. Lucky watched the burgeoning thug throw hay. Must have been a damn big guy who owned the liquor store.

Mike insisted he'd done it to get caught. That he was acting out. As much as Lucky had tried to make the kid feel welcome, he'd kept to himself. So, while the other guys had each other, Gunner had been basically alone. No football team, and, more importantly, no Corey.

And so a week after his eighteenth birthday, he tried to rob a liquor store and landed himself a permanent record.

They moved in perfect unison. Grab a bale. Lift a bale. Throw a bale. They'd obviously done this a thousand times together.

Hm. Maybe that could be useful.

Gunner looked up. His eyes went wide, and the bale tumbled out of his hands.

He bowed his head and brought hand and fist together in front of his bare chest.

Corey threw his bale and looked over a shoulder. "Hey, Lucky.

Look who's here." He looked at the sound system. "Hey, computer, turn down the music."

The volume lowered.

"Mr. Fox..." Gunner's eyes stayed glued to the ground. "I screwed up. I'm sorry. I..."

He stalled out.

Lucky had trusted Gunner and had invested a lot of time and effort in him, and the fact that he could be so humble and embarrassed at disappointing a mentor who was also gay... well, that said a lot.

Handle it carefully. "Look at me, son."

The young man looked up.

Lucky held out his hand.

Gunner grabbed it with a strong grip.

Lucky didn't shake it. Just held it.

"All of us have done stupid shit since Twist ran a bulldozer over us."

Corey had the good sense to blush. Yeah, all of Lucky's boys had been "acting out" in one way or another.

"You just chose to be a bit more public and self-defeating." He squeezed Gunner's hand. The simple fact that the boy allowed him to hold it so long also spoke volumes. "You want a job?"

Gunner's hand contracted and his eyes popped wide. "A job?"

"I don't know if Corey told you, but the other boys are moving to Austin. Ethan, Sam, Kenny." He released Gunner's hand. "So we're about to become seriously short staffed here. Watching you throw hay with Corey made me realize you probably know as much about this farm as anyone."

"They're leaving?" Gunner glanced at Corey.

"I'm staying with the farm," Corey said. "My mom said I could go, but..."

"But the other boys are..." Obsessed was the word Lucky wanted to use. "...interested in pursuing magic, and Corey and I both feel that's better left alone."

Gunner did an actual double take. "You're staying here, too?"

Lucky nodded. "For at least a year."

"Lucky knows wa-a-ay more than me about running a business,"

Corey said, "so I hired him as a manager."

Gunner looked like a kid who'd just received a pony for Christmas.

"Corey? Can I talk to Gunner alone for a minute?"

Corey nodded a lot and grabbed his shirt. "Meet me in the pool, dude."

"Bro." Gunner deflated. "I don't have a suit."

Corey's face contorted. "When have you ever needed a suit here?"

Gunner actually blushed. His eyes met Lucky's, then he looked scared. "It's not because…" He froze. Wow. Lots of issues.

"Find the boy a pair of shorts, Corey." Lucky waved off Gunner's obvious fear that he'd think the gay men were the reason for his modesty. "Other than you, who in the world would want to be naked somewhere Sam might wander past."

Corey hooted. "Woody is hu-u-uge!" Thumbs up. "I gotcha covered, dude." He left.

"Thanks." Gunner stepped closer. "I really don't want you to think it's because of you."

Lucky shook his head. "I don't. I was in the lockers cleaning up more than once when you were in there changing, and it never bothered you."

He nodded, then looked down.

"I talked to your caseworkers, Gunner." How much should he say? "I know more than I should because they kind of think of me as a de facto guardian since your parents are dead."

Gunner looked up. "Why would they think that?"

Really? "Because I told them so." Would Gunner be mad? "Look, you're eighteen now. And an adult, but you're also kind of an orphan, too." Lucky deflated. So many of these boys were orphans, now. "Anyway, it's going to be hard for you to get a job, and I'm serious about needing the help. This isn't charity, it's me hiring someone who knows more about this farm than I do, than any of my other boys knows."

Was that a smile?

Would his deception work? He held up his hands. "One requirement. You know shit can happen any time of the day or night.

Cow's don't give birth during business hours, so I'll need you to live here, too. Does that work? You can start today."

Gunner opened his mouth, then closed it and smiled. "You can take rent out of my pay, right?"

So, he got it. That was okay, too.

Lucky nodded and extended a hand.

Gunner took it, but he startled. "Wait, you mean you need me to move in tonight?"

"Unless you have someplace better to be."

Which he didn't. The grip on Lucky's hand tightened. "Please don't tell the other guys."

Lucky refused to relinquish his grip. "Son, they'll just be glad there's another pair of hands to do the chores. No one needs to know your business."

Gunner smiled and shook Lucky's hand. "Deal."

They released hands.

"I know you're jobless and homeless," Lucky said, "and I'm saying it that directly because I know you need me to. I'm not going to soft talk with you or bullshit you."

Gunner shrank a little.

"I treat everyone here differently because each of you needs something different." Would this make sense? "You need a stronger hand, so if I come down harder on you than the other guys, it's not because I love them more. It's because I love you as much, and I know what you need. You're not the hugs and kisses sort."

And he puffed back up, though he'd likely never admit it.

He nodded.

So did Lucky. "I'm going to tell Corey to put you in the room next to his."

Gunner startled. "I thought that one said, 'Ethan's room.'"

Lucky rolled his eyes. "Ethan spends ninety per cent of his nights in the bungalow, and he's moving away in a month or so…"

Should he go there? Why not. It might help.

"What's wrong, Mr. Fox?" Apparently, Gunner noticed the pause.

Lucky glanced at the empty doorway, more for the look of it than anything, then moved closer to Gunner, dropping an arm around his shoulder. "I'm going to tell Corey this tonight, but he doesn't know yet, so keep a secret for a couple of hours?"

Gunner nodded. That he allowed the arm and was obviously excited about the confidence meant something.

"Theresa's going to Berkley," Lucky said. "In California," he added, just in case.

Gunner's eyes went wide. "Is she dumping him?"

Lucky shook his head. "No, but Corey's going to be fucking lonely with all the other guys and his girlfriend leaving. I will really need you to step up with him."

Question marks wrote themselves across Gunner's face.

"I know that late night talks and hugs are completely not your thing." Although he had yet to shrug off Lucky's arm. "But they're essential to Corey. Please allow him a few chick flick moments."

Gunner barked a laugh.

"Corey talks to everyone."

Gunner nodded. "Mr. Fox?"

Lucky released the boy and faced him directly.

"If we're being straight with each other, don't bullshit me about why you're doing all this for me."

Impressive. "Why do you think I'm doing all this?"

"For Corey." He shrugged. "Why else?"

Wow. This kid had no self-esteem.

Why was he doing it? Why really? No bullshit.

"I'm doing this for me, Gunner." This was the truth. "I've spent my entire life taking care of Ethan and coaching fighters. Teaching and caring are the only things I know how to do, and now Ethan's moving to Austin, and that's what kids do. They go off to college or a job, or whatever, and parents find something new to do." Would any of this make sense? "I've been taking care of four boys for almost a year now. I'd like to help you because it's what I do. And I do care about you Gunner. I really do. In the clubhouse I saw you go from a hateful little shit to someone who endangered his own life for people who didn't give a shit about him."

Lucky shrugged. "What you did six months ago was stupid, but I get why you did it." Well, was that really true? "Well, Dr. Mike explained it to me as best he could." Another shrug. "I like taking care of people, and I think you're worth caring about."

Gunner nodded.

"That straight enough?"

Another nod. "Thanks, Mr. Fox. For everything."

He offered his hand.

Lucky took it.

Gunner pulled him closer and patted one of Lucky's shoulder with his free hand then pulled away and released the hand. "I should go find Corey."

Lucky nodded and the boy ran off.

Baby steps.

Baby steps.

Maestro held a hand to Spook, who glanced at the hand then met Maestro's eyes.

Is this really the only way? the lad sent.

Maestro nodded.

One camera showed a rage of demons racing through a metal corridor, climbing over each other in their bloodlust. Those with wings battling in midair over who would be allowed the privilege of killing their master's sworn enemies.

A second camera showed Mary, blonde and innocent-seeming, leading a horde of zombies. Her gentle innocence belied the powerful, evil witch she was.

A third camera revealed a hundred ETs of every shape and size, each armed with a vicious-looking weapon.

"Do you want what's left of your family in the crosshairs forever?" Maestro asked.

Spook took his hand in a strong grip. He nodded assent.

Maestro turned to Elizabeth.

"We took it too far," she said. "We have to end it here."

He held out a hand.

She took it.

Muscle stared at Maestro through eyes that had aged a hundred years in one. He held his hands out. Elizabeth and Spook each took one.

Over the channel connecting them to everyone back in the clubhouse, back on Earth, several hysterical voices all shouted at once. Ah. They'd realized the truth behind Maestro's gambit.

"I'm sorry, Barry," he said so quietly, Barry would only hear the words after he'd gone over the video a thousand times to see if Maestro had somehow left himself a way out.

He hadn't.

The only alternative had been taking most of Texas, Oklahoma, and Louisiana with them, something Maestro had long vowed would never happen. Not on this timeline.

Pounding from all three doors managed to startle him.

The others jumped as well.

Spook held his hand all the tighter. "Immortal just means they haven't figured out a way to kill you, yet." He smiled. "Of course, you'd be the only one to figure it out."

Maestro squeezed back.

"Doohickey, detonate bomb."

Countdowns were for idiots.

The Tango Triptych might have ended, but the adventures of Ethan Fox and his friends aren't over by a long shot.
Look for "Witches Grow in Threes," Ethan's first story as part of *Tales of Mystery and Woe.*
Available end of 2020/beginning of 2021.

Please enjoy this sample from Morrison "Spook" James' first appearance in the exciting series
Tales of Mystery and Woe: a comedy.
This novel takes place a year before he met (and includes a special guest appearance by) Ethan Fox.
If you don't enjoy it, please remember it was free.

Tales of Mystery and Woe

a comedy

John Robert Mack

Spook

Austin, Texas
Thursday, 10:00pm

Spook was dead.

He'd been killed back in 1961 at the age of seventeen but never stopped walking around and shooting off his mouth. Or so his brother, Ross, liked to say. For the record, Spook hated the word "zombie."

He stood in his basement, arms raised and eyes closed, reciting a spell of demonic summoning. *"O Fortuna. . . velut luna. . . statu variabilis. . . semper crescis. . . aut decrescis."* Dust motes sparkled in the light of a hundred blood-red candles and swirled inside the arcane containment circle painstakingly inscribed on the bare concrete floor.

Spook's "Ye Olde Booke of Shadows" had called for "thee blude of a styll-brything mongrel poured unto the colde, colde stone whilst it screamed its fynal cries of terrour after its throat was verily slitte." But that was impossible, since an animal with its throat slit couldn't cry out in terror anymore. Spook had a deal with the butcher down the road who sold him farm animal blood at cost, just to get rid of the stuff. Close enough.

He continued his spell as he dribbled the cow's blood into the concrete, which ate it up greedily with faint suckling sounds.

Spook hung out with a Goth crowd that'd taught him how to dress the part at a place called Bitter Sweets on Austin's east side. All these years of spell casting and hunting creatures of the night, and Spook had never realized the importance of velvet, leather and platform boots. His short black hair rose in a spikey mess. His normally dark, Mexican skin was made up pale and kohl surrounded his eyes. He wore black leather pants, knee high black boots, a black velvet shirt and a burgundy cowl with the hood down his back so it wouldn't mess up his hair. He had black fingernails and lots of dark, mysterious jewelry where spiders and skulls predominated. Who'd have known it'd be so much effort for an actual zombie to blend into the death-becomes-us crowd?

He opened his eyes and raised his voice. "*Vita detestabilis. . . nunc obdurate. . . et tunc curat. Ludo mentis acie. . .*" His voice dropped an octave and echoed as if he spoke into a much larger space. "*Egestatem. . . potestatem. . . dissolvit ut glaciem.*" The dust motes swirled in a definite vortex within the protection circle and a column of light glowed enough to drive away the shadows and expose the clutter in Spook's basement, pushed to the walls to make room for spell casting.

The illumination revealed the usual assortment of old—but still perfectly serviceable— chairs and tables, a collection of demon banishing swords and daggers laid out for easy access, boxes of clothes bound to come back into fashion someday, a standing mirror of soul capturing and a *Hello Kitty* lamp. An ethereal breeze stirred the various flags, banners and drop cloths.

Faintly, in the background, a chorus in three part harmony rose up to support Spook's voice.

It was working.

He could feel it.

The power started as a tickle at the base of his spine and spread through his nervous system, which was nothing more than a conduit for magical energy since his death and reanimation. Warm. Tingly.

Oh yeah, it was working.

"*O Fortuna. . . velut luna. . . statu variabilis. . . semper crescis. . . aut decrescis.*" Soon, the gate would open and his own personal demonic companion would step through the dimensional rift and shuffle up this mortal coil to—

A happy violin riff cut through Spook's chant to tell him someone had rung the front doorbell.

He faltered, as did the unearthly chorus. But only a moment.

Ignoring the distraction, he raised his voice and focused. The chorus rejoined him and the spell continued. "*Vita detestabilis. . . nunc obdurate. . .*

damn it."

The violin music broke in again, far too quickly this time and joined by a heavily accented little girl's voice. "Hello Kitty, come outside and play!"

"*Et tunc curat Ludo mentis acie. . .* crap."

The theme song interrupted itself to start over.

Person at the door impatient much?

The chorus cut out. Spook lost his place in the spell. "Blast!" His voice still held all the reverb and echo of a demonic overlord.

The maelstrom in the center of the room suddenly and rapidly swirled down into a tiny spot on the floor like water down a toilet in fast forward. The last of the magical energy disappeared into the concrete with a pathetic "thwip."

The *Hello Kitty* theme repeated itself.

With a disgusted snort, Spook glared at the ceiling in the direction of the front door. He pulled at his sleeves and headed for the stairs. "That had better be pizza." As he tramped up the stairs, his Goth boots thundered to suit his mood at the interruption.

He burst through the door into a kitchen obviously decorated entirely from Ikea and headed toward the front door. A more traditional doorbell replaced the bright melody from his downstairs alarm. "If there's no pizza. . . there will be Hell to pay."

Unfortunately, the soft and well-padded carpet in the front hall spoiled the heavy tread of his boots, but he managed two heavy stamps on the hardwood of the foyer to get his steam back up. When the doorbell rang two or three times in rapid succession, Spook yanked the door open as abruptly as he could. "You better have pizza!"

A middle-aged man in a grey trench coat stood with his back to Spook for a moment before turning quickly to face him, his mouth already open to speak.

He did not have pizza. His mouth hung open for a split second before closing as if he'd forgotten what he was going to say or had changed his mind. Holy Columbo!

He looked Spook up and down and then his eyes settled on Spook's face with an expression so utterly blank, it was worse than scorn.

In the bright light of the front hall of a two-story mid-century modern home and surrounded by furniture from Ikea, the burgundy velvet coat and knee high boots were possibly a trifle excessive. And how much make-up had Spook actually applied?

Emotionless, the stranger extended a business card. "I just happened to be passing through your neighborhood and thought you might need some help controlling the demon you're trying to summon."

Spook sucked in a quick breath. How did he know? He grabbed the card. It read:

```
Maestro
Tell me your tale of woe.

Mysteries solved.
```

Spook glanced from the card to the man. "What. . . demon. . . what?" He floundered. "Do I look like someone who would try to conjure—?" He glanced at his reflection in the hallway mirror, suddenly embarrassed at the get-up. With the crowd at Bitter Sweets, it had seemed restrained. Hadn't it?

The stranger, Maestro, spoke gently. "You look like a reject from a Goth *Hello Kitty* convention."

Spook wanted to disagree, but searched deep into Maestro's eyes. He was definitely a fellow mage. Sorcerer? Witch? A powerful one, whatever he was, from the complete sense of control he radiated. Other than the power in the man's eyes, though, he was so bland he'd be nearly invisible in a crowd.

Oooh. Was that just how he liked it?

Spook drew himself up. "How did you know I was summoning a demon? Could you sense a disturbance in the ethereal realm? Ripples in the—"

Maestro snorted. "You are such a little girl." He pointed up.

Spook looked at the ceiling. Nothing there apart from a few cobwebs. Time to call the maid.

The man grabbed him roughly by the arm and dragged him across the porch and onto the front lawn. Spook glanced at the man's hand on his arm. He was stronger than he looked.

The front lawn needed mowing. He'd have to call one of his grand-nephews—

Maestro pointed up again. "Actually, the giant hellsmouth over your house was my first clue."

"Holy spit!" Spook stumbled a step forward as Maestro released him. There, above his home, raged an enormous, swirling tornado of smoke and fire and lightning lit from inside by a sickening green radiance. Spirits and demons flew in and out of it, for all the world like fireflies swarming around a lantern.

In almost sixty years of hunting supernatural evil, Spook had seen *nothing* like it. Nothing even close. He was so ultimately screwed.

Maestro smacked him on the back of the head. "Close your mouth before something evil and smelly flies in. You look like a tourist." The man calmly turned away from the giant funnel of interdimensional power as if it were nothing more than a backed-up sink. "Tell me this isn't your first ride on the merry-go round."

Tearing his eyes away from the hellsmouth, Spook ran to catch up to the stranger who had already opened the back of a green and white VW Microbus.

Maestro dispatched an apepi as it slithered toward one of the myriad bystanders too stupid to realize they should run in terror. As his banishing sword sliced the giant snake in two, the slimy creature exploded into a ball of smoke. One handy thing about most demons: when banished, they popped back to their personal hell without leaving behind an enormous mess. Made it easier to deal with the local constabulary. Also meant they occasionally hunted their killer down for revenge.

He spun and skewered one of Azidahaka's three heads, pulled the blade free and sliced off the other two, sending her back to a very, very hot place.

How had the kid managed to create a dimensional portal *this* bloody powerful? Maestro knew the "kid" had been born in the sixties, but nearly everyone held in magical stasis at a particular age maintained the maturity of that stage. Spook would be seventeen forever.

Assuming he learned to watch his own back and managed to survive the night.

Maestro sliced through a ghast behind the lad.

Spook spun quickly enough to see it evaporate with a high-pitched scream. He glanced at Maestro in embarrassment at letting down his guard and threw out the first thing that came to mind to cover his humiliation. "And you just happened to have a couple of banishing swords in the back of your Mystery Machine?"

His surface thoughts were easier to read than stereo instructions.

"And you don't?" Maestro raised an eyebrow.

Behind Spook, a ghoul chased a middle-aged woman in a housecoat. Maestro raised a hand and intoned a spell. The ghoul evaporated.

Spook stared like a groupie. "Your eyes. . ."

Maestro grabbed him by the shoulders and turned him around just in time for his rising blade to slice a ghost in half. "Yes, yes, yes," Maestro muttered. "They glow purple when I cast that spell. It's very cool. Now you need to get centered and *close that portal.*"

Suddenly, Spook spun out of Maestro's grip, stabbed forward into a ghoul and then quickly flipped his blade backward into a second as it zoomed out of the hellsmouth. "Yeah. . . centering here. Totally peaced out and chill." He pulled a dagger from his belt and tossed it into the center of a cresil chasing a Doberman with obvious lascivious intent.

Maybe the kid wasn't utterly hopeless, after all.

Then he grinned like a puppy eager for a pat on the head, which completely ruined the effect.

"We're kind of on a clock here," Maestro reminded him. "Reporters and cops on the way."

Spook frowned and turned his back to Maestro, bringing his hands together. "Not helping."

With a quiet mutter, Maestro banished the giant hellworm inching toward Spook. "Civilians gonna start dying soon." He let his sword drop to his side for a moment and watched energy swirl and collect about Spook.

"Helping even less," the lad complained. But he did focus better. His energies stabilized into a gentle globe around him.

Spook needed someone directing him. Not good. He'd spent so many years as part of a team, there was no telling how badly he'd screw up on his own. And the fact that he had tried to summon a demon in the first place meant he'd started down a dark and lonely path.

Which, although Spook would never know it, was the real reason for Maestro's visit. He'd seen what he needed to see. Spook couldn't be left alone. Maestro had watched him from a distance for years. It was time to step in.

"Tourist," he teased. He raised his banishing sword and tossed it from hand to hand in a rapid figure eight around his body. "*Lorem ipsum dolor sit amet.*" He spun twice, whirling the sword over his head with his right hand. "*Duo nonumy legimus dignissim.*"

He grabbed it in both hands as it glowed bright white, switched his grip so the point faced the ground. With a guttural shout, he drove the sword up to the hilt into the pavement, dropping to one knee as he did so.

"*Quidam!*"

Lightning crashed into him. A sphere of white light, centered on the quartz crystal in the hilt of Maestro's sword, expanded in a flash out to a distance of about one hundred yards, instantly banishing anything supernatural it touched. Dozens of creatures exploded.

Half a dozen stupid bystanders applauded.

Maestro had to focus hard to keep the spell from destroying Spook as well.

The lad staggered as the hydra he'd been fighting suddenly ceased to exist. He turned to Maestro with shock and awe all over his face. "Who the hell are you, and how have I never heard of you?"

Maestro remained on one knee trying to hold the demons inside the hellsmouth. His grip on the sword tightened as the blade began to vibrate. "Kinda hoping you'd hurry up." Sweat trickled down his forehead and into one eye. The ground trembled.

"Oh. . . right." Spook raised his hands and the echo returned to his voice. "*Sicsercedtau. . . sicsercrepnessilibairavutats anultulevanutrof v!*"

Maestro closed his eyes. Please let it work. He could do it himself, but didn't want to play that card just yet. Please let Spook be able to handle it.

The clouds churned.

The demons screamed.

The giant cyclone of arcane energy swirled down into the roof of Spook's house like water twirling down the drain of a toilet. Great billows of smoke and fire and lightning sucked into the house, and Maestro shifted his gaze to Spook's ridiculously cluttered basement. The entire maelstrom whirled into the center of the summoning circle down there and vanished with an anticlimactic "thwip" that barely managed to blow out the ridiculous and unnecessary assortment of candles.

When he was certain Spook's magic had worked, Maestro loosened his grip on the sword and let himself breathe. The giant glowing bubble faded like so much steam. With the thunderous roar of a demonic gate silenced, Maestro heard the car alarms, the weeping and the distinct sound of police and fire sirens rapidly approaching.

Damn. No rest for the wicked.

Before Spook could start in on some foolish "we saved the day" ritual he'd no doubt had with Percy and Ross, Maestro left the sword sticking out of the road and rose to his feet, motioning the lad closer.

Spook wiped a hand over his forehead and hurried forward, smiling. Maestro reached for the boy, who grinned even more and opened his arms for a celebratory hug.

Maestro snorted. "Don't be ridiculous." He grabbed Spook's shoulders and spun him around so they were back to back. "Don't move," he ordered. "Our work isn't done here."

Maestro pulled out what looked very much like an iPhone. When he touched the screen though, a 2-D hologram screen popped up above it.

Maestro tapped the image. "*Harkle barkle beelzebub*," he muttered. Hopefully, his words were good enough to fool Spook into thinking this was spellwork, too. Sometimes alien technology just worked better, but he couldn't let the little ghoul know about it.

A faint light pulsed out of the device and flashed across the neighborhood, blanketing the block in something not unlike dry ice smoke.

Maestro closed his eyes and sent his gaze outward and upward to look down on his handiwork.

In a gradually spreading circle, every person, animal and insect slowly lowered itself to the ground as if suddenly needing a nap. Cars ground to a halt. A cat about to pounce on a mouse gently fell asleep instead, with the mouse dropping only an inch from its paws.

Opening his eyes, Maestro clicked his tongue at the eerie muting of sound this particular app created. He tapped the device and shoved it into a pocket before turning to face Spook, who walked away and spun a slow circle as he inspected the scene. Shaking his head at Spook's touristy amazement, Maestro pulled his sword easily from the pavement and hurried to the lad's side to relieve him of the other banishing blade.

"That's why you haven't heard of me," Maestro explained. "They won't remember a thing when they wake up."

Spook gestured at the spouting fire hydrants, the crashed cars. "But how do you explain all this?"

Maestro pulled open the back of his van, which even he had to admit looked a bit like the Mystery Machine. "A gas main blew up and knocked everyone out." He tossed the swords into the back and slammed the doors closed.

"Gas main? Really? You expect people to buy that?"

Grabbing him by the shoulders again, Maestro pulled Spook closer and turned him to look out across the street so he was once more facing away. He waved one hand into Spook's field of vision. "Abracadabra." He tapped the device in his pocket.

The yard of the house across the street exploded in a carefully controlled ball of fire. Before ringing Spook's doorbell, Maestro had set the explosives against just such a necessity.

"Jeepers!" Spook rocked back into Maestro.

Maestro pushed him gently but firmly away. "I do expect them to buy that."

People woke up and the sirens roared back full volume right around the corner.

Maestro surveyed the scene. Mayhem and destruction, yes, but no one had been seriously injured. The hellsmouth had been closed. No civilians would know how close they'd come to the Apocalypse. And

Spook would never guess why Maestro watched him. This incident belonged in the "win" column.

Apparently, Spook agreed. "You. . . are a rock star."

Without offering him the satisfaction of a response, Maestro dragged Spook across the lawn and into his house. In the foyer, he released the arm and wandered into the living room, leaving Spook to close the door behind them.

Spook leaned against the closed front door and watched his unusual visitor wander around the living room. Maestro seemed to dismiss most of the furniture but paused to touch the ratty afghan over the back of Ross's old recliner, the only piece of furniture that wasn't new.

Spook's brother loved that chair and even though Spook hadn't seen Ross in months, it helped him feel closer somehow. Maybe it was because he hadn't seen the old fart in so long.

Maestro moved to the fireplace and examined the photos on the mantel. With a deep breath, Spook left the safety of the foyer and joined his guest in the living room. Standing there in a rumpled overcoat, the man looked like nothing. As average and boring as anyone on the street, but the power he'd shown had been incredible.

Had he really just noticed the hellsmouth, or was he there for another reason? Cool if he was. Spook had been alone longer than ever in his afterlife. He didn't like it.

Maestro turned his disquieting gaze on Spook, who stood at Russ' recliner and worried one corner of the afghan. "Don't the cops ever notice there's a VW microbus at an awful lot of gas main explosions?"

"I change cars fairly often."

There had to be some way to connect with this guy, but he was so intensely closed off.

"Why the demon?" Maestro asked suddenly

Wait. What?

"What?" Spook asked.

Maestro didn't respond.

"Oh. . ." Spook didn't want to tell him the truth, so he stalled. "Why does anyone summon a demon? Power."

"Seems like you have a pretty nice setup here." The visitor glanced around the room before leveling his gaze on Spook once more. "Why the demon?"

Spook smoothed out the afghan. "I told you. . . I wanted more power."

Maestro shoved his hands into the pockets of his coat and cocked his head to one side. He needed a fedora. "If I thought that were true," the visitor said, "you'd already be dead. People could have been hurt tonight. They could have died. If you were really delving into the dark arts just to satisfy a craving for power, you'd already be lost." He settled back. "Why the demon?"

Spook moved to the mantle and regarded a photo with Ross. "You won't believe the truth." The photo was Ross, Spook and a very perplexed-seeming Santa Claus. Ross had been much older than the dime-store fat man.

Maestro plucked the photo from the mantle. "This was taken less than a year ago, and I note a suspicious lack of ridiculous Goth apparel. Something changed." He handed the photo over. "Why the demon?"

The photo felt heavy in Spook's hand. "There's nothing ridiculous about Goth apparel." Ross had grown so old.

Maestro leaned against the fireplace. "Ordinarily, I'd agree with you, but on you, it's preposterous. It's like Elvis Presley drag. Not everyone can pull it off. I ask one last time, and then I simply walk out the door." He took the photo from Spook and placed it back on the mantle. "Why the demon?"

Spook stared at the photo. What could he say? It seemed idiotic now that he needed to explain it. When he'd been in the basement last night, looking up spells and drinking Jim Beam, the whole plan had seemed so logical. Tonight? Under the scrutiny of a mage who made Spook's own ability seem feeble and foolish? Idiotic.

With a grunt, the other man pushed himself away from the fireplace and headed for the foyer.

Damn it. He'd leave forever if Spook didn't tell him the truth.

Was he that desperate? Yes.

"I was lonely."

Maestro stopped but didn't turn around.

Spook took down the photo of him and Ross. "Ross was the one who found me after. . . after this happened to me. We were seventeen." Those first days had been full of terror and despair and Ross had held Spook together through it all. "He's not. . . biologically, he's not my brother, but we fought supernatural evil bastards for fifty years. We sort of adopted each other." Even after Ross had married and had kids, the two of them would go off together whenever their mentor Percy found something to kill. Then Percy died.

"Then Ross got old." Spook replaced the photo and faced Maestro. "And one day, he's going to die. And so will his kids. And his grandkids."

"But not you?"

"I'm already dead."

"So you summoned a demon to keep you company?"

Spook shrugged. "At the time, it made a certain kind of sense." He moved closer to the other man. How long before he started laughing? "I told you you wouldn't believe the truth."

"Oh. . . I believe you all right. I mean. . ." He gave Spook a very pointed and critical perusal. "Have you looked at yourself in a mirror lately?"

As Spook stepped closer, he saw himself in the hallway mirror again. Sweat had ruined his make-up. In the sharp light of the overhead lamp, he was a caricature of a zombie pretending to be a real boy playing at being the undead. Ridiculous. "I don't pull it off, do I?"

Maestro regarded him in the reflection of the mirror and, against all probability, he showed only the merest hint of judgment in his face. Maybe Spook didn't need to do this all by himself after all.

"Teach me. Please!" Spook turned to Maestro and took a single step closer. "I've been fighting the supernatural a long time, but I've never known anyone who can do the kind of stuff you did tonight. . . well, except for a couple of evil demons. . ." That was one possibility he hadn't considered. "You're not an evil demon are you?"

Maestro didn't even react to the question. "I'll help you on two conditions."

"Anything."

The scary man held up one hand. "Don't be so quick to make promises." He lowered the hand and stared at Spook for a long time. "Condition one: get rid of the makeup unless you're going out on a Friday night. You look ridiculous."

"Done." He wiped his face with the back of one sleeve.

"Condition two: don't ever try to hug me again."

Spook grinned. "Agreed." This would be easier than he'd anticipated.

"I mean it." The man's face had returned to that spooky lack of expression worse than any amount of disapproval. "You ever try to hug me again, I will sever your soul from your body and send it to spend an eternity in the deepest circle of Hell."

"Can you really do that?" Was he going to smile? Or was he serious?

Maestro didn't respond.

Spook swallowed. "Agreed," he said at last. "For reals."

The other man's hand came up so fast Spook jumped. "Okay, there's a third condition," Maestro said. "No catch phrases. I don't ever want to hear you say 'for reals' again." He grabbed the doorknob and yanked the door open.

"Hey!" How would Spook find him again? He pulled out Maestro's business card. "Your card. . . there's no contact info." He held it up as if Maestro didn't already know what was on it, or, more importantly, what was not.

Maestro glanced at the card and then met Spook's gaze. "I thought you said you'd been on this merry-go-round before." He closed the door between them.

Spook grinned. "Brass ring." He ran up the stairs three at a time to get his laptop and start googling.

Acknowledgements

Thank you, Jackie Claunch, so much, for making my return to Texas a possibility, and also the Tijerina-Trevino family for providing an occasional home-away-from-home. I missed that weird sound grackles make almost as much as I missed y'all. Thanks to Chris, Sarah, Andrew and Jackie for welcoming me back with loving arms.

This novel was largely the product of collaboration with my editor, Lauran Strait, who is strong enough to read fifty pages and say, "Nope. You haven't worked hard enough yet. Try again." And thanks to Jennifer for pointing out I'd gone a little too "Game of Thrones."

About the Author

John Robert Mack currently resides in San Antonio, Texas, the largest small town in the US, where he eats fish tacos at Beto's whenever possible. He teaches dance and writes the column "What Would Oscar Do?" for Out-in-SA, print and online. He has written over a dozen novels, which he hopes to see in print and has recently linked all of them into one large multiverse. Ask him to read tarot for you sometime, but don't be surprised if the cards have nekkid people on them.

To find out more about him, stalk him on all of his social media, and buy his books from his author's page on Amazon.